Nick grabbed her, and suddenly *she* was the one flat on her back. He covered her body with his. "Stop laughing," he growled.

"I'm…trying," she wheezed between giggles. The memory of his shocked look triggered another round of laughter.

Suddenly his mouth was on hers. The crazy man must have thought he could stop her laughter by kissing her.

He was right.

The feel of his lips molding hers stopped her mid-giggle, and suddenly all she wanted to do was kiss him back. She poured every ounce of frustration, hunger, even anger into that kiss. She wanted him, desperately, had wanted him for so long. And even though she knew it was probably a mistake, that she'd hate herself for it later, she wrapped her arms around his neck and pulled him closer, letting him know in every way she could that she wanted this.

UNDERCOVER
TWIN

BY
LENA DIAZ

...aquin (UK) policy is to use papers that are natural, renewable and
...able products and made from wood grown in sustainable forest-
...ng and manufacturing processes conform to the legal environme-

...ed and bound in Spain

MILLS
BOON

First published in Great Britain 2013
by Mills & Boon, an imprint of Harlequin (UK) Limited,
Eton House, 18-24 Paradise Road, Richmond, Surrey TW9 1SR

© Lena Diaz 2013

ISBN: 978 0 263 90386 7

46-1213

Harle... ... UK ... ... natural, renewable and
recyc... ... ... n sustainable fore.. s. The
loggi... ... ... s... conform t... ... le... al env...... ntal
regula...

Printe...
by Bl...

Lena Diaz was born in Kentucky and has also lived in California, Louisiana and Florida, where she now resides with her husband and two children. Before becoming a romance suspense author, she was a computer programmer. A former Romance Writers of America Golden Heart® finalist, she has won a prestigious Daphne du Maurier award for excellence in mystery and suspense. She loves to watch action movies, garden and hike in the beautiful Tennessee Smoky Mountains. To get the latest news about Lena, please visit her website, www.lenadiaz.com.

Thank you, Allison Lyons and Nalini Akolekar.
This book is dedicated to my parents,
James and Letha McAlister. Daddy, you were a true
hero. I thank God for every moment that I had with you.
Mom, you have endured more heartache than anyone
should ever have to endure.
Your strength and grace amaze me. I love you both
and am blessed to be your daughter.

Chapter One

Heather recoiled with disgust and turned away from the couple in the dark corner, their gyrating bodies moving as wildly as the couples filling the dance floor. Every beat of the music hammered at her skull. The smoky haze had her eyes watering. And the rancid odor of the sweaty mass of people seething around her had nausea coiling in her stomach.

Normally a seedy bar wouldn't faze her. She'd been in nearly every major nightclub in northeast Florida, let alone Saint Augustine, because of her job. The free-flowing alcohol lowered inhibitions and made gathering information far quicker and easier than an old-fashioned stakeout ever could. But tonight wasn't about work. Tonight wasn't about snapping pictures of a cheating husband in a compromising position for a couple hundred bucks. Tonight was about finding her sister, going home and soaking away her pounding headache in a tub full of strawberry bubble bath.

She clutched her purse to dissuade any greedy fingers from trying to pilfer her wallet and fought her way to the bar, like a salmon swimming upstream. By the time she found an empty stool to perch on, she'd been groped and propositioned so many times she was seriously considering exchanging her tub of strawberry bubble bath for a tub of hand sanitizer.

The bartender stopped in front of her. But even though his lips were moving, Heather couldn't make out what he was saying over the heavy-metal music pumping out of the speakers. He motioned to her and she leaned forward.

"What are you having?" he shouted.

She shook her head. "Not drinking. Looking for my sister, Lily. She looks like me. Have you seen her?"

"Do you have a picture?"

"I *am* the picture. She looks *exactly* like me. We're identical twins."

He wiped his greasy hair out of his face and squinted at her in the dim light. His mouth curved in a lecherous grin, as if he was considering the possibility of a threesome. "Sweet."

Heather's stomach rolled. She hopped off the bar stool, but the bartender waved for her to wait.

"Check the bathroom," he said. "I might have seen her heading in that direction a few minutes ago." He pointed to the dark hallway just past the couple who'd been enjoying each other so enthusiastically earlier. They both had silly, sleepy grins on their faces now. The guy looked at Heather and winked. She shivered with revulsion.

After thanking the bartender, she braced herself for another battle and fought her way through the throng of people to the pink neon sign that read Females and hung over the women's restroom.

When she pushed the door open, the strong smell of urine and stale beer hit her with gale force. She coughed and waved her hand in front of her face. If her sister wasn't in this bathroom, she was leaving. She'd go home until Nick was finished with whatever emergency his boss had called him about. And this time, when he offered to help her get her sister into an alcohol treatment program, she'd listen.

Just thinking about her new boyfriend of only eight weeks, his sexy half smile, the way his deep voice made her toes curl when he called her darlin', had her feeling better. It was wonderful having someone like Nick in her life. She was so tired of having to be strong all the time, with no one else to share her burdens.

"Lily?" she called out. "Are you in here?" She let the door close and stepped farther into the room. The lighting was even worse in here than out in the main part of the club, for which she was extremely grateful. She didn't want to know what disgusting substance was on the floor, crunching and sliding beneath her feet. "Lily?"

She made her way down the row of stalls, knocking and using the toe of her sneaker to nudge each door open. When she reached the last stall, she heard a noise, like someone taking a deep breath. "Lily, it's Heather. Is that you?"

"Don't come in here." The voice behind the last stall door sounded slurred, but there was no mistaking it.

Heather rolled her eyes. "Lily, are you drunk again? Is that why you called me to come get you?"

"I told you to come at midnight. You're early." Another sniff.

She shook her head in exasperation. It was just like her sister to expect Heather to rescue her, but only on Lily's timetable, on Lily's terms.

"I have to get up early in the morning to meet with a new client. If you aren't ready to leave right now, and you're too drunk to drive, call a cab." She turned and headed for the door.

"Wait," Lily called out, her voice sounding mildly panicked. "Just give me a minute. My car won't start, and I don't have money for a cab."

Because she'd already blown all the money Heather had given her? Money Heather couldn't afford to give her in the first place?

Heather curled her fingers around her frayed purse strap and stepped back to the stall door. "What are you doing in there? Drinking? Haven't you had enough already?"

"Just wait at the bar. I'll be right out."

The airy quality of Lily's words wasn't lost on Heather. Her sister sounded far worse than if she was just drunk. All kinds of scenarios flooded Heather's mind. None of them good. "Open the door."

Cursing sounded from inside the stall. "This is a bathroom. Give me some freaking privacy."

Heather hesitated. Arguing with her stubborn sister wouldn't do any good. It would just make her dig in deeper and fight harder.

"All right, I'll meet you at the bar." She walked to the door, her shoes crunching across the concrete. She stepped into the hall, turned around and tiptoed back inside, easing the door closed behind her. She quietly moved back to the row of stalls, pausing a few feet down from the stall her sister was in, so Lily wouldn't see her through the cracks around the door.

Loud noises sounded from outside the bathroom. Yelling. Feet shuffling. It sounded like people were running. What kind of craziness was going on out there on the dance floor?

Heather ignored the noise and waited. A moment later, the lock on the stall door slid back and Lily stepped out in her ragged jean cutoffs and tank top that showed far more than they concealed, including another new tattoo, a small pink dragon peeking out from the top of Lily's shorts. Her sister couldn't afford to buy her own groceries or gas money, but she could pay for a tattoo? Heather gritted her teeth. She was putting in eighty-hour workweeks—minimum—just to keep up with her car payments and rent. *She* certainly couldn't afford a tattoo, even if she'd wanted one.

She was about to give her sister another lecture on being frugal when she noticed what her sister was holding. In one hand she clutched a dark blue nylon backpack. In the other, she held a baggie of white powder and a rolled-up dollar bill. Heather's stomach sank. Now she knew why her sister was making those sniffing sounds earlier.

Cocaine.

Lily's eyes widened and her face went pale. Heather grabbed the baggie and ran into the stall. She tossed it in the toilet and pressed the handle.

"What are you doing?" her sister screamed. She dropped her backpack and shoved past Heather.

Heather stared in stunned amazement at her sister on her knees on the filthy floor, with her hands in an equally filthy toilet trying to fish out the baggie. Her heart breaking, Heather turned away, but a flash of white in Lily's backpack made her hesitate. She knelt down and pulled out a duct-taped brick of more white powder wrapped tightly in plastic.

Her hands started to shake. At least two more bricks of cocaine peeked out from the bottom of the pack. She couldn't even *begin* to imagine the street value of those drugs, or how many years in prison that would buy.

Lily looked back at her and cursed. "Give me that." She tried to get up, but her feet slid on the slippery floor.

Heather ran with the brick into the next stall and crouched in front of the toilet. She desperately ripped at the tape and plastic.

Lily stumbled in behind her, clawing at Heather's hair. "Stop, don't do it!"

Fire shot through Heather's scalp. She gritted her teeth against the pain and tore at the plastic, scooping the white powder into the toilet, flushing several times, using her body to block her sister until everything was gone but the tape and plastic.

Lily must have grabbed the backpack when she'd chased after Heather, because now she was cradling it against her, as if to keep Heather from taking the rest of her precious stash of drugs. She slowly slid to the floor, black mascara running in streaks down her face. "What have you done?" she moaned.

Sympathy and anger warred inside Heather as she stepped over her sister to get out of the stall. She was determined to leave her there, but she couldn't seem to make her feet move to the bathroom door. How many times had Lily dropped into her life over the years, staying just long enough to blow through Heather's totally inadequate savings account? How many times had Heather woken up to discover her sister gone again, moving on to the next sucker in her life, or her next big scam, or her next drinking binge—usually after stealing one of Heather's credit cards? How many times would Heather let her sister turn her life into a disaster and disappear until the next time Lily needed a place to crash?

Her shoulders slumped. She knew the answer to all of those questions. No matter how many times her twin hurt her, Heather would still love her, and she'd always be there for her. She couldn't walk away and leave her sister, the only family she had, not like this.

She sighed heavily and turned around. "Come on. Let's go home. We'll figure out what to do, together."

"I don't want your help," Lily spat out. "I hate you. I always have."

Her sister's words shot like an arrow straight to Heather's heart. She drew a shaky breath, steeling herself against the pain. "Hate me all you want, but I'm still not going to leave you sitting on this filthy floor." She reached her hand out to help her sister to her feet.

Lily jerked back, like a wounded animal perched on the edge of a cliff, afraid to trust the one person who could save it.

A loud banging noise sounded behind Heather. She whirled around to see the bathroom door being held open as a group of six men dressed all in black rushed inside. Heather instinctively positioned herself in front of her sister.

"Federal officers, freeze!" one of the men yelled.

Federal officers? The man closest to her trained his gun on her while two others hurried down the row of stalls, slamming the doors open, looking in each one.

Heather stared in horror at the three white letters printed across their black flak jackets. *DEA*—Drug Enforcement Administration.

Her boyfriend, Nick, was a DEA agent.

One of the men grabbed Heather and pulled her away from the stall. Another one grabbed Lily and pulled her out into the middle of the room. Lily keened a high-pitched sound and fought to get away.

"Hey, be careful," Heather yelled. "You're scaring

her." She tried to yank her arm away from the man holding her so she could help her sister.

"Let her go."

Heather froze at the sound of the familiar deep voice behind her. The man holding her dropped his hands and stepped back. Heather turned around. The tall man filling the bathroom doorway, his short blond hair glinting in the dim light, was wearing the same dark clothes as the others and the same black flak jacket with the letters *DEA* across the middle.

Nick. Thank God. He'd know what to do, how to help Lily.

The look of shock on his face was quickly replaced with anger. His brows were drawn down and his jaw was so tight his lips went white. He looked mad enough to strangle her, but at least he wasn't pointing his gun at her, like the others. He held his gun down by his side, aimed at the floor.

He was probably furious that she was in the middle of this, and she couldn't blame him for that. She should have taken his advice. She should have tried to convince Lily to go into an alcohol treatment program. Then maybe Lily wouldn't have gotten mixed up with whatever she'd gotten herself into now. Heather had naively insisted she could help her sister on her own, without taking such a seemingly drastic step. But obviously Nick had been right.

Nick holstered his gun and strode toward her.

Heather was so relieved she almost slumped to the dirty floor. "Nick, I'm so glad you're here. Lily is scared. She's not—"

Nick roughly grabbed her arms and spun her around, shocking Heather into silence. He pulled her hands behind her back. She gasped at the feel of cold steel clamping around her wrists. A ratcheting sound echoed in the room, and he pushed her toward the door.

"What are you doing?" she cried out.

"Heather Bannon, you're under arrest." His voice was clipped, cold.

"What? Wait, what are you talking about?"

He paused beside the last sink and leaned down, pressing his lips next to her ear. "You've got cocaine in your hair, darlin'," he growled.

Heather's gaze shot to the mirror. A wild-eyed woman stared back at her, a cloud of white dusting her normally dark brown hair, making it look prematurely gray.

Her horrified gaze met Nick's in the mirror. "I can explain."

"Tell it to the judge." He grabbed her arms and marched her out the door.

IN HER HIGH SCHOOL years, Heather had thought rock bottom was getting an A-minus on her trigonometry final exam, knocking her out of becoming the valedictorian.

In college, she'd thought rock bottom was flunking the GMAT and failing to get accepted into the master's degree program at Jacksonville University.

Later, when she'd been denied the small-business loan she'd wanted to start a private investigation firm, she'd thought that must surely be rock bottom.

But none of those were rock bottom.

Rock bottom was being arrested by her *former* boyfriend—there could be no doubt about that—and being thrown in a concrete-block holding cell that reeked of vomit and urine. A holding cell that currently housed five other women who looked like they could kill someone every morning before breakfast and never bat a false eyelash.

Heather didn't know where her sister was. The police had refused to answer any of Heather's questions about Lily. And no one had come back to update Heather or even give her the infamous phone call prisoners on TV shows always got. Not that she had anyone to call. Lily was her only family. Her friends had given up on her long ago when she'd started working seven days a week to try to build a P.I. business. And Nick... She shied away from that thought.

She was so tired. She wanted to rest her head against the wall behind her, but she was too afraid of lice, or something worse, that might be clinging to the surface. Instead, she stood a few feet away, trying not to touch anything, trying to pretend the speculative looks from the other women didn't send shivers up her spine. She was also trying her best not to give in to the urge to cry.

She was appalled that tears kept threatening to course down her cheeks. She couldn't remember the last time she'd cried, or the last time she'd even wanted to cry. She had Nick to thank for her jangled nerves. He'd judged her without giving her a chance to explain. He'd assumed the worst. Fine. Let him think what he wanted, but if there was any chance he was going to be the one to interrogate her—if anyone ever did bother to interrogate her—she wasn't going to let him see her with red eyes and tearstained cheeks.

She didn't want him to know how much his betrayal had hurt her.

A buzzing noise sounded and the door opened. A policewoman stood in the doorway and motioned for Heather to step out. "Miss Bannon, your lawyer is here."

"My lawyer? But I haven't even had a phone call."

The policewoman shrugged, her lack of interest stamped in her jaded, world-weary eyes. "Do you want to see your lawyer or not?"

Heather figured the police had made a mistake, that the lawyer was there for some other prisoner. But if playing along meant she'd get out of the foul-smelling cell for a few minutes, she wasn't going to argue. She stepped into the hallway.

The door buzzed closed behind her, and the policewoman led her down the hall to a door stamped with the words *Interview Room*. As she went inside, she braced herself, expecting to see Nick or a police officer waiting to grill her with questions. Instead, a stranger in a suit that looked like it must have cost at least a thousand dollars was sitting at a small table. He gave her a friendly smile and stood to shake her hand.

"Miss Bannon, I'm Anthony Greary, your attorney. A mutual friend hired me to help you out of this unfortunate situation."

The door closed behind Heather. She shook the attorney's hand and sat. "Mr. Greary, who is this 'mutual friend'?"

"Someone who prefers to remain anonymous."

The fine hairs on the back of Heather's neck stood at attention. "I don't suppose this friend is the man who gave my sister those bricks of cocaine?"

Greary glanced at the door and cleared his throat. "As I said, I'm here to help."

She had her answer. And it really sucked, because she'd *so* looked forward to a good half hour or more out of her cell. She pushed back her chair and stood. "I think you have me confused with my sister. My name is *Heather* Bannon. My sister is Lily. We're identical twins, but I assure you, we're nothing alike in any way that matters. And I guarantee we don't have any mutual friends."

"There's no confusion. I'm here to get both you and your sister released."

"Why?"

"Let's just say that one of you has something my employer wants returned."

Cold fear iced over Heather's insides. He had to be talking about the cocaine. What would happen if he found out she'd destroyed one of the bricks, and the police had the rest? Her hands started shaking. She clutched them together and gave the lawyer a false smile. "Like I said, there's been a mistake." She strode to the door and banged on the glass window.

A policeman Heather hadn't seen before opened the door, a surprised look on his face. "You have fifteen more minutes, ma'am."

"There's been a mistake. This man isn't my lawyer," Heather said.

The cop looked past her into the room. He shrugged and led her back down the hall to the holding cell. At the door, he paused and pulled a key card from the pocket of his shirt.

"Wait," Heather said, desperation lending her voice a high-pitched tone. She *really* didn't want to go back into that cell. What if the other women had banded together while she was gone? What if they'd formed an alliance, like on those reality TV shows, and had decided to beat up the new girl just for fun, as a way to pass the time?

Panic was making her think crazy thoughts. But crazy or not, she couldn't help the tight feeling in her chest and the way her lungs were laboring to draw an even breath. She had to get out of here. Maybe she could talk to Nick for a few minutes and straighten this out. She hated to beg, especially when she'd rather punch him than look at him, but if she was here much longer they'd have to take her out in a straitjacket.

"Please, I need to talk to Nick Morgan and explain," she said. "He's one of the DEA agents who—"

"I know who he is, ma'am. But Special Agent Morgan isn't here. And he specifically said that if you asked for him, he didn't want to talk to you."

Heather closed her eyes, squeezing them tight against the ridiculous urge to cry again. *How could you, Nick? How could you judge me like this and throw away what we had, like I never even mattered to you?*

She opened her eyes and cleared her throat. "I believe I'm entitled to a phone call. I need to call a lawyer to arrange bail." Not that she could afford it. About the only thing she could offer as collateral was a four-year-old dinged-up Ford Focus that had an outstanding loan balance higher than what the car was worth.

"I'll set that up," he said. "But you need to wait in the cell for now."

She managed not to whimper, barely. The policeman opened the door and impatiently motioned her forward. She steeled herself, took a deep breath and stepped inside. The odor of vomit hit her, making her eyes water, crushing the last remaining shred of affection she'd ever felt for Nick Morgan.

Chapter Two

Heather stood at the counter, rubbing her wrists, before taking the pen the policeman offered her. She could still feel the metal rubbing against her skin, even though the handcuffs had been removed. How long before she could forget that terrible night at the dance club, and being locked up for an entire weekend?

She scrawled her name across the form and handed it to the policeman in exchange for the belongings that had been taken from her when she was arrested. She deliberately checked her credit cards and cash in front of him. If the police didn't trust her and thought she was so dangerous that they had to lock her up, she wasn't going to trust them, either.

Satisfied nothing had been taken, she grabbed her keys. Wait. What good would that do? She plopped the keys back on the counter.

"Sir, officer, my car—"

"Is in the parking lot outside the station."

Relief had her smiling back at him in spite of her intentions. "Thank you." Darn it. She nearly bit her tongue. Why was she thanking him for moving her car from the club where she'd been falsely arrested? Bringing back her car was the least the police could do. Then again, it wasn't this police officer's fault. It was the DEA's fault.

One *particular* DEA agent's fault.

"Don't thank me," the officer replied. "Thank Special Agent Nick Morgan. He dropped your car off this morning, right after you arranged bail." He turned away to help someone else standing beside her.

Why would Nick bring her car back for her? She certainly didn't think it was because he cared about her. If he cared about her, he wouldn't have arrested her. Or at the very least he would have come to see her, maybe even helped her arrange bail. As expected, the bail bondsman had rejected her car as collateral. She'd had to max out almost all of her credit cards to get out of jail. Having already emptied her savings to help Lily when she'd shown up a few weeks ago, Heather now was down to a paltry three hundred dollars in her checking account, and about five hundred dollars of available credit on her last credit card. No, Nick hadn't dropped her car off because he cared. He'd dropped it off because it was his job.

She grabbed her keys and hurried toward the exit. When she stepped outside, she was tempted to drop to her knees and kiss the ground. But she'd already suffered enough humiliation this past weekend. She didn't want to add to it by having someone see her on her hands and knees. Instead, she settled for pausing long enough to take several deep breaths of fresh air, reveling in the pine scent from the nearby trees that was worlds different from the air in the holding cell.

Going home to a hot shower was at the top of her list of priorities. After that, she'd call the client she was originally supposed to meet Saturday morning and try to convince him, without telling him any details, that she'd had an emergency and still wanted his business. She couldn't afford to lose a client right now, not when her business was just beginning to make a profit and she had no more credit cards to fall back on to pay her bills.

Other than groveling to her client, she had no plans to work today, even though it was Monday. She hadn't taken a day off in nearly a year. And there was no way she could work right now. She needed some time to recover from her ordeal, and she needed to talk some sense into her sister. They also both needed to speak to the pro bono lawyer the court had appointed to defend Heather, and figure out what they were going to do about the drug charges.

The police had told Heather that Lily had been bailed out by the slimy lawyer who'd spoken to Heather about their "mutual friend." Heather would talk Lily into firing Greary. Lily would have to somehow pay the man back for the money he'd spent on her and use the pro bono lawyer Heather had been assigned. If Lily was going to survive this fiasco, owing money to a drug dealer's attorney was not the way to start.

When a couple stepped out of the police station, Heather moved away from the door and stood off to the side with her cell phone. She called her apartment three times, but Lily didn't pick up. Sighing, Heather shoved her phone back in her purse and shaded her eyes to look for her car. She spotted her gray Ford sitting in one of the spots right up front.

She headed to her car, but when she unlocked the door and pitched her purse into the passenger seat, she had the oddest feeling someone was watching her. She paused and looked around.

There, at the end of the parking lot, was Nick's massive black four-wheel-drive pickup. It was too far away for her to see details, but she could tell someone was inside. Was Nick watching her? Was he witnessing her humiliation as she left the police station in dirty, wrinkled clothes, her hair a mess, her makeup washed away long ago courtesy of a coarse rag and a filthy bar of soap she'd had to share with five other women? Was he waiting to see how broken she'd be after spending the weekend in jail?

She straightened her spine and got into her car with as much dignity as possible. It took every ounce of control she had not to slam the car door.

NICK TIGHTENED HIS hands on the steering wheel. The passenger door of his truck opened and his police detective brother climbed inside.

Rafe plopped down beside him. "Is that Heather, in the gray compact?"

"That's her."

"You could have come inside and talked to her. That would have been far less creepy than sitting here in the parking lot, like a stalker."

"She wouldn't want to see me."

"How do you know that?"

Nick scrubbed his face and blew out a deep breath. "Because I'm the one who arrested her."

"Yeah, there is that. But you also made me cash in my only chip with Judge Thompson to convince him to reduce her bail so she could get out of jail. Does she know you arranged that for her?"

"No." He glanced at his brother. "And she never will."

Rafe raised his hands. "I'm certainly not telling her,

especially since you owe me, big time. You do realize I interrupted Thompson's weekly golf game?"

Nick winced. "What's that going to cost me?"

"Babysitting. For a month."

The dark cloud that had fallen over Nick since the night he'd arrested Heather lifted, if only a little, and he knew he was probably grinning like an idiot. Being an uncle to his oldest sister's two boys was one of the true pleasures in his life, especially since they loved football as much as he did. If Rafe's new wife was going to have a baby, Nick would gladly welcome another nephew into the family, or even a niece. Hopefully if the baby was a girl, she'd love sports, because the thought of having to sit through a tea party or playing with dolls had him breaking out in a cold sweat.

"Darby's pregnant?" he asked.

"Not yet, but we're working on it." Rafe grinned. "We're practicing. A lot. So I'm sure it won't be long."

"TMI, brother. *Way* too much information."

Rafe laughed but quickly sobered. "You didn't call me out of a meeting to talk about my new bride. What's up?"

"Operation Key West."

"The task force that asked you to raid the club and promptly dumped you when Heather came under suspicion?"

"One and the same."

"I thought you were suspended. You can't be involved with a task force if you're suspended."

"Still suspended, pending an Internal Affairs investigation. But Waverly told me to come here to talk to the head of the task force."

"Here? Why would he want you to meet him at the police station? Why not meet you at the DEA office?"

"I asked the same thing, but Waverly just told me to get my butt over here for a ten o'clock meeting." He shrugged. "I was hoping you might have heard something. Captain Buresh didn't say anything about the DEA dropping by?"

"No, he didn't."

Nick stared through the windshield at the vacant spot where Heather's car had been a few minutes ago. Even now, several days later, he couldn't quite wrap his mind around the fact that Heather had been at that club the night of the raid.

"Maybe the head of the task force is here to discuss another local operation," Nick said. "Maybe Waverly wanted to make sure I met him before he left."

"Why would he want that?"

"Waverly's ticked at me. He might want to make me grovel and apologize for shaming our unit by having a drug-dealing girlfriend."

Rafe cocked his head and studied him. "From what you've told me about her, she doesn't sound the type to be dealing, just the opposite. She's been trying to build a private investigation business for years. She works all the time, putting everything she can into growing her client list. Do you really think she's going to risk throwing that away to deal drugs on the side? Her sister is—"

"Her identical twin."

"Okay. Not what I was going to say, but I'll go with that. Being a twin doesn't make two people the same and you know it."

"Yeah. Maybe. It did surprise me that she didn't let her sister's drug-dealer lawyer bail her out. If Heather had let him help her she could have been out of jail Saturday morning, like her sister. But she didn't, and she ended up staying in jail the entire weekend because of it." He shrugged. "I'm not sure what to make of that."

"You could always talk to her, give her a chance to tell her side."

Nick absently studied the rows of cars in front of the police station. Rafe was right. Heather did deserve a chance to explain. And he hadn't given her that chance. He'd been too angry, thinking she'd betrayed his trust in her. Now that he was thinking more clearly, he knew he'd made a mistake in judging her so quickly. But it didn't matter now. There was no way to fix this.

"I'm not allowed to talk to her now anyway, not with IA all over me. If I'm seen anywhere near her, I can kiss my career goodbye."

"You sure know how to pick 'em."

"What's that supposed to mean?"

"I'm just saying your judgment in women could use some work. You wasted nearly a year of your life with your on-again, off-again engagement to psycho-girlfriend."

"She wasn't a psycho. She was…conflicted."

Rafe let out a shout of laughter. "Conflicted? Now I know you've been talking to my therapist wife way too much."

Nick grinned. "Maybe. But psycho-girlfriend did have a lot going for her."

"Like what?"

"She was hot."

"Everyone you date is hot."

"She was a professional cheerleader. And very…limber."

Rafe smiled. "You've got me there. All I'm saying is that after everything you went through with her, I figured the next time you got serious about a woman you'd pick someone who—"

"Whoa, whoa, whoa. Who said we were serious? We only dated a couple of months. That's way short of serious territory."

"Darby and I only dated a couple of *weeks* before we got engaged."

"That's because her old-fashioned father knew you two had gotten 'friendly' and he shamed you into it. Besides, you two knew each other for years before you started dating."

Rafe rolled his eyes. "Her father had nothing to do with us getting married. And being on opposite sides in the courtroom doesn't count as a relationship. Look, all I'm saying is that you need to take a long hard look at your feelings for her before you do something you might regret."

"Meaning?"

"Meaning, if she didn't really matter to you, on a personal level, do you honestly think you would have twisted my arm to get the judge to reduce her bail? And how many DEA agents would have paid to get a car out of the impound lot and would have driven it to the police station for a woman they don't care about?"

Nick ground his teeth together. "I never told you about that."

"You didn't have to." Rafe gave him a smug look. "I have eyes and ears all over this town. That's part of what makes me a great detective."

"Humble, too."

Rafe shrugged, obviously not caring about Nick's insult. "As I was saying, you obviously care more about Heather than you're willing to admit, even to yourself."

"Since when did you become so touchy-feely?"

"I guess since I married a hot therapist."

"Whatever. I don't want to talk about this anymore. Not that I ever did."

"But—"

"Drop it."

Rafe held his hands up in a placating gesture. "All right, all right. I'll drop it. You said Waverly wants you to meet with the task force. You have to have some idea of why he'd want you to do that. And don't give me the line about apologizing for your girlfriend. That's weak."

Nick let out a deep sigh. Rafe always could read him, like a Jedi knight using the Force to probe his mind. Or was that Spock on *Star Trek?* Either way, it was damned aggravating.

"My DEA buddies tell me the task force still has Heather and her sister in its crosshairs," Nick said. "They think Heather's sister is running drugs for a dealer operating out of Key West. They think Heather's been helping her sister move the drugs, and that Heather flushed that kilo to try to avoid the sting. They believe she would have flushed all of the drugs if she'd had enough time."

His brother's eyes narrowed. "She couldn't have purposely tried to avoid the sting unless she knew about it ahead of time."

"Bingo."

Rafe swore. "That's the real reason they suspended you. Not because you're a terrible judge of character and got mixed up with a girlfriend who may or may not be dealing drugs. They think you tipped her off about the raid."

"If I were them, I'd probably think the same thing," Nick said. "I've been practically living in Key West this past year, building my cover to gather intelligence on the drug activity down there. Maybe they figured I've gone in a little too deep, that the past few months I spent up here were more than an extended vacation. Maybe they thought I was helping move drugs up the pipeline, and that Heather and Lily were in on it with me."

His brother cursed again, impressing Nick. With language like that, Rafe could go undercover as a DEA agent and blend right in with the dealers as if he were one of them. Too bad he'd wasted his talents as a detective and part-time bomb-squad technician in the Saint Augustine Police Department.

"How can I help?" Rafe asked.

"Answer me a question. If you were heading up a task force whose sole goal was to catch a drug dealer with ties to Heather and Lily, what would you do right now?"

"If I was dumb enough to waste my talents as a DEA agent, you mean?"

Nick grinned. "Yeah. That's what I mean."

"If I believed the girls were a lead to a major drug dealer, I'd keep my distance. I'd wait for the dealer or some of his lackeys to show up." His gaze shot to Nick. "I'd use the girls as bait."

"Exactly."

Rafe groaned. "Ah, hell. You want me to keep an eye on your girlfriend for you."

"Ex-girlfriend. And I want more than that. I need you to keep her alive."

HEATHER FINISHED CLEANING the kitchen and stood with her hands braced on the edge of the sink. She stared through the cutout into the family room and shook her head. To say her apartment was a disaster was an understatement. Lily had always been incredibly messy, but this was the worst Heather had ever seen. Lily usually tried to confine her piles of dirty clothes and discarded items to her bedroom. This morning, Heather's entire apartment looked as if a tornado had gone through it.

Probably Lily's way of paying her back for flushing the cocaine.

Heather's shoulders slumped. She slogged her way through the mess to the short hallway that led to the two bedrooms. She paused outside the guest bedroom door and tried the knob. Still locked, like when Heather had first gotten home. She hadn't even seen Lily yet, because her sister was acting like a spoiled brat, hiding behind a locked door with classic rock blasting from the room. Heather banged her fist against the door. Still no answer.

"Come on, Lily. You can't ignore me forever. Open up. We need to talk."

Heather rested her forehead against the door. Maybe she should give up on her sister for now and get that shower she'd been longing for since she'd gotten home. The only reason she hadn't taken a shower already was because when she'd walked into her apartment the smell of rotting garbage coming from the kitchen had nearly knocked her over. How Lily could have ignored that smell was beyond her. It had permeated the entire apartment.

After taking out the garbage, Heather had started setting the rest of the kitchen to rights and one thing had led to another until she'd ended up scrubbing the entire room. Now the thought of a hot shower sounded like heaven. She might even soak her aching, tired muscles in that bubble bath she'd been wanting since Friday. She hurried into her bedroom, shut the door and took off her clothes.

Nɪᴄᴋ ᴘᴀᴜsᴇᴅ ɪɴ the opening to the conference room, surprised to see an assistant district attorney sitting at the table, along with another man Nick had never met. His boss, Zack Waverly, was at the head of the table and motioned for Nick to come in.

Nick shut the door and took a seat beside his boss.

"Nick," Waverly said, "you already know ADA Tom Hicks. He only has an hour window before his next court appointment next door. That's why we met over here instead of at the DEA office."

Nick leaned over the table and shook Hicks's hand.

"And this," Waverly said, motioning to the man sitting at the other end of the table, "this is Special Agent Michael Rickloff. He works out of the Miami office and is heading up the Key West Task Force. He's the one who called and asked us to perform the sting on the club Friday night."

Nick shook Rickloff's hand. "Miami? You're not from Key West?"

"Miami native, born and raised. Key West is my current target, thus the name of the task force I put together. A major drug pipeline is coming up from the Keys into my city, and as you found out, even as far north as Saint Augustine. I want it stopped. And I need your help to do it."

Nick turned to Waverly. "My help? Is my suspension lifted?"

"Assuming you agree to Rickloff's plan, yes."

"But the internal investigation will continue," Hicks said. "And if we find anything that concerns us, you'll be pulled from the operation."

So that was why the ADA was here? To warn Nick to be a good boy? If it weren't for the carrot of having his suspension lifted, he would have gotten up right then and walked out.

Ignoring Hicks, he focused on Rickloff. "What plan? What operation?"

"When you raided the club for us, we were obviously hoping you'd find more than a knapsack with four kilos of cocaine. We were hoping you'd catch Lily Bannon meeting her contact here in north Florida. I wanted a bigger fish than Miss Bannon, to ultimately lead me to the head of the pipeline. Since that didn't happen, I need another way to bring my target down. That's where you come in."

Nick crossed his arms and sat back. "I'm listening."

AFTER PAMPERING HERSELF with a shower *and* a long soak in the tub, Heather was finally starting to feel normal again. She'd clipped her nails short the way she liked them and filed them smooth. She'd styled her hair into long curly waves that hung down her back, and she was wearing one of her favorite pairs of slacks—the soft, copper-colored chinos, with an exquisite pair of Italian leather sandals cushioning her feet—clothes she rarely got to wear because she was usually working.

Her typical work clothes consisted of T-shirts and jeans, things she didn't mind getting dirty or torn if she had to duck behind a Dumpster to avoid her mark catching her with her camera.

Thinking about work reminded her of the disastrous phone call with her client she'd made a few minutes ago—correction, *former* client. He'd been furious that she hadn't called him Saturday, and no amount of apologizing or telling him there was an emergency had soothed him. Now she'd have to work extra hard to be even more frugal until she could get another big case lined up.

Determined not to think about her business and financial woes for now, she straightened the bathroom and went to work on her bedroom. Lily must have searched through all of Heather's drawers hoping to find some hidden money, because every single one of them was hanging open. Heather sighed and straightened the mess, then headed into the living room to tackle the mess in there.

She stood in indecision, not sure where to start. Not only were there piles of laundry, papers and DVDs lying around wherever Lily had chosen to drop them, but some of the drawers and doors in the entertainment center on the far wall were hanging open.

She blinked and studied the room more carefully. Was it a coincidence that her apartment was so horribly trashed, after everything that had happened? This wasn't a typical "Lily mess." It was far worse. The apartment looked like it had been…searched. She'd worried about Greary and his "employer" finding out about the fate of the drugs. Had they broken into her apartment and searched it? She gasped as an even worse thought occurred to her. What if Lily had been home when they broke in?

Her entire body started shaking. She whirled around and rushed back into the hall. She twisted the knob on Lily's door. Still locked. She pounded on the door, praying the awful, sinking feeling inside of her was because she was overtired and overreacting.

"Open up, Lily! Please. I need to know you're okay." She pounded on the door again. No answer. "Are…are you in there?"

Nothing except for the beat of the music, the same music that had been playing earlier, as if it was on a constant loop playing over and over.

Oh, no.

She ran to the kitchen, her gaze darting to every corner, as if someone might be hiding, ready to pounce on her. She yanked the junk drawer open beside the stove and grabbed the skeleton key before running back to her sister's room. She shoved the key in the lock and pushed the door open.

Shock had her frozen, pressing her hand against her throat. Everything in the room was shredded, as if someone had taken a razor-sharp knife and gone on a rampage. Nothing was spared. Not the drapes on the windows, the clothes in the closet that was standing wide open or even the comforter on top of the bed. Everything had been destroyed with a violence that sent a wave of fear crashing through her. And there, on the bed, was a small white piece of paper. A note.

When Heather read what it said, she whirled around and fled from the apartment.

Chapter Three

"You've been building an undercover presence in the Keys for quite some time," Rickloff said.

Nick shrugged. "About eight months, off and on, in preparation for a major op next year. We've been coordinating with the Key West office on that."

Rickloff waved his hand as though that was inconsequential. "That operation is a long ways off. My need is more immediate. I need you to use your cover now, on my task force."

"The Key West office is okay with this?"

Rickloff exchanged a glance with Waverly. "I haven't notified them yet, but I will. That's not for you to worry about. And I'm not asking much here. I just want you to help me draw out the big fish."

A gnawing suspicion started in Nick's mind, the suspicion that Rickloff wasn't being honest with him. Why would a task force out of Miami operate in the Keys without coordinating with the head of the Key West office?

"All right," Nick said. "I'll bite. Who's the big fish?"

"Jose Gonzalez."

"*The* Jose Gonzalez? The top of the food chain in the Keys?"

Rickloff nodded.

Nick snorted and shook his head. "Exactly how do you plan to get Gonzalez? The man has never even had a speeding ticket. Everyone knows he's dirty, that he's the biggest dealer around, but no one can ever get any evidence against him."

Rickloff leaned forward, his dark eyes blazing with excitement. "That's because they've never had the right bait. We've got his girlfriend up on charges that could put her in prison for years. If we make a deal with her in exchange for her cooperation, I think we'll be able to finally get enough evidence on Gonzalez to bring him down."

Nick had feared this would be Rickloff's angle. He'd expected it. But that was before he knew Gonzalez was involved. Using the girls as bait with someone like that was unthinkable, far too dangerous.

He looked at his boss, expecting him to speak up, but Waverly remained silent.

Nick cleared his throat and forced himself to speak in a reasonable tone of voice. "Let me get this straight. Are you saying Lily Bannon is Gonzalez's girlfriend? And that you want to somehow use her to bring Gonzalez down?"

"That's exactly what I'm saying. The two of them met about six months ago on a trip up here in north Florida. They've been a hot item ever since. Our CIs tell us Gonzalez actually thinks he's in love with Miss Bannon. We want to use that against him."

"Are these confidential informants people you've been working with for a long time? You trust them?"

"Absolutely."

"Then tell me how, exactly, you think you can use Gonzalez's affection for Lily Bannon against him?"

"Simple. We want you to be her contact in Key West. We'll make a deal with her. We'll drop the drug charges if she gathers incriminating evidence against Gonzalez and gives it to you. As soon as we have enough evidence to make a case against him, you'll pull Miss Bannon out. In return for *your* cooperation, we drop your suspension."

Nick turned to Waverly. "You do realize this is insane?"

Waverly turned a dull red. "It's risky, yes, but I think it could work."

Nick shook his head. "The problem here is that neither of you fully understand who you're dealing with. Gonzalez is a twisted psychopath. All the other dealers fear him. If anyone crosses him, in any way, he kills them. I don't care how much you think he may care about Lily Bannon. If he suspects for one second that she turned on him, that she's providing evidence to the DEA, she's dead. And exactly what makes you think you can trust an alcoholic and a junkie to hold herself together for this kind of operation? She'll crack under the pressure. And when she does, Gonzalez will pounce. There's only one outcome from this. Disaster. And I want no part of it."

He scooted his chair back from the table and stood. "I'd rather stay suspended than risk a woman's life. I'll take the paid vacation while Internal Affairs investigates me. And I assure you I'll be contacting Lily Bannon to advise her not to help you. It's far too dangerous."

Rickloff shot up from his chair. "You'll do no such thing. We need Miss Bannon's cooperation."

"Don't count on it." Nick strode to the door and

yanked it open. He froze when he saw who was walking through the squad room toward him.

Rafe. And Heather.

Heather looked so pale the freckles on her face stood out in stark relief.

Nick met them halfway. "What happened? Are you okay, Heather?"

She shook her head but didn't say anything.

Rafe reached into his pocket and pulled out a clear evidence bag with a piece of paper inside. "Lily Bannon has been abducted."

THE CONFERENCE ROOM quickly filled with a mix of DEA agents and police officers. Captain Buresh—Rafe's boss—barked out orders, along with Waverly and Rickloff.

Nick stared at the note through the plastic bag.

I've got what you want. You've got what I want.
Let's trade.

The most obvious interpretation was that Gonzalez had abducted Lily and wanted to trade her for his kilos of cocaine.

So much for Rickloff's theory that Gonzalez was in love with Lily.

The second line of the note gave the location for the trade—Skeleton's Misery, a bar in Key West, along with tomorrow's date and the time of 9:00 p.m.

He glanced at his watch. It was eleven o'clock in the morning. That didn't give them much time to come up with a plan to save Lily. As soon as he'd seen the note, he'd run out to his truck to grab his map of the Keys. But when he'd returned, the conference room was in chaos. He'd tried several times to get everyone to be quiet, but no one was paying him any attention.

Rafe was leaning against the far wall, shaking his head, obviously as disgusted as Nick was.

Screw it. Lily didn't have time for this. And neither did Heather. She was sitting as still as a statue in her chair at the far end of the table, so ghostly pale she looked as if she might collapse at any moment.

Enough was enough. Nick raked his hand across the conference room table, sending folders, pads of paper and pens flying. The room went silent and everyone stared at him in shock.

"Now that I have your attention," Nick said, "I want everyone out except essential personnel." He plopped his rolled-up map onto the table. When nobody moved, he glanced at his brother. "Rafe, want to help me explain to everyone who the nonessential people are?"

Rafe grinned. Between him and Nick, they went around the room directing people out the door.

Nick finally closed the door and turned around to a much more orderly, and quiet, conference room. The only remaining people were the same ones Nick had been talking to earlier, plus Heather, Rafe and Captain Buresh.

"You've got a bit of an ego to order all those people out, don't you, son?" Rickloff said.

"Lily Bannon's life is on the line. And we don't have a lot of time to figure out how we're going to save her."

He unrolled the map. Rafe grabbed some of the pads of paper off the floor and helped Nick weigh down the corners so the map would lie flat. Everyone except

Heather gathered around the end of the table, leaning over the map while Nick drew a circle.

"That's Skeleton's Misery," he said, pointing to the circle on the western edge of Key West. "It's a new bar that opened up this year. That's where Gonzalez wants to make the trade."

"Tell me about the location," Rickloff said.

Nick pointed to the street running out front. "It's one of the more isolated bars, at the end of the tourist strip. The street is narrow, more for walkers than cars. The nearest cross streets are a mile south, here—" he pointed to another spot on the map and marked an X "—and two miles north." He marked another X. "The only other access is from the ocean. There's a dock right behind it, again, fairly new. The bar caters more to locals than to tourists, so it won't be as crowded as some of the others, and there shouldn't be a lot of boats at the dock."

"What do you mean it caters to locals?" Waverly asked.

Nick glanced at Heather. Some of the color had returned to her face, and she was watching him intently.

"Heather, would you like some water or a bite to eat?" Nick asked. "Rafe could take you outside, get you something."

Rafe was already heading to Heather's side when she raised her hand to stop him.

"I'm not going anywhere. I want to hear this. I want to know how you're going to help Lily." Her voice broke on the last word and she clasped her hands tightly on the table in front of her.

Nick belatedly wished he hadn't allowed Heather to stay in the conference room when he'd ushered everyone else out, but he didn't have time to argue with her.

"When I say the bar caters to locals," he continued, answering Waverly's question, "I mean it's raw. It's little more than a shanty with loud music. No fancy menus, no live bands, and the people who run the place are ex-cons."

Heather seemed to withdraw into herself and sank farther back in her chair. She was probably imagining her sister in that bar.

"I imagine the courts will insist on keeping the kilos we got from the bar as evidence until the case against Lily and Heather is settled. So we'll need to check some kilos out of the evidence locker to use for the trade," Nick said to his boss. "Do we have that much on hand?"

Waverly shook his head. "I doubt it. Other than that bar raid, we haven't made a cocaine bust in quite some time. Any cocaine we've confiscated would have already been destroyed."

"*We've* got that much," Rickloff said. "Not a problem. I can have an agent bring the drugs down to the Keys and meet up with you."

"Good. We can place a couple of guys up the street here, and down here." Nick pointed to the map. "Gonzalez chose a good spot. There aren't a lot of hiding places. Maybe we could bring a few guys in from the water, have them hide out in a boat at the dock behind the bar."

"All right," Rickloff said.

"We'll have to pick an undercover agent who can pass for Heather in dim light." Nick glanced at Heather. "Five-two, small build, long, curly brown hair, blue eyes. Do you have any agents like that in your Miami office?"

Rickloff shook his head. "I don't have any women in my office."

Why did that not surprise him? Nick shook his head.

He was less and less impressed with Rickloff the more he learned about him.

"I know the Keys office has some women, several of whom might be good candidates," Nick said.

Rickloff shook his head again. "I'm not ready to involve that office just yet."

Nick's suspicion that Rickloff might be trying to hide his operation from the Key West office had just been confirmed. But since neither his nor Rafe's boss were saying anything, he decided to let it go. For now.

"All right. There are five women in our unit here in Saint Augustine," Nick said. "But they're all taller than Heather." He glanced at Rafe. "Do you have any policewomen who could pass for Heather?"

Rafe shook his head. "I don't know anyone that small in stature here."

"There has to be someone we could use," Nick said. "We've got a state trooper headquarters down State Road 16. And the Saint Johns County Sheriff's Office isn't far from here. Or we could even ask for help from Jacksonville. Rafe, could you contact the other offices, see if they have someone available who fits the physical profile? The eye color may not matter. They could wear colored contacts."

Rafe nodded and pulled out his phone, but Rickloff shook his head.

"This is too important to risk using a look-alike when we've got an exact match for Heather Bannon sitting right in this room."

Nick swore under his breath. "You want to use Heather as bait."

"What I want, Special Agent Morgan," Rickloff snapped, "is to ensure that nothing goes wrong with this operation. We have a unique opportunity here. No matter what I've tried over the years, when it comes to Gonzalez, nothing sticks. I would have rather gone with my original plan to use Lily so I could get Gonzalez on drug charges. But they caught Capone for tax evasion. If I have to settle with getting Gonzalez for kidnapping, so be it. As long as I can put him away, that's what matters."

Nick stared at him in disbelief. "What matters is that we catch the bad guys without risking the lives of civilians. And please tell me you didn't just categorize a woman's abduction as a 'unique opportunity.'"

Rickloff's face flushed. "Poor choice of words."

"You think?" Nick crossed his arms. "You have the note. You have the time and location to make the trade. All you have to do is send in a team with an undercover policewoman and four kilos. If Gonzalez or his men show up, great. You save Lily." He thumped his fist on the table. "And you don't risk the life of another innocent civilian by using her as bait."

Rickloff shook his head. "Gonzalez and his men know Lily too well. They'll expect her identical twin to look just like her. They won't fall for a stand-in."

"She'll keep to the shadows. Wear the same clothes, a wig. It will work," Nick insisted.

"If Gonzalez realizes we tried to trick him, he'll kill his hostage."

"You don't know that," Nick said.

"I'll do it." Heather's soft voice broke through the argument and everyone looked at her. She swallowed hard and fisted her hands on the table. "I'll be the bait. I don't want to risk my sister's life by using some other woman to pretend to be me. I'll do it."

Nick braced his hands on the table. "You are not getting anywhere near Gonzalez."

"Tom," Rickloff said, addressing the ADA. "Are you willing to give Heather Bannon the same deal we were proposing for her sister earlier?"

Tom nodded. "We are. Her full cooperation in exchange for dropping the charges."

Heather glanced at Tom. "Drop the charges against my sister, too."

"Done."

"Then it's settled." Rickloff rubbed his hands back and forth. "Agent Morgan, you'll escort Miss Bannon into the bar. I'm not sending a civilian in there alone."

"Right, because you're so worried about her safety," Nick said, not bothering to hide his sarcasm.

"Nick," Waverly admonished. "You don't have anything to bargain with here. If you won't agree to this plan, we'll send a different agent to back up Miss Bannon."

"Really? Who? Who else could you send that has a built-in cover already? If you send someone without a solid cover, you risk Gonzalez thinking the DEA is involved. He'll kill Lily without even attempting an exchange."

Heather sucked in a breath.

Nick immediately regretted his candor. "I could be wrong." He didn't believe that, but he didn't want Heather to give up hope, either.

"Your concern for Heather Bannon's welfare is commendable," Rickloff said. "But you're overthinking this. We'll have backup nearby. She won't be in any true danger."

Rafe made a sound of disgust.

His boss shot him an admonishing look.

"If Gonzalez pulls a gun on Heather," Nick asked, "can your backup get there faster than a bullet?"

Rickloff's jaw went rigid. "If you're convinced we can't protect her, then agree to the plan. You can be the one to protect her. You'll buy us the time we need to move in if something goes wrong."

Nick shook his head. "Find another way to save Lily and bring down Gonzalez. I'll take my chances with Internal Affairs. And Heather can take her chances with the judge."

He strode toward the door and yanked it open.

"Nick, wait," Heather called out.

He half turned, his hand still on the doorknob.

Heather appeared to be struggling for words. She folded her hands on the table and aimed her sad eyes at him like the sights on a rifle. "I can handle this. I'm an experienced private investigator. That might not seem like a big deal to a DEA agent, but it means I've been in a lot of tough, dangerous situations. I'm adaptable and a quick thinker if things don't go as planned. I'm also an excellent marksman, so I can defend myself, or watch your back. I *can* handle this."

"You're still a civilian, untrained in law-enforcement procedures," Nick said, softening his voice, trying to make her understand his concerns. "You shouldn't have to defend yourself against a drug dealer, or worry about watching anyone's back. You're also emotionally involved. That makes you vulnerable. And that makes you dangerous to yourself and everyone else."

Heather's eyes practically flashed sparks at him. "Look, I know Lily is screwed up, but she's still my sister. She's my twin. There's a bond between us other

people—people without twins—can't possibly understand. It's like…we're two halves of a whole. If something happens to her, I don't…I don't know if I could
survive." She drew herself up, lifting her chin defiantly.
"I *am* going to do this, with or without you. But I'd feel
safer if you were the one to help me." Her fingers curled
into fists on the top of the table. "Nick, I'm begging you.
Please. Help me save my sister."

The plea in her voice was difficult to ignore. But all
he had to do was think about her being shot, or worse,
tortured, by Gonzalez or his men, and his resolve hardened. He searched for the words that would make her
accept the reality of the situation. "I've spent months,
years, going undercover with guys like this. They live
by their own code. They don't care about the law. If they
even suspect you're lying, about anything, they'll try to
kill you. Trust me on that."

"I do trust you. I trust you to protect me. I don't have
to know much about the DEA to realize that these men
wouldn't be arguing to get you to work on this case if
you weren't the best agent for the job. I want the best for
my sister. If you don't do this, Lily could die."

Her eyes were bright with unshed tears. It was probably killing her to ask for his help, after what she'd been
through this weekend and his role in it. And watching
her, listening to her, was tearing him up inside. But
how much worse would it be if he gave in? No matter
what angle he used to look at this plan of Rickloff's, he
couldn't see any good coming out of it.

A tear slid down Heather's face and she wiped it away,
her face turning the dull red of embarrassment.

Nick swore beneath his breath and glared at Waverly
and Rickloff. "You're both bastards."

Rickloff nodded. "Maybe I am. Maybe we both are. But when this is over, I have faith that Gonzalez will be behind bars."

"And do you also have faith that Lily and Heather will be alive? And unhurt?" Nick asked, his voice low and deadly.

Rickloff let out a deep sigh. "If you don't agree to help, I'm still sending Miss Bannon undercover with another agent. Is that what you want? For me to put her life in the hands of someone else? Someone who isn't as good as you? Someone who doesn't have as good a cover as you have?"

Nick swore again. He dropped his hand from the doorknob and turned fully around. He stared at Rickloff for a long moment before turning his gaze to Heather. Without looking away from her, he spoke to Rickloff. "All right. I'll go to Key West. I'll help you get Gonzalez and get Lily out of there. But I've got some conditions of my own."

Chapter Four

Waverly crossed the conference room to stand next to Rickloff. "Now listen here, Nick. You don't get to set conditions or make demands. You do what we tell you to do. You do your job." He jabbed his finger against Nick's chest.

Nick grabbed Waverly's wrist and held it in an iron grip. Waverly's eyes widened when he tried to pull his arm back but Nick didn't budge an inch. The look of alarm on his boss's face was almost comical. Waverly had only ever seen Nick in his "charm" mode. A smile, a joke, fast-talking, were Nick's usual methods for getting what he wanted. But when the situation demanded something more, he had no problem taking it up another level. Especially when a woman's life was at stake. And, as much as he hated to admit it, especially when that woman was Heather.

Only the fact that Waverly was his boss kept Nick from shoving his arm when he let go.

"I wasn't talking to *you* when I said I had conditions," Nick said. "I was talking to *her*."

Heather's eyes widened.

"Everyone out, except Miss Bannon," Nick ordered.

He ignored Rickloff's and Waverly's grumblings as his brother and Buresh herded everyone out of the room.

Rafe pulled the door shut behind them, giving Nick a quick nod to let him know he'd guard the door.

Nick stood directly in front of Heather's chair and leaned down, intentionally using his size to try to intimidate her. "You aren't going to Key West," he growled. "With *anyone*."

She raised her chin defiantly and crossed her arms over her chest. "Yes. I am."

"No. You aren't. You're going to stay here. You're going to move in with my brother for a few weeks. He's a police officer, a damn good one. He'll keep you safe in case Gonzalez's buddies come looking for you. I'll go to Key West and try to get your sister out of this mess. But no way in hell are you coming with me."

She was shaking her head before he finished his last sentence. "No. You heard Rickloff. He said Gonzalez will kill Lily if I'm not in that bar to meet him. I am going. With or without you."

"I've been on dozens of undercover operations. What Rickloff is asking you to do sounds too simple, too easy. Nothing in the world of drug dealers is that simple or easy. He's hiding something."

"Like what? Why would he hide anything?"

"I don't know. But it doesn't feel right. It doesn't pass the smell test. I don't trust Rickloff. He's from the Miami office, leading a task force to capture a dealer in Key West. But he hasn't notified the special agent in charge at the Key West DEA office. Something isn't right here. Rickloff's motives are suspect, and this plan of his is far too dangerous and risky."

"Okay, what's the alternative? How do we find my sister and get her back safely?"

He shoved a hand through his hair and blew out an exasperated breath. "I haven't figured that out yet."

"Well, we don't have time for you to figure it out."

Nick stared down at Heather, surprised at how stubborn she was being. She'd always been so easy to get along with. She could be the hard-nosed P.I. when she had to be, but he'd seen the soft, passionate, feminine side of her and had never expected her to defy him like this.

The only time they'd ever argued was after a phone call between Heather and her sister. When Heather told Nick her frustrations about Lily's behavior, he'd flat out told her Lily was a drunk and needed to be in treatment. Maybe he could have worded his conclusions in softer language, but when Heather had insisted her sister wasn't an alcoholic, the two of them had ended up in a heated discussion.

She hadn't backed down one bit and he'd ended up apologizing, even though he firmly believed she was wrong. Now, as he stood in her personal space, purposely trying to intimidate her into giving in, he wasn't having any more luck than he'd had the first time they'd argued. Instead, she stared up at him, her eyes flashing with anger. And something else.

Fear.

She *should* be afraid, for *herself.* But he knew she wasn't. She was afraid on behalf of her sister, and recklessly willing to do anything to help her, even if it meant putting herself in danger. He finally accepted that no amount of arguing was going to change her mind. Intimidation wasn't going to work. He sighed.

"I'll help you get Lily back," he said, "but like I said earlier, I have conditions."

She darted her eyes toward the closed door, as if by sheer will she could get Waverly and Rickloff to step inside. "What conditions?"

"First, we're through, finished. There is no 'us' anymore. And there never will be."

"Agreed."

She answered so quickly Nick was taken aback. He'd been prepared to explain about his job, how he couldn't date anyone tainted by illegal drug activity, even indirectly through a family member. He'd planned to tell her he still cared about her, that he regretted how things had turned out. But there was no point in apologizing now, not when *she* so obviously didn't want a relationship with *him* anymore.

That knowledge stung far more than he would have expected.

He rested his hip against the table. "Second, you do exactly what I tell you to do at all times. I mean it. Exactly what I say. Unquestioningly. If I tell you to get down, you drop on the floor as if someone had swiped your legs out from beneath you. If I tell you to be quiet, you don't even breathe until I tell you it's safe. Can you do that?"

Her eyes widened with alarm, as if she was just beginning to realize how dangerous this mission was.

"O-okay," she said, her voice soft, hesitant.

"Three, you report to me and me alone. I don't care what Rickloff or Waverly tell you. One phone call to them at the wrong place, wrong time, could get us killed—you, Lily and me."

"Why would you think they would ask me to call them?"

"It's what I'd do if I were them."

She nodded. "Okay. Is that all?"

He shook his head. "No, there's one more condition. And it's a deal breaker. You already agreed to my other conditions. Remember that. One of those conditions was to do exactly what I tell you to do."

"I understand."

"Okay. Final condition. We'll go to Key West together, but you'll stay in hiding, in my hotel room with another agent watching over you, while I go to that bar to draw Gonzalez out somehow. I *will* figure out a way to save your sister, but I refuse to use you as bait. It's too dangerous."

She raised her hands in a gesture of surprise and frustration. "How will we save Lily if I'm in hiding?"

"Leave that to me. You have my word I'll do everything I can to save her, but putting you in danger is not part of the plan. I meant what I said. This is the deal breaker. You agree to this or I'm out. And you already know I'm the best agent for the job or Rickloff wouldn't have tried so hard to convince me to do this. So what's it going to be?"

She stared at him for a full minute, frustration and anger warring with each other across her expressive face. Even though she didn't want to agree to his final condition, she obviously knew he was her sister's best shot at making it out of Key West alive.

He glanced at his watch, well aware of how urgent it was to get moving soon or there wouldn't be a chance to help Lily at all.

Heather let out a long breath and glared at him, obviously not happy, but resolved.

"I guess I don't really have a choice," she said. She shoved out of her chair and headed to the door.

"You made the right decision," Nick said.

"I hope so." She paused in the door opening. "Because I've decided Lily's best chance is with someone *other than you.*"

NICK AND RAFE leaned back against the desk in the SAPD squad room. They both had their legs spread, arms crossed, as if they had nothing better to do than to watch the fiasco playing out in front of them.

Waverly and Rickloff stood on the other side of the room with the small group of agents who'd come up from Miami with Rickloff, talking to Heather. Apparently they were giving her last-minute instructions while one of the agents grabbed her suitcase that she'd gone home and packed after telling Nick she didn't want his help. Her refusal to trust him still stung, but he supposed he'd earned that by letting her sit in jail all weekend and not giving her a chance to explain what had happened.

"I heard they're flying out to Key West in the morning," Rafe said. "They're going to a hotel by Jacksonville International Airport for tonight."

Nick grunted in reply.

"They'll arrive at the Key West airport around noon," Rafe said. "An agent from Miami will meet them there with the kilos and drive Heather to a hotel. I might have even heard a rumor about which hotel they'll be using."

"One of those infamous contacts you brag about, I suppose?"

"Yep."

"I don't suppose you also know the name of the Miami agent they've chosen to go to the bar with Heather?"

"I might."

"That could prove useful."

They watched in silence as Heather shook Rickloff's hand. She and the entire entourage headed across the far side of the squad room toward the exit. Heather didn't even look Nick's way.

"Are you sure you've made the right decision?" Rafe asked, stifling a yawn as he, too, watched the group head to the exit.

"Yep."

"If Waverly fires you, I could put in a good word for you at SAPD," Rafe said. "We have an opening for a meter reader. A washed-up DEA agent might be qualified for that."

Nick shoved him.

Rafe shoved him back.

Waverly held the door open for Heather, and the small group headed out front. They stood at the curb, apparently waiting for the van from the airport that was heading toward the front of the building from the end of the parking lot.

"He's not going to fire me," Nick said.

"You sure about that? He seemed pretty ticked that you didn't go along with Rickloff's plan. I haven't seen his face that red since you cleaned him out at poker a few months ago."

Nick sighed. "I miss poker nights. I can't believe you let Darby cancel our poker nights."

"Let her? Are you implying the decision wasn't mine? That she has me wrapped around her finger?"

"I'm not *implying* anything. You're her lapdog. Ruff, ruff."

"I'll pay you back for that."

"Looking forward to it."

"This is serious. You could lose everything."

"Yeah. I know," Nick said quietly. "But I'm still going through with it."

While Heather's luggage was being loaded, she and her entourage got inside the van. Apparently they were all accompanying her to the airport hotel. Nick supposed that was their way of pretending they were actually protecting her instead of sending her into an impossible situation where the odds of her being hurt, or killed, were enormously high.

The van slowly took off, as if it had all the time in the world.

Nick tapped his hand on the top of the desk beside him as he and Rafe watched the van's slow progression. The van turned the corner and disappeared.

"Where is it?" Nick demanded, shoving away from the desk. He grabbed his go-bag of clothes and toiletries from where he'd hidden it inside a small office trash can.

Rafe reached behind him and grabbed a set of keys from out of a folder. "First row." He tossed the keys to Nick, who was already running toward the exit. Nick caught them midair and ran outside. He heard Rafe running to catch him, but he didn't wait.

He sprinted around the corner of the building.

"Damn it, Nick. Hold up."

Nick stopped at the narrow chain-link gate, but only because he didn't have a key to open it. "Hurry," he said, as Rafe pulled his key card from his pocket. "It's a long drive and I've got a lot to do before they get there tomorrow."

"I'm hurrying, I'm hurrying." The gate buzzed and Rafe pulled it open.

Nick ran inside, immediately spotting the car Rafe was letting him borrow from the impound lot. He whistled and ran his hands lovingly over the sleek contours of the red Maserati GranTurismo convertible.

Rafe caught up to him and called him a name that would have given their mother a heart attack, especially coming from her oldest, the son who could do no wrong.

Nick grinned. "You're jealous I get to drive this sweet baby."

"No. I think you're a fool to have chosen this car out of all the ones I told you about. I would have chosen the black Lamborghini over there in the corner. Much less flashy."

"Flashy is the point. It's what my low-life friends expect down in the Keys. Besides—" he opened the door, pitched his go-bag onto the passenger floorboard and paused "—I may need a backseat. You never know when you'll have to carry something, or someone, and need the room."

Rafe exchanged a long glance with him, obviously understanding Nick's meaning. If Heather and her Miami agent ran into trouble, Nick might end up being their only way out. He couldn't do that with a two-seater.

"Don't scratch it," Rafe said as he closed the door. "And no bullet holes this time. There was hell to pay the last time I let you borrow a car. I mean it. Not even a scratch." He ran to the car gate a few feet away and pressed the button that started the gate sliding back on its rails.

Nick started the engine and backed out of the parking space. He would have preferred to get a car from the DEA impound lot, but his boss knew him too well. He'd given express orders that Nick wasn't allowed to check out any vehicles.

As soon as the gate was open wide enough for him to squeeze through, he stomped the accelerator. The car jumped forward like a gazelle, swift and graceful. He waved at Rafe as he zoomed by. He had to ease his foot off the gas to maneuver through the narrow, winding road by the police station. But as soon as he reached US 1, he turned the car south and let the horses run.

Normally when he got to drive one of the impounded sports cars, he would marvel at the perfectly tuned engine or the luxurious feel of Italian leather seats he'd never be able to afford in an entire lifetime of working for the DEA.

But not today. Today he was more concerned with the clock in the dashboard.

He had less than thirty-two hours to figure out how to save Lily and Heather without getting himself or anyone else killed.

Chapter Five

Heather had assumed Nick was exaggerating when he'd described the rough atmosphere of the Key West bar called Skeleton's Misery. But it was just as seedy as he'd said it would be. Still, it's not like she was alone, defenseless. Mark Watkins, the undercover DEA agent assigned to work with her, was sitting beside her. And Rickloff had backup outside somewhere, ready to come to the rescue at the slightest hint of trouble. But even with Mark and backup nearby, a shiver of apprehension still lanced down Heather's spine—because this was definitely *not* a typical bar, and Nick had definitely *not* exaggerated.

She avoided eye contact with the men around them, men who looked like Satan's personal biker gang, draped in black leather and silver chains, and covered with tattoos of snakes, dragons and naked women. She'd glimpsed knives peeking out from beneath some of their jackets. Big knives that made the pocketknife she usually carried around for emergencies—the one she'd had to ditch to board the airplane—look like a harmless toy. And she was fairly certain she'd glimpsed guns beneath some of their jackets, too.

Everyone in the bar seemed to be taking turns staring at her and Mark with open hostility and suspicion while the two of them sat at one of the high-top tables, sipping their beers. She was the only woman in the bar. And from what she could tell, she and Mark were the only "nonregulars." It was as if they'd intruded into someone's home without an invitation, or into a drug dealer's lair where his minions were planning their next big score.

Mark pretended to be absorbed in the football game on one of the TVs suspended from the ceiling. At least, Heather hoped he was pretending.

A large duffel bag sat at their feet, with four bricks of cocaine concealed inside. She didn't want to think about what might happen to her and Mark if Satan's bikers realized what was in that bag. She imagined there would be a violent frenzy, like a group of man-eating sharks scenting blood in the water.

"It's nine-fifteen, Mark," she whispered. "Shouldn't he be here by now?"

"Don't use my real name." Mark's reminder was said in a quiet voice Heather had to strain to hear over the loud TVs and music.

"Look, honey." He pointed to the football game and spoke louder as if for the benefit of those around them. "We're in the red zone. We might pull this one out after all."

Heather rolled her eyes. It was Tuesday night. She and every football fan in America knew that any football game on tonight was either a highlight reel or a replay of an old game. The TV above the bar was tuned to ESPN Classic, which was replaying a Tampa Bay Bucs game Heather had seen firsthand last season in Raymond James Stadium. She'd heard the cannons boom to celebrate the score that clinched the game. Obviously

Mark wasn't a football fan or he'd have known that. Her respect for him plummeted and she shook her head.

Another half hour passed. Angry mutterings started around them. The bartender gave her and Mark pointed looks as if to warn them their presence wouldn't be tolerated much longer.

Heather risked another glance around the room. She didn't know what Gonzalez looked like, but *he* knew what *she* looked like. If he was in the crowd, surely he'd have spotted her by now and would have approached her table. The note he'd left at her apartment had been clear about the time—nine o'clock. Well, nine o'clock had come and gone over forty-five minutes ago. What did it mean that no one had shown up to make the trade? What did that mean for Lily?

She jumped at the feel of a hand on top of hers.

Mark was leaning over, his mouth next to her ear. "I don't like the looks of the guys who just came in. Let's get out of here."

He didn't like *their* looks? Was it possible for someone to be scarier-looking than the men already in this place? Heather started to turn, but Mark put his arm around her shoulder.

"Don't look at them. Let's go." He pitched some tip money on the table and stood.

Heather clutched the edge of her bar stool. "But we can't leave. Lily—"

"We'll figure it out later. We've got to go. Now. Trust me."

Trust me. The last person who'd told her that was Nick. Had she been wrong not to trust him? Had she made a mistake that had just cost her sister her life?

She took a deep breath, trying to stave off the panic that was threatening to consume her.

Mark tugged the strap for the duffel bag over his shoulder and grabbed her hand, hauling her toward the door.

The moment they were outside, reality slammed into Heather like a physical thing, twisting inside her chest, threatening to make her double over and freeze like a terrified rabbit. She had to lock her emotions away. She couldn't give up yet. There was still a chance she could save Lily. *There had to be.*

Mark pressed his hand at the small of her back, urging her to move.

"There are four of them," he whispered a minute later. "And they're definitely following us."

"What about our backup?"

"They should be here any second. I said the code word into my transmitter. They know we need help. That's why we went outside, so Rickloff's men can grab the guys behind us without having to fight every man in that bar. We'll be fine."

Since his fingers were currently digging painfully into her back as he propelled her along, she wasn't so sure that *he* believed everything was fine.

He led her down the sidewalk back toward their motel, which was little more than a collection of cottages a block off the water, with a pool out back and a stage where live bands played every night. Although the sun had set hours ago, the moon was full and bright, guiding their way.

The knot in Heather's shoulders began to ease when the sign for their motel came into view. It wasn't far now, four, maybe five blocks. Unfortunately, the businesses in this section were dark and closed up for the night. Apparently the tourists didn't venture this far down except in the daytime. What had Rickloff been thinking to put them in such an isolated area? Had he realized what he was doing when he'd chosen their motel?

Again Nick's warnings flitted through her mind. He'd seemed unimpressed when he realized Rickloff was from Miami. Was this why? Did he fear that Rickloff would make mistakes because he wasn't familiar enough with the Keys? That sounded like a no-brainer to her, but she'd assumed Rickloff would have had good intel on the area. Looks like she'd put her faith in the wrong people after all. Once she got back to the motel she was going to demand to speak to Rickloff.

"Cross to the other side," Mark's urgent whisper sounded in her ear.

He grabbed her hand and pulled her across the street to the other sidewalk.

"Don't look back," he whispered. "Keep walking."

The worry in his voice sent a sinking feeling through her stomach. He wasn't even trying to pretend anymore that he wasn't concerned.

He suddenly smiled and leaned down as if to say something suggestive in her ear, and casually glanced over his shoulder. He uttered a foul curse.

"Rickloff," he growled into the parrot pin transmitter attached to his shirt, "get some backup over here, now."

He'd called Rickloff by name, something he'd repeatedly warned *her* not to do. And he hadn't used any code words.

They were in deep trouble.

Heather bitterly wished the DEA had allowed her to bring her own gun. She didn't like having to rely on someone else to protect her. And Mark was hopelessly outnumbered if the men behind them all had guns.

Three blocks to go. The registration booth for the motel was dark and deserted, but the lazy tune of "Margaritaville" piped out into the night from the live stage behind the collection of cottages.

Footsteps sounded behind them. So close!

They weren't going to make it to the motel.

"What are we going to do?" she cried out.

Mark's gaze darted to the left and right of the street, as if he was still expecting someone to come to their aid. But the backup Rickloff had promised at the first hint of trouble was nowhere to be seen.

"Mark?" Heather tried not to let her panic show, but his name still came out as a high-pitched squeak.

"When I say go," he said, "I want you to make a run for the motel. Run straight to the back by the pool where all the people should be, right up on the stage with the band if you have to. Tell someone to call the police. You got that?"

"But what about you? What are you going to do?"

"Stall them. Go, Heather, run!" He shoved her forward, dropped the duffel bag and whirled around to face their pursuers.

Heather took off running. Shouts sounded behind her. She didn't dare look back. She pumped her legs as fast as she could, whimpering when she heard the sound of a single pair of footsteps pounding behind her, getting closer and closer every second.

A shot rang out.

She let out a startled yelp. Was that Mark's gun or someone else's?

Tires squealed. Headlights flashed. A car barreled

up the street in her direction. She hesitated. The motel was still too far away. She turned around. A man was charging toward her. She screamed and sprinted to the car, praying the driver wasn't working for Gonzalez, and that he wasn't friends with the man trying to catch her.

Brakes screeched. The sleek red convertible with its top down rocked to a halt beside her.

"Get in."

Heather gasped at the sound of that deep, familiar voice.

Nick Morgan.

He wasn't looking at her. He was holding a gun and appeared to be aiming it at the man behind her. Heather jumped over the passenger door and plopped down onto the seat. She glanced back in time to see the man who was chasing her dive into some bushes on the side of the road.

Nick shoved his gun in the middle console and hit the accelerator. The car leaped forward.

Heather grabbed the armrest to keep from sliding across the leather seat. "There was an agent with me. He's over—"

"I know. Get down."

Remembering condition number two, she immediately turned around and slid off the seat onto the floorboard, or at least as much as she could, folding herself into the tiny space between the dashboard and the seat.

Nick grinned, apparently thinking it was amusing to see her slide down onto the floor. The crazy man was actually having fun.

The car lurched and skidded sideways. Someone lunged over the top of the door on Heather's side of the car and fell into the backseat. Heather had just enough time to realize it was Mark before Nick punched the accelerator again. Someone shouted from a few feet away. Another man cursed. The deep boom of a powerful gun filled the air. Heather jerked in surprise. The crunch and crackle of safety glass told her the shot had punched a hole in the windshield, but the rest of the glass held together.

Nick grabbed his gun, shaking his head and mumbling something about how Rafe was going to kill him. He fired two quick shots and shoved his gun into the console again. The tires screeched as he wheeled the car around in the middle of the narrow street, facing back in the direction he'd come from. The engine roared and the car rocketed forward, flying down the two-lane road into the night.

Heather couldn't move. She was too stunned by what had happened, frozen in place. She stayed curled up, half on the seat and half on the floor, clutching the armrest and console to keep from sliding around.

Nick continued his reckless pace, twisting and turning down side roads. The few houses they passed dropped away until there was nothing but dark trees whipping by.

Mark pulled himself into a sitting position, hooking an arm around the back of the passenger seat in front of him to brace himself, but still no one said anything, as if they were all too shell-shocked from what had just happened, or in Nick's case, too focused on getting away.

Heather caught glimpses of the ocean sparkling in the moonlight through the groves of trees on the side of the road. Nick finally slowed down and turned the car. Heather risked a quick peek and saw he was driving them up a long, sloping driveway. He pressed a button on the sun visor. Moments later he pulled into a garage and pressed the button again. The garage door slowly lowered, cocooning them inside.

After Nick cut the engine, for the space of several heartbeats, no one moved. Nick stared straight ahead as if deep in thought. Finally, he looked down at Heather. "Are you all right?"

She nodded, slowly unfolding herself from her painfully tight position. She turned around and plopped down on the seat. "Why are you here? How did you know we needed help? Where are we?"

He scrubbed his face and rolled his shoulders as if to relieve some stiffness. "You're welcome," he said, his voice sounding bland.

Heather's face flushed hot as she realized how ungrateful she must have sounded. "Thank you. I mean it. Really, thank you, thank you, thank you. You saved our lives back there."

The corner of his mouth quirked up with amusement. "One thank-you would have been sufficient."

Mark leaned in between the bucket seats and wiped a trickle of blood from the corner of his mouth. "You took your own sweet time getting there, Southern boy. They managed to get my gun and were going in for the kill. Cut it that close again and I'll kick your sorry butt all the way back to that alligator swamp you call home."

Nick stared at him in the rearview mirror. "No spoon-fed Yankee momma's boy is going to kick anything of mine."

Heather glanced back and forth between them. They obviously knew each other, but she couldn't tell if they were teasing or about to slug each other. "Um, guys, are we okay here? What's going on?"

"What's going on," Nick said, shoving his car door

open, "is that Rickloff's backup never showed. Which probably means there never *was* any backup."

Mark hopped over the side of the car and dusted off his shorts. "I hate to admit you were right, but you were. You saved our bacon back there."

Heather was still sitting in her seat, trying to follow their bizarre conversation, when Nick rounded the car to the passenger side, leaned over and scooped her up in his arms.

She was too surprised to do more than stare up at him as he carried her into the house.

Mark followed behind. He stopped just inside the kitchen, flipping on the lights, but Nick continued on into the living room with Heather.

"Um, Nick, I can walk. You can put me down."

He didn't bother answering and he didn't put her down. He used his shoulder to flip on the hall light and carried her all the way to the end into what must have been the master bedroom, based on the expansive size of the room. He kicked the door shut behind them and stopped beside the bed.

His brows were a dark, angry slash as he glared at her. The tightness around the corners of his eyes and the way he clenched his jaw told her she might be in as much trouble now as she had been back at the bar.

"Put me down." She tried to sound braver than she felt. The last time she'd seen him like this, he'd slapped her in handcuffs. She wasn't sure what to expect. She squirmed in his arms, anxious to get away from him.

He suddenly released her. She dropped to the bed and hadn't even stopped bouncing on the mattress before he came down on top of her.

The shock of his warm body pressed against hers had

her mouth going dry. For a moment they just stared at each other. His body was rigid. His Adam's apple worked in his throat several times, as if he was struggling for words. Heat flooded through Heather, tightening her stomach. She was appalled that she was getting turned on, because it was quite obvious Nick wasn't suffering from the same affliction.

He looked as if he wanted to strangle her.

She didn't have to ask him why. She already knew. He was still furious that she'd jeopardized his career back at that nightclub in Saint Augustine and that she'd gotten him mixed up in this mess tonight. Although, really, it wasn't her fault. And he wasn't supposed to be here anyway. Was he? Actually, if she looked at it that way, he really didn't have a right to be angry at all. If anyone should be angry it was her, because he hadn't adequately warned her about the dangers. He should have tried harder to get her to *not* go along with Rickloff's plan. And just as soon as Nick quit glaring at her, she'd find the courage to tell him so.

"You could have been killed tonight." His voice shook.

Heather blinked in surprise. *That's* why he was upset? "You were *worried* about me?"

"Hell, yes, I was worried about you. You shouldn't have agreed to Rickloff's plan. I told you I didn't trust him, and you still insisted on plowing ahead. I'm on suspension. I'm supposed to be sitting at my house in my favorite recliner, which—I might add—is a hell of a lot more fun than being shot at. What do you think would have happened tonight if I hadn't disobeyed orders and come down here to keep an eye on you?"

She was pretty sure she wouldn't have survived the

night without him, but she didn't think it was a good idea to say that out loud. He was already shaking, and from the tension in his body against hers, she guessed he was still fighting his own battle not to throttle her.

She swallowed hard. "I...ah...don't really know."

His mouth thinned and his eyes flashed. He shook his head and rolled off her to sit on the side of the bed, as if he couldn't stand to look at her anymore.

Heather scrambled up on her knees beside him, searching for the words that would ease his temper. She remembered he'd found humor in her thanking him repeatedly back in the car. She cleared her throat. "Thank you, again, Nick. Really. Thank you, a hundred times."

He closed his eyes briefly, still shaking his head.

She tried again. "I'm...ah...really grateful you aren't sitting at home in your comfortable recliner."

He shot her an irritated look.

She sighed and straightened her legs, sitting on the edge of the mattress beside him. "Are you going to tell me how you ended up coming to our rescue? It sounded like you and Mark know each other, and that he was expecting you tonight."

He let out a long, deep breath. "When you refused my help, Rafe and I dug around and pulled some strings to get some information. When I found out that Mark was the agent you'd be working with down here, I contacted him. He and I used to work together out of the Fort Lauderdale office. He kept me posted on where you two were going to be. I rented this house because it was near enough to your motel and the bar to be useful, but far enough away and remote enough that it made a good hiding place if it came to that."

He twisted around to meet her gaze. "I borrowed a

fast car in case I needed to make a quick getaway. Then I followed you two as closely as I could manage without being too obvious. I figured something was wrong when I never once ran into any other agents. If Rickloff was backing you up the way he was supposed to, someone should have challenged me earlier in the evening for keeping tabs on you two. No one ever did."

Heather scrambled off the bed and stood facing him. "I don't understand. Why wouldn't there be any backup? Rickloff's goal was to catch Gonzalez or some of his men when they swapped Lily for the cocaine."

He cocked a brow. "Rickloff's *goal* is to catch Gonzalez. Period. You're a pawn, and so is your sister. Don't forget that."

She wasn't sure she bought Nick's cynical version of what had happened. Surely a high-ranking DEA agent like Rickloff wouldn't be so cavalier with the safety of two civilians just so he could catch a drug dealer. There had to be another explanation for what had happened tonight.

"Why do you think Gonzalez didn't show?" she asked.

"Oh, I think he probably did. He just didn't let anyone see him. He would have come there to point you out to his men."

"What? Wait. What do you mean? We were there waiting to meet with him. We had the cocaine… Oh, my gosh. The cocaine! We lost it. If we don't have that cocaine we don't have anything to trade for Lily. What will we—"

He grabbed her arms. "Don't you get it yet? If Gonzalez was planning on a trade, he'd have shown himself.

Tonight wasn't about a trade. Gonzalez set this meeting up for an entirely different reason."

"What reason is that?"

"He wanted you to come to Key West."

"But…I don't…" She twisted her fingers together in confusion. "Why would he want that?"

"For exactly the reason Rickloff said in the meeting yesterday. Gonzalez cares about Lily. He doesn't want to lose her. But he's a powerful man who maintains that power because people are afraid of him. If word gets around, and it will—it always does—that his mistress and her sister lost his drugs, or that either of them is helping the DEA, he'll lose face. He can't afford that. So he has to come up with an alternate plan. He wants to figure out how to save face in front of his men, but still keep Lily."

Heather nodded, trying to follow his reasoning. "Okay. And he cares about my sister, so hurting her is the last thing he'll do, right?"

"Based on the information I gathered last night and earlier today from my informants here in the Keys, yes. I think he really cares about her and he'll do whatever he can to protect her, as long as it doesn't mean giving up his reputation of power in front of his men."

Relief loosened the tightness in her chest. "Thank God. That means Lily is okay."

He stared at her for a long minute. "I don't think you've thought this through yet if you think things are going well here. Rickloff didn't back you up, even though he thought Gonzalez or his thugs would meet you at the bar. What does that tell you?"

She blinked in surprise as things started clicking together in her mind. "Rickloff is working for Gonzalez?"

He smiled, looking mildly amused at her conclusion. "No, I don't think so. From what Mark told me on the phone last night, Rickloff has an ego the size of the state of Florida. He's not the type to be at the beck and call of a drug dealer. He'd consider it beneath him. I believe he really does want to put Gonzalez in prison, partly to make the streets safer, but mainly because that would catapult his career to a higher level. At the least, he'd get a promotion. And if he has political aspirations, which Mark assures me Rickloff does, putting someone like Gonzalez away could be the perfect platform to put him in office."

"But Mark and I could have been killed."

He closed his eyes, his forehead wrinkling as if he were in pain. "Yes, you could have." When he looked at her again, there was tenderness in his eyes that reminded her of how he used to look at her. *Before.*

"We'll stay here tonight," he said. "I'll call the Key West DEA office and bring the special agent in charge, Dante Messina, up to speed on what's going on. He can run interference with the police about the shooting back in town, in case anyone called it in. Tomorrow morning, I'll take you to meet him and we'll get this all sorted out."

He gently pushed her hair out of her eyes. "Try not to worry. Dante is far more reasonable than Rickloff. I've worked with him quite a bit this past year while on assignment down here. And I promise you I'll do everything I can to find your sister. Okay?"

She blew out a shaky breath. "Okay. I just hope she's—"

Red and blue lights suddenly lit up the room, flashing against the thin blinds covering the only window. Nick lifted Heather out of his way and ran to the window. She followed him, but he frowned at her and pushed her back as he lifted one of the slats to look out.

She caught a glimpse of a police car sitting in the driveway, pulled all the way up to the garage door. Both car doors opened and two policemen got out.

"I guess you were right," she said. "Someone in town must have reported the shooting and given a description of your car to the police."

Nick dropped the blinds back in place, shaking his head. "If they're the police, how did they find us?"

"Your car—"

"Is in the garage. They couldn't have seen it. And there aren't any other houses for miles around. That's why I chose this location. No one could have seen me pull the car into the garage."

Her fingernails bit into her palms. "So what are you saying?"

"What I'm saying is that I don't know what's going on. Maybe they're real cops, maybe they aren't. Maybe someone saw us when we made the turn down this road. They thought the cracked windshield looked suspicious so they called it in. Then again, maybe not."

He started to reach for the phone attached to his belt when a door slammed somewhere in the house.

His eyes widened. "Mark. No, damn it." He rushed around Heather and strode to the door. "Stay here." He hurried into the hallway, firmly closing the door behind him.

Heather couldn't resist a quick peek through the blinds. The slamming door must have been Mark going out front, because he was now standing on the walkway talking to the two police officers. Heather clutched her hand to her throat, fervently hoping Nick's worries about the policemen were unfounded.

One of the policemen suddenly drew his gun and pointed it at Mark's chest. A gunshot rang out. Mark flipped backward onto the lawn.

Heather screamed. The policemen swiveled toward her, looking right at her.

She dropped the blind and flattened herself against the wall.

Oh, no, Mark. No, no, no.

Where was Nick? Was he already outside? Were they going to shoot him next?

Oh, no, please.

Muffled footsteps sounded through the house.

Heather clapped her hand over her mouth to keep from making any noise. Was that Nick? Or someone else?

Oh, God. Please let Nick be okay.

The footsteps pounded down the hallway, closer, closer. If that was Nick, wouldn't he have called out to warn her?

Heather whirled around. Nowhere to hide. She ran toward the door and lunged for the vase on the dresser as the door flew open. She swung the vase like a bat, aiming at her attacker's head.

The man's arm jerked up. The vase thunked against his forearm and fell to the floor, exploding into a dozen pieces.

Heather shoved at him and tried to escape through the doorway.

An iron grip clamped around her wrist and brought her up short.

"Heather, it's me," Nick's harsh whisper sounded near

her ear. He flipped off the light switch, plunging the room into darkness.

She sagged against him, wrapping her arms around his waist, hugging him. "Nick, oh, my gosh. You're okay. They shot Mark. I thought you were outside, too, that they were going to shoot you."

"The men who shot Mark had disappeared by the time I made it to the front door." His voice was still a harsh whisper, as if he was afraid of making much noise. "They could be anywhere. We've got to get out of here."

He grabbed her wrist and pulled her down the hall toward the main room, forcing her to run to keep up with his long strides. He must have flipped the lights out when he ran to get her because the entire house was dark except for the moonlight filtering through the French doors off the back of the main room and through the skylights overhead.

"Can't we just grab Mark, get in the car and get out of here?" Heather whispered.

He peered out through the glass panes in one of the back doors. "The police car is blocking the garage. I can't get the car out." He pulled out his cell phone. "Shade the screen to help conceal the light," he whispered.

She did as he said. "What are you doing?"

"Calling for backup." He pressed a button on the screen.

A soft "pfftt" sound echoed through the room. One of the glass panes in the French door next to them exploded.

Heather let out a startled yelp.

Nick pushed her down onto the floor. He aimed his gun toward the front of the house and fired off three quick shots. He shoved his phone in his pocket and threw open the door behind them.

"Come on." He grabbed Heather's wrist.

They took off running, with Nick pushing her ahead of him, using his body to block any attack from behind.

"What are we going to do?" Heather called back to him.

"Get to the woods," he said. "We'll use the trees for cover. I'll try to hold them off until we can get help."

They practically flew across the soft grass toward the woods behind the house.

Another shot rang out behind them.

Nick swore and pushed Heather harder. He fired a shot, then yanked Heather behind the first stand of oak trees.

HEATHER STARTED TO SLOW.

"Don't stop," Nick whispered harshly, urging her forward with his hand on her back. "Get to that next stand of trees. The bushes are thicker there, more cover." He had to get some distance between them and their pursuers.

When he thought they'd gone far enough, he pulled Heather to a stop. Her breathing was loud and choppy. He needed her to calm down, or anyone within ten yards of them would hear her breathing.

"Shouldn't you call for backup now?" she panted between breaths.

That last shot had shattered his phone holstered at his hip, but he wasn't about to tell her that. She was already so scared her face was ghost-white.

"In a minute," he said, trying to think of a lie that would make sense. "The screen is too bright. It will let our pursuers know right where we are."

She nodded, probably remembering the shot the last

time he'd tried to use his phone. The person who'd shot the French door had a silencer, which told Nick far more about the men who were after them. They definitely weren't cops. And at least one of them was a highly paid assassin. The average drug dealer thug couldn't afford a silencer.

"Nick," Heather whispered, her breathing slower and much more quiet now. "Mark is hurt. Shouldn't we try to go back and—"

He stared down at her. "I figured he was just playing dead for the gunmen, because he lost his gun back in town. He *was* wearing a Kevlar vest. And so are you. Right?" At her hesitation, his eyes narrowed. "Please tell me Rickloff didn't send you and Mark into that bar without bullet-resistant vests."

Heather blinked at him and swallowed hard. "I seem to remember him saying something about not being able to conceal a vest beneath T-shirts and shorts like tourists wear in the summer."

Nick swore viciously and shoved his gun back into his belt. He yanked his shirt over his head and threw it on the ground. He tugged at the Velcro straps of his vest, wincing when the ripping sound seemed to echo through the trees.

"What are you doing?" Heather shook her head when he lowered the vest over her head. "Wait, you can't do this. You're the one who should be wearing this, not me."

Ignoring her pleas and her struggles, he tugged the straps, tightening them around her.

"No, stop it." She batted at his hands. "I am not going to be responsible for you getting hurt or killed. Stop it."

He grabbed her arms, holding her tight to stop her

struggles. "Condition number two. Be quiet. And stop fighting me."

Heather instantly stilled but she continued to glare up at him. The woman was adorable when she was angry. Nick barely managed to squelch a threatening grin as he finished tightening the straps on the vest. He didn't want to give her the impression they were in the clear now and everything was okay.

Because they weren't, and everything was definitely *not* okay.

"Fine," she whispered. "I'll wear the vest, but at least give me your backup gun. I'm an excellent shot. I can help."

He peered around the trees, watching for movement in the dark woods behind them. "What makes you think I have a backup gun?" he whispered.

"Because *you're* not the idiot who went into Satan's biker bar without a bulletproof vest. I'd bet my life, and I totally am, that you have a backup gun."

His mouth twitched and his gaze shot to hers.

The branch above them popped and cracked. Leaves and bark rained down on them. The assassin with the silencer must have spotted them and fired off a shot.

"No time," Nick whispered in a harsh voice. He grabbed Heather's right wrist with his left hand in an unbreakable viselike grip. "Come on. We're going to do the only thing we can do right now."

"What's that?"

"Run like hell."

Chapter Six

Nick pulled Heather behind a tree, holding her close as he scanned the woods around them. When he looked back down at her, the sick feeling in her stomach told her what he was about to say.

They were in serious trouble.

He held his finger to his lips in a shushing gesture. He held up one finger then pointed to their left. He held up two more fingers and pointed to their right.

Heather's heart stuttered in her chest as she realized what he was telling her. Two men on one side, one on the other. They were surrounded. She nodded to let him know she understood. When they took off again, instead of pushing her in front of him, Nick held her glued to his side, guiding each of her steps, as if to ensure she didn't make any noise.

The sound of something snapping off to their right made Heather jump. She stumbled and stepped on a stick that snapped in two from her weight.

The large crack seemed to echo around them like a beacon. Nick tensed and froze, waiting, listening. A shout, something in Spanish, sounded off to their right. Nick took off, towing Heather with him, no longer trying to be quiet. They raced through the woods, hopping over fallen logs, dodging around trees as fast as they could go, trying to outrun their pursuers.

Heather cursed her short legs. She'd never cared before that she didn't have the long legs of a model. But right now she'd do anything for those longer strides so she wouldn't hold Nick back. If it weren't for her, he'd be perfectly safe. He wouldn't have given her his bullet-proof vest and the men chasing them wouldn't be catching up.

Shouts sounded behind them. Footfalls pounded the ground.

Heather's breaths came in short pants. Nick was half dragging her along with him, forcing her to run faster than she'd even thought she could run. She knew she couldn't keep up this pace very long. The stitch in her side was already so painful she was clutching one hand against her ribs to try to keep going.

Ahead, moonlight glinted off the ocean, visible through breaks in the trees. In the daytime, Heather would have welcomed the sight. She longed to explore the thin, rocky, seashell-strewn strips of sand and clear blue-green water beyond. But seeing that water, inky-black in the night, get closer and closer, meant only one thing—they were trapped. With the ocean ahead and gunmen behind, there was nowhere else to go.

Nick shoved Heather behind a tree. He whirled around and squeezed off two shots into the woods behind them. A guttural scream of pain echoed through the woods.

"Vámonos, vámonos!" someone else, farther off, shouted in Spanish.

"Good grief, how many of them are there?" Heather whispered. She breathed in huge gulps of air, clutching her side.

Nick swiveled toward her. "Can you swim?" he asked, his voice low and urgent.

"I'm a Florida native. Of course I can—"

"Go." He waved toward the water visible through the trees. "Swim out about fifty feet. Then swim parallel to the shore, south, back toward town." He pointed toward his left.

She hesitated. "What about you? Aren't you coming with me?"

"I'll try to take out a few more of our pursuers and lead them away from the water. I'll catch up with you. Just swim south." He gestured to the left again to make sure she knew the direction.

"Nick, I'm a good shot. Give me a gun."

He pressed his lips next to her ear. "I'm not willing to bet your life, or mine, on your marksmanship under pressure, not as long as there's a safer alternative. Now go."

A footstep sounded near them.

"Go," he mouthed, making a shooing gesture with his hand.

Heather fisted her hands in frustration. She whirled around and took off toward the ocean, stepping as quietly as she could, staying close to the trees for cover. Part of her was furious that Nick didn't trust her to help. But the other part was well aware of how even the most highly trained people—law enforcement officers, soldiers—were notoriously inaccurate with firearms when in a high-pressure situation. She had only ever fired at targets, and the shooting range certainly wasn't stressful in any way. Maybe Nick was right not to trust her ability to shoot in this type of situation. And if he was worrying about her, he couldn't adequately defend himself.

Crashing noises sounded in the woods, moving north and off to the east, away from her. Nick's plan was working.

Hating herself for leaving him, but knowing there wasn't much she could do without a gun, Heather lunged between the last two trees. She sprinted onto the narrow strip of sand. Her foot hit something hard and she went sprawling onto the ground. A conch shell. Heather shoved it away and climbed to her feet. She made her way more carefully to the water that was only a few feet away.

She didn't stop. She ran right into the warm water. When she was chest deep, she turned around to look back toward the beach. Thankfully, she didn't see anyone. Following Nick's orders, she swam farther out. Her waterlogged shoes kept trying to pull her down. She toed them off under the water and let them drop. She debated pulling off the vest, too, but she quickly discarded the idea. Nick had risked his life to give her the vest. She wasn't going to ignore his sacrifice by throwing the vest away.

The thought of him being shot sent a flash of panic straight through her. She stared back at the dark line of trees at the edge of the sand. What if he was hurt? What if he was lying in the bushes bleeding right now? Suddenly the fact that she'd been imprisoned in that filthy jail cell all weekend faded to insignificance. Nick had done what he'd done because it was his job. It wasn't fair for her to hate him for that, especially since his honor and protectiveness toward women were some of the very traits that had drawn her to him in the first place.

When they'd first met, it was on a beach very different from this one, back home. Nick had noticed a guy bothering her who didn't understand what "no" meant. He'd sent the other guy on his way. Then he'd grinned at her and called her darlin'. If any other guy had called her that she'd have thought he was being condescending. But there was nothing condescending about Nick. He was just pure Southern charm rolled up in a hot package, impossible to resist.

Every muscle inside her tightened at the thought of leaving him in those woods. She desperately wanted to go back and find him. But if she went back she could be a liability again, slowing him down, making him vulnerable.

No, she had to trust him and go along with his stupid conditions. He'd earned that trust a hundred times tonight, and she had to keep the faith that he knew what he was doing.

She drew a deep breath, then another, and submerged beneath the water, swimming farther out. When she thought she might be far enough from the shore, she rose, sticking her head out of the water just enough so she could breathe.

The tiny strip of sand that couldn't legitimately call itself a beach was still clear. No sign of her pursuers. But no sign of Nick, either.

Another shot rang out, startling her at how close it sounded. She drew a deep breath and submerged, swimming underwater again. She rose several more times for breaths and to make sure she was swimming in the right direction, parallel to shore. Each time she didn't see anyone. And each time she went right back under.

She hated condition number two, hated following Nick's orders unquestioningly. If they both survived this night, she was going to renegotiate his stupid conditions.

The next time she surfaced for air, she let out a small yelp before recognizing the figure swimming toward her. Nick. He quickly reached her with his powerful strokes. She would have thrown her arms around his neck with sheer joy that he was okay, but his grim expression held her back.

"Good job," he said. "You did great. You swam farther than I thought. We can cut back to shore now."

"What about the gunmen?"

"They're a good clip north of us, but the trail I laid won't fool them for long. They'll loop back to try to find us. We don't have much time. We need to get back to the house and take either the patrol car or my car, whatever works, and get out of here."

They struck out swimming side by side toward shore.

"How many were there? Were those cops after us, too?" Heather kicked her feet to try to keep up with him.

"I didn't see the supposed cops. But there were five men in the woods."

"Five?" Heather squeaked.

"Don't worry. I shot three of them. The odds are in our favor now."

"Oh, goodie," Heather grumbled.

Nick grinned. They were in the shallows now. He took her hand and pulled her with him back to shore and into the trees.

He stopped and squatted down by a twisted oak. He pulled his gun from under a pile of leaves where he must have put it before swimming out to get her. While he dusted off the dirt and grabbed whatever else he'd stored in the pile of leaves, Heather glanced anxiously around, keeping watch. Nick stood and grabbed her hand again, pulling her behind him through the woods. They rounded a clump of trees and suddenly they were on the front lawn of the house. Heather was surprised and relieved. She hadn't realized they were this close.

The police car was no longer parked out front. Had the fake cops left? Or had they just hidden their car to make Nick and Heather think they'd left?

Her breath caught in her throat as they ran past Mark's body, still lying on the grass. A reddish-brown stain darkened his shirt and spread down one side. She tugged her hand, trying to pull it out of Nick's grasp so she could stop and check on Mark.

Nick's fingers tightened around her wrist. He wouldn't let her stop. "Keep going."

The urgency in his voice had her pulse pounding in her ears. Had he seen something? Heard something? He pulled her at a dead run to the front door, then pressed her up against the side of the house, again using his body—his half-naked body, dressed only in jeans, *without* a bulletproof vest—to shield her. Heather wanted to scream at him and tell him how ridiculous and reckless he was being with his own safety, but she didn't want to distract him, so she stayed silent. For now.

He held up one finger to his lips again, then held his palm out telling her to wait. He crouched down with his pistol out and dove in through the open front door. An agonizing ten or fifteen seconds later, he pulled her inside. He shut and locked the front door, waved her to silence again and disappeared down the long hallway.

It was too dark to see many details, but Heather could see the back door was closed. They'd left it open when they ran out that same door earlier this evening. Or had they? Had Nick closed it just now, when he came inside, before he pulled her inside with him? Had he had enough time to do that?

Her throat tightened at the sound of running feet. Nick ran from the hallway into the living room. He ran past her in a whisper of sound, heading into the kitchen. A door creaked, footsteps sounded. Was that Nick? Or someone else making those sounds?

She inched her way back toward the front door. Should she run for it? Go for help? Nick had said there weren't any other houses on this road. Where would she run? Back to the ocean?

She stopped. No, no, she couldn't run. She couldn't leave Nick, not again. If only she had a gun. She chewed her bottom lip. Nick didn't seem inclined to give her his backup gun. But did Mark have a backup gun? Had he mentioned that? She couldn't remember.

A noise sounded from the garage to her right. Her knees started to shake. She had to do something. She couldn't stand here waiting to be rescued, especially if Nick needed help. She squinted in the dim moonlight from the skylights. The end table by the couch had several statues on it. The dolphin statue looked heavy enough to crush a man's skull if she put all her weight behind it. The idea of actually hitting someone with it had her stomach churning, but if that's what it took to save Nick, she'd have to do it.

She pushed herself away from the wall and hurried to the statue before she lost her courage. Someone rushed into the room. Heather whirled around, lifting the statue before she recognized Nick's familiar silhouette.

He stopped in front of her, his white teeth flashing in the dark. "You can put the dolphin down," he teased. "The house is clear. I'm going to get Mark."

Heather clutched the heavy statue to her chest. It was the only weapon she had and she wasn't giving it up until Nick was safely back inside.

He opened the front door, holding his gun up at the ready. He leaned out before he ran outside, leaving the door cracked open behind him.

Heather rushed to the door and peered out. Nick was on the front lawn, crouching down next to Mark's body. He pressed his fingers against Mark's neck as if checking for a pulse. He hoisted him up on his shoulders and turned back toward the house. Thank goodness. Mark must still be alive or Nick wouldn't have risked his life to grab him.

Heather held the door open, closing and locking it after Nick came inside.

"I heard someone in the woods in the side yard," Nick whispered. "Get to the garage. Now. Go."

Her mouth went dry. She pitched the dolphin statue on the couch and led the way through the dark house, sorely wishing she could flip on a light. She held the door open to the garage so Nick could pass through with Mark.

"Is he going to be okay?" Heather asked.

"I don't know." His voice was tight, a harsh rasp full of pain and regret.

He rushed past her and heaved Mark over the side of the car into the backseat.

She ran to the passenger side of the car, stealing a quick look over the side at Mark. His chest rose and fell. He was still breathing, but just barely.

A muffled noise sounded from inside the house, followed by a dull thump.

Nick jerked his head toward the car, motioning for Heather to get in. He disappeared back into the house.

Heather bit the inside of her cheek to keep from calling out to him. What was he doing? She got into the car and turned in her seat, her gaze fastened on the dark maw of the open door that led into the kitchen.

Another thump sounded from inside the house, followed by a low moan.

Heather leaned over the side of the car, looking at the shelving for some kind of weapon. Why hadn't she kept the statue? She gasped when a dark shadow moved into the garage. Nick, again. The man was going to be the death of her the way he kept disappearing and reappearing. She pressed her hand against her chest, her heart beating so fast she could hear it pulsing in her ears.

Nick gently eased the door to the house shut, dug his keys out of his pocket and ran to the car.

He jumped over the side and plopped down onto the driver's seat. "You said you wished you had a gun earlier. Just how good a shot are you?"

"I grew up on a farm. I've been shooting since I was ten. I guarantee I can outshoot you."

"Unfortunately, you just may have to prove that. The door to the house has hinges on the inside, meaning there's no way to brace it from out here." He laid his pistol in his lap and reached down, yanking up the leg of his jeans. A small holster was strapped to his calf. He pulled out a .38 snub-nose and handed it to her. "If anyone comes through that door, don't hesitate, shoot them."

She nodded, grateful to finally have a weapon, and turned around in her seat, aiming at the door that led back into the house.

The garage door squeaked as it began to rise.

Heather swallowed hard. She felt so exposed knowing the door was opening behind her, but she kept her gun trained on the house door as Nick had told her to do.

The doorknob rattled. The door flew open. Heather didn't wait for someone to step out. She squeezed the trigger, aiming at the middle of the dark opening.

The shot was deafening in the confines of the garage. A man screamed and fell through the doorway onto the concrete floor behind the car.

"Hold on," Nick yelled.

Heather grabbed the back of her seat with her left hand as the car rocketed forward out of the garage. She kept her gun trained on the door to the house.

"Ah, hell. It's the freaking O.K. Corral around here. Get down," Nick yelled.

Heather dropped down into the seat.

Shots rang out behind them as the car flew down the driveway. Nick slid down in his seat, too, trying to take cover while steering the car. The already cracked windshield shattered and sprayed bits of glass all over the inside of the car.

The car fishtailed into the road out front. Nick slid up higher in his seat and yanked the steering wheel hard left, then hard right. He punched the gas again.

Metal pinged as a bullet hit the back of the car. Nick gunned the car down the road. As soon as they rounded a curve, he sat straight up in his seat and wrestled the steering wheel to keep them from going into the ditch on the far side of the road. The car straightened out and practically flew down the narrow two-lane road back toward town.

When the car quit swerving, Heather stowed her gun in the console and climbed into the backseat.

"What are you doing?" Nick demanded.

"Checking on Mark."

"Hang on, I'm turning."

She held on to the back of the seat in front of her as Nick swerved onto a side road, tires screeching. He continued his mad dash, flying down street after street, passing more and more houses as they got closer to town.

"How's he doing?" Nick asked, turning onto another road, but at a less-frantic speed than before.

Heather pulled Mark's shirt open and found the entry hole in his chest, about halfway down his rib cage on the right side. She pressed her hands against his injury, applying pressure. "The bleeding isn't that bad now, but he's still unconscious. We have to get him to a doctor."

"Check his pockets for his phone. Mine is…waterlogged."

Heather wondered why he hadn't hidden his phone, just like he'd hidden his gun, to keep it dry when he swam out after her. He must have forgotten. She kept one palm pressed against Mark's wound while she fished into his pockets. When she found his cell phone, she pressed a button and was relieved that the light came on and five bars showed they had service. "You want me to call 911?"

"No. Call this number instead." He rattled off a phone number and Heather punched it in.

She handed him the phone, then pressed both palms against Mark, trying to stop the bleeding.

Nick spoke in some kind of DEA combination of code words that made no sense to her. When he hung up, he set the phone in the console next to his gun.

"We're ten minutes from the hospital. Backup's on the way."

"You sure about that?" she asked. "I don't remember backup working out so well the last time."

She saw his quick grin in the rearview mirror. She didn't think she'd ever met someone before who could smile or laugh so much when people were trying to kill him. She had a feeling he might have actually enjoyed tonight if she hadn't been there to slow him down or force him to have to protect her instead of going after the bad guys.

Some of the tension drained out of her shoulders. Maybe the worst was over now. Maybe they really would make it out of this mess alive.

"You were right," she called out over the sound of the wind rushing by. "About everything. I should have trusted you back in Saint Augustine when you warned me about Rickloff's plan."

His grin faded and his jaw tightened. "You've got nothing to apologize for. You were put in an impossible situation. You're a civilian. You never should have been given the choices Waverly and Rickloff gave you."

"I realize that now." She shoved her wet hair out of her face. "But there's still the question of what to do about my sister. I don't even know if she's alive."

"We'll figure something out. Trust me."

"I do."

He gave her a sharp look in the mirror before looking back at the road.

Heather wasn't sure what that look meant, but she was willing to bet it had something to do with *him* not trusting *her*. Since her arrest at the nightclub, she and Nick had never sat and discussed what had happened. Would it make a difference in his feelings toward her if they sat down and talked? Or would he even give her a chance to explain her side?

A few minutes later, the squeal of tires sounded behind them. Nick checked the mirrors. Heather jerked around in her seat. A car had just swerved from a side road and was rapidly gaining on them. The headlights blinked three times.

Heather half stood, holding on to the back of Nick's seat for balance. She reached for the snub-nose she'd left in the console.

Nick grabbed her hand before she could get the gun. "Hold on, Annie Oakley. Those aren't the bad guys. That's our backup."

She plopped back down, grinning over his Annie Oakley comment. Either she was too exhausted and relieved that backup had arrived to think clearly anymore, or his warped sense of humor was contagious.

Minutes later, as promised, they were at the hospital. Nick pulled up to the emergency room entrance. The backup car pulled right up behind them and two men jumped out. They both wore wrinkled shirts and jeans, as if they'd pulled on whatever clothes they could find when Nick's call came in. They immediately flanked Heather.

Nick scooped Mark up out of the backseat and preceded them in through the emergency room doors. A nurse saw them and her eyes widened with alarm. She ran around her desk and grabbed a wheelchair. Nick set Mark in the chair and braced him so he wouldn't fall out.

One of the agents put his hand on Mark's shoulder, anchoring him to the chair. "I've got this."

Nick nodded his thanks, and the agent rushed off with

the nurse and Mark through the swinging doors into the heart of the emergency room.

Nick introduced himself and Heather to the remaining agent, who said his name was Tanner, and that the other agent who'd gone with Mark was named Chuck.

Another nurse stopped next to them and handed Nick a hospital gown to replace the shirt he'd left in the woods when he'd given Heather his vest. He murmured a thank-you and shrugged the gown on as he spoke to Tanner.

Heather was surprised at how much blood was smeared on Nick's abdomen. Mark must have bled all over him when Nick picked him up out of the backseat. She quietly offered up a quick prayer for Mark's safety and tuned back in to what Nick and Tanner were saying.

It soon became clear they had never met each other before.

"Wait. Nick, you don't know this man but you called him for backup?" she asked.

"I called the satellite office here in Key West and asked for help. Tanner and Chuck were barhopping nearby so they answered the call."

Tanner rolled his eyes. "We were working, not barhopping." He waved his hand at his clothes. "It may not look that way, but half my job involves dressing down to blend in."

Heather smiled at him. "I understand. I do that a lot, too."

"You're DEA?"

"Oh, no. I'm a private investigator. But half the time I either meet prospective clients in bars or end up meeting informants in bars. It's an unfortunate downside to my job."

"Ah." He didn't look impressed, and Heather felt

her face grow warm with embarrassment. She probably seemed like a bumbling amateur to an experienced DEA agent.

"Don't worry, ma'am," Tanner said. "We'll take good care of both of you. Let's go find somewhere a bit less out in the open and figure out what's going on."

"Go ahead. I'll catch up," Nick said. "I'm going to check on Mark." He hung back while Tanner led Heather down the hall.

"Wait a minute." Heather stopped and turned around. Nick was going to let her out of his sight, with an agent he'd only just met? Knowing how protective he was, that didn't sit right with her. She stared at him suspiciously.

He raised a brow in question and crossed his arms over his chest. That action made the hospital gown mold to his body. Heather's eyes widened and she gasped in shock.

A growing red stain saturated the part of the gown covering Nick's lower left side. That wasn't Mark's blood.

It was Nick's.

Chapter Seven

Nick plucked at the fresh hospital gown, hating the necessity of wearing the darn thing. His jeans, lying on the emergency room countertop beside the bed he was sitting on, were bloody where the bullet had scraped across his hip. He didn't relish the idea of putting the jeans back on, but he couldn't exactly walk out in the flimsy gown he'd worn while the doctor had sewn him up.

A knock sounded on the door. Before he could say anything, the door flew open. Heather stood there, her two DEA agent shadows standing behind her. Two more agents had arrived a few minutes ago and were guarding Mark, just in case someone came in the hospital to seek him out and finish what they'd started.

"Give us a minute, okay, guys?" Heather called over her shoulder. She didn't wait for an answer. She shoved the door shut, tossed a small bag onto the countertop and put her hands on her hips. Her deep blue eyes were practically shooting sparks as she glared at him.

Nick's curiosity about what was in the bag was no competition for the vision standing in front of him. He couldn't have moved to pick up that bag if he'd wanted to. He was too busy just trying to draw a normal breath.

He crossed his arms and tried to appear unaffected,

but boy did she look good. Someone had given her a
fresh white T-shirt and jeans, both a size too small by
some standards but pretty near perfect by his. Every
curve was outlined for his hungry gaze. He swallowed,
hard, and reluctantly dragged his gaze up from her generous breasts.

"Is there a problem?" he asked, barely able to get
the words out past his tight throat. He swallowed again
and reminded himself she was off-limits. She wasn't
his girlfriend, not anymore, not if he wanted to keep his
job. He'd have a hard enough time as it was explaining
to Waverly how he'd ended up in Key West in a firefight when he was suspended and was supposed to be
in Saint Augustine.

"You got shot," Heather accused.

"Uh, yeah. A little bit."

"A little bit?" she choked out. "Why didn't you tell
me you were hurt?"

"We were busy trying to escape without getting
killed."

She shook her head and fisted her hands at her sides.
Her gaze went to the items sitting in the tray next to his
bed. Her eyes widened and her mouth fell open.

He probably should have hidden his phone.

She strode toward him and grabbed his ruined phone
from the tray. When she held the twisted piece of metal
up, the bullet hole was clearly visible. Her eyes flashed
daggers at him as she tossed the phone back onto the
tray. "Waterlogged, Nick? You said your phone was waterlogged."

"I'm pretty sure I said it was broken." She sure looked
good when she was angry. Her skin was flushed a del-
icate pink. Her long hair flew out around her and her

breasts pushed against her too-tight shirt as she put her hands on her hips.

Nick clutched the edge of the bed to keep from reaching for her.

She narrowed her eyes. "No, you said the phone was waterlogged. You *implied* you forgot to leave your phone on the beach with your gun when you went into the ocean. I thought that was odd for you to forget something like that. Now I know you didn't. You lied to me."

He shrugged, unimpressed by that accusation. He lied all the time. It was his job. If lying meant keeping her from worrying and keeping her safe, that's what he would do. "I didn't want you to worry about an insignificant injury."

"Insignificant? You call a gunshot insignificant?"

"Through and through. A handful of stitches." He gave her his best frown when what he really wanted to do was pull her against him and remind himself how well her curves fit against his hard planes. There was only one reason he could think of for her to be this upset. She still cared about him. After the way he'd treated her, that surprised him. And pleased him. Blood started pumping to a part of his body that left his brain slightly dazed from lack of oxygen.

"I could have helped you," she insisted. "When did you get shot?" She reached past him, tore the plastic bag open that she'd carried in and dumped out a pair of jeans, a shirt, and miraculously, a pair of tennis shoes that looked like they just might fit.

She grabbed the blanket from the foot of the bed and tossed it over his lap. Then she began tugging at the fastenings on his hospital gown, apparently intent on helping him change clothes. He wondered just how far she'd go with that, and he couldn't seem to dredge up any desire to refuse her help.

She pulled the gown off and pitched it on the countertop. "Well? When did you get shot?"

He had a feeling if he told her he'd gotten shot just as they'd reached the woods after running from the house, that she'd never let him hear the end of it. He decided a vague reply was the safer route. "I'm not really sure. It didn't even hurt."

Actually, it had hurt like hell, but he wasn't going to admit it.

She rolled her eyes and helped him slide his arms into the clean shirt. "*I'm* sure that it did. I don't buy for one second that you don't know when you were hit." She stepped back, apparently deciding he could button his own shirt, and raked her hands through her hair.

"I'm tougher than I look," she said. "I don't want you giving up your Kevlar vest for me and running into a firefight. And if I'd known you were injured, I could have helped, somehow. I could have dressed the wound to make sure you didn't lose too much blood, for one thing. I have enough on my conscience without adding you to the list."

"Like what?" He didn't bother with the top two buttons on his shirt. He grabbed the fresh jeans and lifted a leg to put them on.

Heather's eyes widened and she whirled around. "What do you mean, like what?" she asked.

Nick smiled at her sudden nervousness and tossed the blanket back on the bed to make it easier to pull on his pants. "You said you had enough on your conscience. Like what, for instance?"

He pulled the clean jeans on, wincing when they

tugged on his stitches. The fact that he was partly turned on from ogling Heather's breasts and staring at her curvy backside didn't help with the snug fit. He was extra slow and careful with the zipper, since he was forced to go commando.

She threw her hands in the air. "What do I have on my conscience? Really? Everything! Mark being hurt. You being hurt. And Lily, God knows it's my fault she's in this mess."

Nick stilled. "What do you mean it's your fault?"

She peeked over her shoulder, as if to make sure nothing was exposed that shouldn't be before turning around to face him.

Good grief, the woman was adorable. She acted as if she'd never seen him naked before. Then again, they'd only slept together once, the night before the raid on the club. And speaking for himself, one time with the little firecracker wasn't enough, not even close. It would have to be, of course, which meant he'd probably spend the rest of his life wanting her and wondering what could have been.

That thought had his mood taking a dive south.

He grabbed his wallet from the tray and shoved it into his pants pocket. "How is it your fault that Lily's in this mess?" he repeated.

A knock sounded on the door.

"Come in," Nick called out. He didn't miss the look of relief that crossed Heather's face. He made a mental note to ask her that question again later, when they were alone.

Chuck and Tanner stepped inside.

"About ready?" Tanner asked.

"Just about." Nick sat back on the bed and grabbed the pair of shoes. "How's Mark doing?"

"He's still in surgery," Chuck said. "But the doctor said his prognosis is good. We'll keep agents guarding his room until he's stable enough to be transferred to a Miami hospital."

Heather stepped forward and pushed Nick's hands away. She grabbed one of his shoes and gently slid it onto his foot. He stared at her in surprise. It had been hurting like crazy trying to bend down to put his shoes on, so he appreciated her help. But he couldn't fathom why she was being so nice and concerned after he'd left her in jail all weekend. He owed her an apology, at the least, and here she was trying to take care of him.

He thanked her and forced his attention back to Tanner. "Did you find the men who were after us?"

"Not yet, but we did find the police car. It was stolen right out of a parking lot earlier tonight. Pretty bold. And it proves this whole thing was planned. Nothing spur-of-the-moment about it, that's for sure."

Heather finished tying Nick's shoes and stepped back. "How will I know the real cops from the fake cops when I go back to my motel?"

"You're not going back to that motel," Nick said. "Gonzalez's men will be watching, hoping you'll return."

"But my suitcase, my clothes—"

"We've got that covered, ma'am," Tanner spoke up. "We've already had someone pick up your things. And as soon as the police release the crime scene at the house you rented," he said, addressing Nick, "we'll get your stuff from the house. But that might be a while. In the meantime, give me a list of what you'll need and I'll send someone to a store to get it."

"Thanks. I appreciate that. I assume you'll put Heather and me up at a hotel in town tonight?"

At Chuck's nod, he continued. "You said the police are processing the scene. Were they able to identify the men I shot in the woods behind the house? And the one Heather shot in the garage?"

Heather shivered and wrapped her arms around her waist. She might think she was tough, and maybe she was, but obviously the idea of shooting someone—no matter how much they deserved it—didn't sit right with her. Nick hated that she'd had to experience that. No matter how many times he was forced into that kind of situation, it still ate at him every time he had to hurt someone or take a life. Heather wasn't in law enforcement. She hadn't signed up for that kind of burden. Waverly and Rickloff deserved a special place in hell for using her and abandoning her when she needed their protection.

Tanner and Chuck stared at him in surprise. "Are you saying you shot someone? Both of you?"

"Yes," Nick answered slowly, studying them both. "I shot two men back in town who were trying to kill Mark. I shot three more in the woods and Heather shot one in the garage. It's possible they weren't all killed and some of them got away before the police got there." He glanced back and forth between them. "Are you telling me no one found *any* bodies?"

Tanner shook his head. "Not a one. They did find blood in the garage, but they figured it was Mark's. How certain are you that you actually hit anyone?"

Nick crossed his arms, insulted they'd even asked. "I never miss."

"Neither do I," Heather said, crossing her arms as well and looking just as insulted as Nick felt.

Tanner motioned to Chuck, who nodded and pulled his phone out of his pocket as he stepped out of the room.

"We'll notify the police to make another sweep, see if they can find a blood trail in the woods. But that may not be possible until daylight."

"Put the hospital on alert for gunshot victims and make sure they notify the DEA if anyone comes in for treatment," Nick said.

Tanner nodded. "Will do. We've already set up hotel rooms for the night under some aliases. You two will be in a two-bedroom suite. Chuck and I will be in the room next door, just a phone call away or a knock on the wall if you need us. Tomorrow morning we'll take you to our office. Our boss wants to debrief you on everything that happened."

"Have you spoken to Waverly or Rickloff?" Nick asked.

"We spoke to Rickloff. He claims there was a miscommunication, a mix-up about the name of the bar. He claims his men wanted to provide backup but didn't know where to go."

"A miscommunication?" Nick said. "That's what they call it these days?"

"Call what?" Heather asked.

Incompetence. Actually, he was beginning to wonder if Heather's original suspicions about Rickloff were right, that he might be working for Gonzalez. But he wasn't going to air that thought in front of fellow agents without facts to back it up.

"Never mind," he said, in response to Heather's question. He eyed Tanner. "Since this is the only hospital in Key West and the men who tried to kill us know we grabbed Mark, it's a pretty safe bet they'll assume we're here, too. I bet they've already got someone watching this place. We can't just walk out the front doors."

"We can take you through the ambulance bay."

Nick shook his head. "Not good enough. This was a well-planned attack with plenty of manpower and a cleanup crew, or else you'd have found the bodies." He slid a glance at Heather. "They didn't get what they came for. *You.* So I'm betting they're not going to just say forget it. They'll be worried we'll go into hiding, so they won't want to miss us leaving the hospital. They'll watch everyone who comes in or out."

"Then what are we supposed to do?" Heather glanced worriedly back and forth.

"Does this hospital have a medevac helicopter?" Nick asked.

Tanner shook his head. "No. When we have trauma cases, Ryder Trauma Center in Miami sends their chopper to airlift the victims. That's an hour out, and they won't send the medevac for something like this." He grinned and pulled his phone out. "But I do know where we can get a chopper."

HEATHER TUCKED THE last of her hair up underneath the ball cap and critically inspected her reflection in the hospital bathroom mirror. The T-shirt hugged her chest almost indecently. And the jeans were snug, too. The nurse who gave Heather her clothes had been just a little smaller than Heather. The sneakers were tight, too, but at least she wouldn't trip over her own feet when she ran outside. Would Gonzalez's men recognize her in this outfit? It certainly didn't conceal much, other than her hair.

"Heather," Nick's deep voice called through the door. "The chopper's a minute out. We need to hurry."

She tugged at her T-shirt, trying to stretch it out some more, but gave up. She sighed and opened the bathroom door.

Nick stood in the opening. He swallowed, his Adam's apple bobbing in his throat. "You're not going to fool anyone in that outfit, even with the ball cap," he said, his voice oddly tight.

"What choice do I have?"

"I'll grab you a lab coat on the way out."

He'd been luckier than her at getting clothes that fit. He'd rolled the sleeves of the dress shirt up to his elbows, giving him a rakish, sexy appeal that had Heather clutching her hands into fists to keep from reaching for him. No one should look that good after the horrible night they'd just experienced.

Thinking about the men possibly watching the hospital, she shivered. The night and all its dangers were far from over.

Whump. Whump. Whump. The sound of the helicopter's blades sounded overhead.

Nick automatically glanced up, as if he could see the helicopter through the ceiling. "Chopper's here. Let's go."

Heather stepped out of the bathroom, her borrowed sneakers painfully squeezing her feet.

"This way." Nick led her out the door and down the hall to their left.

They could hear the sound of excited voices coming from the front of the hospital. Having a helicopter touch down in the parking lot was definitely not the norm. The DEA agents had cleared the lot right in front of the emergency room doors to make space for the chopper.

"Come on," Nick urged, pulling Heather with him

to the exit. "We have to time this just right." He held the door open, and Heather ran with him outside, to the parking lot out back.

Less than a minute later, Nick drove their borrowed car down the side road next to the hospital. Heather leaned over in the passenger seat to look out Nick's window. "Fake Nick" and "fake Heather," both DEA agents from the Key West office, wearing exactly what Nick and Heather had been wearing when they got to the hospital, ran out of the emergency room doors and into the waiting chopper—a chopper that had *Bubba's Seafood* written on the side.

That explained Tanner's grin when he said he could get a helicopter.

Heather wouldn't have believed for one second that the shirtless man pretending to be Nick was really Nick. Nick's abs were much more defined and his biceps were twice as big.

"Do you think we fooled Gonzalez's men?" she asked.

"I sure as hell hope so." Nick punched the accelerator and the car leaped forward.

Chapter Eight

A knock on the hotel room door had Nick waving Heather into the first bedroom. He drew his gun and leaned back against the wall.

"Who is it?" he called out.

"Tanner."

Nick leaned over and looked through the peephole before unlocking the door. Tanner hurried inside and Nick locked the door behind him.

Heather stepped out from the bedroom without waiting for Nick to give the all clear. He barely resisted the urge to remind her of condition number two as he holstered his gun. The only reason he didn't was because he didn't want to embarrass her in front of the other agent. But she was going to have to learn to be more careful. What would she have done if it hadn't been Tanner at the door?

He shook his head and waved Tanner over to the couch.

"How did it go?" Nick asked.

"Hard to say. We didn't notice any vehicle activity on the ground when the chopper took off, other than your car leaving the hospital. The agents tailing you didn't see anyone else following. I'm not sure what to think. Either Gonzalez didn't have anyone watching and we went totally overboard getting that chopper—which, I might add, is going to be fun to explain on my next expense report—or he's a lot smarter than I thought."

"I've never met the man in person, but I've met plenty who have while I was building my undercover identity this past year," Nick said. "He's got a reputation for being on top of things and isolating himself behind layers of front men. If his thugs were the ones after Heather and me, I guarantee they were watching the hospital."

Heather plopped down on the opposite couch. "If? What are you saying? That Gonzalez might not have been the one who went after us?"

"I'm just open to all possibilities until proven otherwise," Nick said. "Tanner, have your men interviewed any witnesses who saw the shoot-out near the bar?"

"We're still canvassing that area. No witnesses yet, but that's no surprise in that part of town. The drug trade has a wrap on that area."

"What about my sister?" Heather asked. "Has there been any word about her? Other than the note from the men who abducted her, I haven't heard anything. I don't even know if…if she's alive."

"I'm new to this case," Tanner said. "Can't say that I really have much background, other than what Nick gave me in the hospital. But I *can* tell you that your sister and Gonzalez have been an item for quite some time. If it makes you feel better, I seriously doubt he'll hurt her if he can avoid it. That's not what he wants at all. The fact that he went after you with so much manpower, and that he didn't even seem interested in the duffel bag of drugs, tells me he's trying to make a public statement.

And stealing a police car on top of everything else, well, that's definitely out of character for him. He doesn't normally tangle directly with law enforcement. He's got too much to lose."

"I'm not sure I understand," she said.

Nick scooted forward on the couch opposite from her and rested his forearms on his knees. "What Tanner is saying is that if Lily were dead, Gonzalez would have no reason to go after you. The fact that he did go after you is a good indication that he's still trying to figure out a way to save face and prove that he's still in control of his empire. Plus, if he killed Lily, he'd dump her body…"

He cursed his poor choice of words when Heather blanched and wrapped her arms around her waist.

"I'm sorry," he said. "I was just trying to say that if your sister was dead, we'd know about it. Gonzalez wouldn't try to hide what he'd done. Just the opposite. He'd want everyone to know that the woman who'd stolen from him had paid the ultimate price, as a warning to others."

She nodded, some of the color returning to her face. "I hope you're right, that she's unharmed."

Nick exchanged a glance with Tanner. The worried expression on Tanner's face told Nick they were both thinking the same thing.

Lily might not be dead, but "unharmed" was a stretch.

Even if Gonzalez eventually let Lily go, a man like him wasn't going to ignore the fact that his mistress had stolen from him, which was exactly what Nick's informants had basically confirmed when he'd arrived this morning. The rumor was that Lily had gotten into a fight with Gonzalez and took off with the kilos.

Nick figured the odds were about seventy-thirty that

Lily had already experienced Gonzalez's wrath, and that her suffering wasn't going to end until—if—she was rescued.

HEATHER WAS STILL exhausted the next morning when Nick dragged her out of bed at the unholy hour of seven o'clock. But fear for her sister had her quickly showering and getting dressed without complaint. They'd rushed over to the Key West DEA office, and now she was sitting in the lobby, doing nothing but watching the seconds on the clock tick by while Nick met with Dante Messina, the special agent in charge.

Why she wasn't being included in that meeting made no sense to her. Lily was her sister, after all, and both of their futures were on the line. Those two facts should have ensured that she was allowed inside the DEA "hallowed offices" instead of relegated to the lobby with Tanner and Chuck babysitting her. She wasn't sure if they were really worried about her safety or whether their job was to make sure she didn't run away. She didn't get the feeling these DEA agents trusted her any more than Nick did.

The clock on the wall showed that Nick had been gone for over half an hour. Heather let out a deep sigh.

Chuck looked up from the newspaper he was reading in the chair across from her. "Are you sure you don't want anything, Miss Bannon? I can send Tanner out for Starbucks or Mickey D's."

Tanner, sitting next to Chuck, cocked a brow. "Or I can send Chuck out to get whatever you need."

His quick glance at the door to the other room told Heather he was just as anxious as she was to find out what was going on. Heather vaguely wondered what

Chuck and Tanner had done to draw the short straw and be stuck in the lobby with her.

Before she could tell them she didn't want anything, the door opened.

Heather jumped to her feet, expecting to see Nick. Instead, Dante Messina—whom she'd met briefly when they first arrived—strode out of the room and stopped in front of her.

"Miss Bannon," he said. "Thank you for waiting. We're ready for you now." He held his hand out toward the open doorway.

"Thank you." Heather preceded him into the room and Dante followed behind.

As soon as she stepped inside, she stopped and stared in amazement.

Dante moved past her and spoke in low tones to three men standing beside one of the computer monitors on the left side of the room.

"Impressive, isn't it?"

Heather jerked around at the sound of Nick's voice. He was standing beside her, grinning as if everything were perfectly fine. As if none of the horrible events yesterday had ever happened. Then she noticed the tiny lines around his eyes, the tension in his stance. Nick wasn't fine at all. He looked…worried.

"It *is* impressive," she answered. "I've never seen anything like it."

"Neither have I. And I've been in a lot of DEA offices around the country. I have to admit I've got a bad case of technology envy right now."

Heather could understand why. This office was unlike anything she'd ever seen, except maybe in a movie. There were no cubicle walls. The entire room was open, with three enormous semicircular tables that stretched from one side to the other, in tiers, all facing the front like stadium seating in a theater, or maybe a NASA control room. Agents sat at the various workstations, talking into headsets or typing at their state-of-the-art computers. An electronic map of the Florida Keys was currently displayed on the screen at the end of the room, with live pictures of different parts of the Keys being flashed down the left side.

Dante finished his conversation with the three men he was with and waved at Nick and Heather to join them.

"Come on," Nick said, resting his hand on the small of Heather's back. "That's our cue."

They headed down the stairs and went through a side door with Dante and the three other agents. Though smaller than the room they'd just come from, this office had the same theater-style screen on the far wall, showing the same live shots.

Dante didn't sit behind the desk that dominated one side of the room. Instead, he and his agents sat in the well-worn group of chairs arranged in a circle in front of the desk. Heather couldn't imagine Nick's boss giving up his position of power by sitting with his agents like Dante. Nick led Heather to one of the chairs and sat beside her. He squeezed her hand as if to reassure her, then let go.

"These men are my section leaders," Dante said, directing his comments to Heather.

He introduced each man and Heather shook their hands.

"I'm sorry I left you waiting so long," Dante apologized. "But I had to gather some facts together and hear Nick's side of what happened before I spoke to you."

"No problem." She glanced worriedly at Nick. He gave her a reassuring nod.

Dante rested his forearms on his knees. "I understand you and your sister were arrested for possession of cocaine, with intent to sell."

Heather jerked back in her chair as if she'd been slapped.

"I'm not judging you," Dante assured her. "I'm fact-finding so I can make some decisions."

"Fine. The *facts* are that my sister had cocaine in her possession because she's mixed up with a drug-dealing boyfriend who took advantage of her vulnerability. I tried to destroy the drugs to keep her from using them or from doing something worse, as you said, like selling them." She directed her next statement to Nick. "I'm not a drug dealer."

Nick's eyes widened. His reaction told Heather he'd never considered that she was. Well, it would have been nice if he'd bothered to tell her that. She crossed her arms and faced Dante.

"The boyfriend you're referring to is, of course, Jose Gonzalez," Dante continued. "He's a major trafficker of cocaine through the Keys to Miami, and on to other cities like Saint Augustine. Nick tells me that Waverly offered you a deal, that if you helped him get Gonzalez he'd drop all charges against you and your sister. I have a problem with that, because Gonzalez is on my turf. Rickloff is out of the Miami office and never consulted me. If he had, I wouldn't have offered you a deal."

Heather shot a desperate look at Nick, but she couldn't read the hard expression on his face. What was going on?

"I don't understand. I signed an agreement. I was sent here with Agent Watkins…" She swallowed hard against the tightening in her throat and flushed with guilt because Watkins had been injured, but she plowed ahead. "I did exactly what I was told. I'm cooperating in every way that I can."

He held up his hand to stop her. "I'm not nullifying your deal. I can't. It's legal and binding. I'm just saying that I agree with Nick. It was a bad deal, a lousy idea, and if anyone had consulted me—which they didn't—I would have explained to them how stupid it was."

"I don't understand," Heather said.

"As far as I'm concerned, Waverly is responsible for Watkins being hurt and for you and Nick almost being killed. Not to mention, he didn't provide backup. Rickloff isn't an idiot. He knew what would happen. I can only conclude one thing. He wanted Gonzalez to abduct you."

Heather's hand flew to her throat. "That's insane."

"No, that's desperation. Rickloff has been after Gonzalez for a long time, with no more success than I've had. He wants to get him, badly, so that blinded him to the dangers. I can't imagine he wanted you hurt. There's nothing to gain by that. But it's logical to assume if Gonzalez's men grabbed you they'd have taken you back to one of his private compounds. Rickloff wanted to follow you to that compound to capture Gonzalez."

He stood, picked something up off his desk that appeared to be a remote control and crossed to the screen on the far wall. The pictures changed, revealing a more detailed map of the Keys, with several red Xs on it. He waved his hand to encompass the entire screen. "Gonzalez has dozens of homes throughout the Keys and south Florida. Most are protected like military compounds, with the latest security gadgets and a full staff of security guards. There are some remote houses, too, on smaller islands, basically little blips of land just a mile or so across that you won't see on most maps. Gonzalez likes to go from compound to compound like a game of musical chairs, because he knows we're watching. The problem is, he has several look-alikes, much like Saddam Hussein had in Iraq. We're never quite sure where the real Jose Gonzalez is at any particular time. It's an old-school trick, but effective."

He tossed the remote back on his desk and sat down again. "We really don't know which house Gonzalez thinks of as his real home, which brings me to my point. We have no way of figuring out where your sister is without searching every compound, every little island he owns. No judge is going to give us a warrant to do that, and Rickloff knows that. I believe he was hoping to get Gonzalez to kidnap you so he could follow you to where Lily was being held. Armed with that information, he could get a search warrant. I'm sure he thought it would be a simple in-and-out procedure, no one gets hurt. But, as usual, he underestimated Gonzalez."

Heather stared at the map. All those Xs made her slightly nauseous. Finding Lily was starting to look like an impossible task. "But if what you're saying is true, about all those compounds, how would Rickloff have known where to go if Gonzalez kidnapped me?"

Dante twisted sideways in his chair to pick up something from his desk. He held it out in his palm—the parrot transmitter Mark was wearing on his shirt in the bar.

"This isn't just a microphone," Dante said. "It's also a homing beacon. I believe Rickloff planned to use that to find you after you were taken. Since Mark was still wearing the pin when he was taken into the E.R., the nurse who cut off his clothes put this in the bag that contained his belongings. That bag was put in his room. None of my agents noticed the pin or realized what it was until there was an attempt on Mark's life this morning at the hospital. Even though we had him sequestered in a remote room under a fake name, one of Gonzalez's men found him and tried to kill him."

"Oh, no. Is he…okay?" Heather asked, her nails biting into her palms.

"Yes. Fortunately we had him well guarded, but the man who tried to kill him was killed in the scuffle, so we couldn't get any additional information out of him. Regardless, my point is that Rickloff made some terrible mistakes. I could have told him what outcome to expect if he paraded you in public for Gonzalez's men to see. Rickloff and Waverly may make deals, but Gonzalez doesn't. Your sister—"

"Lily."

He nodded. "Lily. She's been living with Gonzalez for a while. She—"

"Wait, wait," Heather said. "Everyone keeps saying my sister was Gonzalez's girlfriend. Now you're saying they were living together. You just showed me that he owns entire islands. That means he's wealthy, right?"

Dante frowned, not looking pleased at her interruption. "Yes. He's quite wealthy actually. He owns many legitimate businesses that we believe he uses to launder his drug money. But yes, he's rich."

"Does he normally spend money on the women he associates with? Does he buy them cars, clothes, things like that?"

"Of course."

"Then why did my sister show up in Saint Augustine a couple of weeks ago flat broke, driving a car that wouldn't even start the night we were arrested?"

The room went silent. Heather looked at each man, including Nick, waiting for someone to answer her, but no one did. "None of you have thought about that?"

"It's a valid question," Nick finally said. "One wouldn't expect that Gonzalez's mistress would have a rattletrap car and no spending money. I have no idea what this could mean, but I think Dante's men should look into it."

"We will," Dante assured them. "But back to my original point. Your sister knows how the system works, that if she destroyed Gonzalez's drugs, she'd be dead. So, when his lawyer talked to her in jail, I assure you the first thing she told him, regardless of how much she may love you, is that you're the one who flushed that cocaine. She probably told him you tricked her somehow into taking the drugs in the first place. Basically, she gave him what he wanted, a way to place blame on someone else and not hurt her. But by doing that, she moved you to the top of Gonzalez's hit list. I imagine his lawyer was supposed to bail you out of jail so Gonzalez's men could abduct you. When that didn't work, he took Lily and tempted you to the Keys with that note. Going to Skeleton's Misery was like offering yourself up as a gift. The end result was inevitable, that Gonzalez would send someone to kill you. Lucky for you, Nick stepped in. Unfortunately for Nick, it cost him his job."

Heather froze, her heart stuttering in her chest. "I don't…I don't understand," she whispered. "Nick?"

His jaw tightened. "When Dante called Waverly to report what happened, Waverly fired me for not staying in Saint Augustine and for coming down here without permission."

Heather's stomach twisted into a hard knot. She knew Nick loved being a DEA agent. It seemed to matter more to him than anything else.

Including her.

If he hadn't hated her before, he must hate her now. "But you were a hero. You saved Mark and me."

"Exactly what I said to Waverly," Dante said. "If it weren't for Nick, Agent Watkins would be dead. Of that I have no doubt. And you would probably be in one of Gonzalez's compounds right now being interrogated by Gonzalez or one of his men. Nick saved both of you, several times from what I've heard. He's extremely good at what he does, which is why I offered him a position on my team. Unfortunately, he turned me down."

"What?" Heather grabbed Nick's hand. "Why would you do that? You shouldn't lose your job because of me."

He gently pulled his hand back. "For the same reason I defied Waverly by coming down here in the first place. I don't want you to get hurt. And now Dante wants to put you in danger just like Waverly. I'm not going to allow that. After this meeting, you and I are going back home, to Saint Augustine."

Panic bloomed inside Heather, making her legs shake. "I can't go back, not without Lily."

"I agree," Dante said. "And I have a plan to help get her back."

Nick swore, leaving Heather little doubt that he knew exactly what Dante's plan was.

And he didn't like it.

"Okay, what's the plan?" she asked.

Dante grinned. "We're going to play the identical twin card."

Chapter Nine

"You're proposing the same ill-fated plan Waverly proposed," Nick said, his voice low and menacing.

"Close, yes, but far less dangerous, because I'll make sure she's protected," Dante said. "Miss Bannon, believe me when I tell you I would never have agreed to Rickloff and Waverly's plan had they asked me ahead of time. But the wheels are in motion and two agents were nearly killed. That sends the wrong signal to the bad guys. If I don't bring Gonzalez down, I might as well declare open season on all my agents. To get him, I need inside information, which has proved exceedingly difficult with Gonzalez. His men are so afraid of him they're loyal without question." He leaned forward in his chair. "I'm proposing a twist in the original plan. Instead of presenting yourself as Heather, I want you to pretend to be Lily."

Heather blinked, not certain she'd heard him correctly. "Excuse me?"

Nick mumbled something that sounded like "stupid plan" and "dangerous" beneath his breath.

Heather clutched the arms of her chair in frustration. "If Gonzalez has my sister, how can I pretend to be her in public? Everyone will know I'm a fraud."

Dante shook his head. "Last night, no one thought you were Lily. You didn't dress like her or act like her, because you weren't trying to pretend to be her. Gonzalez had no problem sending men after you because you were obviously *not* your sister. But if you can convince everyone you're Lily, he has to be more careful. If his men grabbed Lily in public, he'd be sending the message his mistress had defied him, and he'd be forced to kill her. But he doesn't want to kill her. So, instead, he'll come after you himself and try to bargain with you so you'll go with him without making a fuss, allowing him to save face and not hurt his girlfriend."

Heather shook her head. "This is all so confusing. But I'll do whatever I can to save her. How will your plan do that?"

"After forcing Gonzalez out into the open, we'll be able to follow him back to see where he's holding your sister. Then we can get a warrant and raid the compound and free Lily. The beauty of it is that I then get to charge Gonzalez with kidnapping. I'll take that to get him off the streets. Of course, we'll have to figure out how to make all of this happen, without Gonzalez taking you prisoner as well."

Nick swore. "Yet another reason not to use her in this crazy scheme. There's no way to guarantee her safety. Your plan isn't any better than Rickloff's or Waverly's."

Dante frowned at him. "Waverly sent a civilian with one agent and no backup. That was stupid. I'll send her in with plenty of backup. And we'll have every possible escape route covered."

Nick shook his head. "There has to be another way to find Gonzalez and rescue Lily without putting Heather in danger."

"We have no way of knowing where Gonzalez is holding Lily. We need a way to narrow it down. If you have a better plan, please, tell me. I'm listening." Dante leaned back in his chair and folded his hands behind his head.

"Send your men to all the local bars," Nick said. "Let them infiltrate Gonzalez's network and gather information, find out where he is. Use all this fancy equipment and resources you have to launch a rescue operation."

"That will take too long—weeks, months. Even though Gonzalez has hidden Lily's thievery from most of his men, his close inner circle has to know what happened by now. He can't afford not to punish her. And he's not going to wait weeks or months."

The unspoken conclusion seemed to weigh on everyone in the room. Lily was still in danger, mortal danger.

Nick glared at Dante. "What, exactly, do you want Heather to do?"

"One of Gonzalez's men's favorite hangouts is a marina a couple of miles north of here. There's a restaurant on the boardwalk that's considerably more tame than Skeleton's Misery. We'll have men inside and out, and scattered throughout the marina. Heather will wear a wire and sit as bait, waiting for Gonzalez to approach. She'll walk outside with him and we'll cause some kind of commotion to let her escape. Then we'll follow Gonzalez without him realizing it."

"Won't he smell a trap?" Nick asked.

"Possibly. I didn't say the plan was perfect, just that I don't have a better one."

"I don't think he'll show," Nick insisted.

"You may be right," Dante said, his tone matter-of-fact as if that didn't really matter. "I'd give it fifty-fifty odds. But even if he doesn't show, having Miss Bannon pretend to be Lily will stir things up. That might increase the activity in the compound where Gonzalez is holding the real Lily. If Gonzalez thinks the DEA is going all out to trap him and find Lily, he may have his security doubled or tripled where he's holding her." He gestured toward the screen on the far wall. "We've got eyes on all of his major holdings. If he starts making changes, we'll know about it. Once we know where she's being held, we can do everything the old-fashioned way, get down to basics and perform twenty-four-hour surveillance until he makes a mistake. Then we'll get that warrant and go in."

Nick stared down at the floor for a moment. Heather watched him carefully. She trusted his judgment. She wanted to save her sister, and she believed Nick was her best chance. If he didn't want her to go along with Dante's plan, she wouldn't. She'd learned her lesson. But if he did agree to the plan, she'd do whatever it took to help.

Nick looked up and met her gaze. "Do you want to do this?" he asked quietly.

"I want to save my sister. If you think this is our best shot, then yes, I want to do it. It's your decision."

His brows rose in surprise. He stared at her for a full minute before blowing out a breath and sitting back. "All right, Dante. Reinstate me and put me in charge. I plan every single detail down to which men come along, where they sit, even what weapons they have. The second I feel antsy, I pull Heather out. You either agree to my terms, or we're leaving."

Heather couldn't help but smile. Nick was all about conditions, and he was reciting condition number two to Dante.

Dante slapped his hands on his thighs and grinned. "Agreed." He stood and held his hand out to Nick.

Nick rolled his eyes and stood to shake his hand. "You had this planned all along, didn't you?"

"You bet. Waverly's loss is my gain. Welcome to my team. When do you want the operation to take place?"

Nick looked at his watch. "Might as well do it tonight. We'll plan everything out right now. Then you can work on putting all the pieces in place while I take Heather back to Saint Augustine for a couple of hours."

Heather frowned. "Why would we go back home?"

"Because if you're going to pretend to be your sister, you've got to look like her. That means finding the perfect clothes, which my sister-in-law can help with. But more importantly, it means going where I have a special contact with very special skills."

Heather stared at him suspiciously. He looked like he was suddenly enjoying this way too much. "What special skills?"

He grinned. "Tattoos."

HEATHER BALKED AT the entrance to the tattoo parlor. The look of distaste on her face as she stared at the sign over the door was priceless. Nick knew he was having far too much fun teasing her, but he also knew she was far too uptight and nervous for tonight's dangerous operation. He needed her to loosen up, to have some fun, to relax. And if he enjoyed himself along the way, so be it.

She bit her lip. "Are you absolutely sure it won't hurt? And that the tattoos won't be permanent?"

Nick grinned. "Permanent wouldn't be so bad, would it?" He leaned down next to her ear. "Show me yours and I'll show you mine."

She rolled her eyes.

Nick winked and pulled the door open, ushering her inside.

"I still don't see why we had to fly all the way to Saint Augustine for this," she grumbled.

"This is my home turf. I know whom to trust here. And we couldn't risk anyone in Key West finding out about you getting these fake tattoos. They have to believe the tattoos are real, that you're Lily, for this to work."

She stared up at him. "You were just teasing me about having a tattoo, right? I know you don't have any."

"You sure about that?" He dipped his head again, his mouth hovering next to her ear. "We only made love once. Are you sure you saw every…single…inch of me?"

Heather blinked, her face flushing an adorable shade of pink.

Nick laughed out loud, thoroughly enjoying himself.

"Can I help you folks?" A man shorter than Heather, with tattoos completely covering his arms from shoulder to wrist, stepped in from the back. When he saw Nick, he smiled and held out his hand.

"Hey, man, it's been a while. You here for a touch-up?"

Heather stared at Nick in surprise. He could practically see the thoughts whirling through her mind as she tried to figure out where his tattoo might be. She deliberately turned her back on him, pretending to study a book on the counter that contained dozens of designs.

"Nope, I'm not here for me today, Mitch. This is Heather, a friend of mine."

Heather turned around and shook his hand, but she didn't look at Nick.

"What can I do for y'all?" Mitch asked.

In answer, Nick pulled some copies of Lily's mug shots out of his shirt pocket. He and Heather had stopped at the station earlier for the photos. They were the only pictures that clearly showed Lily's tattoos.

Mitch didn't even blink when Nick handed him the pictures. Apparently mug shots weren't anything new to him.

"I need you to reproduce these tattoos on Heather. I need them to look exactly like the pictures, but they need to be temporary, lasting no more than a couple of weeks."

"Afraid to commit, huh?" He smiled at Heather. "Don't worry, you'll fall in love with my artwork. I guarantee you'll be back once this starts to fade. You'll want me to make everything permanent."

"Don't count on it." She allowed him to lead her to a chair that resembled the kind in dentist offices.

The bell above the door rang. Nick turned and smiled with genuine pleasure. He stepped over to greet his brother and sister-in-law.

HEATHER TRIED NOT to be too obvious with her interest as she watched Rafe Morgan enter the shop. She'd only met him once, after she'd called 911 about her sister's abduction and he escorted her to the police station. She'd never understood why he'd been the first to arrive after her 911 call, since he was a detective and not a uniformed officer. But he must have been close by and responded when the call came in.

She hadn't really noticed much about him at the time because she was so focused on her sister's disappearance. But now, seeing him standing with Nick, she was struck by how alike they were in height and build, but how very different they were in other ways. Rafe had dark hair and dark eyes. He didn't smile nearly as much as his blond brother, or laugh the way Nick tended to do. Rafe was definitely the more serious of the two.

"Heather?" A soft voice had Heather turning around. She'd been so busy staring at Nick and his brother that she hadn't realized the petite woman who'd come inside with Rafe was now standing beside her chair. Mitch was a few feet away, in his own little world, studying the pictures of the tattoos as if he were Michelangelo preparing to paint the Sistine Chapel.

"You must be Nick's sister-in-law," Heather said, offering her hand and a smile.

The woman shook Heather's hand and returned her smile. She pushed a thick strand of dark hair back from her face. Her chic-looking bob swished back and forth every time she moved. Her suit was perfectly tailored to fit her tiny figure, and looked like it cost more than Heather could earn on a month of stakeouts.

"Yes, I'm Darby. Mind if I sit down?"

Heather shook her head, and Darby pulled a folding chair from nearby and sat. "Nick called Rafe earlier this morning and asked if I could pick up some clothes for you. He said you might have some pictures I could use to get some outfits for the case you're working on. I'd love to help. I know all the specialty shops around here. I can find whatever you need and make it back before Mitch is finished."

Heather shot a glance at Nick. He was still talking to his brother, but he was watching her.

"Um, what exactly did Nick tell you about me?"

"All he said was that you were going undercover on a case together." She hesitated, glancing at Nick before continuing. "But I know Nick fairly well," she said, lowering her voice. "I can tell he cares about you. I've never seen him so…focused on anyone. I know you two have some sort of past, but Rafe wouldn't give me any details." She grinned. "Even though I tried everything I could to get him to tell me, after Nick called this morning."

Heather sighed. "I wish you were right about Nick, but I'm afraid if he's focused it's because he doesn't trust me. Let's just say, he's judged me and found me lacking."

Darby frowned. "Hmm. Maybe you're right. I could have sworn…well, it doesn't matter. How about it? Are you going to let me pick out some clothes for you?"

Mitch laid out his tools on a tray beside the chair and waited expectantly. He was obviously ready to get on with his plans to pepper Heather's arms and torso with tattoos.

Heather grimaced and leaned in close to Darby. "Thank goodness he's not going to give me any real tattoos. I can't imagine having someone stick me with needles and paint my skin permanently."

Darby's eyes sparkled with mischief. "It's not as bad as you think. And the right tattoo, in the right location, can drive a man crazy."

Heather laughed, surprised a woman as conservative-looking as Darby might actually have a tattoo. "Are you saying that you—"

Darby nodded, her face flushing a light pink. "Now give me those pictures so I can go shopping. By the time I'm done, you won't recognize yourself."

Heather gave her a wan smile. As she passed copies of Lily's pictures to Darby, she felt her face flush warm. She wished she had other pictures of her sister, but these were the only ones. She and Lily didn't exactly go for photo ops when Lily blew into town.

Darby's eyes widened. "Are these—"

"Mug shots. Yes. That's my twin sister. Is that a problem?"

Darby cleared her throat and shoved the pictures into her purse. "Of course not. Just leave everything to me."

Chapter Ten

Leaving everything to Darby had been a colossal mistake.

Back at the hotel in Key West again, Heather desperately searched her suitcase one more time and shook her head in disbelief. Darby had taken her shopping assignment to the extreme. She'd bought three outfits, probably to give Heather a choice. But every single one was far too risqué. Even the underwear was like what her sister would wear. The bras were tiny scraps of lace that would barely support her. The panties looked like neon silly string. There was no way Heather could wear this stuff.

She wanted to make others believe she was Lily, yes, but she couldn't dress quite as…revealing as her sister did. She'd mentioned that to Darby. She was sure of it, and yet everything Darby had bought was too short or too tight or just plain too indecent for Heather to even consider wearing.

She sighed and flipped the suitcase closed. Instead, she pulled some of her own clothes out of the closet. She mixed and matched, trying to figure out something that would work. The above-the-knee skirt and short-sleeved blouse would have to do. Mitch's amazing artwork would show just fine with this top. That's all that mattered.

Nick was sitting at the small table next to the kitchenette studying a map spread out before him when she walked out of the bedroom.

His brows climbed to his hairline and he rolled his eyes. "Please tell me that's not what Darby bought you. Didn't you give her the pictures of Lily?"

Heather glanced down at her ensemble. It's not like she'd tucked the blouse in or anything. She'd left the last three buttons undone and had even dared to tie the ends of the blouse together. For goodness' sake, her belly button was showing. No one who knew her would ever expect her to dress like this, not even on one of her forays into the bar scene while doing her P.I. job.

"The clothes Darby bought didn't work out, so I had to get creative with some of my old clothes." She waved her hand at her blouse. "This is like something Lily would wear."

Nick laughed. "No. It isn't." He pushed back from his chair and strode toward her.

"How would you know? You only met her once. The night you threw both of us in jail."

He stopped in front of her. "We're not having that argument tonight. We have too much to do."

She crossed her arms over her chest. "Have you even seen the cell where they house the women prisoners? It's disgusting. It smells like pee."

His lips twitched. Lucky for him, he didn't smile, or she would have been tempted to kick him in the groin.

"No, I didn't know it smelled like…pee," he said. He grabbed her hand and pulled her toward the bedroom.

"What are you doing? I thought you wanted to get to the bar by nine."

"You're not going out looking like that. No one would believe you were Lily." He let her hand go and flipped the suitcase open on top of the bed. He pulled out a pink tank top with spaghetti straps. "How about this?"

She shook her head and held the top against her. "Look how short it is. It would barely cover my breasts."

He stared at the shirt for a moment. He swallowed hard and cleared his throat. "Right." He grabbed another shirt out of the suitcase and held it up.

Heather shook her head. "Too low-cut. I'd fall out."

Nick's gaze shot to her chest, as if he were trying to imagine just that thing. His mouth tightened and he balled up the shirt and tossed it onto the bed. He dug around in the suitcase some more. "Aha." He pulled out a leopard-print tank and held it up. "Long enough to, ah, cover you and not too low-cut."

She took the shirt and held it up, eyeing it critically. "There's something that isn't quite right about this." She understood the spaghetti strap on the right side. But what held it up on the left side? The neckline didn't even look straight. She was seriously having doubts about Darby's so-called shopping expertise. "I'm not even sure I know how to put this on."

Nick pulled a short black miniskirt out of the suit-case and handed it to her. "You'll figure it out. Hurry. We should have left ten minutes ago."

She huffed and headed into the bathroom to change. A few minutes later, she stared at herself in the mirror, horrified.

A knock sounded on the door. "I've got your shoes. Or, at least, I think these are the right shoes. They're black. That matches everything, right?"

"I am not wearing this…this…outfit," Heather said, raising her voice so he could hear her. "I look like a hooker."

The door opened. Heather's gaze shot to Nick's in the mirror as he stepped in behind her. He set a pair of six-inch stilettos on the countertop.

Heather gasped. "I can't possibly wear those…those medieval foot-torturing devices. I'd break my neck."

He grinned. "Medieval torture, huh?" He cocked his head to the side, studying her reflection. "I don't think that's the way that's supposed to work." He tugged the left side of the shirt off her shoulder. "There. That looks better."

Heather stared into the mirror. One side of the shirt was held up by the spaghetti strap. The other side hung low, revealing far more of her breasts than she'd ever revealed in public before, except maybe at the beach in a swimsuit. Even then, she wasn't sure she'd shown off this much skin. She shook her head. "I can't do it. I can't go out like this. The top is—"

"Perfect. It shows off your lovely…tattoos." His grin broadened, letting her know he'd substituted tattoos at the last second.

She eyed the artwork Mitch had so painstakingly painted on her arms and upper body. The pink dragon peeked out of the top of her skirt. She'd blushed profusely the entire time Mitch was working on that particular tattoo. Her skin had felt as though it was on fire, especially when Nick sat down beside her, watching every stroke, after Rafe and Darby left on the shopping trip.

"That one's my favorite," Nick breathed next to her ear.

She shivered and refused to meet his gaze.

He picked up the shoes and held them out. "I can't wait to see how you look in these." The teasing laughter in his voice told her he knew how hard it was for her to stand here in this outfit, and he was having fun at her expense.

"No," she said. "I told you I'm not wearing those. And I'm not wearing this ridiculous outfit. I'll put my own clothes back on." She turned to leave, but he didn't budge an inch.

His thighs pressed up against hers and his chest rubbed against her breasts. He set the shoes on the countertop and braced his hands on the sink, trapping her.

"How did you and your sister grow up in the same household and end up so completely different?" His voice was low and husky. There was no mistaking the heat in his gaze, or the way his pulse was slamming in his chest. She could feel every beat of his heart against hers.

"Let me guess. You prefer the way my sister dresses."

"I didn't say that. But dressing so…minimally…does have its advantages." He winked.

Heather didn't know what to make of his flirty mood. She tried to focus on her memories of the jail cell to combat her softening feelings toward a man she could never have, but with Nick standing so close, all she could think of was how good his hard body felt against her soft curves. And how perfectly…edible he smelled.

He reached up and traced the barbed-wire tattoo on her left bicep. "So, how did two identical twin sisters end up so different?"

Heather cleared her throat and took a step back to put some space between them. "Lily was always, ah, competitive, jealous, I guess. She thought I was the favorite. And she…" She shivered when Nick smoothed his fingers up her other arm, lightly tracing the outline of one of the swirling flower tattoos.

"And she…what?" He slid his hand up her shoulder.

"She left home when she was sixteen. Dropped out of school. I didn't see her for a long time. I only recently…"

He gently massaged her shoulder, making her skin flush hot wherever he touched her.

"Go on," he urged, both of his hands heating her skin, leaving a fiery trail in their wake. "You recently what?"

"I…I don't remember what I was going to say. Nick, what are you doing?"

His nostrils flared and he dipped his head down toward her, but before his mouth claimed hers, he hesitated. Time seemed to stand still as Heather looked into his eyes, so close to hers.

"Nick?" she breathed, waiting, hoping.

He shuddered, his brow furrowing as if he were in pain. Then he stepped back and turned away. "I'll wait in the living room. Don't change clothes. What you're wearing is perfect for pretending to be your sister. If you want to get Gonzalez to notice you, that's the way to do it."

His voice was hard and cold, with none of the warmth she'd heard earlier. He stalked from the bathroom, leaving her wondering what in the world had just happened.

"Don't forget condition number two," Nick said.

Heather clutched his hand, afraid she wasn't going to be able to do this. He had her backed up against the wall in the dark hallway to the bathrooms in the marina restaurant, pretending to be amorous in case someone saw them, but he was actually giving her last-minute instructions.

"Heather, did you hear what I said?"

"Condition number two, yes, got it." She glanced down the long hall toward the main room of the restaurant. She had to go out there, by herself, in this horrid outfit, and pretend to be okay with that while she waited for a dangerous drug dealer to approach her. She clutched Nick's hand even harder.

He cursed and gently eased her grip, bringing her attention back to him.

"Sorry," she whispered.

"It's okay. What's condition number two?" he asked. "I need to make sure you've got this."

"I hate your stupid conditions."

"I know, but tell me anyway."

She rolled her eyes. "Condition number two—I do exactly what you tell me to do at all times. I remember. And don't worry. I've got that ear thingy in. I'm not going to try to wing it on my own. I'm scared enough as it is."

His mouth twitched. "Earwig, not ear thingy. And why are you scared? It's just a restaurant, nothing like the bar you were in before. There are no fewer than ten DEA agents in here undercover, plus me. You're surrounded by people who want nothing more than to keep you safe. Nothing's going to happen, as long as you follow instructions. The second I feel it's not safe, I'm pulling you out. If I tell you to leave, you jump out of your chair and hightail it out of here. Some of the agents will follow you out. If I tell you to duck down, you—"

"Yeah, yeah. I drop to the floor. You reminded me of all your conditions a million times on the way over here. I've got it. And I've got *this*. I didn't dress up like a two-bit hooker for nothing. I'm not going to humiliate myself looking like this without doing everything I can to make this work. I don't want to have to come back here again. I want this to end tonight."

His hand circled her waist and he pulled her close. "Trust me. You don't look like a two-bit hooker."

"I don't?" she whispered, her breath catching in her throat at the heat in his gaze.

He shook his head. "I'd pay a lot more than two bits." He winked.

She drew a sharp breath and shoved his hand away. Without another word, she whirled around and headed for the high-topped table reserved for her. Her dramatic exit was ruined when she lost her balance on the ridiculous stilettos and almost fell. She grabbed the back of a chair, forcing a smile when the startled man in the chair turned.

With a slower, more sane pace, she made her way to the table. She climbed onto the bar stool, certain she looked like a fool trying to keep from flashing everyone as she tugged on her miniskirt.

When a waitress stopped by, Heather ordered her sister's favorite drink, tequila, straight up. But when the drink arrived, Heather only pretended to sip it. The smell alone told her she'd be gagging or half drunk in minutes if she really drank any.

It didn't take long for someone to notice her. A tall, thin man with coffee-colored skin threaded his way through the crowd to her table. She could see him out of the corner of her eye, but she focused instead on watching the people at the other tables, eating dinner.

"Stranger approaching at two o'clock. He's not Gonzalez, but he might be one of his men," Nick's voice spoke in her ear through the two-way transmitter.

Heather couldn't help but jump when his voice first sounded. Hopefully no one noticed.

"Mmm-hmm." She raised her glass for a pretend sip.

"Lily." The man she'd seen approaching was suddenly standing beside her chair. "What are you doing here?" He glanced around, as if afraid someone might see him with her.

Her pulse sped up. This man obviously knew her sister, and expected she would know him, too. She tried to focus on what Nick had told her to do. Lowering her glass, she crossed her arms on the table and tried for a world-weary expression.

"What do you think I'm doing? I'm having a drink."

He leaned in close, still not looking at her directly. He kept scanning the room as if he was afraid someone was watching him. "Obviously, but why here?"

"Why not here?" she countered. "Where else should I be?"

He quirked a brow, facing her directly this time. "Does Gonzalez know you left the compound?"

"Be evasive," Nick's voice whispered through the transmitter in her ear.

Heather moved her glass in tiny circles on the table-top. "I couldn't say if he knows or not. He doesn't own me. He doesn't tell me what I can or can't do."

The man's brows lifted. "How much have you been drinking?"

"Not enough." She lifted the glass and held it to her lips. Then she set it back down and wiped her mouth. "Say whatever it is you want to say and go away. You're ruining my good mood."

He shook his head, his face reddening. "If Gonzalez realizes you left, there won't be a safe place within hundreds of miles for you to hide. You'd better go back, now, before he realizes you're gone."

"Go back where?" She purposely slurred her words, trying to give him the impression she was a little tipsy, to explain why she wouldn't know where Gonzalez was.

He shook his head. "Come on. I'll take you back."

Excitement pulsed through her. Could it really be this easy? He was offering to take her to where Gonzalez was holding her sister. She took a slow, deep breath, trying to remain calm. "All right, I guess. This place is boring anyway. You'll have to drive though. This tequila's already gone straight to my head."

He gave her a quizzical look. "Drive?"

Shoot. What had she done? She was being too specific, which could ruin everything since she didn't have a clue where Gonzalez's compound was. Why would he balk at the word *drive?* Was the compound so close they could walk there? Or was it so far away they would have to fly, or take a boat? She wasn't sure what to say.

The transmitter crackled in her ear. "Play up how much you drank. He's getting suspicious."

She grinned and lifted her drink again. "What? You don't think I could do it? Drive to the compound?" She giggled, trying to make him think she thought the idea was ridiculous, too.

"You really are wasted." He pulled the drink away from her and shoved it out of her reach. "Come on. My boat's out back. I'll try to sneak you into the compound before all hell breaks loose."

"Okay, walk outside with him but stay close to the restaurant," Nick's voice whispered in her ear. "Try to get him to tell you where the compound is. If he doesn't, ditch him and go back inside to wait for Gonzalez."

She slid off the bar stool. She immediately had to clutch the table for support when her feet wobbled in her outrageously unstable stilettos.

The man with her cursed and grabbed her arm, steadying her. He obviously thought she was too drunk to walk, because he held her close and guided her out of the bar.

"We're with you," Nick's voice whispered. "But you're too close to him. Put some distance between the two of you. And under no circumstances are you to get anywhere near his boat. Make an excuse. Say you have to go to the bathroom, whatever it takes. We'll follow his boat when he leaves and see where he goes. With any luck, that will give us the location of the compound where Lily is. Now back away. You're still too close."

With any luck? Meaning if she didn't get on the boat, this might all be for nothing and they might not find Lily? Heather frowned, but did as Nick had told her. She pulled away from the man beside her.

"I can walk," she said, slurring her words again. "Just lead the way. Um, where are we going again?" She threw the last part in, hoping he'd say the name of the island where the compound was, if indeed it was on another island, which she assumed because of him saying they would take his boat to get there.

"To the compound," he said.

Her hopes plummeted as the boats sitting at the dock came into view. If she couldn't get him to give her the location, she'd gained nothing. What if they lost him once he took the boat out? What if Gonzalez didn't show, and this was her only shot?

"I know, I know," she said, forcing another giggle. "But where is that again? I can't seem to keep it straight in my head." She tapped her temple and wobbled on her heels, this time on purpose.

He ignored her question.

"Go back to the restaurant," Nick hissed in her ear.

Heather kept walking.

When they reached the stranger's boat, he held out his hand to help her. "Come on."

She should have backed away. She should have told him she had to go to the ladies' room as Nick had suggested. But she hesitated. This man knew where Lily was.

"Why are you still standing there?" Nick whispered. "Go back inside the restaurant."

"Hurry up," the stranger said, waving his hand for her to step over the side of the boat. "I'm telling you, if Gonzalez figures out you managed to leave without him knowing, it's not just you who's in trouble. It's me and the other guys who are supposed to be guarding the place."

"Don't you dare," Nick's furious voice whispered in her ear, as if he'd just realized she was seriously considering getting into the boat. "Get out of there," he demanded.

She glanced down at the man's hand in front of her. If she stepped into that boat, she'd see her sister again. Or would she? What if this was a trick? But if she didn't, she was back at the beginning, no closer to finding her twin than she'd been on day one. How much more time did Lily have if she wasn't rescued? A week? A day? An hour?

"Heather." Nick's voice was a low growl. "Condition number two."

She stiffened her spine. "I'm sorry," she whispered. "I have to do this."

"What?" The man's brows lowered in confusion.

"Nothing." She smiled and took his hand.

Nick cursed in her ear. He sounded out of breath, as if he was on the move.

Heather stepped over the side of the boat, and all hell broke loose.

Chapter Eleven

The hand holding Heather's went slack. The man in front of her crumpled to the floor of the boat. Behind him stood the man Dante had shown her a picture of earlier, to make sure she'd recognize him.

Gonzalez.

In his hand was the gun he'd used like a hammer to knock the other man unconscious.

Heather stood frozen, staring into the eyes of the man who'd taken her sister. Gonzalez started to raise his gun. A man suddenly lunged from the shadows beside the boat and launched himself at Gonzalez, slamming into him, propelling both of them over the side and into the water. The splash sent up a plume of water that would have drenched Heather if someone hadn't grabbed her and pulled her back.

Like ants pouring out of an anthill, a dozen DEA agents converged onto the docks from their hiding places behind bushes, boats and even the cars parked near the dock. Two agents standing at the water's edge discarded their jackets and guns and jumped into the water where Gonzalez and the other man had disappeared.

"Miss Bannon, this way, please." The man who'd pulled Heather out of the boat tugged her backward. The big white *DEA* letters on his jacket reassured Heather that he really was an agent and wasn't one of Gonzalez's men, but the fact that he wasn't Nick had her stomach clenching with dread. Where was Nick? Had something happened to him? She replayed the last few moments in her memory.

The man who'd taken her to the boat crumpling to the floor.

Gonzalez standing behind him with a gun in his hand.

Another man launching himself at Gonzalez.

A very familiar-looking man.

Heather's gaze flew back to the boat and the crowd of men standing there.

"Please tell me that wasn't Agent Nick Morgan who went into the water with Gonzalez."

"Well, yes, ma'am, it was."

She tugged out of the man's grasp and ran toward the water's edge. Or at least, that was her plan. She'd only gone about five feet when her right heel wobbled, she lost her balance and she went sprawling onto the asphalt.

Her mind had just enough time to register that her miniskirt was hiked up around her hips before someone hauled her to her feet and tugged her skirt back into place. From the sounds of the cursing in her ear, she knew exactly who'd come to her rescue this time.

Nick.

She was so relieved that he was okay that she didn't even care that he was yelling at her in front of everyone for being so stupid and foolishly risking her life. And she didn't care that he was dripping wet. All she cared about was that he wasn't dead.

She threw her arms around his waist and held him tight. "Thank God you're okay."

He stiffened and grabbed her arms, forcing her back. He grabbed one of the agents nearby. "Higgins, get Miss Bannon back to the hotel. Take another agent with you and try to keep her from causing any more trouble until I get back."

"Yes, sir." Higgins motioned another agent over. "Miss Bannon, come with us, please."

Without another word, Nick stalked off and joined the group of men surrounding a very wet, very angry-looking Gonzalez, who'd been fished out of the water.

Heather wanted to jump into the water herself, or maybe throw one of those DEA flak jackets over her head, anything to shut herself away from the other agents giving her curious looks. They'd seen her hugging Nick. And they'd seen him push her away. He'd treated her like a stranger and spoke to her as if she were a recalcitrant child. Perhaps if she were a child, or a stranger, he'd at least have asked if she was okay. Instead, he'd been too busy putting as much distance between them as he could, as quickly as he could.

As if she didn't even matter.

"Miss Bannon?" Higgins gave her a quizzical look. "Are you okay?"

His kind question and gentle voice had her tearing up. Why couldn't Nick have shown some compassion, an ounce of caring, instead of being so disgusted with her? She didn't have cocaine in her hair this time, but he'd still treated her as if she had the plague.

In front of everyone.

She gave Higgins a tight smile. "I'm fine. I'm ready to go. Thank you."

He nodded and led her toward a waiting car. She kept her head up, her back straight, refusing to let Nick have the satisfaction of thinking his treatment of her mattered. It was all her fault, really. She'd forgotten about condition number one. The words Nick had said to her at the police station couldn't have been more clear when he'd listed his first condition for agreeing to help her.

We're through, finished. There is no "us" anymore. And there never will be.

She'd been in total agreement at the time, right after she'd gotten out of jail. She'd wanted nothing to do with him, either. But just being near him the past few days had reminded her how much she was attracted to him, how much she admired him for the work he did, how much he cared about helping other people. Seeing the lighter side of him with his brother and sister-in-law at the tattoo parlor had reminded her how warm and loving he could be, a side of him she'd enjoyed so much when they first met, but which she'd seen so little of in the past few days.

How could she have allowed herself to fall for him again only to be rejected again? He didn't want her. He didn't care about her. All he cared about was his job and appearances.

She wouldn't forget again.

THE SOUND OF voices woke Heather. She bolted up in bed, blinking to focus in the dimly lit hotel room as she clutched the covers to her chest. Her pulse was pounding so hard she could hear it echoing in her ears.

The low murmur of a deep male voice sounded again, and Heather slumped with relief. Nick. He was in the main room of their hotel suite, talking to the two agents guarding her. A few moments later, she heard the sound of a door closing. The other agents must have left.

She glanced at the bedside clock. Two in the morning. Good grief. What had Nick been doing out this late? Had he helped interview Gonzalez? That thought had her fully awake. If he'd spoken to Gonzalez, he might know where her sister was. The DEA could be on their way right now to rescue her. She fervently hoped so.

She shoved the covers back and hopped out of bed right as her bedroom door flew open. She gasped and pressed her hand to her throat before her mind registered that it was Nick standing in the doorway.

She drew in a shaky breath. "You scared me." She lowered her hand to her side, grateful the only light in the room was from the moonlight filtering in through the blinds. She was only wearing a T-shirt and panties, and after Nick's treatment of her back at the dock had reminded her about condition number one, she wasn't exactly comfortable parading around in her underwear.

"Did you find out anything from Gonzalez? Do you know where my sister is?" She reached for the light blanket at the foot of the bed to wrap around herself.

Nick stalked toward the bed, stopping just short of touching her. The tightness of his jaw and the way his eyes narrowed dangerously had Heather's survival instincts screaming at her to run. She resisted the cowardly urge because she knew Nick would never hurt her—not physically, anyway—and her pride had taken too much of a beating already tonight. She wasn't about to let him bully her.

He leaned down toward her, obviously trying to use his size and strength to intimidate her.

It was working.

"What were you thinking?" he bit out, his voice a tight rasp. He grabbed her arms and lightly shook her.

"What were you thinking when you stepped onto that boat?"

His shaking her and talking to her in that condescending, sarcastic tone was the proverbial last straw. She was through with his conditions, through with him bullying her, through with him ordering her around. She picked up her feet and dropped right out of his arms. She twisted and threw all her weight at the back of his knees.

He crashed to the floor like a rock.

Heather crouched beside him, ready to lecture him on manners, but the sight of big, tough Nick lying flat on his back, blinking up at her with such a look of astonishment on his face, tugged at her funny bone. A giggle burst between her lips.

Nick's eyes narrowed in warning.

Another giggle escaped. Heather clasped her hand over her mouth, but it was hopeless. She started laughing so hard tears streamed down her face.

"Oh, oh, my gosh." She wiped her tears. "The look on your face when you…" She laughed again, so hard her stomach hurt. She clutched at her middle, drawing big gasping breaths between laughs.

Nick grabbed her and suddenly *she* was the one flat on her back. He covered her body with his. "Stop laughing," he growled.

"I'm…trying," she wheezed between giggles. The memory of his shocked look triggered another round of laughter.

Suddenly his mouth was on hers. The crazy man must have thought he could stop her laughter by kissing her.

He was right.

The feel of his lips molding hers stopped her midgiggle, and suddenly all she wanted to do was kiss him back. She poured every ounce of frustration, hunger, even anger into that kiss. She wanted him, desperately, had wanted him for so long. And even though she knew it was probably a mistake, that she'd hate herself for it later, she wrapped her arms around his neck and pulled him closer, letting him know in every way she could that she wanted this.

He responded to her surrender like a starving man at a banquet. He peppered her with kisses, ran his tongue across her skin, suckled her until she cried out with pleasure. In a whisper of cloth her shirt was gone. A quick tug and her panties disappeared, too. Nick pushed himself off her for the briefest of moments as he tugged off his clothes. And then he was back, his naked skin heating hers, the light matting of hair on his chest scraping across her breasts, his arousal prodding her belly.

She shivered with wanting, longing for him to hurry and make her his. She couldn't bear the pleasure-pain of his wandering hands and sweltering kisses much longer.

"Nick, please…" she breathed against his neck.

Her urgency was matched by his. He pressed another quick kiss against her lips, then pulled back.

"Give me a minute. I'll be right back."

Suddenly, he was gone, leaving her lying there, wondering why he'd run out of the room. But then he was back, and at the sound of a foil packet tearing open, her face turned warm. He was putting on a condom.

And then he was lifting and carrying her to the bed. He pushed her back against the mattress, doing sinful things to her neck, making her want him even more than she ever thought possible.

He suddenly grabbed her hips and pushed himself inside her in a long, deep stroke.

She cried out from the pleasure washing through her. Nick rasped her name and began to move again, building the tension inside her, higher and higher. He praised her, telling her how beautiful she was, how much he wanted her, as he stretched and filled her, bringing her closer and closer to the peak.

When she thought she was about to explode from the pleasure, he slowed his strokes and leaned down and kissed her again. He feathered his hands across her hypersensitive skin, learning every curve. Whenever he found a particularly sensitive spot, and her breath caught, he would pause and lavish her with more attention, as if to wring out every ounce of pleasure he could.

He shuddered, and Heather knew he was close. He kissed her again, then reached down between them, stroking her with his fingers as he thrust harder and faster into her. Heather drew her knees up, shouting his name as her climax washed over her, exploding through her body in a wave of pleasure so intense tears ran down her face.

Nick pushed fully into her, filling her, saying her name as he stiffened against her in his own climax. He shuddered again, collapsing on top of her for the barest of moments, then rolling to the side with her clasped tightly in his arms, as if reluctant to let her go.

As they lay together on the bed, their chests heaving from exertion, his hands stroking her bare back, she realized she'd never felt so complete as when she was in his arms. He couldn't have made love to her the way he had if he didn't care about her. He'd only yelled at her on the docks because he was worried about her. She knew that now.

She fell asleep with a smile on her face.

HEATHER'S DEEP, EVEN breathing told Nick she'd fallen asleep.

He continued to hold her and stroke the velvet-soft skin on her back. As his own skin cooled and the blood began pumping to his brain again, he realized what a terrible mistake he'd just made, in so many ways.

When he'd opened the door to her room, he hadn't meant to go on the offensive. He'd planned their conversation on the drive back from DEA headquarters. He was going to sit her down and calmly remind her how dangerous this mission was. He was going to remind her they'd had to be extra careful because her barely there outfit wouldn't allow her to wear a bullet-resistant vest. He was going to remind her how crucial condition two was, that he'd set that condition out of concern for her safety, not because he wanted to boss her around.

But then he'd stepped into their hotel suite and had relived every agonizing moment of the encounter with Gonzalez as he briefed the two agents protecting Heather. He was furious with himself for agreeing to a plan that had put her in danger. A week ago, he wouldn't have even considered it. But after being with Heather these past few days, after seeing how deeply she cared about her sister, he'd realized she would be devastated if Lily died, and she'd never forgive him if he hadn't done everything he could to save her. He'd selfishly allowed his emotions to rule his head and had gone along with a far too dangerous plan.

Remembering Heather's blatant disregard for her own safety, how she'd been only a few feet from that sick, twisted psychopath, how he'd had a gun in his hand and could have easily killed her, all of that had his nerves stretched taut. When the agents stepped out of the suite, he'd been on the edge of desperation to assure himself that Heather was okay. He'd run to her room and had thrown the door open.

Her scantily clad body had been bathed in moonlight, her breasts pressing against her threadbare T-shirt, the lacy edge of her panties peeking at him beneath the hem. All the blood had pumped from his brain to another part of his anatomy. He wanted her, badly, wanted to feel her silky skin rubbing against his, hear her sexy little cries in the back of her throat when he plunged inside her. Wanting her, knowing he couldn't have her, had him clenching his jaw so tight his teeth ached.

So instead of holding her against him, he'd held her at arm's length, and his frustration that he couldn't do more than that had him saying things he shouldn't have said. Then she'd dropped him on his butt and started laughing, and all he could think about again was how much he wanted to kiss her. Just once, he'd told himself. One kiss, then he'd leave. But one kiss hadn't been enough, could never be enough.

He let out a deep sigh. The smile that was still on Heather's face, even in sleep, told him far more than she realized. That smile and the gift of her body tonight told him she'd forgiven him for arresting her and for abandoning her in that cell when he could have easily gotten her out.

But he didn't deserve her forgiveness, and he shouldn't have made love to her, because there was no turning back. There was no future for them. There was no way to pretend she'd never been arrested, that she hadn't broken the law to try to save her sister from going to jail—not without giving up his career. For him, being a DEA agent wasn't just a job. It was his life. It was who he was. He couldn't give that up, not if he had a choice.

He tucked the covers around her, then picked his clothes up off the floor and quietly walked to the door.

"Nick?"

He turned at the sound of her sleepy voice. "Yes?"

She propped herself up on her elbows. "You're leaving?"

He cleared his throat. "I'm going to my room. We both have to get up in just a few hours. We should get some sleep."

Even in the near-darkness he could tell she was weighing his words, searching for the truth hidden in them. He owed her the truth, and the sooner she knew it, the sooner they could both focus on the case again. And somehow find a way to move on.

He drew a deep, bracing breath.

"Don't say it." Heather's voice was frosty. "You don't have to say anything about…us." She laughed bitterly. "Condition number one, right?"

He briefly closed his eyes, hating the sound of hurt in her voice. "I'm sorry. It's not that I don't care about you. I—"

"Oh, please. Spare me, okay? I wanted you. I knew it was a mistake, that nothing had changed. My bad. What's done is done. Just tell me what happened with Gonzalez. Did you interview him? Did you find out where my sister is?"

He hesitated, feeling awkward, despising himself for hurting her. He also wasn't sure what to tell her. She'd find everything out in the morning, but if he told her what he'd learned, she wouldn't get any sleep, and she'd make herself sick with worry.

"Nick? You know something. Tell me." Her brows were drawn down and she was clutching the covers like a lifeline.

He sighed and chose a half truth. "Gonzalez didn't tell us where Lily's being held."

She closed her eyes briefly, as if she was in pain. "But did he at least tell you she's okay?"

"We don't know yet."

"But—"

"I'm sorry. There's nothing else I can tell you right now." Coming in here had been a mistake, one that he sorely regretted. He opened the door.

"Because you *can't* tell me, or because you won't?"

He answered without turning around. "Does it matter?"

"Yes."

"Because I can't. I honestly don't know if Lily is okay or not."

But he had every reason to believe she wasn't.

The silence stretched out between them. He finally turned around to look at her. She stared at him, as if she was deciding whether or not she could believe him.

"Thank you," she finally said, her voice firm, cold. "Thank you for telling me the truth."

He curled his fingers into his palms. He gave her a curt nod and stepped out of the room.

Chapter Twelve

For reasons Heather would understand all too soon, the DEA had taken Gonzalez to a secret location an hour north of Key West. Nick sat in the conference room beside Heather, waiting for Gonzalez to be brought in.

Heather was pale this morning, with dark circles under her eyes. She'd barely eaten anything for breakfast, no matter how much Nick cajoled and tried to talk her into taking care of herself. Knowing this was his fault had guilt eating him up inside.

Unfortunately, once she heard what Gonzalez had to say, she was probably going to go from bad to worse.

Part of what Nick couldn't tell her last night was that he'd spent several hours at the docks, creating a cover story for what had happened. It was imperative that Gonzalez's capture be kept secret. But there had been several people who'd seen the swarm of DEA agents converging on that boat. Those people would see a story in the paper this morning that Nick had helped plant, a story that described a fiasco, painting the DEA as having mistakenly targeted a local fisherman thinking he was dealing drugs. But they'd found nothing. Their tip had turned out to be wrong, and there were no arrests to report.

The story would make it look like the DEA had bungled an investigation, a small price to pay for the agency to cover up what had really happened and to keep their original mission intact. Or at least, partly intact.

The true story from last night had changed everything.

"Are you sure you want to do this?" Nick asked. "You don't have to meet with him."

"I have to find my sister." She swallowed hard. "Or at least find out what happened to her. I'll talk to him. Did he…did he say why he wanted to talk to me? I mean, he knows I'm not Lily. So why would he insist on seeing me?"

Nick knew exactly why Gonzalez wanted to speak to her. Originally he'd thought it was kinder not to tell her ahead of time, because it would just drive her crazy hearing it from him, then having to make the long drive to speak to Gonzalez and ask the questions that would be going through her mind. Now Nick was second-guessing that decision. Maybe he should try to soften the blow by telling her himself, now, before Gonzalez came in.

"Look," he said, turning in his chair to face her. "I couldn't tell you this last night, but you're going to find out in a few minutes so I'm going to go ahead and tell you. When we brought Gonzalez in, he insisted that he wasn't—"

A knock sounded on the door. Before Nick could tell the agent on the other side to wait, the door opened. Two DEA agents came inside, flanking Gonzalez, who had chains dangling from his wrists and legs as he shuffled into the room.

Heather's complexion turned ashen. Regret curled inside Nick. He definitely should have warned her before they got here. She was in for a shock, and she was already shaking and looking impossibly frail. But there was no going back now.

Gonzalez's dark brown eyes went straight to Heather and never wavered, even as the agents wove chains from his cuffs to two shiny new steel hooks that had been bolted to the top of the table this morning for this very purpose. That was one of several things Nick had insisted on before allowing Heather anywhere near the man.

Another thing he'd insisted on was that Heather wasn't going to meet with Gonzalez alone. Gonzalez had been adamant, wanting to talk to her by himself. But Nick had refused to budge an inch, even when Dante had ordered him to do so. Nick had threatened to pull Heather out altogether to make his new boss back down.

Thankfully, Dante hadn't called his bluff, because Nick wasn't so sure he had enough influence on Heather right now to make her agree to let him pull her off the case.

"We'll be right outside if you need anything," one of the agents said.

Nick nodded his thanks and waited until the agents had left before addressing Gonzalez.

"All right, Mr. Gonzalez. You have your audience with Miss Bannon, as requested. If you threaten or insult her in any way, this meeting is over. Understood?"

Gonzalez's honey-brown eyes focused on Nick.

"I'm perfectly aware of your conditions, Agent Morgan," he said, in a thick accent. "And I assure you, I have nothing but Heather's best interests at heart."

Heather suddenly reached for Nick's hand beneath the table. He flicked his gaze up to hers in surprise, but she wasn't looking at him, so he threaded his fingers through hers and gave her a reassuring squeeze.

"The only thing I want to hear from you," Heather said, her voice surprisingly strong, "is where my sister is. I want her to be safe and I want to bring her home."

"We both want the same thing, I assure you. I love Lily very much, and I want nothing more than for her to be safe and as far from Key West as possible."

"If that's the truth, why are you holding my sister hostage?"

"You misunderstand, Miss Bannon. I'm not the one holding your sister hostage."

Heather's eyes widened. She looked at Nick as if for confirmation. He gave her a slight nod. If anything, her face turned even more pale.

"What are you saying?" she asked Gonzalez.

The chains attached to his wrists rattled on top of the table as he tried to reach his right hand across to Heather. When the links pulled him up short, he grunted and clasped his hands together.

"Miss Bannon, allow me to explain. Do you recall when Lily visited you about six months ago and asked you to go to a convention with her?"

"I don't see how that's relevant, Mr. Gonzalez," she replied. "How is my sister? Have you hurt her?"

He shook his head. "I assure you, I've done nothing to harm your sister. As far as I know, she is alive and well."

Heather's breath caught. "As far as you know?"

"Please, let me explain," he said. "The convention? Do you remember?"

"Yes, yes, I remember. It was one of those identical twin things, where they bring twins from all over the world to meet up and make friends. She begged me to go with her and I couldn't take the time off from work, but she was insistent. So I went with her to registration so she could get in—they only let pairs of twins register. But then I went back home. Why are you asking me about the convention?"

"Because that's where I met Lily."

Her brows drew down in obvious confusion. "I don't understand."

"I was one of the attendees."

"But that doesn't make sense. The only people who are attendees are…"

He nodded. "You've figured it out, I see. I'm not Jose Gonzalez, the man holding your sister. I'm Luis Gonzalez, Jose's identical twin brother."

HEATHER FRANTICALLY SHOOK her head, certain she couldn't have heard him right. "You're not Jose Gonzalez?"

"No. I'm not."

She looked to Nick for confirmation.

"We've fingerprinted him," Nick said. "He's definitely not Jose. The DEA never realized Jose had a twin, but that's the only explanation."

"But…you know my sister?" she asked Luis, her voice hesitant.

"Yes. As I said, we met at the conference. Like you, I did not want to go. But my brother wanted to go." His mouth twisted with disdain. "Not because he wished to socialize, but because he wanted to use it as a front for some deal he was planning. Then he met Lily, and they hit it off."

Heather tried to make sense of what he was telling her. "You sound bitter about that."

"I am. We both liked Lily when we met her. But my brother…he takes what he wants. And he wanted her."

Heather studied his facial expressions, his eyes, trying to decide if she believed him. "Are you a drug dealer like your brother, Mr. Gonzalez?"

"No, Miss Bannon, I am not. I am a businessman. My brother's activities grieve me deeply, but no matter what I do I can't seem to dissuade him. However, when I realized what had happened to Lily, I couldn't sit back and ignore it. I had to do something. That's why I'm here."

His thick Spanish accent made it difficult for Heather to understand him. She had to think for a moment about what he'd just said for it to make sense. "Then you know what happened to my sister and where she is?"

"I know she was taken against her will several days ago from your apartment in north Florida. And I know she's with my brother right now—again, being held against her will—in one of his compounds, but I don't know which one. I've been trying to find out. I want Lily away from my brother as much as you do. I don't want her hurt."

Heather rubbed her temple, trying to relieve the dull ache that had started. "If you don't know where she is, why did you want to talk to me? What were you doing at that dock last night?"

"My men have been on the lookout for information to help me find Lily. As soon as I heard she was in that bar, I headed over, hoping she'd somehow gotten away from my brother. But when I got there I found out one of my brother's men was talking to you inside the bar. I knew he was trying to lure you outside to kill you. I figured out which boat was his and waited."

"You were there to…protect me?"

"Yes."

She gave a harsh laugh. "You didn't protect me, Mr. Gonzalez. You destroyed my best chance to find my sister. That man was going to take me to see her."

"Heather," Nick said, "it's possible he may be telling the truth. We had a team of agents looking into Luis's background last night, proving his identity. Everything is checking out. And what he says about the man who took you to the boat is valid. That man was one of Jose Gonzalez's most trusted men, known for doing his dirty work. It's highly unlikely he would have thought you were really Lily. We believe he knew exactly where Lily was, and that you were her sister, and he was going to take you out into the ocean to kill you."

Heather shivered and wrapped her arms around her waist. "Then I guess I owe you both for saving my life last night." She dropped her face in her hands. "It's hopeless. There's nothing else I can do. All of this was for nothing. No one is going to lead me to my sister."

She straightened and put her hand beneath the table to clasp Nick's hand again. She hated that she was leaning on him right now, after last night, but she needed his strength, his reassurance. He owed her that much, at least, for making love to her then rejecting her. She squared her shoulders.

"What is Jose Gonzalez planning?" she asked Luis. "Is he keeping my sister alive just long enough so he can tell her that he killed me? Is that what he's doing? Or is she even alive at this point?" She thumped her fist on the table. "All these silly fake tattoos were a waste. No one ever believed I was Lily."

"If I may disagree, Miss Bannon," Luis said, "I don't think it's a waste at all. If I didn't know Lily so well, I would have completely fallen for your trick. I believe most people in my brother's employ would think you were Lily as well. The only ones who wouldn't are his bodyguards and the men he trusts the most, men who have been around Lily long enough to be able to tell you two apart."

Heather studied him for a moment. "You're saying pretending to be Lily can actually work then?"

"In the right circumstances, yes."

"And yet, you were able to tell I wasn't Lily. How could you tell?"

"It's not your looks that give you away. It's how you hold yourself, how you walk. Lily is a bit more, ah, more of a free spirit. She has attitude. You're more like a librarian playing dress-up."

Nick let out a snort of laughter beside her.

She glared at him and he sobered.

"What do you mean by 'right circumstances'?" she asked.

Nick squeezed her hand beneath the table, capturing her attention. "While you and I have been trying to use your likeness to Lily as our angle to find her, Dante's men have been canvassing the Keys and following up on leads. They believe they may be able to determine exactly where Jose is holding her within a few days. The problem is that, even once they figure out where his compound is located, there isn't much they can do through legal channels. Unless someone actually sees Lily and swears out an affidavit that she's being held against her will, we have no justification for a warrant."

"How about the fact that someone tried to kill us, twice? Isn't that enough for a warrant?"

"No. It isn't. We don't have a firm link between what

happened and Jose Gonzalez. We don't have anything with which to make a case. That's where the 'right circumstances' come in. Once we determine where Jose is holding Lily, we'll have to do something, cause a diversion, to get Jose to leave the island. Then we'll use Luis and you, pretending to be Jose and Lily, to gain access. We'll go in with enough force to take over and, hopefully, rescue Lily."

"Hopefully?"

"Hostage situations are always tricky. No guarantees. We have a lot of details to work out. You won't be bait again. I won't allow that. And you aren't physically going to the island. If we use you at all, we'll do it through a video hookup, to speak to some of Jose's men. I'm not putting you in harm's way again."

"But—"

He held up a hand to stop her. "I mean it. There is absolutely no circumstance under which I will foolishly allow you to be put in danger again. I won't shut you out. You can stay here and listen or even help us plan. But that's it. Once everything is set, I'm taking you back to the hotel. And tomorrow morning you'll go back to Saint Augustine. You can do the video hookup remotely, without being anywhere near Gonzalez."

Heather glared at him and crossed her arms.

Nick rapped on the table.

The door immediately opened and Tanner leaned in and looked at Nick. "You're ready?"

"Yes. Tell Dante to get everyone in here. It's time to come up with a plan that will end this once and for all."

Chapter Thirteen

Nick shoved the car into Park in front of the hotel.

Heather reached for the door handle, but Nick grabbed her arm.

"Wait in the car. I'll come around and open your door."

"I assure you that's not necessary. I don't need a man to open my door for me."

Nick's mouth hardened into a thin line. Heather could tell he was irritated with her. That was her fault. She'd been sarcastic and argumentative all day. Then again, that was *his* fault for giving her false hopes last night about the two of them, then rejecting her and then insisting she had to go back to Saint Augustine in the morning while the rescue plan went forward without her.

"Good to know," Nick said, his tone short and clipped. "But we aren't on a date and I'm not playing the gentleman. I'm your bodyguard tonight, which means you sit in the car until I come around and get you out."

He didn't wait for her response.

She grabbed her purse, fuming that she had to wait like a child for him to open her door, but she followed his ridiculous order anyway. He scanned the area several times as he made his way around the hood of the car to her side.

His gun was in his right hand, pointing down to the ground as he opened her door.

Seeing that gun squelched Heather's irritation. It reminded her just how serious everything was, and that she was still in danger. Nick was determined to protect her, no matter how she treated him.

Her shoulders slumped. She'd acted like a spoiled brat all day. She resolved to be polite the rest of the short time they had together. The man was going to risk his life for her tomorrow. The least she could do was to treat him with respect.

She got out of the car and Nick shut the door behind her. He waved for her to precede him up the walkway.

She started up the path.

A small pop sounded, followed by a buzzing noise as something flew through the air from the shrubs beside the hotel.

Nick raised his gun.

Too late.

He grunted, his face contorting with pain as his gun dropped out of his hand. He fell onto the pavement, convulsing.

Twin darts stuck out of his thighs, attached to a long, curly wire. He'd been hit with a Taser.

Heather drew a breath to scream, but her throat closed in shock as a slim figure stepped out from behind the shrubs, holding the Taser. Heather would have known that face anywhere. She saw it every morning when she looked in the mirror.

Lily.

THE SPEEDBOAT SLAPPED against the water as it accelerated away from the dock. Heather held on to the railing to her left as she sat on the rear bench seat beside Nick. They were handcuffed together, and Nick's right arm was cuffed to the railing to his right. Her sister sat about six feet in front of them with her back facing them, beside the man driving the boat—the same man who'd dumped Nick into the trunk of Lily's car, and had then forced him and Heather into the boat at gunpoint. The man might be the muscle behind this abduction, but Lily was definitely the one calling all the shots.

As their speed increased, the ride leveled out. The nose of the boat rose out of the water and the boat practically flew out into the ocean. They weren't running with lights on, but it wasn't like they were going to hit anything. There was nothing and no one else out here this late at night. No one to report a suspicious, unlit boat flying across the ocean. No one to call the police and send help.

Heather clutched Nick's hand. "What are we going to do?" she whispered.

His fingers squeezed hers and he leaned down toward her. "We're going to survive. We'll worry about escape later. Do whatever your sister tells you to do. Don't give her a reason to pull the trigger."

Grief welled up inside Heather, nearly choking her. "I'm so sorry. This is my fault. You were right all along. It was too dangerous. I put you in danger by being here. And all along my sister was only pretending to be abducted. She played me. And I don't even know why. But you're going to pay the price. They're going to kill us. They're going to take us out in the middle of the ocean and dump us."

She eyed the dark water passing by them so fast. "There are sharks, lots of sharks, way out here. I read that somewhere."

Nick squeezed her fingers again. "Take a breath, sweetheart. Try to calm down. I don't think they're going to dump us in the ocean. If they wanted us dead they could have shot us in the parking lot. Instead, they went to a lot of trouble getting us in the car, driving us to the dock and getting us in the boat. They have plans for us."

She shivered. "What plans? Why is Lily doing this?"

"I have no idea. We'll have to keep our wits about us and take advantage of any opportunities we get to escape. Just try to stay calm and pay attention to everything. You never know what detail could save our lives. Take slow, deep breaths before you hyperventilate and pass out."

She took slow, deep breaths, but it wasn't helping. Her heart was pounding so hard it hurt to even breathe. Her sweaty palm kept slipping off the railing.

"Lily is blocking my view of the instrument panel," Nick whispered. "Can you see it?"

Heather leaned to the left. "I see some big, digital numbers. Why?"

"I need to know how fast we're going so I can calculate our distance. What numbers do you see?"

She rattled off everything she could see, which wasn't much. Most of the instrument panel was a blur from this distance.

"Good. That second number is the speed. Let me know if it changes." He studied his watch and mumbled something under his breath, as if he was doing calculations. He looked up in the sky.

"What are you doing now?" Heather whispered.

"Figuring out which direction we're going." He leaned down close to her. "Find the Big Dipper. You know what that is?"

"Of course." She looked up and found the collection of stars above them that looked like a cooking ladle. "There it is."

Nick nodded. "If you mentally connect the two stars at the end of the ladle it forms a line that points to the North Star."

"Oh, I see. Cool. So…we're going south."

"More or less. Now look for Orion's Belt." He watched Lily and the driver for a moment. Then he pointed up to the sky. "There, see those three stars?"

It took longer this time, but Heather finally saw what he was pointing at. "Yes. What does that tell us?"

He lowered his hand. "They form a line that's roughly east-west. So we're going—"

"Southwest, right?"

Nick smiled. "Right." He looked at his watch again. "And if we're maintaining a steady speed, we're about thirty miles southwest of the dock where we boarded the boat. Keep an eye on that speed gauge."

Heather leaned to the left. The numbers were the same. "How is this going to help us?"

He let out a deep sigh. "It won't, unless we can get to a phone wherever we're going, and unless Dante can do some detective work back in Key West and figure out which dock we took off from. I didn't see any landmarks when they opened the trunk and pulled us out. But we were only in that trunk for about thirty minutes, so that limits the possibilities." He shrugged. "It's a long shot, but it might help."

Heather tightened her fingers on his. "You're kind of amazing. If anyone can get us out of this, you can."

He shook his head, his mouth flattening. "I don't know about that. But we're about to put that to the test."

"What do you mean?"

He pointed to a dark shadow on the horizon. "Because it looks like we're about to reach our destination."

The dark shape came closer and closer, revealing itself as an island, perhaps no more than a mile across from one end to the other. Of course, there was no way to know how deep it might be.

Nick's hand tensed beneath Heather's. She looked up at him in question, but he wasn't looking at her. He was staring straight ahead, clenching his jaw, as the boat slowed and gently bumped against the dock.

The driver of the boat turned around and pointed his gun at them.

Lily dangled a small ring of keys in front of her before tossing them onto the bench between Nick and Heather. "Unlock your hand from the railing and toss me back the keys," she told Nick.

"Lily," Heather said. "Why are you doing this? I was worried sick about you, thinking you were being held against your will. I—"

Lily laughed, cutting her off. "Your concern for me was exactly what I was counting on. That's why I drove up to Saint Augustine in that rattletrap car and acted like I was down on my luck. I wanted you to feel sorry for me and follow me down here to the Keys. But you were too worried about your precious job and your precious clients. I had to change my plan. It worked. I got you down here. But I'll admit that my first attempt to grab you at Skeleton's Misery was a bit pathetic." She laughed. "I've got you now though. And thanks to your DEA boyfriend, I'm about to get everything I've ever wanted, everything I deserve."

"It was you all along? Not Jose Gonzalez who was after me?"

Lily didn't answer. She motioned with her gun at Nick.

He finished unlocking the cuffs from his right hand and let them drop against the railing. He turned to unlock the second set of cuffs that imprisoned his left wrist against Heather's right one, but Lily shook her head.

"Toss me the keys," she said.

He threw them to her. She caught them and shoved them into the pocket of her cutoff shorts.

"Come on." She waved her hand toward the side of the boat. "Get out and go stand on the shore. We'll get out behind you."

"But I don't understand," Heather said. "Why are you—"

Nick squeezed Heather's hand. She obeyed his unspoken warning and didn't say anything else. He helped her step over the side of the boat. The stiffness in his posture as he walked beside her down the dock told her he was just as worried as she was.

Was Lily planning to leave them stranded on a deserted island, to let them die of exposure or starvation? Was she going to shoot them in the back as they stepped off the dock?

Or did she have something far worse planned?

LILY HAD SOMETHING far worse planned.

Nick pulled Heather to a stop when their five-minute trek through the woods brought them into a clearing.

Fifty yards ahead stood a concrete block structure, no bigger than a garden shed. A single light beside the open door cast a dim yellow glow across the clearing.

"Keep moving," Lily called out from behind them.

"If we go in there," Nick whispered, in a voice so low Heather almost couldn't hear him, "we're dead."

"What do we do?" she whispered back.

A gunshot boomed behind them.

Heather screamed.

Nick dove to the ground, pulling her with him and covering her body with his. Her right arm was twisted painfully because of the handcuffs, but Nick still managed to block her from any harm.

When Heather looked up, she realized the bullet had hit the dirt just inches from where she'd been standing. Lily stepped toward them, stopping six feet away. She held the gun they'd taken from Nick, pointing it directly at him. The driver of the boat remained silent, but his gun, too, was aimed their way. Heather didn't know which one of them had taken the shot, but from the dark look in her sister's eyes, she wouldn't be surprised if it had been Lily.

Lily's lips curled back in a sneer. "Get up and get into that shed, or the next shot won't be a warning."

"Stall her," Nick whispered. "Keep her talking." He rose, pulling Heather up with him.

"Go on," Lily said, her voice hard.

"You owe me an explanation." Heather tried to sound far braver than she felt. She couldn't seem to move past the fact that her own sister was holding a gun on her. "I did everything for you. I tried to help you. Gave you money, food, clothing. I was there for you, always."

Lily let out a harsh laugh. "You were never there for

me. You were the golden one, Daddy's perfect little girl, the one who could do no wrong. You got everything. I got nothing. That ends today. Go on. Get in the shed."

When Heather didn't budge, Lily slowly moved her gun to point squarely at Nick. "I said, move."

Nick pulled Heather with him toward the building.

"When we reach the door," he whispered, "I'm going to smash the light. We're going to run to the left, around the corner of the shed into the trees." He spoke quickly, his words a low rumble in his chest.

They were twenty feet from the shed. Fifteen.

"When we run, stretch your handcuffed arm out behind you and I'll keep mine as far right as I can to keep you directly in front of me. Remember, Heather, I'm the one wearing a Kevlar vest. I don't want you in the line of fire. Do you understand?"

Ten feet.

"Heather?" he whispered, his voice low and urgent.

"I understand," she whispered back.

Five feet.

"Get inside and shut the door behind you," Lily called out. She didn't sound close, like maybe she and the driver had stopped a good distance behind them.

They stepped to the doorway. Suddenly Nick slammed his fist into the carriage light, shattering the glass and plunging everything into darkness.

"No!" Lily screamed behind them.

A shot rang out. Dust flew up from the concrete wall next to Nick's head. He yanked Heather to the left, half lifting her as he positioned himself between her and their pursuers. They slid around the corner of the building. Another shot boomed behind them. A pinging noise echoed through the trees to their left.

"Faster," Nick urged, his whisper a harsh exhalation of breath near Heather's ear.

They entered the woods on a well-worn path. Heather assumed Nick would steer her off the path so they could try to hide, but he didn't, possibly because the foliage was so thick.

"Heather," Lily called out from behind them. "This wasn't the plan. Stop running or I'll shoot!"

"Keep going," Nick said. "Just a few more feet."

At first Heather didn't know what he meant. But suddenly they were out of the woods, running toward a massive structure, a rambling one-story house that seemed to go on forever. Nick must have seen the whitewashed sides of the house reflected in the moonlight, and that's why he'd kept running down that path.

He didn't slow as he urged her forward. They could have gone faster if it weren't for their awkward position with her arm behind her and his held in front of him, but still it seemed they practically flew across the short expanse of dirt that separated the woods from the house.

Footsteps pounded on the path.

Nick urged Heather around the left side of the house.

Another gunshot rang out just as she ran around the corner.

Nick grunted and fell against her, knocking her to the ground.

He was sprawled on top of her, twisting her arm at an impossible angle. The pain was blinding, as if someone had rammed a fire-hot poker into her right shoulder. She gritted her teeth against the urge to cry out and shoved at Nick to get him to move.

"Nick, Nick, get up. Come on, please." Was he shot?

She didn't know. All she knew for sure was that if they didn't get up, right now, they were both going to die.

"Come on." She twisted around, using her left hand to shove at him. Her right hand hung useless at her side. Tears of pain ran down her face as she tried to ignore the fiery agony in her shoulder.

Nick blinked, looking dazed. He gasped for breath, as if air had just rushed into his lungs. He heaved himself to his feet. "I'm okay. Let's go."

He grabbed her shoulders to pull her up and she let out a shriek of pain before she could stop herself.

His eyes widened, but before he could say anything, footsteps pounded from around the corner. Nick turned and kicked the nearest door. It sagged but didn't open. He kicked it again, grunting with the effort. This time the wooden frame burst into splinters and the door crashed open, slamming against the wall.

Heather ran inside before he could grab her shoulder again. She held her right arm with her left hand, trying to immobilize it as much as possible. A hall opened up on their left and right. She started to go right, but Nick steered her to the left again. He pulled her inside the first open door, a bedroom.

He didn't shut the door. Instead, he urged her back against the wall while he stood in front of her, facing her, inches from the open doorway, once again blocking her with his body.

"What—" she started to whisper, but he vigorously shook his head and pressed his right hand against her mouth. The metallic taste of blood on her lips had her blinking in horror. Nick's hand was covered with blood. He must have cut it when he punched the light.

Since he was watching her so closely, she realized

he was waiting to make sure she knew to be quiet. She nodded to let him know she understood, and he dropped his hand. Heather wanted to check his injury, but she followed his lead, being as still and quiet as she could. Her lungs ached with the need to draw a deep breath, but instead she focused on breathing slowly so she wouldn't make any noise. She felt so exposed, so vulnerable, waiting for a bullet to come crashing through the wall.

They both stood motionless in the nearly pitch-black room, waiting, listening. It seemed like time crawled, but it was probably only a few seconds before the sound of muted voices reached them. A man's deep voice, followed by a woman's softer, but somehow harder, voice. Lily.

The words they said weren't clear, but they must have agreed to go the other way, because their footsteps faded off toward the other end of the house.

Nick pulled away from Heather. He motioned for her to follow him this time as he stepped back out of the room into the hallway. He started to turn right, but apparently changed his mind. He tugged her into the bathroom opposite the bedroom. He opened a drawer and felt inside it for a moment, then he opened another drawer. He grabbed something, shoved it into his pocket and glanced out into the hall again before pulling Heather out with him.

Instead of finding another room to hide in, he quickly retraced their steps back to the door he'd ruined and out into the night. They hurried across the side yard and headed into the brush and trees.

Again Nick surprised Heather by stopping a few feet in. He fumbled with something, but Heather couldn't tell what he was doing. Her shoulder was aching so much

she was having trouble concentrating. She still couldn't
move her right arm, but it was blessedly starting to go
numb.

Her own pain reminded her about Nick's injured
hand. She wanted to help him, but he seemed to be just
fine and there really wasn't anything she could do.

She shuffled anxiously from foot to foot, turning to
look back toward the house. She expected Lily or the
man with her to come bursting outside at any moment.

She felt a tug on her hand and heard a click.

Her mouth opened in surprise when the handcuffs fell
from her wrist. Another twist and the cuffs unclicked
from Nick's wrist, too, and dropped to the ground.

In answer to her unspoken question, he held up a cu-
riously bent safety pin. That must have been what he'd
gotten from the bathroom.

"Go," he whispered next to her ear, pointing in a di-
agonal direction off to their left. "I'm right behind you."

Chapter Fourteen

Nick squatted down in front of Heather. He'd pulled her to a stop a few feet from the water's edge, still deep in the cover of the trees and brush. She was sitting on the forest floor, cradling her right arm as she tried to catch her breath.

He gently swept her bangs out of her eyes. The corners of her eyes were tight, and she didn't even seem to realize that every once in a while she let out a low moan. He hated to see her in such pain, and he hated that he'd been the cause of that pain.

"Why aren't we going to the boat?" she pleaded, sounding on the verge of panic. "We should run down the beach until we get back to the dock."

"We can't go back to the boat. That's where they'll expect us to go. Besides, I saw your sister pocket the keys when we docked." He didn't tell her that he planned to go back to the house to get those keys. It was their only chance. He'd get those keys no matter what.

Even if it meant he had to kill her sister to do it.

Without being handcuffed to Heather, he had more freedom to plan and attack. But right now, there was something more pressing to take care of.

He eased himself to her right side.

"What…what are you doing?" Her voice sounded wary.

"You know what I'm doing. It has to be done." He gently wrapped his fingers around her right forearm and braced his other hand against her rib cage.

She winced and tried to pull away, but he held on tight.

"Let me go," she pleaded. "It will hurt." A whimper escaped between her clenched teeth.

"I know, baby, but if we don't get your shoulder back into the socket, the blood flow might be restricted and you could permanently lose the use of your arm. Plus, it will feel a lot better. After."

"It's not the 'after' that I'm worried about. How many times have you done this?"

"Counting this time?"

"Yes."

He grinned. "Once."

Her eyes widened.

"I've seen it done a couple of times, though."

"Oh, gee, that's reassuring."

He tightened his hold on her arm and began to gently pull it toward him.

"I'm ready." She squeezed her eyes shut. "Just do it."

He laughed but didn't let up the pressure on her arm.

She opened her eyes. "Aren't you going to pop it back in?"

"I'm working on it. If I try to force it, I could break your arm or damage the muscles even worse. Just give it a minute and let me know once you feel it snap back in place." He continued the long, steady pull. "Talk to me. It will help take your mind off the pain."

"Okay." She scrunched her eyes shut. "Uh, why did you make us turn left instead of right when we went into the house? And later, when we ran into the woods. Every time, you turned left."

"Because most people turn right when they're under duress. It's instinctive, probably because most people are right-handed. So I try to go left if I can, to throw off my pursuers."

She opened her eyes. "You make it sound like you run from people on a regular basis."

"It's part of the job. If you're undercover, dealing with dangerous people on their turf, there are times when you're going to have to run."

"Okay, ouch, it hurts." Her breaths came out in choppy pants.

"I'm sorry, honey. Just a little longer." He hoped he was right. It was killing him watching the pain lance across her face. But he had to stretch the muscles out slowly or he'd end up tearing them.

"When you fell…" Heather panted for a moment. "When you fell against me by the house, did you get shot? I mean, you were wearing your vest, and you seem fine, but…" Her voice drifted off and she clenched her jaw.

"Yeah, the bullet knocked the breath out of me. Stunned me for a second. God bless whoever invented Kevlar."

She laughed, then inhaled sharply.

He increased the pressure, and Heather let out a little whimper.

He was about to give up when he felt a slight movement in the muscles of her arm.

"It's in. It's in," she gasped.

He gently lowered her arm and sat back. "Are you

sure?" He felt along the top of her shoulder, feeling for a gap.

"I'm sure. It already feels a lot better." She opened her eyes. "Thank you."

Unable to resist the temptation of her lips so close to his, he framed her face with his hands and gave her a gentle kiss. When he pulled back, her eyes were wide and searching.

He dropped his hands. He needed to keep reminding himself that they weren't together anymore, and never could be. Touching her was dangerous in so many ways.

He cleared his throat. "Be careful with that shoulder. Don't lift your arm up too high or back behind you. It could pop right out again."

She let out a little sigh. He wasn't sure if it was because of that kiss, or something else. "I don't understand what's going on. Why would Lily do this? What does she hope to gain?"

He sat down next to her. He was quiet for several seconds as he listened to the sounds in the woods around them. Something small scurried off to their right, some forest creature probably out looking for dinner. A night bird let out a chirp, reassuring him that no humans were close by.

Lily and her helper were probably holed up in the house, figuring out their strategy. He doubted they'd chance trying to find him and Heather until the sun came up, which was still several hours away. Hopefully by then Dante and his men would have figured out that he and Heather were missing, and they'd be canvassing Key West, looking for witnesses. Maybe someone had seen them head out in the boat, and Dante would send in the cavalry.

But Nick wasn't counting on it.

And he hoped to hell that Lily and her minion didn't have infrared goggles.

"INFRARED WHAT?" HEATHER whispered, her voice slurred from lack of sleep.

Nick grinned. He'd hated waking her—not that she seemed fully awake even now as they walked through the woods—but he didn't feel safe staying in one place very long.

"Goggles," he said. "Keep your voice down."

"But you said no one was out here," she whispered, lowering her voice. "And the sun isn't up yet. You said Lily wouldn't come looking for us until sunrise."

Nick held a branch out of her way. "Just keep moving," he said. "And stop talking so much." He squeezed her waist to soften his words.

After Heather had fallen asleep, he'd dozed for about twenty minutes, a power nap, the way he'd trained himself to do whenever he was on a stakeout with a partner. But once he'd thought about the possibility of Lily having infrared equipment, he couldn't get it out of his head.

Lily had access to an incredibly powerful and expensive speedboat. And the house on this island wasn't exactly cheap. The generator alone had to have cost thousands of dollars. Lily obviously had access to the best equipment Jose Gonzalez's money could buy.

Which meant she and the man with her could be out here right now, hunting Heather and him down with all kinds of advantages.

His only choice was to go on the offensive, which meant he was circling back toward the house from another direction. He hadn't told Heather that yet because he didn't want to scare her. He'd decided their best option was to go back in the house and search for a weapon and a phone, assuming the house had a phone. On a small, remote island like this, there was probably at least a satellite phone somewhere. And if this was one of Gonzalez's houses, which Nick was willing to bet it was, the odds were also high there were more guns inside. Drug dealers tended to keep a heavy arsenal wherever they were at all times.

He already knew Heather was good with a gun. Her bullet had found its target with incredible accuracy, even under extreme stress, when she'd shot one of their pursuers in the garage a few days ago. So if he armed both himself and Heather, they might have a chance.

Provided she could shoot her sister if she had to.

Hopefully it wouldn't come to that. With the sun coming up in less than an hour, they couldn't afford to wait for their hunters to find them.

It was time for the hunted to become the hunters.

"STOP RIGHT HERE," Nick whispered.

Heather stopped, and peeked through the shrubs. The white coquina shell exterior on the house glowed in the predawn gray light filtering through the trees. Birds chirped, lending an eerie normalcy to a situation that was anything but normal. Presumably, inside that house her sister and a stranger were waiting, with guns, to kill her and Nick. A ripping sound had her looking over at Nick in question. He had his shirt off and was undoing the straps that held on his vest.

"Oh, no, not again." Heather held out her hands and shook her head. "You are not giving me your vest again. Last night you got shot. If you weren't wearing your vest you'd have been killed. I mean it. I will not put that on. I'm putting my foot down this time."

A minute later she was wearing the vest and glaring at Nick as he tugged her shirt down over it.

"Glare at me all you want," he said. "It's not going to change my mind."

She put her hands on her hips. "If you get shot, you'd better hope it kills you. Because if it doesn't, I will."

"Thanks for the warning. Now you need to be really quiet so I can sneak inside and look for some weapons. I don't want you being so noisy the bad guys find us out here."

"Too late for that," a voice said behind them.

Nick and Heather whirled around.

A man stood several feet away, his face hidden in shadows. But there was no mistaking what he was holding and pointing directly at them—a rifle.

Nick shoved Heather behind him as the other man stepped forward.

Heather leaned over so she could see the gunman.

Gonzalez.

The only question was, which one? Jose or Luis?

Did it even matter?

Either way, they were in a world of trouble.

"You're supposed to be in the shed," he said. "I should have known Lily would screw this up. You might as well go on into the house while I straighten this out." He gestured with his rifle. "Move."

"Luis, right?" Nick asked.

Gonzalez nodded.

"You do know Lily has another man inside the house with her?" Nick said, as he turned around. He put his hand at the small of Heather's back, guiding her toward the house, sheltering her with his body as always—even though she was the one with the vest on this time.

She seriously wished she could shake some sense into him.

"If you're trying to make me angry or jealous so I'll make a mistake, Agent Morgan, don't bother. Lily and I planned this down to the last detail. I know who's in the house with her."

The ruined side door was still sagging open and Luis ushered them in through the opening.

"Lily," he called out, as they rounded the corner into the long hallway. He passed through the archway on the other side into the massive living room and waved Nick and Heather over to one of the couches. He kept his rifle trained on them, his hand steady, his eyes never wavering. "Lily," he called out again.

Footsteps sounded in the hallway, echoing on the wooden floor. Lily rounded the corner. Her eyes widened in surprise when she saw Nick and Heather sitting on the couch.

Heather's stomach tightened and she dug her nails into the soft material of the couch cushion to keep from jumping up and going to her sister. She wanted to talk to her, to plead with her, to make her see reason.

But she couldn't very well do that when her sister was holding a pistol.

"Well, well," Lily said. "This is a surprise." She strode forward, her hips swaying beneath the long T-shirt she'd obviously slept in, which barely reached the tops of her thighs. Her hair was mussed and she smoothed her hand over it as she reached Luis.

She smiled seductively and reached up and kissed his cheek.

He wrapped his free arm around her and pulled her close. "Miss me?"

"Always. You were supposed to be here last night. What took you so long?"

He ran his hand up and down her back, never taking his eyes off Nick and Heather. "The DEA didn't trust me. They talked to me for hours and didn't let me go until this morning. I made them think I needed to go set up some logistics to help with their planned assault on Jose's compound."

"Do they know Heather's missing yet?"

"If they did, they wouldn't have let me go. I figure they'll send an agent over there this morning to check on them. Then the search will begin. Far too late." He glanced back toward the hall, then looked at Lily. "Did you take care of our friend?"

Lily plopped down on one of the chairs. "Yep. We won't have to worry about him ever telling any of Jose's men that we double-crossed him. It's all going to go down just like we planned."

Heather shivered, and Nick wrapped his fingers around hers.

"You double-crossed your sister," Nick said to Lily. "You double-crossed the man who helped you kidnap us. And now you plan on double-crossing Jose." He flicked a glance at Luis. "How sure are you that she won't double-cross *you?*"

A flash of unease passed over Luis's face. "Shut up. You don't know anything about her. She loves me. And she wants to make things right. My brother has spent his whole life spilling his evil drugs into this world. And Lily got caught up in that because you," he spat, glaring at Heather, "took everything that belonged to her. You

shut her out and didn't try to help her. She did everything for you. She's the one who worked so hard, but you
stole everything from her. That stops today. She and I
will bring down my brother, stop his evil, something the
DEA should have done years ago. We're the good guys
here, not you. We're going to end my brother's tyranny
and start a new life together."

Heather shook her head. "Is that what Lily told you?
That I took everything from her? Lily, is that what you
believe? Explain this to me. Because I remember everything totally differently. I worked hard all my life for
what little I have. And I tried to include you, but you
pushed me away at every turn. Yet every time you came
to visit me, I gave you money I couldn't afford to give.
And you took it and left and I never saw you again until
the next time you needed money."

"You lie," Lily said. "You were the favorite. You were
given everything. And when you gave me money it was
only right, because you owed me that money, for ruining my life."

"Enough," Luis said. "My brother will be here soon
and we need to prepare. Lily, get dressed. We'll put these
two in the shed where they should have been in the first
place."

Lily narrowed her eyes at him. "It wasn't my fault.
Raul was incompetent. He let them escape."

"Well, then, it won't be a problem for us to put them
in the shed now, will it, now that incompetent Raul is
gone?"

The tone of his voice was mildly sarcastic. Heather
tensed, sensing there was trouble between these two.
Trouble between two people holding guns didn't bode
well for either her or Nick.

Lily whirled around and stomped back down the hall.

Luis sat down across from them, his gun steady. "Lily is a good girl," he said, sounding slightly defensive, as if he needed to make excuses for her. "She's not accustomed to having to use a gun and breaking the law."

Heather snorted. "Right. That's why she was in Saint Augustine with four kilos of cocaine."

He glared at her.

Nick put his hand on top of her thigh, as if to remind her to be careful what she said.

"Lily is a good girl," Luis repeated. "It was…difficult for her to go through with this plan. But she has a good heart and she knows this is the best way. The world will be a better place without my brother. And you—" he nodded at Heather "—you must pay for your sins against her. Your death will be quick. This entire house, and the shed out back, are wired with explosives. All of Jose's houses are wired this way, so he can destroy them if his enemies try to take him. Well, we are going to use that against him today. And as I said, your death, and yours—" he looked at Nick "—will be quick and painless."

"Let Heather go," Nick said. "She never did anything to hurt Lily, or you."

"Neither did you," Heather insisted. "This is crazy. Luis and Lily are both crazy."

Luis's eyes flashed. "I do not have time to argue with you." The whump-whump sound of a helicopter sounded overhead.

"It is time. My brother will be here soon. We must hurry and put you in the shed. Come."

"Why don't you want us here when your brother gets

here?" Heather asked. "Are you afraid we'll tell him the truth, that you're double-crossing him?"

Luis's jaw tightened. "It is not a double cross," he said, his accent thicker than usual as he practically spat out the words. "When you fight Satan, it is God's work."

"Is that what you think you're doing?" a voice asked from the doorway. "God's work?"

Jose Gonzalez stood at the opening to the family room, five men standing beside and behind him. One of the men was holding a squirming Lily.

Luis jerked around but the rifle was snatched from his hands by one of Jose's men.

Nick grabbed Heather and pulled her to her feet. He shoved her back into the corner and stood in front of her.

"I have no quarrel with you, Agent Morgan, or Miss Bannon," Jose's smooth, accented voice said. "My quarrel is with the traitor I call family, and the woman I once called my love."

"I still am," Lily insisted. "It was Luis who tried to betray you, not me. I was going to warn you."

"Ah, so that is why, when my men and I arrived by boat and sent the helicopter as a diversion, we found you hiding in the trees with your gun pointed at my helicopter."

"I was…confused. I thought you were Luis."

Luis let out a roar of rage.

"Enough," Jose said.

Heather tried to see around Nick, but he smoothly stepped in front of her and blocked her view.

"Please take my brother and his lover away," Jose said. "I do not wish to see them anymore."

Heather couldn't see what was happening, but she

could hear her sister cursing and Luis yelling as they were apparently shuffled out of the house.

"As I said," Jose's cultured voice rang out after the noise died down. "I have no quarrel with either of you. Please, have a seat."

"Have your men put their guns away first," Nick said.

"Fair enough. Put the guns away. There are no enemies here."

Nick pulled Heather to the couch and they sat. Jose sat across from them in his business suit, looking like he was preparing to share a cup of *café con leche* and churros with friends. Two men stood beside him, their pistols in holsters at their waists, their massive arms hanging down at their sides. They would have looked like a couple of palace guards if it weren't for their khaki shorts and T-shirts.

Jose pulled a cell phone out of his pocket and put it on the coffee table in front of Nick. "Agent Morgan, your DEA friends are on their way here with an arsenal at their disposal. Apparently my brother told them that I was holding you hostage. I would appreciate it very much if you would please tell them not to blow up my island and that you are not a prisoner here. Both of you are free to go when your friends arrive. There are no drugs here and I have not broken any laws."

Nick grabbed the phone. "What about Luis and Lily?"

"Luis and Lily will be taken care of. This is a…family matter."

Heather jumped to her feet. "Let my sister go."

Nick stood beside her and grabbed her around the waist. "Let me handle this."

Heather gave him a terse nod. Nick would protect Lily. He wouldn't let something bad happen to her.

"Deliver Luis and Lily into my keeping," Nick said. "They'll both stand trial and will be put away behind bars."

Jose slowly rose to his feet, shaking his head. "I am sorry, Agent Morgan, but that is not how this is going to work. You see, certain events over the past few weeks have put me in a…delicate position. I have been made to look weak."

"You mean because I destroyed your cocaine," Heather spit out.

"Condition number two," Nick said. "Be quiet."

Heather stiffened against him but didn't say anything else. For now.

"I, of course, do not know what you mean," Jose said. "I have no cocaine. I do, however, have a family business and rely on my reputation to run that business. My reputation cannot survive having my own brother and lover turn against me and get away with it."

"They won't get away with it," Nick insisted. "They'll go to prison."

"This is not a negotiation, Agent Morgan. I am trusting you to make that phone call. Do not break my trust, for I would not want us to become enemies. I must go now. Your DEA friends will come here and take you and Miss Bannon back to the mainland. But I do not choose to be here when they arrive." He strode across the room. His men followed, but kept a close watch on Nick as they stepped through the archway.

"Wait, wait, you can't leave with my sister." Heather started after them, but Nick grabbed her and held her back.

"Stop it, you little fool," he said. "We're lucky to be

alive. I assure you Jose Gonzalez doesn't give second chances."

"But what about my sister? If he takes her, he's going to kill her."

"Which is why I'm going to stop him, but not by running after him and his armed bodyguards when I have no weapons." He handed the phone to her and rattled off a number. "Call Dante and tell him what's going on. Tell him not to shoot at the house. I don't want us blown up. And stay right behind me."

She hurried after him as he headed down the long hallway. She punched the buttons he'd told her and held the phone to her ear as he led her into a bedroom. She waited for the call to go through. Nick yanked open drawers and rummaged through them. Then he headed into the walk-in closet.

"What are you looking for?" she asked.

"Guns," he called out, his voice muffled.

The phone crackled in Heather's ear and Dante's voice came on the line. Heather hurriedly interrupted him. "Sir, this is Heather Bannon. I'm with Agent Nick Morgan. We—"

Heather gasped and clutched the phone to her ear. Lily stood in the doorway, holding a pistol. One side of her face was covered in blood. The gun dropped from her fingers and fell to the carpet.

"I'm sorry," Lily gasped. "For everything. I got so screwed up. I never meant to hurt you. I just wanted to scare you." She coughed. Blood dribbled out of her mouth and dripped down her chin. "Help me." Her eyes rolled up in her head.

"Nick!" Heather screamed. She lunged forward and caught her sister as she crumpled to the floor.

Chapter Fifteen

Gunshots erupted outside the house, the rat-a-tat-tat of automatic weapon fire. Heather cradled her sister's unconscious body and scooted farther down into the cast-iron claw-footed tub. Hot tears slid down her face and plopped onto her sister's hair.

Seeing Heather look so devastated was killing Nick inside, but he couldn't worry about her feelings right now. He'd be lucky if he kept her from being killed, because Armageddon was taking place outside the house.

"Why won't she open her eyes?" she blubbered.

Nick squatted down beside the bathtub. Hopefully it would protect both of the women if any shots came through the bathroom wall. It was the best cover he'd been able to find when the shots started outside.

But if the explosives went off, a fancy tub would be worthless. He needed to get them both out of the house.

Heather looked up at him with wide, tear-bright eyes. "She can't die, Nick. She can't die without knowing how much I love her. How sorry I am."

Nick gritted his teeth. "She knows you love her. And you've got nothing to be sorry about. You didn't do anything wrong."

"But—"

"But nothing. Just wait here. I'm going to see if there's a way out without running the gauntlet outside. I'll be right back."

He ran out of the bathroom and into the hall. He'd reluctantly agreed to put his Kevlar vest back on when Heather had insisted. With the cast-iron tub surrounding her, he figured she was as protected as she'd be in a vest. And he wouldn't be doing her any good if he got shot and couldn't come back to help her.

He ducked down under the windows by the front room and hurried to another bathroom at the front of the house, instead of the one at the back where Heather was. The thicker walls of the bathroom would hopefully lend him some protection. He stood in the tub and lifted the blinds to look out the window.

Dante's men were in a firefight. What neither Dante nor Nick knew was exactly who they were fighting—Luis's men or Jose's men. When Heather had called Dante, his men were already landing on the island. A few minutes later, the gunfire started.

Nick peeked out the window and watched the woods. He counted five different gunmen from his vantage point, based on the muzzle flashes.

A pinging noise sounded and he ducked back, cursing at the small hole in the Sheetrock just inches from where he'd been standing. Another bullet pinged through the wall. He dived down onto the floor, using the tub as a shield. Two more bullets shot into the room. Someone must have seen him looking out the window.

Going out the front was suicide. He needed to find another way for Heather and Lily to get out of the house. He grabbed the cell phone Jose had given him earlier and punched Dante's number.

"Dante," a breathless voice answered.

"It's Nick. We're pinned down in here, and if Luis's statements can be trusted, this whole place is wired with explosives. What the hell is going on? I've got gunfire coming through the walls."

"It's not from us. I swear it's like someone's purposely shooting at the house. We're trying to take them out. We've spotted both of the Gonzalez brothers a few times, but they've got a lot of men protecting them. I can only assume their men are either shooting it out with each other or us. Hell, I don't know who's shooting at whom. It's a screwed-up catastrophe out here."

Nick swore again. "Luis must have had more men hiding in the woods when he came in here. He said he wanted to blow up the house. I've got to get the women out of here. What's the situation out back?"

"Not much better than out front. Your best bet might be to hang low and wait it out."

Another bullet pinged through the wall. The ceramic sink shattered, raining dust and needlelike shards all over the room. Nick covered his head, hissing as the shards pricked his skin like a hundred volts of electricity all over his arms.

"We're sitting ducks in here. I'm taking the women out the east side of the house into the woods. We'll head to the water. Can you cover us?"

"I'll reposition some men. We'll do what we can."

"Give me three minutes."

"You got it."

Nick ended the call and shoved the phone back into his pocket. He grabbed one of the towels hanging on a bar above him and raked the ceramic shards from his arms, leaving a bloody trail across his skin.

He tossed the towel down, lunged to his feet and ran into the hallway. He sprinted down the hall back toward the other bathroom. He didn't want to take the women out into that firestorm outside, but if he could get into the cover of trees, they'd have a much better chance than in here. The house was a death trap of bullets and explosives.

He ran down the hallway and whirled around the corner into the other bathroom.

The tub was empty. Heather and Lily were gone.

THE SOUND OF a voice drifted down the hall. Nick crept forward, following the sound. He held Lily's gun at his side, pointing to the floor. It was a man's voice. Luis? Jose? The voice stopped.

Sweat popped out on Nick's forehead and ran down the side of his face. His gut tightened with dread as he crouched down by the last doorway where the sound had come from. This room was on the back of the house. Thankfully no bullets were pinging through these walls, but there was no guarantee there wouldn't be at any time. The rat-a-tat gunfire was still strafing across the yard.

He raised his gun and swung around the doorway.

Oh, God. No.

For a moment, time stood still as his mind tried to take in the bloody scene.

Luis Gonzalez sat slumped against the far wall. The only way Nick knew it was Luis was because he wasn't wearing a suit as Jose had been earlier. His face and chest were covered in blood. Arterial spray covered the ceiling and walls, and blood was still gurgling from the gaping wound in his jugular. The knife Luis had apparently used to cut his own throat lay in his lifeless hand beside him.

And on the floor at his feet lay Lily and Heather. At first, Nick wasn't even sure which one was which. They were naked, side by side, their eyes closed. It was as if Luis had undressed them and posed them as his last act of vengeance, so no one would be able to tell the two apart.

And they were both covered in blood.

Nick shoved his gun in his holster and ran to the two women. He felt for a pulse. Both of them were still alive, but unconscious.

To the casual eye, the women were identical, especially with their matching tattoos. But Nick knew every inch of Heather's body. He knew the tiny little round scar on her forehead from when she'd had chicken pox as a child and had scratched herself. He recognized the smattering of freckles on her shoulders from when she'd suffered a serious sunburn a few years ago.

Perhaps the most telling of all were her no-nonsense fingernails, clipped short so they wouldn't get in her way—unlike Lily's nails, which were long and perfectly manicured, painted a hot pink.

He sank down next to Heather and gently felt along her body, searching for injuries. When he felt the back of her head, he found a large bump, and his hand came away bloody. He sucked in a sharp breath.

A whisper of sound came from the hallway. Nick grabbed his gun and pointed it at the opening just as Jose Gonzalez stepped into view.

Jose held his arms in the air. His gaze swept the room, his skin turning a pale gray beneath his tan. He stared at his brother a moment. Then he looked above him. If possible, his skin turned even whiter.

"Grab your woman and get out of here," he said. "Luis started the countdown. The house is going to blow." He pointed to the far wall.

Nick looked up. He swore when he saw the square box on the wall that resembled a security system keypad. But the bright lights on the readout showed numbers that were counting down.

They had less than a minute.

"Grab Lily. She's still alive." Nick shoved his gun in his holster and lifted Heather into his arms. "We'll make a run for it. My men out front are going to lay down cover fire. We'll go out the door on the east side and run into the woods."

Jose slowly shook his head and lowered himself to the floor. He gathered Lily up in his arms and cradled her against him. "No. You go. I'll stay here with my brother. And the woman I loved."

"Don't be a fool. I can't carry them both, and I won't have time to come back for her. If you love her, carry her out of here." He glanced at the readout. "Forty-five seconds. Come on. Let's go."

Heather stirred in Nick's arms. She moaned and opened her eyes. She gasped in recognition. "Nick, what are…" She turned her head and let out a scream. She squirmed and struggled in Nick's arms, but he held her tight so she couldn't get down.

"Let me go!" she yelled, her voice breaking on a sob. "Please. I have to help Lily."

"Jose," Nick urged. "Come on. We only have thirty seconds!"

"Thirty seconds?" Heather whispered, confusion in her tone.

Jose laughed bitterly. "This little firefight has brought down my empire. You and I both know I'll never see the light of day if I go to prison. I didn't mean for any of this to happen, but it did. Luis turned some of my own men against me. I'm finished whether I go to prison or not. At least this way, I'll be with the woman I love. Now go. Get out of here. You may have already waited too late."

Nick looked at the numbers counting down and cursed viciously. He whirled around and ran out the door, up the hallway.

Heather twisted and flailed in his arms. "No, no, don't leave my sister. Nick, oh, God, please don't leave her there!"

The devastation and panic in her voice were like shards of glass to his soul. He steeled himself against her heartbreaking pleas and ran outside.

"Let me go, put me down. I have to help her!"

Nick ran across the side yard. Gunshots continued to ring out, but Dante must have provided the cover he'd promised because none of the bullets hit him or Heather. He clasped her hard against him to quell her struggles so he wouldn't fall while he ran into the woods.

Once on the path, he tossed her on his shoulder, steeling himself against her tearful sobs and pleading to go back for her sister.

He grabbed his cell phone and punched Dante's number, running as fast as his legs could carry him through the thick brush.

When Dante's voice came on the line, Nick yelled into the receiver. "Get your men back from the house, now. It's going to blow!"

He dropped the phone and clutched Heather against him, running faster, faster. The sparkle of blue-green water beckoned in a break in the trees. He yanked Heather back down off his shoulder, clasped her to his chest and jumped into the water.

The world exploded in a fiery ball around them.

Chapter Sixteen

He shouldn't have come to Lily's funeral. Nick knew Heather didn't want him there. She'd made her feelings, or lack of them, perfectly clear by ignoring his requests to see her when they were both in the hospital.

But he couldn't stay away. Part of it, a very large part of it, was guilt. Which was why he was standing here, against doctor's orders, beside some oak trees, using one of the trees for support so he could watch Lily Bannon's memorial service taking place fifty yards away.

He acknowledged that part of the reason he was here was to see Heather again. To catch a glimpse of her brown, wavy hair tumbling down the back of her black dress. To mentally caress the curve of her face as she kissed a white rose and placed it on top of her sister's casket.

There were only a handful of people sitting in the dozen or so white chairs set up in front of the gaping hole in the ground. Apparently Lily hadn't had a lot of friends. And the lack of family members was almost embarrassing. He didn't even know if Heather had any family, and that somehow bothered him even more than his guilt.

He'd loved her almost from the first moment he'd met

her. And although he knew her personality, the goodness inside her, the work ethic that was as much a part of her as breathing, he didn't know much about her past, what had shaped her into the person she was today.

He hadn't taken the time to learn.

He'd chosen his career over her. And the only time she'd ever asked him for anything—*please save my sister*—he'd failed her, utterly and completely.

The service was over. He hadn't planned on Heather seeing him there. He'd come to pay his respects, to offer a silent prayer, but he'd intended to step back behind the tree so no one would see him when the funeral came to an end. But he'd been too lost in his thoughts to remember to conceal himself.

Now it was too late.

Even from fifty yards away, he could see Heather's shoulders tense when she looked his way. An older woman standing next to her put her hand on Heather's arm, said something to her. Heather shook her head and started walking toward Nick.

He straightened away from the tree, gritting his teeth against the nausea that action caused and the tug of the material of his suit across the still-tender skin on his back. The explosion had singed the hair on his head and blistered the skin from the back of his neck to the back of his calves. Only his feet had escaped without burns because of his shoes. But thankfully Heather hadn't received any burns. She'd had a concussion from when Luis had knocked her unconscious. And she had half drowned by the time Dante's men had fished them both out of the water. But thank God she hadn't been burned.

She came to a stop about three feet away, the same

distance someone might give to a stranger, as if they'd never been anything more than that to each other.

Maybe they hadn't. Maybe he was the only one who felt like his heart was being ripped from his chest every time he thought about the explosion, and how close Heather had come to dying. He certainly hadn't realized how much she meant to him, not until she nearly died in his arms.

"What are you doing here?" she asked, her blue eyes flashing, her hands fisted at her sides.

"I came to pay my respects."

She laughed harshly. "Your respects? To the woman you killed?"

He winced.

"Why did you do it?" Heather demanded. "Why didn't you put me down and grab Lily? I could have run out of that house on my own two feet. You could have saved her. But you chose to let her die. Why?"

He felt the blood rush from his face. He stared at her, incredulous, shocked. Was that what she thought? That he chose for Lily to die? He shook his head. "I didn't want her to die. You had a huge bump on your head and had lost a lot of blood. You'd been knocked unconscious—"

"But I came to. I told you to put me down. You chose not to. There was still enough time to save her."

"You were pale, shaking. Your eyes were unfocused. I knew you had a concussion. I couldn't risk you trying to run out on your own. You wouldn't have made it. You couldn't have run fast enough. The only *choice* I made was to save you. I couldn't save you both."

Her skin flushed and she opened and closed her fists several times, as if she were fighting the urge to slap him, or slug him. If it would make her feel better, he'd gladly stand there and let her.

She didn't hit him. Instead, she drew a deep breath. "You saved my life, several times. I know that. And I thank you for that. But…" Her lips compressed into a hard line and she swallowed. The bright shine in her eyes told him how close she was to losing her composure.

It nearly killed him not to reach out and draw her close, cradle her against him. But he wasn't sure he had the strength to take a step, even if she'd wanted him to hold her, which he knew she didn't. The most severe burns, the ones on his right calf, were sending sharp jolts of fire racing across his nerve endings. It took every ounce of strength and stubbornness he had not to sag against the tree for support.

She blinked several times, fighting tears. She finally let out a pent-up breath, back in control. "I'm sure you feel like you did the right thing on that island, and I am glad to be alive. But I could never look at you again without seeing the face of my sister lying there in a drug dealer's arms while you forced me to leave her there to die." Her voice broke on the last word and she drew another shaky breath. "I don't ever want to see you again."

She turned around and marched across the grass, back to the only person still standing by the graveside, the older woman she'd spoken to earlier. The woman put her arm around Heather's shoulders and led her toward the parking lot.

Nick prayed he wouldn't disgrace himself by blacking out while he waited for Heather to get into her car. His legs started shaking violently, but still he fought against the white-hot agony. He didn't want Heather's sympathy, and he'd be damned if he let her see how weak he'd become.

When her car rounded a curve out of sight, Nick's brother stepped from behind the cluster of oak trees and shoved the wheelchair up behind him. Nick collapsed into the chair, hissing when his back pressed against the hard vinyl.

"Thanks for waiting," Nick said from between clenched teeth.

"I didn't want you to look like any more of a fool than you already do," Rafe said. "You know it was totally stupid coming here. You've probably set your recovery back a couple of weeks. She would have been really impressed with your intelligence if she'd realized you sneaked out of a hospital to go to a funeral where you weren't even wanted in the first place." Rafe pushed the chair across the grass toward their car.

Nick winced with each bump of the wheels. "I didn't come here for her."

"Yeah. Right."

The agony pulsing through Nick's back and legs was making his vision blur. But it was no worse than the pain of knowing that his brother was right. One of the reasons he'd insisted on coming here was that he'd held a small grain of hope that—if he had the courage to speak to her—Heather might be happy to see him. He'd hoped she might find it in her heart somehow to forgive him.

But now he knew that had been just a dream.

HEATHER SAT IN her car at the curb as she'd done every day this week, and the week before, doing nothing but thinking. Thanks to her sister's one selfless act, she had the luxury of sitting and thinking, of doing nothing, because she could afford to.

Lily had purchased a life insurance policy, a rather large one, and she'd made Heather the beneficiary. The generous settlement seemed like Lily's way of paying her sister back for everything she'd taken from her. It had certainly come in handy, because Heather couldn't focus or concentrate on work ever since the disastrous trip to Key West. Her fledgling private investigator business was on hiatus, and she wasn't sure she even wanted to start it up again.

Thanks to Lily, she didn't have to.

The life insurance policy had been paid for in a lump sum. The only way Lily would have been able to do that was with money from one of the Gonzalez brothers. Heather had wrestled with her conscience for weeks before cashing the insurance check. She'd finally decided that since the Gonzalez brothers had helped to destroy her sister's life, the least they could do was to make some kind of restitution, even if it was from the grave.

Heather had done a lot of looking back in the past few weeks, because she couldn't move forward until she understood how she'd gotten here, why everything had gone so horribly wrong. Talking to her relatives had been, well, an enlightening experience. She'd learned things she'd perhaps suspected, but had never been completely sure of. She'd cried over and over in the days since, but the tears had finally dried. She'd finally made her peace with her sister, and herself.

But there was one more person she needed to make peace with.

That's why she was sitting in her car on the curb in front of a house she'd never been in, hungrily watching the front windows, both hoping and fearing for the glimpse of a familiar profile. It had taken several trips and finally an all-out bribe at the DEA office to get Nick's address. But now, she couldn't seem to work up the nerve to even walk to the door.

Just like yesterday.

And the day before.

And the day before that.

She closed her eyes and rested her forehead against the steering wheel. Why couldn't she work up the nerve to get out of her car?

"What are you doing here?"

She jumped at the sound of the voice beside her. Rafe Morgan was crouching down next to her open window. The frown and tension around his mouth told her he wasn't a bit pleased to see her.

"I'm sorry," she said. "I didn't mean to intrude. I'll leave." She reached for the keys in the ignition.

"The hell you will." He stood and opened the door. "Get out."

"I'm sorry, what?"

"You heard me. Get out or I'll drag you out."

She blinked, and let out a shriek of surprise when he reached in across her and unbuckled her seat belt. He hauled her out of the car and started walking up toward the house with her in tow.

She pulled back, desperately trying to stop him. "What are you doing? Stop it right now. Let me go."

He ignored her struggles and forced her all the way to the front door before finally letting her go.

Heather yanked her hand back and rubbed her aching shoulder, the one Nick had popped back into the socket.

She was still going through therapy, and Rafe's rough treatment had it throbbing.

His face flushed as he glanced at her hand rubbing her shoulder. "I didn't realize I was hurting you. My apologies."

Heather dropped her hand. "It's an old injury. You didn't know."

He gave her a curt nod. "I couldn't let you leave again without talking to Nick."

This time it was her turn to flush. "Again?"

"I come over here every afternoon after work to check on Nick. And every evening about this time you end up sitting out front, trying to gather the courage to knock on the door. Well, I'm tired of waiting for you to develop a backbone. So I'm taking the decision out of your hands." He turned the knob and shoved the door open. "After you." He swept his hand out in front of him.

Heather balked at the threshold. "Wait, what do you mean you come over here to check on him? Is he sick or something?"

"Or something. He's out back where he is every day at this time. I don't mind telling you that I think you treated him like crap, and he doesn't deserve that. I wouldn't let you near him except that I know the idiot will be happy to see you. Mainly because he's a little bit drunk and too stupid to know better."

Heather's stomach sank. "He's…drunk?"

"Only a little. He just got started. You've caught him at a good time. Now go talk to him. I don't care what you're here to say. Just get it over with. Either make up with him or make sure it's a clean break. Get it all out so he can move on with his life." He wrapped his hands around her waist and physically set her in the foyer as if she were a doll.

She was too shocked to do more than blink at him and move her mouth like a fish, but no sounds came out.

Rafe shut the door in her face, leaving her alone in the darkened entranceway.

Heather reached for the doorknob, intending to step right back outside, but the pictures on the wall caught her attention. She slowly lowered her hand. There were dozens of photographs, family pictures, there could be no doubt. She recognized Nick in some of them, laughing or smiling, the Nick she remembered from when they'd first started dating, the charmer who called her darlin' and made her heart melt.

Her breath caught when she saw a rectangular strip of pictures affixed to the expensive wallpaper with a thumbtack, a black and white collection of five pictures of her and Nick, taken in a photo booth at the local fair. She'd forgotten about that day, had assumed she'd lost those pictures somewhere. She never would have expected to find them on the wall in Nick's house.

For the first time since she'd left him standing in the cemetery after saying those horrible things to him, hope flared inside her that he might yet forgive her. It gave her the courage she'd lacked all week, and had her walking through the house toward the sliding glass doors that opened onto the backyard.

She paused with her hand on the door handle. He was standing with his back to her, staring at the creek that ran behind his house.

Leaning on a cane.

Why did he have a cane? She shoved the door open and stepped onto the back deck.

Nick held up a half-empty beer bottle but didn't turn around. "If you're going to lecture me again, brother dearest, at least wait until I'm drunk to do it." He tilted the bottle and took a long drink.

Heather stepped off the deck onto the grass, a flash of anger finally giving her the courage she'd been lacking. She marched across the grass and grabbed the beer bottle out of Nick's hand.

His eyes widened, then narrowed as he tried to swipe the bottle back from her.

She held it out of his reach and tilted it so the liquid ran out onto the grass.

He glared at her. "What do you want? An apology? Well, forget it. I'm fresh out."

"Why are you using a cane?"

His mouth tightened, but he didn't answer.

"Rafe said you've been drinking a lot. Is that because of me?"

He turned and headed back toward the house. It nearly broke Heather's heart to see him leaning so heavily on the cane. She hurried after him.

"Stop, Nick. We need to talk."

He ignored her and climbed the steps to the deck. The grimace on his face told her how much it hurt him to do that. She followed him all the way to the door, but when he didn't turn around, she rushed to stand in front of him, blocking his way.

"Move," he said, bending down as if to intimidate her with his height.

Truth be told, she was intimidated. He had several days' growth of stubble on his face and his hair looked like it hadn't been cut in a month or more. His hazel eyes had darkened with anger and he looked as if he wanted to beat her over the head with his cane.

She swallowed and reminded herself that he didn't hate her. If he did, he wouldn't have kept her pictures in the foyer.

"Now who's the coward?" she accused. "Big, strong Nick Morgan running away from a woman."

He braced himself against the sliding glass door, his frown ominous as he held up his cane for her to see. "Not so big and strong anymore, in case you hadn't noticed."

Sympathy flooded through her, but she knew he wouldn't welcome her pity, so she struggled to keep it from showing. "Is that because of the explosion?"

He gave her a curt nod.

"I didn't know. I'm sorry."

He leaned on the cane again and stared at her for a full minute, as if trying to come to a decision. Finally, he let out a deep sigh. "Most of the burns were second degree. They healed fairly quickly. But some tree sap stuck on my right calf burned clean down to the muscle. I'm on disability until the doctors decide I can go back to work again."

"Oh, Nick. I'm so sorry."

"It's not your fault," he said, his voice losing some of its anger. "None of it was. It wasn't anyone's fault. It just…happened."

She put the flat of her palm on his chest.

He stiffened, but she didn't move her hand.

"I know that now," she whispered. "I know it wasn't your fault. It wasn't your fault that any of those terrible things happened." She took a step closer and tilted her head back to look him in the eyes. "Lily's death wasn't anyone's fault but her own. I'm so sorry that I ever blamed you. I don't blame you anymore."

He stared down at her, searching her face, her eyes, for the truth. "What are you saying?" His voice was raw, raspy.

"I'm saying that I was…confused, hurting, and I wanted you to hurt, too. Because I'd just lost my sister. I wanted, I needed, someone to blame. So I blamed you. But it wasn't your fault. I know that now. And it wasn't my fault, although I believed it was for a long time. There are a lot of people I can blame—myself, Lily, Luis, Jose—but not you."

He reached up and slowly, as if he was afraid she'd reject him and turn away, traced his fingers over the curve of her cheek. "I'd rather you blamed me than yourself," he said, his voice gruff.

"Can we go inside and sit down?" she asked. "Your leg must be hurting, and I need to explain a few things."

He nodded and pulled the door open for her to go inside.

He limped in after her and lowered himself to the couch, grimacing as he did so.

Heather wanted to soothe his pain away, to run her fingers across his battered leg. But this truce, or whatever it was, that they'd just made was tenuous at best. She didn't want to push too hard. Not yet. She sat down in the chair beside the couch, with a foot of space separating the two of them. So close, and yet so very, very far.

"I never told you about my childhood, about growing up with Lily. And I won't bore you with all the details now except to say that it was…rough. From as far back as I can remember, Lily always seemed to resent me.

Oh, we had happy times, but they were when we were very young. Our parents died when we were little and we were raised by relatives, shuffled back and forth. It never bothered me. I always seemed to thrive and excel at school. But Lily was just the opposite. It got really bad after she turned fifteen." She rubbed her hands up and down her arms.

"I always felt like it was my fault somehow, like maybe I shouldn't have tried so hard at school. Or maybe I shouldn't have made so many friends. Lily and I grew further and further apart no matter what I did. And then, on our sixteenth birthday, she ran away. I didn't see her again until a couple of years ago—the first time she stopped in to ask me for money."

Nick watched her intently, as if he were eating up every detail of her life.

"The point is, I always felt like I'd let her down somehow, like her failures were my fault. Like I should have done something more to help her. That's why it was so important to me to try to…save her…when I thought she'd been kidnapped. That's why I was willing to give my life for hers. I felt I owed her that."

Nick shook his head. "You didn't owe her anything."

"Oh, I know that now. Because I was just a child, you see. I couldn't have known what was happening."

Nick closed his eyes briefly before looking at her again. "Lily was abused, wasn't she?"

"Yes." She reached out and took his hand in hers. She was relieved when he didn't pull away, but he wasn't really holding her hand, either. He was letting her hold his hand, without responding one way or the other.

Heather swallowed against the lump in her throat. "After Lily's death, I searched out my relatives. I hadn't kept in touch over the years, but I learned that several of them suspected what I'd never realized, that one of my uncles had abused her. He's dead now, so it's not like I can try to pursue any legal action against him. But at least now I know why Lily was so angry and resented me so much."

Nick gently squeezed her hand.

She felt that touch all the way to her heart.

"She resented you because he never…touched you," he whispered.

"Yes. I don't know why he chose her as his victim."

"You can't blame yourself for anything that happened. You were a child."

She pressed her lips together, nodding. "I know. I don't. It's like I'm…at peace now. Now that I know what happened, and why everything went so wrong between Lily and me, I can forgive her. I understand how torn up she was inside, why she longed for someone to really care about her but never felt she could turn to me. I honestly believe she wanted to protect me from the truth, but that she still couldn't move past her resentment that I was the one who escaped, even though she's the one who ran away."

"I'm glad you don't blame yourself," Nick said, looking wary. "But why did you feel you needed to tell me this?"

Her heart broke at the guarded look in his eyes.

"Nick, I love you. I needed you to know why I said all those horrible things, and that I regret every single word. I'm at peace with my past, except for the part where I hurt you. I love you. And I'm here to ask you to forgive me."

"I forgive you," he whispered. "And I love you, too."

Heather let out a breath she hadn't realized she was holding. "Thank you. That means so much to me, to know you forgive me." She let go of his hand and stood. She hurried across the room, desperate to get out of the house before he saw her tears.

"Hey, where the hell are you going?" Nick called out from behind her.

"Home," she called back as she hurried into the foyer.

The front door opened, and Rafe and his wife Darby stood in the opening. They were smiling until they spotted Heather. Rafe's eyebrows rose and his smile faded.

"I thought you two, I mean, I could have sworn that you would have…" His words trailed off and his mouth tightened with disappointment.

"I…ah, need to go home now. Thank you for letting me speak to your brother."

"Don't let her step one foot out that door," Nick growled from behind her.

Heather stepped forward, but Rafe nudged his wife back behind him and crossed his arms, lounging in the doorway.

"Detective Morgan, I'd appreciate it if you would get out of my way." Heather was trying hard to hold back her tears. She would be mortified if she cried in front of all these people. It was hard enough to leave without having an audience to her humiliation.

"Heather Bannon, turn around and explain what the hell you think you're doing. You can't tell me you love me then walk out the door."

Heather glared at Rafe. "You aren't going to move, are you?"

He slowly shook his head. She could have sworn he was trying not to laugh.

She huffed out a deep breath and turned around. "Fine. Have it your way," she said to Nick. "I didn't want you to see me cry, okay? Well, look your fill. These are tears. I'm a strong woman but sometimes I can't help but cry. There. Satisfied?" She crossed her arms and stared at the floor, gulping in deep breaths.

Nick limped toward her and stopped a few inches away. He gently nudged her chin up. "Why are you crying?"

"Because I love you, you stubborn man."

"Okay, maybe I'm a little slow here, because I've never been in love before. But I don't get the connection."

Heather shoved his hand away from her chin. "Do I really have to spell it out?"

"Um, yeah. You do."

She huffed again and fisted her hands beside her. "You're a DEA agent. My sister was a drug dealer's girlfriend. Heck, let's be honest. She was basically a drug dealer, too. I had felony drug charges against me. Yes, they were dropped, but only because I helped with a case. I know what all of that means. It means we can't be together. So forgive me if it makes me sad, okay? Now can I go?"

"No."

"What do you mean, no?" she practically screamed at him.

He put his arms around her and gently but steadily pulled her against him. "I love you, Heather Bannon. And you love me. I chose my career over you once. That was the biggest mistake of my life. I won't make that mistake twice. And no, you aren't leaving. Ever."

She blinked at him. "Ever?" she whispered.

He leaned down and gently kissed her lips. "Ever," he repeated.

"But…but…your job means so much to you."

He sighed and shook his head. "I have a past, too. A cousin, whose life was destroyed by drugs. When he died, I vowed I'd grow up to be a DEA agent, that I'd help stop drugs from pouring into our streets. I was sixteen. And yes, I still meant that vow. But, honey, I can help people without being a DEA agent. I didn't think it was that simple before, but I've lived the past four weeks, ten days, and—" he looked at his watch "—thirty-two minutes without you. That's the longest I ever want to be without you again. I can find another job. But I'll never find another you."

"What a nice thing to say," Darby's voice sounded from behind Heather.

Nick frowned.

Heather turned around, blushing fire-hot when she saw Darby and Rafe both standing in the doorway. She'd forgotten all about them. Darby's eyes were misty. Rafe was grinning as if he'd planned this reunion all along.

As Heather thought back to when he'd pulled her out of the car earlier, she realized maybe he had.

She grinned back at him.

Nick grabbed her hand and hauled her into the living room, cursing under his breath. For a man walking with a cane, he could move at a pretty fast clip. He practically dragged her toward the opening into the hallway.

"Hey, wait, where are you two going?" Rafe called out. He and Darby ran into the living room behind them.

"I need some privacy to tell Heather that I love her," Nick yelled as he pulled Heather down the hall.

Rafe stepped into the hall behind them. "But you al-

ready told her you loved her. We heard you." His voice
was thick with laughter.

"Yes, we did," Darby agreed.

"I need to tell her again." Nick opened a door and
shoved it, slamming it against the wall.

Heather's face went even hotter when she saw the bed
and realized this was Nick's bedroom. She glanced back
over her shoulder. Rafe was leaning against the wall, his
grin bigger than ever.

Darby stood beside him, her eyes dancing with
amusement.

Nick tugged Heather's arm, pulling her into the room.
He hooked his cane on the edge of the door and slammed
it shut.

Laughter sounded from the hallway.

Nick rolled his eyes and threw the cane on the floor.
He pulled Heather into his arms and kissed her soundly
on the lips. When he pulled back, he framed her face
with his hands. "In case I forget to tell you later, I love
you."

"I love you, too. Um, why would you forget to tell
me?"

He grinned. "Because I'll be too busy *showing* you."

Heather shoved out of his arms.

Nick didn't like that. His brows lowered and he took
a halting step toward her without the aid of his cane, as
if to pull her back into his arms.

Heather held up her hand to stop him. "What about
condition number one?"

"Condition number one?"

"Yeah, you know. The one that said we're through, finished. That there is no 'us' anymore. And I'm pretty sure
you said there never would be." She crossed her arms.

His face reddened. "I might have been, ah, hasty when I said that. Let's forget all about that."

"Okay. What about condition number two?"

His mouth quirked up. "The one where you do exactly what I tell you to do? At all times?"

"Mmm-hmm."

"I kind of like that one."

She raised a brow.

He grumbled something under his breath. "Okay. We'll forget that condition, too. If we have to."

"We definitely have to. Now for the third condition."

He waved his hand. "That one said you report to me alone, not Rickloff or Waverly. Obviously that doesn't apply anymore."

"I'm proposing a new third condition."

He stopped directly in front of her, close, but not touching. His eyes held a wary look. "What condition?"

She uncrossed her arms. "That you love me, always, no matter what. And that you don't try to impose any stupid conditions again, ever."

He cocked a brow. "You get to set conditions, but I don't?"

"Works for me," she teased.

He grabbed her and swung her up into his arms. "I agree to condition three, but everything else will have to be renegotiated." He limped with her to the bed.

"Wait, I have one more condition," she squeaked.

He dumped her on the bed and followed her down, covering her with his body. "I'm losing my patience. Make it quick."

"I want you to show me your tattoo."

He blinked, then let out a shout of laughter.

Heather clapped her hand over his mouth. "Hush.

Rafe and Darby might hear us. And we still have to re-negotiate new conditions."

He grinned and smoothed her hair back from her face. "That's exactly what we're about to do, darlin'. Negotiate." He leaned down and whispered exactly how he would negotiate, exactly how he would wring an agreement out of her to his every demand.

* * * * *

He knew he couldn't just grab her dad's records away from her and leave. As much as he dreaded having to offer her comfort, and knowing what it was going to do to him to be that close to her, he was all she had.

She made a face. "I don't like to cry. It just messes up my face and gives me a headache."

She met his gaze and he marveled at how blue her eyes were. He'd thought from the beginning that they were lovely. "I think you have the most beautiful eyes I've ever seen."

He had a sudden need to swallow—hard. Here they went again. Just like before, he sat perfectly still and hoped like hell that she didn't kiss him, because he was already very much on the edge.

She's your responsibility. Your responsibility.

He leaned forward, his gaze moving from her eyes to her lips. Then, as she let her eyes drift shut, he brushed her mouth with his.

DIRTY LITTLE
SECRETS

BY
MALLORY KANE

First published in Great Britain 2013
by Mills & Boon, an imprint of Harlequin (UK) Limited,
Eton House, 18-24 Paradise Road, Richmond, Surrey TW9 1SR

© Rickey R. Mallory 2013

ISBN: 978 0 263 90386 7

46-1213

Harlequin (UK) policy is to use papers that are natural, renewable and recyclable products and made from wood grown in sustainable forests. The logging and manufacturing processes conform to the legal environmental regulations of the country of origin.

Printed and bound in Spain
by Blackprint CPI, Barcelona

Mallory Kane has two very good reasons for loving reading and writing. Her mother was a librarian, who taught her to love and respect books as a precious resource. Her father could hold listeners spellbound for hours with his stories. He was always her biggest fan.

She loves romantic suspense with dangerous heroes and dauntless heroines, and enjoys tossing in a bit of her medical knowledge for an extra dose of intrigue. After twenty-five books published, Mallory is still amazed and thrilled that she actually gets to make up stories for a living.

Mallory lives in Tennessee with her computer-genius husband and three exceptionally intelligent cats. She enjoys hearing from readers. You can write her at mallory@mallorykane.com.

For Michael: Hang in there, baby. I love you.

Chapter One

Everything had been planned—from every lock that had to be picked, to every step through every corridor. The Louis Royale Hotel's popular restaurants had cleared out by midnight and most of the diners had moved on to more exciting places or gone home. The hotel's bar was popular for lunch and predinner cocktails, but most serious partiers ended up on Bourbon Street by late evening.

It had been simple to slip in with the last of the late diners. Simple to take the elevators up to the tenth floor. And it was a snap to pick the lock on the fire stairs door to the penthouse suite that took up the entire eleventh floor. The hotel still used the original ornate metal keys, although the guest rooms also had computerized security card locks.

The hotel was the perfect place to kill the senator. And tonight was the perfect night. His offices and the senate floor in Baton Rouge were too public and too secure. The locked gates of his home just outside of that city put the Louisiana State Legislature's security measures to shame. It was laughable that the man who'd

erected a fortress worthy of a paranoid potentate was so
lax about his safety in a hotel. But then, a lot of people
assumed a hotel's penthouse suite was innately secure.
Tonight, for Senator Darby Sills, that assumption would
prove to be a fatal mistake.

Crouching in the fire stairs to wait for the perfect
moment was also a snap. Boring, cramped, but simple.
The layout of the penthouse suite was perfect. The elevator doors opened into the sitting room. On the left
wall were the double doors to the master suite and on
the right was the door to a second, smaller bedroom.

It was after midnight, one twenty-seven, to be specific. The senator and his staff were due to have breakfast with the local longshoremen's union at eight o'clock
in the morning. He'd probably sent his staff off to their
rooms by eleven, eleven-thirty at the latest. Sills insisted
that his employees maintain a routine. He liked to say
that any man or woman worth their salt should be in
bed by eleven and up by seven. Not that Senator Sills
abided by that rule. No one in public life could maintain a healthy, structured sleep schedule.

Although few people were aware of it, Sills was an
insomniac. He rarely got four hours' sleep a night. At
home, he'd sit in a rocking chair in his study, smoke
his pipe, sip Dewar's scotch and read. It was widely
rumored that his staff had the unenviable task of keeping the senator and his scotch separated when he was
on the road.

The plan to kill Senator Sills allowed seven minutes
for the job, start to finish. Best scenario, Sills would be
in the sitting room, reading. A quick entrance through

the service door, a muffled shot, right in the middle of Sills's chest, a rapid escape and down the fire stairs. If Sills had already retired to the bedroom, seven minutes would be stretching it, but it could still be done.

Next, change to the clothes hidden in the fire stairs while descending to the first floor, then walk through the bar and out the door as if nothing was more important than heading left toward Bourbon Street. Seven minutes, one bullet, and the greedy bastard would be dead.

LANEY MONTGOMERY CLOSED the connecting door between the penthouse suite sitting room and the adjoining bedroom with an exhausted sigh. She'd thought the senator would never stop editing his speech. He was pickier than usual tonight.

She kicked off her heels and collapsed on the king-size bed, too tired to lift her arm to check her watch. The last time she'd checked, it had been after two, and she had to get up at six to make any final changes to Louisiana State Senator Darby Sills's speech before his eight o'clock breakfast meeting with the local officers of the Longshoremen's Association.

But as much as she wanted to just turn over, grab a corner of the bedspread for warmth and drift off to sleep, she couldn't. She had to brush her teeth, take off her makeup and set her phone's alarm first. She felt around for her phone, then remembered that she'd left it on the printer cart in the sitting room.

With a weary sigh, she sat up. For a brief moment she fantasized about leaving the phone where it was and calling for a wakeup call, but she couldn't spend three hours—not even three hours while she was asleep—without her phone. As Senator Darby Sills's personal assistant, she'd be the one called if anything happened. Whether it was a change in the number of people attending the longshoremen's breakfast or a frantic text from the governor about some issue facing the legislature, it came to her phone.

She closed her eyes. Maybe nobody would call tonight. And surely she'd hear her phone through the door. Just as she began to sink into the soft bed, she heard a loud yet muffled pop through the connecting door, then a thud. Was that pop a bottle being uncorked? Had the senator smuggled in a bottle of scotch?

Ready with her "remember what the doctor said about your liver" speech, she vaulted up and knocked briskly. "Senator? I forgot my phone," she called, then opened the door and stepped through.

The desk chair where Senator Sills had been sitting just two minutes before was empty. Laney glanced toward the wet bar. The senator liked his Dewar's on the rocks. "Senator," she called. "Where did you get—?"

Then she saw the scarecrow-thin shadow looming in front of her.

Laney's hands shot up in an instinctive protective gesture. "What? Senator—?"

The shadow took on a vaguely human outline—a silhouette completely cloaked in black. It came toward her and she recoiled. "Who are you?" she cried. "Where's the senator?"

The person in black lifted its right arm and pointed at her.

Laney blinked and tried to clear her vision. Surely there was something wrong with her eyes. "Senator—" she started, but stopped when something in the person's hand caught the lamplight, gleaming like silver.

"No!" she cried, her subconscious mind recognizing the object before her brain had time to attach a name to it. She dived, face-planting on the hardwood floor in front of her bedroom door. A muffled pop echoed through the room and her skull burned in white-hot pain. Her head was knocked back into the baseboard behind her. Her cry choked and died as her throat seized in fear.

What happened? What hurt so bad? Again, her brain was slow to catch up to her intuitive subconscious. Finally she understood. *I've been shot.* Whimpering involuntarily, she drew her shoulders up and pressed her forehead into the floorboards as hard as she could. She wrapped her arms around her head, grimacing in awful anticipation as she waited for the next bullet to slam into her.

And waited. There were no more pops. Instead, she heard footsteps coming toward her. They echoed hollowly on the hardwood floor.

One step. Two. She thought about moving. Pictured herself propelling backward through the door to her room and slamming it. But it didn't matter how brave she was inside her head. In reality, she couldn't make her frozen limbs move. All she could do was cower.

Three steps. He was coming to check and be sure

she was dead. He was going to shoot her again, at point-blank range. She didn't want to die. "No—" she croaked. "Please—"

The elevator bell dinged.

The footsteps stopped. The man whispered a curse. Laney held her breath. Who was on the elevator? Who would have access to the penthouse? Had someone heard the shots?

The footsteps sounded again, but this time they were quicker and fading, as if the man were retreating. Laney opened her eyes to slits, bracing for the sharp, nauseating pain. She had to know where the man was—what he was doing.

When she raised her head, a moan escaped her lips. The shooter whirled and something silvery and bright caught the light again. He was holding the gun at shoulder height, pointed right at her. She gasped and tried to shrink into the floor. At that instant the distinctive sound of elevator doors opening filled the air.

The man turned as if to glance over his shoulder, then disappeared through the service door to the left of the elevators. His footsteps echoed, warring with the electronic sound of the doors.

With a massive effort, Laney lifted her head. Coming out of the elevator was a bellman carrying a bottle of Dewar's scotch. She pointed with a trembling finger toward the service door and cried out, "Help. He's getting away!" Only it wasn't a cry. It was nothing more than a choked whisper.

The bellman saw her then. He dropped the bottle, which thudded to the floor without breaking. "Oh,

God!" he cried, running over to kneel beside her. "Oh, God. Are you all right? What happened? Where are you hurt?"

"Senator—" Laney forced herself to say. She pointed toward the desk. "The senator—"

The young man twisted to look in the direction she was pointing. "Oh, God," he said again.

"Help him," she whispered.

"I can't—" the bellman started. "The blood—"

Laney pushed herself to her knees. "Senator!" she cried out as she crawled toward the empty desk chair, hoping against hope that the gunman hadn't killed him. That somehow the shot had missed him and he had taken shelter under the desk, wounded maybe, but alive. As she crawled closer, she saw his back. He was lying next to the chair, crumpled into a fetal position. Blood made a glistening, widening stain on the Persian rug.

"Senator!" she cried again, shoving the chair out of the way. Twisting, she pinned the bellman with a glare that ratcheted up the throbbing pain in her head. "Call the police," she grated.

She put her hand on the senator's shoulder and carefully turned him onto his back—and saw his eyes, open and staring and beginning to film over.

"Oh, no," she whispered. "No, no, no." She shook him by the shoulder. His jacket fell open and she saw where the blood was coming from. A small, seeping wound in his chest. She cast about for something to stanch the bleeding, even though she knew it was too late. She looked back at his eyes and her heart sank with a dread certainty. There was no need to stop the bleeding. He was dead.

Behind her she heard the young man on the house telephone beside the elevator. "Hurry!" he said shakily. "There's blood everywhere."

Laney knew she ought to be the one on the phone, calling the police, taking care that no one but them knew what had happened. Senator Sills was dead and it was her responsibility to him and to the legislature to keep that information away from the press and the public. But her head hurt so badly and her vision was obscured by a red haze. Defeated by pain and sadness, she curled up on the floor next to the senator, one arm under her head.

Behind her, the bellman spoke into the phone. "No. I'm telling you, it's Senator Sills. I think he's dead."

NEW ORLEANS POLICE Detective Ethan Delancey stared down at the body of Senator Darby Sills, sprawled on the floor of the penthouse suite in the Louis Royale Hotel in the French Quarter. Blood stained the Persian rug beneath him. This was going to be ugly.

"This is going to be ugly," Detective Dixon Lloyd's voice came from behind him.

"Morning, partner," Ethan responded wryly. "Nice of you to show up." He'd gotten to the hotel fifteen minutes earlier. But then he didn't have a wife or a house in the lower Garden District like Dixon did. His apartment on Prytania Street was less than ten minutes from the French Quarter in rush hour, much less at four o'clock in the morning.

"Hey, give me a break," Dixon said. "Did you see how many reporters are already outside? Not to mention rubberneckers. I had to call the commander to round up more officers for crowd control."

"Everybody in New Orleans will know Senator Sills is dead before the sun comes up," Ethan said glumly.

"Probably already do. I hate politics."

"You?" Ethan countered. "Try being Con Delancey's grandson." Like his older brother Lucas and his twin cousins, Ryker and Reilly, Ethan had become a cop, hoping to separate himself from the tarnished legacy of his infamous grandfather, Louisiana Senator Con Delancey. But like them, he'd quickly found out that the name Delancey was an occupational hazard in New Orleans, no matter what the job was. There was nowhere in the state of Louisiana—or maybe the world—that his surname didn't evoke a raised eyebrow and a range of reactions from an appreciative smile to unbridled hostility.

"I think I can relate," Dixon said, "since I'm in the family now."

"You two finished catching up on family gossip?" Police Officer Maria Farrantino interrupted. "I'm sure it's been a couple of hours since you've seen each other." She stood on the other side of the body, the toes of her polished boots avoiding the pool of blood by less than two inches.

Ethan sent her an irritated glare.

Unfazed, she continued. "I've got the second victim over here. The first officer on the scene took her statement. The EMTs are working on her now, and CSI hasn't gotten to her yet."

Ethan looked at the young woman who was sitting on a straight-backed chair with her head bowed and one hand holding back her dark, matted hair as an EMT applied a bandage to the side of her head. Draped over her knee was a wet cloth that was stained a deep pink, the same color as the large spot on her white shirt. According to the statement the first officer had given him, she was Senator Sills's personal assistant and had surprised the killer in the act. She'd told the officer that she'd dived to the floor when the killer had turned his gun on her, but hadn't been quick enough to escape injury.

Ethan's gaze slid downward to the short black skirt that had ridden up to reveal a pair of class A legs ending in bare feet.

"Yo, Delancey," Dixon said and waved a hand across his field of vision. Ethan blinked and turned his head.

"What?"

"Ah, you're back to earth," Dixon said. "Have you talked to the medical examiner yet?"

Ethan shook his head.

"Your choice. The M.E. or the injured victim with the killer legs that go on forever?"

"Legs. No question," Ethan muttered.

Dixon winked at Ethan as he headed toward the man bending over the senator's body.

"What's her name?" Ethan asked Farrantino as he squinted at the scribbled words on the officer's statement. He was going to have to ask that the officers receive penmanship lessons.

"Let's see. Montgomery. Elaine," Farrantino answered.

Montgomery. His gaze snapped back to the witness just as the EMT finished with the bandage and she raised her head. He took in her features for the first time. Could her name be a coincidence? With a sinking feeling in the pit of his stomach, he thought about the late, infamous lobbyist Elliott Montgomery, comparing his memory of Montgomery's narrow features and dark blue eyes to Elaine Montgomery's face. It didn't take much imagination to see the resemblance. The slender nose, full mouth and high cheekbones looked a lot better on her than they had on him, though.

So, Senator Darby Sills's personal assistant was the daughter of the ruthless lobbyist for the Port of New Orleans unions. Ethan frowned. Was this case about to get even uglier? "Looks like the EMTs are done with her. What about the crime scene techs?"

Farrantino glanced toward the two young men in CSI jackets. "It's probably going to be another five minutes or so before they can get to her."

"Fine," he said. "I'll see how far I can get." He stepped up to her with a small spiral notepad in his hand. "I'm Detective Ethan Delancey. I hope you feel up to talking for a bit, because I need to ask you a few questions. You are—?"

"I'm—Elaine Montgomery. Laney."

"Okay, Ms. Montgomery. Can you tell me what happened here? Briefly?"

She had closed her eyes and was touching the area

around the bandage the EMTs had applied with her fingertips. "What?"

"What happened?" he repeated.

"A man shot Senator Sills and when I walked in, he sh-shot me."

"Did you see the man shoot the senator?"

Her face seemed to crumple a bit. "No."

"Where was Senator Sills? Was he still alive?" Ethan had barely gotten the question out when Farrantino gestured to him.

He excused himself and walked over to the officer, who handed him a cell phone. "Sills's," she said. "You might be interested in some of his recent calls."

Ethan checked the phone's incoming call log. "'Senator Myron Stamps,'" he read. Then a little farther down, "'The U.S. federal minimum-security prison at Oakdale, Louisiana.'" He looked up at Farrantino. "That's where Congressman Gavin Whitley is. Here." He handed the phone back to her. "Take this and retrieve all the calls and times and the texts as well as voice mails."

"How far back?" Farrantino asked.

"Far as it goes," Ethan said. "Get me the list. We might want to talk with all of them. And set up an interview with Whitley and Stamps *this* morning. I want to find out why they were calling Sills."

"Are you thinking this has something to do with Kate Chalmet's son's kidnapping?"

Ethan thought about his brother Travis, who'd come home to New Orleans eight months before, to find out that he had a son and that the four-year-old had been kidnapped. "Could be. Whitley claimed that it was Sills's money that paid for the kidnapper."

"I remember," Farrantino said, then nodded toward Elaine Montgomery. "The crime scene techs are ready for her."

"What do the EMTs say?" he asked.

"They want her checked out at the E.R. just in case. They think the wound is superficial, but they want a CT scan to rule out internal bleeding."

"Okay. As soon as I'm done here, I'm going by the E.R. to see if I can get in a few more questions. Otherwise it's going to be hours before I can finish with Whitley and Stamps and talk to her again."

As Farrantino gave him a nod and headed toward Laney Montgomery, Ethan's partner returned to his side. "Okay," Dixon said. "We've got a preliminary time of death. The M.E. said he's been dead two, maybe three hours at the most."

"Great. The hotel's been cordoned off and everyone is being questioned. Thankfully there are no conventions or weddings scheduled for today. The only event is—or was—the longshoremen's breakfast, where the senator was scheduled to speak."

"Yeah. Still, I doubt our murderer has been hanging around for hours waiting to see if we can pick him out of a crowd," Dixon said wryly.

"Farrantino is bringing in Myron Stamps for questioning, and arranging with the warden at Oakdale to question Gavin Whitley," Ethan said. "Both of them called Sills within the last couple of days. I want to know exactly where Stamps is now and where he was all evening. And I'm going to get every single phone call and every visitor Whitley has had since he went inside." He didn't have to tell Dixon why he wanted to talk to them.

Dixon nodded. "It must have really rankled to be under indictment like Whitley or facing certain loss in the next election like Stamps, and know that Sills came out of the kidnapping scandal smelling like a rose. I'd be surprised if both of them hadn't wanted to kill Sills. But do you think Whitley could have arranged this from prison?"

"No. I don't think he has the connections or the cojones to set up something like that at all, much less handle it from prison. But we'd better check it out." The two of them stepped aside as the body of Senator Darby Sills was rolled out the door.

"Okay," Ethan said. "I'm going by the hospital to talk with Elaine Montgomery, because I'm probably going to be tied up all morning with those two."

"You know we've got to bring Travis in."

Ethan grimaced. He sure as hell didn't want to make his older brother come in for questioning, especially after everything Travis had been through in the past months. He'd like to give Travis and Kate and their son, Max, time to recover and heal from Travis's months as a hostage and Max's kidnapping ordeal. They needed time to get used to being together, to being a family.

"I know," Ethan said dejectedly. "I'm sure I'll be hearing from the D.A. within the next hour or two, making sure I've questioned him as a person of interest in Sills's death, despite the fact that there was no evidence connecting Sills with the kidnapping. I'll call him in a little while." He looked at his watch. "He'll be up and out on a run by six. Maybe I can be done with him before Farrantino gets Whitley and Stamps set up."

WHEN ETHAN GOT to the emergency room and flashed his badge in order to get in to see Laney Montgomery, he found her lying on a gurney in cubicle three with a bandage on her temple, looking miserable. As he peered in, he saw her wipe her eyes with her fingertips. He stepped in through the curtain. "Hi," he said. "How's your head?"

"Who are you?" she said, sniffling.

"I'm Detective Ethan Delancey. I talked with you for a few minutes at the crime scene."

"Oh, right." She lifted her hand to touch the edges of the bandage. "I'm sorry. This has just been so—" Her voice cracked and her face crumpled. She covered her mouth with her hand.

"Hey," Ethan said, glancing behind him at the closed curtain. He didn't want the nurses to think he'd made her cry, and he sure didn't want her to get so upset that she couldn't talk. He stepped closer to the bed. "You've been through a lot. But everything's going to be okay."

"No it's not." She looked up at the ceiling. "Senator Sills is dead. I had just left him, not five minutes before. I should have—"

Ethan waited, but she bit her lip and didn't continue. "Should have what?" he asked.

She spread her hands helplessly. "I don't know. Been there? Done something?" Her voice was rising in pitch.

He laid his hand on her arm and squeezed reassuringly, then realized what he'd done and snatched it away. "You couldn't have done anything. Not against a gun. If you'd tried, you'd probably be dead now, too.

"What we have to do now is try to catch the person who killed him and bring him to justice."

Laney cut her eyes over to him. "You can catch him, can't you?" she said, as if she were saying *you can leap tall buildings and stop a bullet with your hand, can't you?*

He felt as though he were letting her down just by being human. He smiled at her. "I'm going to do my best," he said. "But to do that, I need to ask you some questions. Do you think you can answer them for me?"

She stared into his eyes. "Yes," she said. "Yes I can."

"Great," he said, reaching out and patting her hand. "You said you'd just left the senator. Where did you go?"

"I went to my room. I was staying in the second bedroom of the penthouse suite. When I went back into the sitting room to check on the senator after I heard the pop, he wasn't sitting in the desk chair. Before I could look for him, I saw the man dressed in black. He spotted me, he lifted his gun and I dived to the floor."

"Was the senator dead or alive at that point?"

She shook her head despairingly. "I don't know. I wasn't able to get to him until the elevator came and the shooter ran out." Her eyes glittered with tears and her hand kept darting up to her temple and stopping a fraction of an inch above the bandage. "Do you think he was lying there alive? Do you think if I'd gotten to him earlier—?"

"You can't worry about that. You were in danger. If you'd tried to get to him, the man could've gotten off a better shot. You could be dead, too. Plus, as good as the technology is, there's no way to pinpoint the second when he died. So let's take it one step at a time. You came in. The figure in black saw you, shot at you. You dived to the floor. How far away was he?"

"I don't know. Ten feet or so?" She closed her eyes. "Why are you asking me all these questions? I told the first officer all this and he wrote it down."

"Why do you think the shooter missed you?"

She frowned. "He didn't miss."

"He barely grazed your temple."

Laney peered at him sidelong. "Maybe he didn't expect me to drop to the floor."

He gave her a little smile. "Did he fire a second time?"

"No, but then you know that. You've got your CSI people and you've got the gun, don't you? And all the bullets are in the wall or the floor?"

"That's right. But he could have fired into a sofa or a pillow or something. So you only heard two—"

The nurse came in, followed by an older man dressed in blue scrubs.

"All right, Ms. Montgomery," the nurse said. "We're going to take you to get a CT scan. It won't take long, but the doctor wants to be sure you don't have an injury inside your brain that could cause bleeding."

"After they finish, I can go home, right?" Laney directed the question to Ethan. Her blue eyes pleaded with him.

"No. I'm afraid not," Ethan said. "One of the officers will take you to the police station as soon as the hospital releases you." He caught himself before he asked her if there was someone she'd like to call. That was a reflexive statement he used with witnesses all the time.

He hadn't been here ten minutes and he'd made a serious mistake. He'd been way too nice to her—way too sympathetic. He needed to start asking the tough questions. Because he didn't know what had happened in that suite yet. For the moment, Elaine Montgomery was playing three roles in this murder case—witness, victim and possible suspect.

MORE THAN FOUR hours later, Ethan looked through a two-way mirror at Laney Montgomery. She looked sad and miserable and bored. He couldn't blame her. He'd left her at the E.R. at around six o'clock, which meant she'd been here at the police station, waiting for him, for four hours. Her face and neck still weren't completely clean of blood, and a small dark spot on the bandage told him the graze on her temple was still bleeding a little. He had the EMT's report and he'd just printed out the E.R. doctor's assessment of her and the results of the CT scan. Her injury was minor. It was going to be painful for a few days, but there was no internal bleeding or damage.

As if she'd read his thoughts, she lifted her gaze to the mirror and glared at him. Or that's the impression he had. It felt as though she was staring right into his eyes, although he knew she couldn't see him through the two-way mirror. She knew he was there, though. He could see it in her suspicious gaze. He glanced away as if they'd held each other's gazes too long.

She closed her eyes and rubbed her temple gingerly, just below the edge of the bandage. Her expression changed to a wince. She looked at her fingernails, then began picking at one with a thumbnail. Even from this far away, Ethan could see the tiny leftover stains from the fingerprint ink.

He ran a hand over his face, feeling the day's growth of beard. He'd been running ever since he'd gotten the call at four o'clock this morning. By the time he'd gotten back to the station from the hotel, Travis was there, waiting to be interviewed. Then he'd taken a few minutes to review the reports from the crime scene unit, the first officer on the scene and the medical examiner, before spending almost an hour bringing Commander Jeff Wharton up to speed. He and Dixon had just finished questioning Myron Stamps and Gavin Whitley, a process that had taken over two hours, not a pleasant experience. Stamps had shown up with his lawyer. The phone call with Whitley had been a three-way, involving his attorney. Ethan's jaw ached from gritting his teeth while nearly every question he or Dixon asked was parried by their shysters.

As Dixon came into the viewing room, Laney yawned. She covered her mouth with her hand, even though there was no one in the room with her. Then she winced and patted the bandage with her fingertips again.

"She's had a long night," Dixon commented.

"She's not the only one," Ethan said, suppressing a yawn of his own. "Where'd you run off to?"

"I ran down to the lab to see what the crime scene techs found outside the penthouse service door and on the stairs."

"What'd they find?"

Dixon pulled out a notepad. "Black scuff marks, probably made by leather- or synthetic-soled shoes. Not rubber. A few fibers of black fleece, like from a sweatshirt or hoodie. That's about it. No indication of how long they might have been there."

"Fingerprints?"

"They dusted the service door's handle and the railing at the top of the fire stairs, but didn't get anything except some smudges that probably came from the shooter's gloves. There was gunshot residue in the smudges."

"That's something, I guess."

Dixon shrugged. "They're not finished with the penthouse suite or Laney Montgomery's room yet, but there's nothing conclusive."

Ethan turned to look at him. "Anything on the gun or bullets?"

He nodded. "The gun is untraceable—big surprise. The bullets were fired from the gun that was found at the scene. The partial print on the gun barrel hasn't been through the system yet."

"What did you think about Whitley and Stamps?"

"I think they're telling the truth, at least about where they were last night," Dixon said.

"You know, Stamps is kind of pitiful, isn't he? I mean

his wife's dead, and they never had any children. Apparently he's got no one except a housekeeper."

Dixon nodded. "It's hard not to believe him, isn't it? Home by himself. Can't say whether his housekeeper can vouch for him because she went to bed early with a headache."

"Yeah," Ethan agreed. "That was either a sad but honest accounting of his lonely evening at home or a truly clever way to avoid having to depend on someone lying for him. The housekeeper went to bed early, therefore she can't say if he was there or not."

"I think I do believe him. He seems as though the kidnapping and his trial have taken all the starch out of him."

"And I guess Whitley's alibi is solid," Ethan said wryly, his eyes on Laney as she uncrossed her legs, recrossed them and pulled her raincoat more tightly around her.

"I don't like him a bit—and that goes double for his lawyer."

"Pretty slick, aren't they?" Ethan sighed. "But unless Whitley got his attorney to come over here and pop Sills, I'm not sure how he could be involved. At least we know he was where he says he was."

"I wouldn't believe Whitley if he told me his name was Whitley," Dixon said. "But no matter what I think, those alibis are good. Still, that doesn't mean one or both of them couldn't have hired someone."

"Stamps doesn't have any money—or at least none we know about. And like I said, I can't see Whitley."

He thought about something. "Who went through their financial records during the kidnapping case?"

"No idea, but I'm going to check," Dixon said. "Seems like I heard that Whitley had a couple of big deposits and payouts that matched the time frame of the kidnapping. That's when Whitley tried to implicate Sills, but the forensic accountants couldn't find any proof of where the money came from."

"The amounts matched exactly the amount of money that Bentley Woods deposited in Chicago. With all Whitley's whining about Sills, I'll bet the senator's records were subpoenaed, too," Dixon responded. "No sense reinventing the wheel, if they're already there in the case file."

"Good point. You want to check on that?" Ethan asked.

"Yep. And you're going to tackle Elaine Montgomery," Dixon said, not a question.

Ethan nodded toward the glass. "I'm going to find out what she's holding back."

"Holding back?" Dixon asked him. "What do you think she's holding back on?"

"I don't know, but I can see it in her eyes. She's hiding something."

"You can see it in her eyes," Dixon said, his voice sounding choked, as if he were trying to suppress a laugh. "Those big blue ones?"

"Bite me," Ethan muttered.

"Come on Delancey. You've seen her for what, maybe ten minutes total, and now you can read her mind?" He paused before continuing. "Or maybe it's not her mind you're interested in. Last night you were all about her legs."

"Don't be crass. She's our only witness *and* she's a victim. Look at her." Ethan gestured toward the glass as Laney wet her lips, then clamped a hand tightly over her mouth as if she were holding back tears or a scream as she stared into space. "There's something on her mind and it's not just the murder of her boss."

"She looks nervous, but lots of people are terrified of being questioned by the police."

"Nope. She's hiding something," Ethan muttered, his gaze still on her. After a moment, he said to Dixon, "So what are you up to now?"

"You don't want to double-team her like we did Whitley and Stamps?" Dixon pressed.

"No," Ethan said with exaggerated patience. "I think I can handle her alone."

"Okay, if you're sure. One thing I'm going to do is check with the CSI folks about what they've pulled from the hotel room. I'm afraid we're not going to have much, if all the guy did was sneak in, pop the senator, try to take her out, then hightail it out of there. We'll probably be lucky to get anything other than what was found on the fire stairs. Then I'll get started on pulling the Chalmet kidnapping file and see what they got on Sills."

"Okay. I'll talk to you later then."

"Watch yourself in there," Dixon said as he left.

Ethan stepped out of the viewing room and into the interview room.

Laney Montgomery looked up from inspecting her fingernails. "You know, I was printed when I started work for Senator Sills," she said, holding up her hands, palms out. "I tried to tell them but nobody would listen to me."

Ethan sat down without speaking.

"In case you're not familiar with state government policy," she went on, "employees of any public official are required to be fingerprinted. My prints are on file, here and with the FBI."

Ethan picked up one of the folders he'd brought into the room with him and paged through it. "According to the information I have, you're not a government employee. You're an independent contractor working directly for Senator Sills."

"I still had to declare my allegiance to the United States and to Louisiana and be fingerprinted and photographed before I could go to work for him. About thirty seconds of listening to me could have saved the police department about a pint of ink," she finished drily.

Ethan looked back at the page in front of him, waiting to see what she would say next.

She glanced around the room, then looked at the mirror. "Is everyone else staying in there to watch?" she asked, nodding toward the mirror.

"In there?" Ethan asked.

The look she sent him was equal parts disgust and irritation. A "you don't think I'm that dumb, do you?" expression. "The room behind the mirror."

"Nobody's in there now," he said as he sat down in a wooden straight-backed chair and tipped it backward onto two legs. He watched her.

She sat silent for a few moments, casting about for

something to settle her gaze on, then she looked directly at him. "What?" she said.

He raised his eyebrows.

"Stop trying to make me say something by being silent."

He lowered the front legs of the chair to the floor. He liked that she wasn't easily rattled. But he wasn't fooled by her outburst. She'd turned a favorite tactic of his back onto him. Break a silence with a noncommittal comment or an attack on the other person. But he knew how to play this game. "Okay. I'll stop being quiet. Is there something you want to tell me?"

Her gaze stayed on his face and her mouth turned up slightly. "No. Is there something you want to tell me?"

Chapter Two

Ethan was startled, and intrigued. With those few words, Elaine Montgomery had managed to turn his tactic around again. She was on a mission to stay in control, to manipulate him. Well, it wasn't going to work. This interview was not going to be easy, but it was definitely going to be interesting. He liked a challenge, and Laney Montgomery was definitely a challenge.

"Sure," he said. "I introduced myself earlier at the emergency room, but I think you might have been given something for pain. So in case you don't remember, I'm Detective Ethan—"

"I remember," she said flatly. "You were nicer then."

"Delancey," he went on as if she hadn't interrupted. "My partner, Dixon Lloyd, and I responded to the murder of Senator Darby Sills this morning."

"Detective Delancey, how long are you going to keep me here?"

He stood and stepped toward her, then propped his hip on the edge of the table, his thigh less than two inches away from her right hand. "It won't be too long. I just want to expand on our earlier discussion. Why don't you go through what happened from the moment you heard the noise from the sitting room? You told me that you walked in on the murderer within a couple of minutes of the sound of the first shot."

She scooted her chair away from him and turned it toward him. "It was probably no more than twenty-five seconds," she corrected.

"Twenty-five seconds," Ethan said, jotting a note. "So what did the suspect do once he'd shot the senator?"

"During that twenty-five seconds? I don't know. I was opening the door and going into the sitting room."

Ethan sighed. He appreciated, but didn't like, her type of witness. She wouldn't let any fact slip by. Her account would be as accurate as she could make it. She wouldn't voice any assumptions either, unless he specifically asked her to. "Fine. What did he do when he or she saw you?"

"He, I think, judging by his build. He was thin, but that was about all I could tell in the dark. He turned toward me, lifted his gun hand and shot me."

Ethan knew the answers to a lot of these questions, from the officers on the scene, from the crime scene unit and from the few seconds he'd talked with Laney earlier, but he wanted to hear her version. "Right or left hand?"

"Right hand."

"And what did you do?"

"I saw the gun and hit the floor," she said, touching the bandage gingerly. "Not quite fast enough, though."

"So you didn't actually see him pull the trigger."

"No, technically that's true." She lifted her gaze to

his and lifted one brow. "But I would like to go on record as saying that I believe the same man who shot the senator shot me."

Ethan laughed at Laney's statement of the obvious. "Thanks for that insight, but that's not what I'm asking. My question is, did he fire the weapon with one hand or did he support his gun hand with his other?"

"I have absolutely no idea," she responded. "I wasn't looking at him when he shot me. Why would that even matter?"

"Mannerisms. Sometimes we can eliminate people based on how they handle a gun."

"When he first raised his hand, he just held the gun out, like this." She demonstrated. "Then I dived, he shot and I felt a burning pain here." She indicated the bandage.

Ethan waited a couple seconds, but she didn't continue. "What happened then?"

"My face was flat against the floor, my eyes were closed and my head was throbbing. At first, I was sure the shot had gone right through my skull. I expected a second bullet." She blinked and a small shudder vibrated through her shoulders. "But he didn't shoot again. I heard him walking toward me," she said, clasping her hands tightly together. "I heard one step, then two, then three. I knew he was coming to check me, to be sure I was dead. I remember praying, *Dear Lord, I don't want to die.*"

Ethan hadn't taken his gaze off her. Her eyes glistened with tears. Her fingertips and knuckles were white. She had believed that moment would be her last.

He didn't speak. He waited for her to compose herself and get back to her description of what had happened.

With a small shrug, she said, "Then the elevator bell rang."

"The elevator?" Ethan echoed. She'd caught him off guard. He'd still been with her, in that awful endless moment when she'd feared dying. He'd been there, luckily only once or twice. But he'd known that helpless, hopeless fear. "What did the killer do?"

"He stopped and listened. I did, too. I was holding my breath. I mean, I didn't know who was on the elevator. It could have been somebody from the hotel staff or his accomplice. Who had access to the penthouse?" She suppressed a shudder. "Then I heard those shoes again."

"Those shoes?"

"What?" She seemed unaware of what she'd said. "Oh. Shoes. Right. His shoes sounded funny on the hardwood floor."

"Funny how?"

She gave him a puzzled look. "I'm not sure." Her voice held a tone of incredulity. Obviously, she wasn't used to being flummoxed.

"Come on, Elaine. You noticed them. Try to remember why."

Laney closed her eyes for a few seconds, then shook her head. "I don't know. They sounded—" she spread her hands out in front of her "—hollow? No. That's not quite right."

Ethan wrote down what she'd said, then looked up. "What does that mean? Hollow?"

"I don't know. I can't explain it."

"Okay. You were saying he headed the other way when the elevator bell rang. Which way?"

She closed her eyes again, then lifted a hand and pointed toward the left. "That way, toward the service door. When I opened my eyes my head started hurting and I must have moaned, because he turned back around and pointed his gun at me again. That's when the elevator doors started to open. He stood perfectly still for a second or two, like he was trying to decide whether to shoot me or run." She barked a soft, wry laugh. "He ran. Out the service door."

"He dropped the gun as he took off?"

She nodded. "Oh, and he was wobbly." She held her hands out and waggled them side-to-side. "The way he ran. Awkward, like he was about to fall down."

"Wobbly," Ethan repeated. "Had he tripped? Maybe hurt an ankle or twisted a knee?"

"No. I didn't notice anything like that. He just seemed unsteady on his feet."

Disappointed, he wrote down "wobbly and awkward." If the shooter had an injury, it might make him easier to find.

"The gun was found about halfway between the senator's body and the service door, and about seven feet away from you. Why did he drop it?" It was one of those things he couldn't figure out. Why leave the gun there? It didn't make sense. It telegraphed to anyone who cared to think about it that the piece would be untraceable. But there was no logical reason for the shooter to have abandoned it.

"I don't know."

"So who was on the elevator?" he asked her.

"A bellman carrying a bottle of Dewar's. Obviously, as soon as I left the room the senator called down and ordered it. I tried to tell the bellman that the killer was getting away, but my voice wouldn't work right. He saw me, though, and tried to help me." Her fingers went to the bandage. "I pointed toward the desk and told him to help the senator, but he was all freaked out by the blood, so I crawled over to the senator's body, and yelled at the bellman to call the police."

"You told him to call the police?" Ethan said. "Apparently he called hotel security instead."

"Did he?" she asked. "Oh. That's right. The security guard did show up first."

Ethan went back to his chair again. "Tell me more about the shooter. You said he was thin. What else? What did he look like? What did he have on?"

"He was about my height, thin and bony and dressed all in black. Had a black ski mask that covered his whole head. He was holding the gun—until he dropped it on the floor."

"Did you pick up the weapon or touch it in any way?"

"No," Laney said. "I know better than that. I've watched my share of *Law & Order*." Her hand went up to push her hair back, but her fingers skimmed the bandage and she grimaced.

Ethan scowled to himself. She was a little too sure of herself, a little too proud of what she knew. He'd love to tell her that about eighty percent of what she saw on *Law & Order* was as fictional as the names of the characters. But despite the fact that she got her forensic knowledge from a police procedural TV show, she was pretty smart. And despite the seriousness of the situation and his growing irritation at her attitude, he was fascinated by her. She had a confidence and a quick intelligence that he thought he'd like a lot under a different circumstance. For instance, if they were dating.

Forcing his attention back to the questioning, he watched her as he said, "But you did move the body, didn't you?"

She started and brows shot up. "I did," she said. "I'd almost forgotten. I touched his shoulder and turned him onto his back. I shouldn't have done that, I guess."

While he let her think about that mistake, he consulted the statement of the first officer on the scene as well as his own notes. "Officer Young said you recognized something about the suspect?"

"I recognized something he was wearing," she corrected deliberately.

Ethan leaned back in his chair again. "What was that? I thought you said he was all in black."

"I did. But right before he ran, when he turned back toward me, something caught the light. It was a belt buckle. It looked like silver, but it was big. I only saw part of it. It looked like his shirt was covering more than half of it, but it reminded me of the belt that televangelist guy wears. The guy that always dresses in black. He's got that cowboy hat with the little silver things on it."

Ethan paged to the officer's report of his interview with her at the scene. She had told him essentially the same thing. He considered what she'd said and what was written in the statement. It was the closest she'd come to an outright lie. He'd bet next month's salary that she knew exactly who Buddy Davis was. "So are you saying the killer was wearing a Buddy Davis Silver Circle belt buckle?"

"Buddy Davis. That's him. Like I said, I didn't get but a glimpse of it, but that's what it looked like to me," she said, then narrowed her gaze. "But it couldn't have been Buddy Davis. He wouldn't kill anybody, would he?"

Behind the narrowed gaze, Ethan saw that look again. That guarded caution. Combined with pretending that she didn't know who Buddy Davis was, it made him suspicious. Was she holding back something about the killer? Something about the belt buckle or about something else he'd been wearing? "I don't know. People are never predictable. The question is, do you think he would? Do you think it was Buddy Davis in that room?"

Laney looked down at the table. With one neat, unpainted fingernail, she traced a scratch in the scarred surface. "The guy was thin. But I can't really tell you anything else about him."

"Any other distinguishing marks? Did you recognize anything about the man?"

"If you mean about his appearance? No. I don't think so."

"What did you think when you first saw the buckle?"

"I guess my first thought was Buddy Davis, but I didn't consciously think, *Oh, I wonder if that was Buddy Davis that just killed Senator Sills.*"

"Have you ever met Davis?"

She pressed her lips together again. "I have. Yes."

"Where?"

Her fingernail traced the scratch again and she spoke without looking up. "He and Senator Sills are—were friends. Everybody knows that. They golfed together about once every week or two."

Ethan was becoming more fascinated and more irritated with her every minute. Everything she said sounded perfectly reasonable, but it was obvious that she considered the consequences of every word she said first. He was more convinced than ever that she knew more than she was telling him. A lot more.

Now if he could only break through her confident demeanor and figure out what she was so carefully hiding from him. Would mentioning her father put a crack in that mask? "What about your father. Elliott Montgomery, right? He knew Senator Sills, didn't he? Isn't that how you got your job?"

Now she was the one caught off guard. And irritated at his implication. After a slight pause, she spoke. "My father. I wondered how long it would take before you brought him up. I assume you know he died last year. Heart attack."

Ethan remembered, now that she'd mentioned it. "I'm sorry."

"Thank you. But to answer your question, yes. He and Senator Sills had known each other for years."

"Were they friends?"

Her face shut down. If he had not been certain before that she was not telling him everything, he certainly was now. He waited for her answer.

"I don't think 'friends' is the word my father would use."

"What word would he use?"

Her gaze snapped to his. "What?"

He knew she'd heard him. He didn't answer.

"I don't know," she said finally. "Acquaintance? Business colleague?"

"Enemy?"

"No," she said quickly. "Why would you say that?"

He changed direction. "Did your father know Buddy Davis?"

"I'm sure they'd met, at least," she said. "I don't remember Davis ever coming to our house. And I don't remember ever seeing them together."

Nice. Clever, evasive answer. Ethan almost smiled at her sheer audacity. "So is that a yes or a no?" he persisted.

She looked at him in silence for a moment and he could see the wheels turning in her brain. "It's a probably," she said.

She was good. He had to give her that. He had to admire her careful consideration of every question before answering. No assumptions. No guesses. What could he do with a probably? He had to act on it. He picked up his phone and pressed a button.

"Farrantino here," a brisk female voice said.

"Hey. Get Buddy Davis in here for questioning," he said. "ASAP."

There was a pause. "Buddy Davis?" Farrantino repeated. "The evangelist? That Buddy Davis?"

"That's the one. Problem?"

"No, sir." Farrantino's crisp tone was back. "I'll get right on it."

Ethan hung up. Laney had listened with unabashed interest.

"You're going to bring him in and question him just based on something I think I saw for about half a second?"

Ethan assessed her. "You think I shouldn't?"

"No. I mean, no, I don't think you shouldn't. I just—"

He waited.

She moistened her lips. "I don't know if I could swear that the logo was Davis's. I only saw a corner, maybe a little more. It did look like it, though."

He didn't comment. He just went on with his questioning. "So the killer, who had heard the elevator and wanted to get away, turned around enough that you could see a big gaudy belt buckle he was wearing?"

Laney shot him a suspicious glance, probably because of the tone of his voice. He hadn't meant to let his skepticism show, but maybe it wasn't a bad thing that she wondered if he believed her.

"Yes," she said shortly.

"Why?"

"He didn't say."

Ethan pressed his lips together, partly in irritation, partly to hide his smile. "Why do you think?"

"I think he was wondering if he had time to shoot me again."

"Hmm. Apparently he decided he didn't."

"Apparently."

"So what happened next?"

"Like I told you, he ran out the door and the bellman came in and called the police—well, hotel security—for me."

"Right," Ethan said. "And why was that?"

"Why was what?" she echoed, genuinely puzzled.

"Why him? Why didn't you call?" Ethan watched her. She was looking at her hands, and she seemed more at ease, now that they had left the subject of her father and Buddy Davis and were back to talking about what had happened.

"I was trying to get to the senator, to see if he was alive, so I yelled at the bellman to call."

"Didn't you have your phone with you?"

She shook her head. "No, I didn't," she said with exaggerated patience. "As I told the officer at the hotel, I'd left it on the computer table in the sitting room. I was trying to make myself get up and go back in there to get it when I heard the pop."

"The pop?" Ethan knew what she was talking about, but he wanted to hear her tell it. He'd read the hotel reports from the hotel's security guard and the first responding officer.

"You know, Detective, this might go a lot faster if you'd stop trying to trip me up. I've been over the pop I heard through the connecting door, too. I'm sure it's in the first responding officer's report." She gestured toward the folder open in front of him.

"I'm not trying to trip you up. And yes, the officer mentioned the sound you heard. But I'm asking you the question. I'm going to be asking you about a lot of things you've already told other people."

Her brows went up. "Yes, sir. Understood, sir," she said. "I heard the pop, so I got up to check on the senator. Then I—"

"Hang on. What did you think it was?"

"The pop?" She shook her head.

"You had an opinion about what you thought it was. Tell me."

"I'd rather not say," she replied. "It's not relevant."

"You let me decide what's relevant," Ethan said. "You just tell me."

She glared at him, but answered. "It was loud, but for a second I thought it might be a cork. Senator Sills enjoys a scotch now and then."

Ethan took mental note of the wry tone of her voice. "Did you hear anything else?"

She nodded, then winced. "A thud, as if something had fallen."

"And what did you think that was?"

"At the time I didn't know. But obviously it was when the senator fell."

"What time was that?"

"I'm not sure." She paused. "Don't the electronic locks on the rooms keep track of entries and exits by room number and time?" she asked.

Ethan smiled to himself. He liked the way she thought. Her attention to detail. His estimate of her level of intelligence kept going up. She was extremely smart. Irritatingly smart. Strangely enough, he liked that about her. "They can, but the hotel doesn't have that function turned on. The security guard said it would be cost-prohibitive to hire enough people to handle the amount of data all the comings and goings would dump into the computer."

"That's too bad. I can't imagine how the killer timed his attack on the senator so perfectly. I had just left the suite after making the last changes to the breakfast speech."

"I was wondering the same thing," Ethan replied evenly. He met her gaze.

She frowned. "You don't—oh, come on," she said, exasperated. "You don't think I'm involved in this? That's ridiculous. Senator Sills was my boss."

Ethan shrugged, watching her closely. Truth was, he didn't think she'd had anything to do with killing the senior senator. It was another attempt to catch her off guard. He wanted her rattled. Rattled and talking. "You surprised the killer, but he didn't kill you. He left you alive, knowing you might be able to identify him."

"He left me alive because someone was coming. But he knows I can't identify him. He was covered from head to toe in black. He *shot me*. Why would he do that if I were involved?"

"Maybe *he* wasn't there at all. Maybe you made him up."

"Oh, give me a break. You cannot be serious." She glared at him.

Ethan just watched her.

Her expression changed from irritation to surprise to frustration. She spread her hands. "Okay, then. I guess I'm getting the picture. So tell me, Detective. Am I under arrest? Should I have a lawyer? And don't bother telling me that if I was innocent I wouldn't need one.

You might not think much of police shows on TV, but they do teach people a few things, like exercising their right to an attorney."

Finally, she was agitated. Her cautious demeanor was cracked. Ethan was glad. The confident, controlled person he'd seen in the hotel room and who'd walked into the interview room as if it belonged to her was gone, and in her place was a woman who had at the very least witnessed a murder and whose protective wall was cracking, piece by piece. And he knew—he *knew*—that he was getting closer to what she was hiding.

"I wouldn't dream of telling you that innocent people don't need lawyers. But you aren't under arrest. You are the victim of a crime and its only witness. You don't need a lawyer. I don't think you had anything to do with the senator's death. I do, however, think you're not telling me everything—"

"Why wouldn't I tell you everything?" she interrupted, spreading her hands. "I have nothing to hide."

"Really?" Ethan said, leaning back in his chair. "I think you do. I asked you before if your father's relationship with Sills was the reason Sills hired you. You didn't answer, but it's true, isn't it? The daughter of the infamous Elliott Montgomery, who lobbied for the Port of New Orleans Import/Export Council for over forty years, happens to be hired as Senator Darby Sills's personal assistant? How likely is that?"

A muscle ticked in her jaw for an instant, then she took a deep breath and let it out in a sigh. Then a little smirk quirked her lips. "Oh, come on, Detective *Delancey*. Nepotism has been a long and honored tradition in Louisiana. You of all people should know that. It has worked for generations without undue harm to anyone. Senator Sills was kind enough to let me intern with him for a year while I was getting my master's in political science." Her shoulders straightened. "He was pleased with my work, so he hired me. I don't see anything wrong with that."

Ethan gave her a hint of a smile. "Neither do I," he said.

She raised her brows. "Then what was all that?"

"Just demonstrating how you aren't telling me everything." He spent a few moments perusing his notes, not that he needed to. He wanted to keep her hanging for a little while, to demonstrate that he had the upper hand. Finally, he asked, "Is there anything else about the killer that you noticed?"

"No. I don't think so. The desk lamp was the only light, so the room was pretty dark. And of course he was in solid black."

"Not solid black," Ethan reminded her.

"No," she said, looking at him assessingly. "You're right. There was that belt buckle."

"Why do you think a killer who worked so hard to hide himself would put on something as distinctive as a Buddy Davis silver belt buckle?"

Laney shook her head. "I don't know, maybe to frame him."

Excellent guess. "But you're absolutely certain that's what you saw? You would swear under oath that it was one of Buddy Davis's solid silver belt buckles?"

"I told you, I'm not that certain. I thought the glimpse I got looked like one of them, but I can't swear to it."

"What *would* you swear to under oath?"

She shrugged. "I guess I'd say that I saw a large, oval silver belt buckle. I only saw it for a second and didn't see the whole thing because the man's shirt was covering it. I did see what looked like an engraved arc—possibly part of a circle, and an image inside the arc that looked like the edge of a crown. So if it wasn't Buddy Davis's Silver Circle belt buckle, it certainly bore a strong resemblance."

"That's about as precise a description as I've ever heard, even from experts," Ethan said, and meant it. She was an excellent witness. Irritating, but excellent.

"As Kate Hepburn said to Spencer Tracy in *Desk Set*, 'never assume.'"

"What? Desk set?"

Laney waved her hand. "Never mind. My dad loved the really old movies and the older TV shows, so I know way too much about them."

Ethan had never heard of the movie and he doubted seriously that it mattered, so he went on with his next question. "Describe what you did and what you saw when you crawled over to check on the senator."

"I was hoping he'd done what I had—dived to the floor, hidden under the desk, something. But—" She shook her head and a shadow crossed her face. "He was dead."

"Did you touch him?"

She nodded, pressing her lips together. Ethan noticed that her eyes shone with tears. "Yes. I turned him over to see where he'd been shot. But as I said before, his eyes were…dead."

"Then what did you do?"

"I listened to see if I could hear him breathing, and I felt his neck, trying to find his carotid pulse. By that time the security guard was there. Almost no time later, the police officers showed up, and then you." She spread her hands as if to show him that she had nothing else.

Ethan watched her thoughtfully, letting the silence stretch, as he had earlier. He waited to see if she'd break the silence this time, because, while he had no idea if the information she was guarding so closely had anything to do with the murder of Senator Sills, he knew with a hundred-percent certainty that she was still holding back.

After a few moments, she looked at her watch. "It's after noon. I need to call the senator's family. I have to tell them—"

"That's been taken care of," he said with a wave of his hand. She'd broken the spell of silence without revealing anything—again. She was good. He'd like to have her on his team in a fight.

"What is your precise position on Senator Sills's staff?"

She fixed him with a frosty glare. "My *precise position* is personal assistant to Senator Sills."

Ethan nodded and jotted "personal assistant" on his pad. "And what are your duties as the senator's personal assistant?"

If possible, the glare turned even colder. Had he sounded sarcastic?

"Pretty much what you'd expect. I wake him up every morning, make sure his meals are to his liking and on time. I type up his personal correspondence, update his social media pages, keep up with his appointment calendar and his committee schedules, and—"

"So you're his secretary."

Her shoulders stiffened. "No. He has a secretary. She works in Baton Rouge. I travel—traveled with him wherever he went."

"Okay. You're more of an administrator."

"I suppose you could say that. I do a lot of administrative work. I also edit the memos and letters the secretary sends over for his signature, and often, I stamp them with his signature stamp. Especially all the congressional letters we send out in response to constituent problems."

"You also travel with him and stay with him?"

Ethan hadn't figured her shoulders could get any more stiff, but she managed it. "Many of my duties are last-minute. So yes, I generally will stay in an adjoining room near him in case he needs something in the middle of the night."

"What kind of things did Senator Sills need in the middle of the night?"

Now she was becoming visibly angry. "Last night he worked on his speech until after eleven o'clock," she said through gritted teeth. "So I didn't finish typing the last revision until after midnight. Then—"

The door to the interview room opened and Ethan's partner stepped inside, smiling in a friendly manner.

"Afternoon, Ms. Montgomery. I'm Detective Dixon Lloyd."

Elaine Montgomery gave Dixon a smile like nothing he'd seen from her yet. "Nice to meet you. Please call me Laney. You must be Good Cop, because Detective Delancey here is definitely Bad Cop."

"You have no idea," Dixon said.

At the same time, Ethan asked loudly, "What's up, Dixon?"

Dixon handed him a file folder. "We got the report back on the weapon that killed Senator Sills. There's a partial print on the barrel. Probably not enough for a positive ID. It could be marginally helpful along with other evidence."

"Did they check it against Ms. Montgomery's prints?"

Dixon nodded. "First thing. No match."

"I didn't touch the gun," she said.

"And therefore your prints were not found on it," Ethan said evenly.

"You want me to stay and play good cop?" Dixon asked, obviously noticing the tension between them.

"No," Ethan said firmly.

At the same time, Laney said, "Yes."

"Okay, I'm going," Dixon said on a laugh, reaching for the doorknob. "Oh," he said, reaching into his pocket and coming out with a piece of paper. "Here's a note I was told to give to you." He handed it to Ethan.

Ethan skimmed it. "Is he serious?" The note was from Commander Wharton. He wanted an in-person report from Ethan about the Whitley and Stamps interviews. "He should have the transcriptions on his desk by now."

Dixon shrugged. "I'm just the messenger."

"Did he ask you to come, too?"

Dixon shook his head.

"That figures. I suspect his real question will be if I've interviewed Travis." Ethan sighed. "Wait for me outside, will you, Dix?" Ethan said.

He turned to Laney. "Despite my partner's amusement, this is a very serious matter, Ms. Montgomery," Ethan said. "I realize that you are a victim, just like Senator Sills, but you're also the only witness to his murder. I don't have to tell you how much publicity is going to be surrounding this case, especially in light of Congressman Whitley's involvement in the kidnapping of Max Chalmet."

"Oh, you certainly don't have to tell me anything about that, Detective *Delancey*. I read the paper. I'm perfectly aware of the latest scandal involving the Delanceys."

Ethan bristled. "The *scandal* didn't involve the Delanceys. The scandal was the kidnapping plan cooked up by Gavin Whitley, who by the way did his best to implicate your boss."

"Congressman Whitley was mistaken. Senator Sills had nothing to do with that."

"And you would know because—?"

"I know because I'm—" She paused. "I was his personal assistant."

"The fact that you worked for him isn't proof that

he wasn't involved in the kidnapping. You say you know. How?"

"I handled all his correspondence. All of his phone calls go through me."

"All?" Ethan laughed. "Can you prove that?"

"I—" She stopped and Ethan knew she'd gotten to the place where he'd been ever since she'd said *I know because*— Of course she couldn't prove it.

Ethan pushed back his chair and got up.

"Oh, good. Are we done now?" Laney asked, sliding her chair backward. "Because I have a lot to do. There is a checklist a mile long that includes who all is to be notified, who is to be invited to the wake and to the funeral, *where* the wake and funeral are to be, how the family should be brought in—"

Ethan held up a hand to stop her. "I get the picture. Are you the only one who manages all that?"

"No. I believe the office of the governor and the office of the president of the senate handle most of it, but they'll be calling me—in fact, I'll need my phone."

"Nope. You're not going anywhere or making or receiving phone calls until I'm finished with you, and right now I've got to go see my commanding officer. So while I'm gone, I need you to write out your duties as Senator Sills's personal assistant, and write an accounting of your and the senator's time from the moment you got to the hotel."

Laney's shoulders stiffened. "Then I'll ask you again. Am I under arrest?"

"No," he said, "but I would rather you didn't leave."

She looked at him, irritation evident in those eyes again, but she didn't speak.

"If I think of anything else I'll have one of the officers let you know," Ethan said as he opened the door and left the room.

Chapter Three

"What do you need, Delancey?" Dixon asked after Ethan closed the door to the interview room. "I'm late. I've got officers on the way to Sills's home to confiscate all his personal records. We're still waiting to hear from the court order filed with the bank."

"Did you check the Chalmet kidnapping case file to see if they already requested his bank records?"

"Yep. We got his checking and savings accounts and CD records. What we're waiting on is access to the safe-deposit box."

"Good," Ethan said.

"So has she mentioned anything about Sills having trouble with anyone or receiving threats from anyone?"

"Not yet, but then, I only started questioning her." Ethan rubbed his eyes. "But I've got to tell you, I'm not happy about the names that have already popped up."

"What names?"

"You know who she is?"

"Yeah. Elaine—Montgomery."

Ethan nodded grimly.

"Wait a minute. Montgomery—" Dixon frowned. "Her father wasn't the lobbyist—?"

"Yep. Elliott Montgomery."

"So the lobbyist's daughter is working for a prominent state senator who's been known to be influenced by the large interests represented by the Port of New Orleans lobbyists and unions," Dixon said.

"And who just got murdered. Yeah. But that's not the biggest shocker," Ethan replied.

"It isn't? What else have you got?"

"Did you talk to her at the crime scene? Or anywhere?"

"No. I left her to you. I've been dealing with the mundane, day-to-day stuff."

"Yeah, well, it serves you right. You're married. You *shouldn't* be talking to pretty young witnesses."

"What about the big shocker?"

"Right. Get this. According to her, the man who shot Sills was wearing a great big silver belt buckle. She saw it when it reflected the light. Want to guess what she saw on it?"

"No." Dixon grimaced.

"A crown and circle."

Dixon stared at him. "Please tell me you're kidding me."

"Not even a little bit. She claims a patch of bright silver caught the light. She only caught a glimpse of it but she's sure she saw a part of a circle and the corner of a crown."

Dixon pushed his fingers through his hair. "Is she willing to testify to that?"

Ethan shook his head. "I don't know. She's sure of what she saw, but she only saw part of the buckle. The rest was obscured, apparently by the shirt. A really good defense attorney could probably make her look at worst like a liar and at best, like that graze on her temple is causing hallucinations."

"What do you think? Think she really saw that belt? Delancey, do you think Buddy Davis shot Senator Sills?"

"I don't know," Ethan said. "But I know what I've got to do. I've sent Farrantino to pick up Buddy Davis and bring him in for questioning. I'm not looking forward to that. Talk about a media circus."

Dixon smirked. "You sent Farrantino? I'd love to be a fly on the wall when she confronts Davis. Everybody in the state knows his reputation for *paying attention to* pretty women."

Officer Maria Farrantino was tall and lithe, with long black hair. Even with her hair pulled back and dressed in the androgynous police uniform, she was a knockout. "I figured he might come in just to get to ride in the car with her," Ethan said. "But do not tell her I said that."

"Did you warn her to watch out?"

"Didn't get a chance," Ethan said.

"Like hell you didn't. Oh, she's never going to forgive you. It should be interesting with Davis and his wife together in the car. I don't think I'll stick around for the fireworks—Benita Davis's or Farrantino's." Dixon checked his watch. "I've got to get going," Dixon said.

"Yeah, and I've got to go tell the commander what he's already read on the transcribed interviews," Ethan said on a frustrated sigh. "Let me know if you find anything interesting in Sills's house, like records of blackmail or proof that he bought or sold votes in the legislature."

Dixon laughed. "Right. You'll be the first to know."

LANEY MONTGOMERY DIVIDED her attention between the door through which Detective Ethan Delancey had just disappeared and the mirror on the wall in front of her. She wondered how many people were standing on the other side of that mirror, watching her. Then she wondered just how paranoid she was to think that. Still, she figured there was one person in there at least—the handsome, arrogant detective.

She wondered if the "note" Good Cop had given him was real, or just an excuse to let him get out of the room for a few minutes.

She had a childish urge to stick her tongue out— maybe even stick her thumbs in her ears and waggle her fingers. But Detective Delancey apparently already thought she was hilarious. She hadn't missed him suppressing a smile every so often as he listened to her answers to his questions. There was no need to make him think she was also immature.

She wondered why he, a Delancey, had become a police detective. Like everyone else in Louisiana, she'd heard of Con Delancey, the infamous politician who was beloved by his constituents. The word was that although the Delancey patriarch had provided generous trust funds for each of his grandchildren, they all worked—several as police officers, either in New Orleans or in Chef Voleur on the north shore of Lake Pontchartrain, Con Delancey's hometown. She'd also heard that the Delancey men were charming as well as handsome. She was forced to agree with the handsome part, but she was still waiting to see the charming side of Detective Ethan Delancey.

She glanced at the two-way mirror again. Almost as powerful as the urge to stick her tongue out was the urge to turn her back on the mirror, or better yet, just get up and walk out of the room and the police station, leaving Ethan Delancey to like it or lump it.

But she didn't have the nerve to do either. His tone when he'd told her he'd *rather* she didn't leave had sounded like an order. If that were the only consideration, she might risk it. After all, he'd admitted she wasn't under arrest. But to her dismay and chagrin, she realized she didn't want to let him down. For some reason, she didn't want to see disappointment in his blue eyes. She liked it better when they sparkled with humor or danced with what she would like to think was interest. *Interest?* She didn't mean interest. She meant amusement. She wanted to make him laugh. He seemed much too serious. His face didn't have the natural creases that laughter pressed into the skin around eyes, cheeks and mouth. His mouth was wide and straight, and he had a strong jaw and his eyes were killer sexy. She'd love to see them crinkled in laughter. The most she'd managed to coax out of him was a slightly crooked smile so small it might be better labeled a smirk.

She rubbed the back of her neck and closed her aching eyes. She felt grimy and exhausted. She hadn't slept a wink and it was—she peeked at her watch—after two in the afternoon. Almost twelve hours since she'd surprised the murderer in Senator Sills's suite.

She considered banging on the mirror and asking for a quiet place to lie down and take a nap. Or maybe she could sleep in here. She scanned the walls for a light switch, but didn't see even one. Did that mean the lights were controlled from outside the room? She'd watched the television versions of police tormenting suspects to obtain information, even confessions. Were some of those stories true?

She was beginning to see why suspects confessed, even if they were innocent, at least on TV shows. She was about ready to declare that she had shot the senator because he made one too many changes to his speech, if it meant they'd let her go home and take a shower. She was exhausted, and her head was pounding. She wanted privacy. *Craved* it. She wanted to be at home, in bed with the covers pulled over her head. And she wanted to stay there until this nightmare was over.

But she'd never been able to just stick her head in the sand—not even as a little girl. She'd been born with the talent—or curse—of an almost uncanny intuition. Her mother had died when she was eleven, but she'd known, years before, that her mother was sick. She'd also figured out that her mother's illness was not the kind that was talked about in public. Then, later, she'd realized that her dad's late nights and mysterious meetings with people like Senator Sills were also best kept as secrets. Even though she didn't know exactly what went on, she always knew that there was something wrong about them.

Her first thought after she'd recovered from the shock of seeing the senator dead was that her life, from that moment on, would never be the same. Her brain had gone into fast-forward, detailing the consequences of any action on her part a week, a month, a year in the future, like a desert highway that stretched on to the horizon and beyond.

She would be tied up with inquiries, hearings, trials for who knew how long. Her career was toast, and privacy was something she might never have again. She was smack in the middle of the biggest murder case to hit New Orleans since Con Delancey's personal assistant had killed him twenty-five years ago.

Then a more immediate concern hit her. The killer had seen her. Did he realize she couldn't identify him? Did he care? The idea that the person who had killed Senator Sills in cold blood was out there, maybe waiting for a chance to kill her was terrifying. For an adrenaline-soaked second, her limbs tightened in an almost uncontrollable urge to run.

But where? She was in the police station, probably the safest place in the area, at least for now.

Once she'd calmed down and settled into the hard-backed chair again, she thought about the senator and reflected on how selfish she was being. Quelling the urge to touch the bandage above her temple, she reminded herself harshly that she was alive. The senator was dead. Her dad was dead. But each of them in their way had left her a legacy—a heavy, burdensome legacy that she would have to unload before she could ever be free of the past.

Exerting an almost superhuman effort to keep her face expressionless in case there were people on the other side of the mirror watching her, Laney pulled the legal pad the detective had left on the desk toward her and began to write down her duties as personal assistant to Senator Darby Sills.

By the time she finished documenting everything the senator had done since he'd arrived at the hotel the afternoon before, Detective Delancey was back.

As he closed the door, she asked, "How much longer are you going to keep me here?"

"Why? Have you got some place you need to be?" Ethan snapped, frowning.

She lifted her chin at his tone. "Actually I do. I'm going to be receiving a lot of phone calls—condolences, questions, comments. I'd like to have my phone so I can check my messages periodically, if you don't mind."

He nodded toward the legal pad. "Did you finish giving me a written accounting of your duties and Senator Sills's and your movements yesterday?"

"Yes. It's all here. Can I get my phone and purse so I can go?"

Ethan turned toward the mirror. "Have Ms. Montgomery's belongings brought down here," he said.

While they waited, he leaned back in his chair and watched her. Those blue eyes on her made her extremely uncomfortable. But she did her best not to show it. She pulled the legal pad to her and read over what she'd written—or pretended to.

Even without looking at him, Laney felt Ethan Delancey's presence. She'd noticed last night in the penthouse suite that the feel of the whole room changed the moment he walked in. From the first instant she'd laid eyes on him, she noticed an energy about him that seemed almost palpable. She remembered glancing around to assess others' reactions to him, but most of the other people in the room were going about their tasks as if nothing was different. Was it just her?

And now, as tired as she was, as sick of this room and the police and the questions as she was, she still felt that same energy. But there was something else, too. Something calming or soothing. All her tension and exhaustion didn't fade away, but it occurred to her that she'd felt very alone and uneasy while he'd been gone. Now that he was back, she felt safe.

She glanced up to catch him watching her. Her heart rate shot up and she quickly dropped her gaze back to the pad. On second thought—maybe that feeling of safety was just wishful thinking—or a hallucination.

He said something she didn't catch. She looked up. "What?"

His mouth quirked into a ghost of a smile. "I asked if you're ready to go. Were you falling asleep?"

"No," she snapped, then blinked as she realized he had her purse and her phone. Her gaze went to the door, which was closed, then back to him. Had she dozed off for a few seconds? Long enough for someone to bring her things in without her even noticing?

"Hey," she blurted as she realized he was playing with her phone. "What are you doing? That's my phone."

At that instant, another phone rang. "Don't worry. I'm just using it to call my phone. There," he said as the phone stopped ringing. "Now you've got my phone number. And I've got yours."

She looked at him, puzzled. "Why?" she asked.

"Just in case," he said. "If you think of anything else that might be pertinent to the case, or if you need anything, you can just call me." He pushed her phone across the table to her.

With a shrug, she slid it into her purse. "Okay, thanks." She stood and sidled past him toward the door.

"Laney," he said, his voice close to her ear.

A shiver slid through her as she turned her head.

"Stick close to home. Don't go out alone, especially at night. The killer knows who you are."

The shiver became a frisson of fear gripping her spine. "But he knows that I have no idea who he is, right? I mean, I couldn't see anything except that mask."

"And the belt buckle," Ethan reminded her. "And Laney, we're holding on to that clue. Don't tell anyone about it. Not the press, not anyone in the government. Not *anyone*."

"You think someone in the legislature might be involved?"

"I don't know. Right now, I'm proceeding as if everybody's involved until I can eliminate them."

She shrugged, reached for the doorknob, then turned back. "But I'm not a suspect, right? You still know I didn't have anything to do with the senator's murder, don't you?"

"I can't totally rule you out as a suspect yet, but no. Personally, I don't think you're involved," he said. "However—"

"However what?" she asked. To her dismay, her voice quivered slightly.

"You could be in danger," he said.

Although she already knew she could be targeted by the man who'd killed Senator Sills, his words ramped up the chill of fear inside her. "In danger. From the murderer?"

"He knows who you are. I'm going to have one of the police cruisers in the area drive by your house every few hours, just to be safe."

He reached around her and opened the door. She caught the clean scent of soap and shampoo. "I'll walk you out."

As they walked down the hall from the interview room, two well-dressed men were standing near the front entrance to the station, straightening their ties and talking in undertones to each other. Laney recognized one of them, Senator Myron Stamps.

Beside her, Ethan muttered a curse. He laid his hand reassuringly on the small of her back.

Reassuring, yes. His warm hand felt like a promise of safety, but she couldn't help but be suspicious at the timing. Had he set up this *accidental* meeting to see how she would react when confronted by one of the two members of what Senator Sills had called the "Good Ole Boys" club? It had been long rumored that

Sills, Stamps and Whitley, a trio of older politicians in the Louisiana Legislature, had taken bribes and kickbacks from businessmen and lobbyists in the import/export businesses to keep taxes low and look the other way when certain illegal substances were brought in through the Port of New Orleans. In fact, the kidnapping of Dr. Kate Chalmet's little boy had been a warped plan to keep Stamps in office so the graft and corruption could continue.

As if he could hear Laney's thoughts, Senator Stamps turned. Unsure what to do or say, meeting him in the middle of the police station, Laney pasted on a small smile and nodded.

Senator Stamps stepped forward. "Laney," he said, reaching out a hand toward her, but Ethan stepped in front of her. "Excuse us, Senator," he said evenly.

"I just wanted to speak to Laney," Stamps countered, and spoke to Laney as if Ethan wasn't there. "My dear, you must be in shock and terrified." Stamps squinted at the bandage on her head. "Oh, my dear, were you shot?"

Laney opened her mouth, but Ethan deflected the senator again. "I'm sorry, Senator. It's probably best if y'all don't communicate."

Stamps frowned as Ethan guided her past him. Beyond, Laney saw the other man, probably Stamps's lawyer, scowl. Was his disapproval aimed at Stamps, at Ethan—or at her? She nodded to him as well, but he just glared at her.

Laney held her tongue until Ethan had opened the door to the squad room and guided her through and out the front door of the station house.

"Why did you do that?" she demanded, once they were walking down the concrete steps.

"Do I have to remind you that you are a victim in this case, as well as my only witness, and Senator Stamps is a person of interest. You shouldn't be talking to him."

"Not that. Why did you walk me right past them?"

Ethan frowned. "That was an accident."

"You mean you weren't hoping for an encounter? You weren't hoping someone would say something incriminating?"

"It didn't hurt my feelings that Stamps confronted you."

"He wasn't confronting me. He was offering his condolences."

"His lawyer should have stopped him. Didn't you see the look he sent him?"

"I can't say if it was aimed at Stamps or you or me."

Ethan said, "Listen to me. You need to be careful. Don't take any unnecessary chances. Don't go out alone at night."

"So you do think I'm in danger. But not from Senator Stamps, surely?" she asked. "I thought you figured any threats would come from Buddy Davis. Assuming he was the man in black."

Ethan glanced around as they stepped off the bottom step and onto the sidewalk. "Watch what you say in public. And as for threats or danger, until I have some concrete evidence, I'm considering everybody dangerous, especially to you."

Laney frowned at him. Suddenly, his voice had gone harsh.

"You've got my number. If anything, and I mean anything, odd or unusual happens, you call me. Got it?"

She angled her head for a second. "Yes, sir," she said, still not sure how she felt about his seeming certainty that something could happen to her. "I will call you at the first sign of a roach, a scorpion or a thug with a gun." She smiled.

But Ethan didn't. He scowled at her. "This is not a game, Laney." He reached out and touched the bandage on her temple. "I'm not trying to scare you. I'm trying to make sure you stay safe. The killer shot at you because he wanted you dead. If his aim had been a quarter-inch lower, you would be."

Chapter Four

By the time Laney got home, it was after five in the afternoon, fifteen hours since Senator Sills had been killed. She flopped down on the sofa, too tired to even kick off her shoes. Her eyes filled with tears, mostly from reaction to the long, awful night and day. The sight of the senator dead on the floor and the feel of the bullet grazing her temple seemed at once glaringly real and a terrifying nightmare.

She hadn't minded working for the senator, but she hadn't particularly cared for him as a person. Of course she was sad that he was dead. Sad for him and for his two daughters. They would be devastated. One of them had a new baby. The senator had been so excited and so proud. She'd never met them, but she wondered if she ought to call them.

What would she say? She couldn't tell them anything about the murder, couldn't tell them anything she'd seen or heard. She couldn't tell them about the man in black. Ethan Delancey had warned her not to talk about the case and he'd told her that the police had taken care of notifying the senator's family. It was likely that the only thing she would accomplish would be to upset them.

The senator's daughters were not the only people she didn't know how to handle. She had dozens of messages on her phone from people who had called while she'd been stuck in that interview room at the police station. And by the time she'd gotten into her car and headed home, her phone was ringing almost constantly. She had no idea what to say to any of them either.

She'd turned the ringer off and done her best to ignore the vibration whenever it rang. Now as she sat on the couch in her living room and tried to relax, she heard it vibrating in her purse, which sat on the table in the foyer. With a sigh, she pushed herself to her feet and retrieved it. Back on the couch, she started playing messages and returning calls. There were several from Senator Sills's other staff members, wanting to know what had happened, was she okay, had she seen anything. She tried to keep her conversation with each of them short and her answers generic and vague, but every single staff member, from his secretary to his campaign manager, begged her to tell *just* him or her and swore they would not tell a soul.

While she talked to them the calls kept coming in. She screened several more and was surprised and irritated to hear other legislators' staffers, whom she knew as speaking acquaintances, asking the same questions that Sills's staffers had ask—was she all right, had she seen anything, if she'd tell them what happened they wouldn't tell a soul. She deleted their messages. The last message was from her best friend, who'd sounded so frantic that Laney immediately called her back and did her best to assure her that she was fine.

By the time she'd listened to probably forty calls and returned more than twenty of them, her head was hurting and she was so tired that she could barely move. But staying on the couch in the clothes she'd worn for the past thirty hours or more was not an option.

With a great deal of effort, she pushed herself up off the couch and forced herself to walk to the kitchen and open the refrigerator. The contents included a carton of milk that was probably out of date, a take-out box of Chinese food from—she counted backward—four days ago, a carton of eggs, a package of shredded cheddar cheese and two cans of decaffeinated cola. She considered a cheese omelet, but even that sounded too difficult. Sighing, she closed the door and drew herself a glass of water from the dispenser on the front.

Before she could even take a swallow her phone rang again. She looked at the display. It was a number she didn't know. Probably another congressman's staffer, fishing for information.

As she went into her bedroom, she turned the phone off. She put it and her glass of water on the nightstand and looked at her bed. She wanted to collapse into it and fall straight to sleep. But there was one thing she wanted more than sleep. A shower. She headed to the bathroom, discarding clothes along the way.

Within seconds, she was under the hot shower spray. Again, the tears welled in her eyes. Weariness, sadness, fear. She could take her pick of emotions. Standing there with the warm water loosening her tense muscles as it washed away the dirt and grime, she knew what she was really crying about. She'd been there. Right there in the room, a few scant feet from the man who had murdered Senator Sills in cold blood, and she hadn't been able to do a thing about it. She couldn't even identify him.

In that moment, staring up at him from the floor, she'd felt more helpless than she ever had in her life. Helpless and terrified and crushingly guilty.

She'd never been Senator Sills's biggest fan, mostly on behalf of her father, but she had never wished him dead. But he was dead, and for the life of her, she couldn't figure out what she could have done to save him. Her brain began inventing scenarios—what if she'd not gone to her room when she did? What if she'd jumped up immediately when she heard the pop?

Ethan's voice came back to her from the E.R., when he was being nice. *You couldn't have done anything. Not against a gun. If you'd tried, you'd probably be dead now, too.* The words weren't very comforting, but somehow, they helped. Or maybe it wasn't the words. Maybe it was him. The timbre of his voice. During that brief time, unlike the interrogation at the police precinct, he'd spoken gently, even kindly. When his eyes turned smoky and soft, she would believe anything he said.

She closed her eyes and let the hot water cascade over her, washing her fear and guilt down the drain, at least for a while. The image of Ethan Delancey's hard-planed face and smoky eyes helped her relax. As she washed, she realized that her hands were lingering on certain areas of her body and her languid relaxation was morphing into a pleasurable tension. Not the sharp, electric tension of fear and guilt. No. This was different. It swirled, building slowly, spiraling from the deepest center of her desire out to her suddenly sensitized skin. She lifted her head and let the shower spray caress and tease her breasts. As she drew a deep, moisture-laden breath, the water began to cool.

She shivered and wrenched off the water taps. Quickly, she ran a towel over her body, which suddenly felt too heavy to lift. Wrapping a terry cloth robe around her and using the damp towel to squeeze the last droplets of water out of her hair, she headed into her bedroom and threw back the covers.

Then she dropped the robe and slid into bed. She snuggled under the covers with a relieved sigh. Closing her eyes, she searched her brain for the image of Ethan's smoky eyes, but that spell was broken. As she'd turned off the hot, seductive shower and dried her body, she'd also turned off the hot, seductive daydreams.

It was as though stepping back into the cool real world had erased all that. Now all she could picture was Ethan's mouth as it twisted into an annoying smirk at things she'd said, or inverted into a frown when he didn't like her answer. It was obvious that he could turn the kindness on and off at will. And clearly, his default attitude was officious and annoying. She wondered how that worked for him when he wanted information from witnesses or suspects.

Her last thought before she fell asleep was that she needed to get her dad's financial records before it occurred to Detective Ethan Delancey to get a warrant for them.

SHE WOKE TO the sound of gunfire. A muffled pop that had her cringing, paralyzed with fear, until she fought her way to consciousness and realized she'd been dreaming. She opened her eyes to darkness and lay there, listening. Two more pops sounded, and then—a car's engine revved and tires squealed.

Laney collapsed back into the bedclothes, her limbs quivering with relief. The pops were nothing. Just a car's engine backfiring. She wasn't in the hotel room facing a killer. She was home in her own house. She was safe.

Safe. The word immediately conjured Ethan's words. *I'm not trying to scare you. I'm trying to make sure you stay safe.* With those words and the memory of his smoky eyes reassuring her, she relaxed and drifted toward slumber. But her fickle brain began to wonder what time it was. Sighing, she glanced over at her silent phone, then with a groan, reached out and picked it up.

Turning it on, she saw the time. Eleven-thirty. She'd been asleep for about four hours. Then with a cringe of dread, she looked at her phone log. There was a long list of numbers she didn't recognize. But she saw a missed call from her Aunt Darla, in Philadelphia. That meant that Senator Sills's murder had made the national news.

She pressed redial and spoke to her father's sister for a few minutes, assuring her that she was all right and declining to come to Philadelphia to visit. She explained to her aunt that she had to stay here during the investigation into the senator's killing. She didn't mention to her that she'd been a witness or a victim.

When she ended the call, she turned the phone off

again, feeling much less guilty and somewhat self-righteous that she'd interrupted her much-needed sleep to check her messages. As soon as she closed her eyes, she fell asleep and dreamed that it was Ethan who got off the elevator and rescued her from the murderer.

THE NEXT TIME she woke, it was to a loud banging that set her heart to racing. She reached for her phone to see what time it was, but it was turned off. So she threw back the covers to get up—and discovered that she was naked.

For a second she just stared at herself in disbelief. She had never gone to bed completely naked before—and with wet hair, too. She must have been exhausted. The last thing she remembered was the exquisite sensations the hot water sluicing over her skin caused.

The banging forgotten, she closed her eyes, but it started again and a loud familiar voice cried, "Laney! Laney Montgomery! It's Ethan."

Ethan. Detective Delancey. What was he doing here? She jerked the sheet up to cover her breasts, then sniffed in embarrassed amusement. She was alone in the room. *For now.*

She pushed the covers back and got out of bed, wondering what she could throw on that would sufficiently cover her nakedness. And what the hell was Ethan Delancey doing outside her door at—whatever time it was in the morning anyhow?

She scurried into the bathroom, trying to suppress the urge to cover herself with her hands as if he could see through the walls. She splashed water on her face and glanced in the mirror. She'd gone to sleep with wet hair and this morning it looked like Medusa's snakes. She ran her wet hands through it, trying to smooth it. Then she looked at the robes and gowns on the back of the door. No. She wanted her terry cloth robe. It was white and thick and covered her from chin to toes. Likely the most modest piece of clothing she owned, as long as the sash at the waist stayed closed and the front flaps didn't slip.

But where was it? She glanced through the bathroom door at her bed. There it was, right where she'd left it last night. She tiptoed over to the bed and quickly threw it on. She wrapped the robe tightly around her and cinched the sash as tightly as she could. Then she hurried down the hall to the front door.

Just as she reached to unlock the deadbolt, Ethan banged again. "Laney? Are you in there? I swear if you don't answer the door I'm going to break it down. Are you okay in there?"

She took a deep breath. "I'm—I'm here," she said. "Just a minute."

"Laney? It's Ethan."

"I know," she cried. "Hold on." She finally got the door open.

Ethan was standing there, on her front stoop, his pressed white shirt unbuttoned over a white T-shirt and his hair uncombed. "Thank goodness," he said when he saw her. "I was afraid something had happened to you. Do you know that your phone is off?"

She nodded.

"Well, turn it on. Don't you know people are trying

to call you? I called several times. I figured you might have turned your phone off while you were asleep, but it's eight-thirty."

"Eight-thirty? Oh, my God. I slept for over twelve hours."

"Well, that's good, I guess," he said. "Aren't you going to invite me in?"

Laney glanced behind her. "I—uh, well I just got up and—" She instinctively stepped out of the way as he walked inside, closing the door behind him. He surveyed the foyer and the rooms that opened onto it—the living room to his right, the kitchen directly in front of him and a hallway to his left. There were three doors on the hall—bedrooms and a bathroom he figured.

Laney watched him take in her little house. His expression didn't change, but his head moved slightly in what she thought might be a nod.

"Got coffee?"

"I can…make some," she said with a vague gesture toward the kitchen. But then she stopped. She had no reason to extend hospitality to him. He'd shown up at her door banging and making a scene. She turned to face him. "What are you doing here?" she asked.

She started to put her hands on her hips, but felt the terry cloth sash give a little and decided a better idea would be to fold her arms across her middle, anchoring the robe in place.

He headed into the kitchen. "The coffee's not made," he said, looking at the pot and then at her.

"No, it's not," she said. "I asked you a question."

"I'm here because I need you to come in to sign your statement. Can you be there at ten?"

Laney looked at her kitchen clock. "That's barely over an hour from now."

"Yeah," he said, opening the cabinet above her coffeepot, spotting a can of coffee and retrieving it. "Plenty of time."

He inspected her pot, emptied the reusable filter, rinsed it and refilled it with fresh coffee. He filled the carafe with water and poured it into the pot, then turned on the power.

"No," she said. "It's not plenty of time. Oh, and please, make yourself at home," she added sarcastically.

He glanced at her, first in puzzlement, then understanding. "I figured I'd better make the coffee if I wanted some, since you're busy holding your robe together," he commented, a small smile curving his lips. It wasn't wry but it wasn't kind either. It was more... suggestive.

His gaze drifted downward to the neckline of the robe. It took all her willpower not to look down. But she couldn't stop her face from heating up. She knew she was blushing.

"What's the matter?" he asked, studying her face. "You said you got over twelve hours of sleep. You obviously showered, by the look of your hair."

She shot her fingers through her damp hair, smoothing it as well as she could.

"Is that—" he inclined his head toward her hair "—going to keep you from getting dressed and down to the station by ten?" He didn't take his eyes off her, just stood there, waiting for her to answer.

"No," she said through gritted teeth. "Of course I can be there by ten, if that's what I have to do."

"Great," he said. "I'd appreciate it." He turned back to the coffeepot, watching it drip. After a couple of moments, he looked back at her. "Shouldn't you be getting ready?"

"Shouldn't I—" Laney drew a deep breath. Although the vestiges of the dream in which Ethan heroically saved her from the black-clad monster in the hotel room still lingered, she couldn't remember for the life of her what had made her think that it would be romantic to be rescued by him. He was arrogant, impatient and rude. In fact, she was sure if he had the occasion to rescue her, she'd never hear the end of it. She cleared her throat. "I thought I'd have a cup of coffee first," she said coldly.

"Okay," he said. "Good idea. Where are your mugs?"

"Here," she said, pulling one from the cabinet and edging past him to pour it full of coffee. She turned and handed the steaming mug to him. "Please," she said with a smile. "Keep it. Drink the coffee on your way to work."

He looked at her in mild surprise, gave her that same little smile he'd shown her earlier, lifted the cup in a coffee salute, then turned on his heel and left her house, stopping to salute her one more time at the front door.

Laney poured herself a mug of coffee, although what she wanted to do was slide back down under the warm covers and go to sleep again. She knew, however, that by the time she did something with her hair, dressed and drove to the police station, she'd be lucky if it wasn't after ten.

She headed to her bedroom to put on underwear and clothes, but first, before she took off the terry cloth robe, she looked at herself in the full-length mirror on the back of the bathroom door. Had Ethan known that she had no clothes on under her robe? She'd thought the thick cotton was the best thing to cover her, but now, trying to see what he'd seen, she realized with embarrassment that a fluffy white bath robe and wet hair said nothing so much as *I'm just out of the shower and didn't bother to dress.*

BUDDY DAVIS, FOUNDER and pastor of the Silver Circle Church on the North Shore of Lake Pontchartrain and owner of the Silver Circle Broadcasting Network and Circle of Faith Ministries, sat in the interview room with his wife and business partner, Benita. The two of them had their heads together and Benita seemed to be doing most of the talking.

Ethan watched them through the two-way mirror in the viewing room. Maria Farrantino stood at his side.

"You sent me out there to get them on purpose, didn't you?" she asked.

"What? Me?" Ethan said innocently. "Nah. I'd have gone yesterday, but they were up in Jackson. Thanks, by the way, for bringing them in."

"He practically groped me, right there in front of his wife. And she acted like I was coming on to *him*."

"He does have that reputation. Remember when that

female deacon in his ministry accused him of sexual harassment?"

"*You'll* be accused of sexual harassment if you do anything like that again."

"I apologize for his actions, Farrantino, but you know you're going to have to take them home, too. I'll call you when they're done."

"Oh, no. No. No. No. Their chauffeur followed us. He's waiting for them in their limo. They do not need a ride home."

"They'll need to be escorted from the building," he said teasingly.

"Don't push it, Delancey."

"Seriously, I didn't mean to put you in that situation," he said. "I'm planning to walk them out."

"I can do it," she retorted. "Don't think I can't handle him."

Ethan shook his head. "No. I want to do it. I'm working on a theory."

"Hey, fine. Do what you want. I'd be happy if I never saw that skinny Richard Petty wannabe again." She left the room.

Ethan turned his full attention back to Davis. He did look like a pale copy of the legendary NASCAR race driver in his black cowboy shirt, tie, leather jacket and jeans, and sporting a graying mustache. Against all the black, the signature silver belt buckle he wore stood out like a beacon. Small replicas of the buckle circled the black cowboy hat that completed his outfit. As they'd walked through the station, Buddy had shaken hands with and spoken to every single person he passed. And the whole time, Benita, his wife of thirty-some years, had clung to his side, her arm through his, and smiled and greeted people right alongside him.

Davis's wife was an interesting specimen. She was several inches shorter than Davis and the description that came to Ethan's mind was lean and hungry. Even though she had to be in her late fifties or early sixties, she wore a sleeveless top and a short denim skirt with cowboy boots. She obviously spent a lot of time either outside or in a tanning bed. He was reminded of an obsessed runner whose primary goal in life was zero body fat. She was leaning near Davis's ear with her hand on his shoulder and talking rapidly.

Ethan was not looking forward to this interview. He'd questioned his share of celebrities, local and national, and he knew that he was going to encounter outrage, defensiveness, entitlement, pompousness, irrational demands and probably a quick dismissal with those words every police officer dreads hearing. *I want my lawyer.*

He sighed as he walked around from the viewing room to the interview room. He'd give it his best shot until they cut him off. He'd no sooner stepped through the door when Benita attacked him verbally.

"What's your name? I'm going to report you. How dare you send a rookie bimbo to bring us in here, without even a courtesy call ahead of time? This is an outrage. I've got a good mind to demand to see your captain."

"Benni," Buddy Davis said gently, placing a hand over hers. "Why don't we listen and see what the young man has to say." He turned his mild blue eyes to Ethan. "Are you a detective, son?" he asked, smiling.

"Yes, sir," Ethan said. "Detective Ethan Delancey." He chose to respond to the evangelist rather than to his strident, outraged wife. He'd heard bits and pieces of Davis's sermons on television. The man was as hellfire-and-brimstone as any TV preacher Ethan had ever heard. But he'd never met Davis. The contrast between Buddy Davis the evangelist who dressed outrageously and drove a fancy Italian sports car while he shouted and ranted about love and tolerance, and Buddy Davis the polite, kindly husband who calmed his wife and subtly offered amends to Ethan, was astonishing.

"Delancey," Buddy said, smiling. "I never met your granddad, although I'd have liked to. He was a powerful and influential man. I was sad when he died."

"Thank you, sir," Ethan said as Benita continued her tirade.

"And another thing," she said stridently. "Why have we been dragged in here against our will? What on earth—"

"Against your will?" Ethan interrupted. "Surely the officer didn't force you? Please tell me she didn't handcuff you or hold you at gunpoint."

Benita flushed. "Of course not. If—if she had, I would have already called our lawyer. But she practically threatened us."

"Practically," Ethan repeated thoughtfully. "I see." He greeted Davis, smiling at him. "Mr. Davis—" he started.

"*Pastor* Davis," Benita cut in.

"I beg your pardon," he said. "Pastor Davis, I'm sure you've seen the news about Senator Sills."

"Of course he has," Benita said. "It's all over TV, radio and the internet."

Davis patted her hand again. "Benni, he's just doing his job. Let me answer his questions and we can be on our way."

"Ma'am," Ethan said, turning his attention to her. "If I have to, I'll separate you. I need to be able to question Pastor Davis without you interrupting."

Her face twisted in anger, but before she could speak, Davis's hand squeezed hers. With a grimace, she tossed her head as if to say, *Go ahead, but you're going to regret it.*

"Thank you. Now, Pastor Davis," Ethan said. "I take it you've seen the news?"

"Yes," Davis responded. "It's awful. Someone murdering Darby Sills right there in his hotel room."

"Did you know the senator?"

"Why, yes. We are—or we were—good friends. We've played golf together for years."

Ethan nodded. "That's right. Senator Sills's personal assistant, Elaine Montgomery, told me that." He threw the name out, then paused, waiting for a reaction. Buddy Davis didn't react, but Benita appeared to be almost in apoplexy from biting her tongue. "You know who she is, right?"

"Who? Elaine?" Davis asked. "Oh, yes, of course. Pretty thing, isn't she? She must take after her mother, because she's certainly better-looking than her old dad." Davis laughed.

"Her dad. That would be Elliott Montgomery. You knew him?"

"Excuse me, *Detective*. I don't mean to butt in, but why are you asking *us* about Senator Sills's murder?"

"We're talking with everyone who knew the senator, starting with those he had spoken with recently."

"That certainly does not include us."

Ethan addressed his answer to Buddy. "There was a call from the senator's cell phone to your phone yesterday."

"What?" Benita snapped. "Buddy? Did you talk to Senator Sills?"

Buddy looked at her. "I—I'm not sure," he said.

"Where's your phone, Buddy?" she asked him.

"Right here, in my pocket."

"Let me see it."

Buddy pulled his phone out and handed it to Benita. She bent her head and studied it, punching a button here and there.

Ethan divided his attention between Buddy and Benita. Their relationship seemed odd. As hellfire-and-brimstone as Buddy was when he preached, he was as meek as a lamb sitting here talking to his wife. Benita, for her part, was loud and insistent on his behalf but soft-spoken, even cautious, when talking to him. What was up with these two?

"Here it is," Benita said. "The call came from Senator Sills's cell phone but it's showing as a missed call. I knew Buddy hadn't talked to him. Here, Buddy. Take your phone." She handed it to him, then turned back to Ethan. "Will there be anything else, Detective?"

"As a matter of fact, yes. I have a few more questions. Pastor?" he addressed Buddy. "I was asking about Elliott Montgomery. Did you know him?"

"Montgomery?" Buddy repeated.

"The lobbyist, honey," Benita said, patting Buddy's hand. She turned to Ethan. "We met him a few times at political functions or charity events," Benita answered. "I don't recall ever meeting his daughter, though." She shot a glance that was at once possessive and filled with suspicion at her husband.

"I just know her from going to Darby's office, Benni. And I saw her a few times when she was younger, with her dad." He paused. "Did something happen to her, Detective? I certainly hope she wasn't there—"

"Buddy!" Benita snapped.

Ethan shot her a look. What was that about? Was she trying to shut him up before he said something incriminating? "No, sir. Nothing has happened to her. You were saying?"

Buddy frowned at him. "I was saying?"

"You said you certainly hoped that Elaine Montgomery wasn't there."

Buddy's frown deepened and he looked at Benita.

"Don't worry about it." She laid a hand on his arm. "He was just expressing his hope that Ms. Montgomery was all right. Now, is that all?"

"Pastor," Ethan said, ignoring Benita. "Where were you at around two a.m. on Wednesday morning?"

Buddy squinted at him. "Two a.m.? When? Yesterday?"

"Yes, sir," Ethan said. "About thirty or so hours ago."

"Well son, at two a.m. I'm pretty sure I was at home asleep." He looked at his wife. "Right, Benni?"

Ethan noticed that as strident and interruptive as Benita had been throughout the questioning so far, she was uncharacteristically tight-lipped now. "Ms. Davis?"

She looked up. "What? Oh, sweetie, of course you were." She inclined her head toward Buddy while nodding at Ethan. "Snoring like a freight train. We haven't slept in the same room in years. I can't sleep a wink if we're in the same room, with all that honking and blowing going on. But he's always in bed by eleven." She swallowed. "Always."

Buddy nodded placidly.

"And what about you, Mrs. Davis?"

"Me? You mean where was I when the senator was killed? What a ridiculous question. Are you suggesting that I might be a suspect?"

"My job is to ask questions, ma'am. Could you please answer?"

"Ask Buddy. I was at home in bed asleep, too."

"But the two of you were in separate rooms. So really, neither one of you can swear that the other was at home."

"Hmm, Benni? I think the boy's got a point there," Buddy said with an appreciative smile.

"Don't be ridiculous," Benita snapped at the same time. "We were there, in the same house, all night."

Ethan let the silence stretch for a moment, to see if either of them would break it. Benita was back to biting her lip and Buddy just stared at a spot on the desk.

After about forty seconds, Ethan spoke. "So exactly what time did you last see your husband that night?"

"Well, it had to be close to eleven, didn't it, since as I just told you, he goes to bed by eleven."

"*Had to be?* You don't remember for certain?"

She glared at him. "What I don't remember is the past few nights being any different than our usual routine."

Nice, Ethan thought. Benita Davis was quick and careful.

"What about you, Pastor Davis? What time do you remember last seeing your wife that night?"

"What night was that again?" Buddy asked, looking at his wife.

Ethan started to answer, but Benita broke in. "I think that's enough." She stood, making a production out of checking her watch. "We have to be somewhere. Are we under arrest, Detective?"

"No, ma'am," Ethan said. "I just have a couple more questions."

"Let's go, Buddy. We're leaving."

Buddy frowned at her. "Benni, we shouldn't be rude. That's not the Christian way. You know what I always say. *Be kind, live life and—*" he stopped, glancing down at his hands.

"*Love your neighbor,*" Benita said with a smile that looked stiff to Ethan. "That's exactly what you say, and what a wonderful rule for living life. Don't you agree, Detective?"

That was odd. Ethan studied Buddy for a moment, watching him perk up and continue talking about the

Christian way to live one's life. When Buddy was done, he gave Ethan a small smile and sat back in his chair, looking satisfied and smug.

On the other hand, Benita was a mini-volcano ready to explode. Her frustration and anger had been building ever since she walked into the station. It seemed that Buddy's short soliloquy only added heat to her fire. Ethan was absolutely sure that she was going to blow her top within about twenty seconds. He studied her. When she finally blew, would she accidentally spill something she didn't intend to? He could hope, he supposed.

There was nothing Ethan would like more than to burst Benita's angry balloon, and he knew exactly what would do it—whether or not the evangelist or his wife were guilty.

He stood. "I want to thank you for coming in," he said, smiling at them both. "I hope that if anything else comes up, I can speak to you again."

"I'm not sure why you would need to talk to us again. We have nothing to do with Senator Sills or anything that happened to him."

"In any case, I need to warn you not to leave town. We may need to question you again."

"You may—?" Benita repeated. "You *may* need to question us again? This is unconscionable. Well, I *may* need to speak to Leon."

Leon was, of course, New Orleans Police Department Superintendent Leon Fortenberry. Ethan smiled at her, hoping the right amount of wistfulness showed. "I think that would be a really good idea. I receive my orders from Superintendent Fortenberry's office. So I'd actually welcome you speaking directly to him. He can discuss with you how vital your cooperation is to our investigation."

"Fine. We're going there right now." She held out her hand to Buddy, and he took it and stood.

Ethan nodded reluctantly. "That's your prerogative, Mrs. Davis." He turned to Buddy. "Thank you, Pastor." He paused, looking at Buddy's waist. "You know, that belt buckle of yours," he said. "I couldn't help but notice it when you came in. It's pretty distinctive."

Buddy beamed. "Why thank you, son. I'm really proud of that. Did you know Benni designed the logo? Silver Circle. It stands for our Silver Circle of Faith."

"Silver Circle of Faith. What is that?" Ethan asked.

"Wait a minute. What's got you so all-fired interested in the silver belt buckle anyhow?" Benita asked sharply. "What's it got to do with anything?"

Ethan feigned surprise as he turned to her. "Why, nothing. I was just admiring it. Have I upset you in some way?"

Benita glared at him. "You haven't upset me. I just want to know what that belt buckle's got to do with Sills's murder."

Ethan spread his hands. "I wasn't suggesting it had anything to do with it. Please forgive me if I gave you the wrong impression. I was just curious."

"Oh, please," Benita huffed. "You brought us here to question us about Senator Sills's murder. Now, suddenly you're talking about belt buckles. You'd better do a better job than that of explaining yourself."

"There's nothing to explain," Ethan went on, mildly. "I merely made a comment. Do *you* have any reason to think the buckle has something to do with the senator's murder?"

An odd expression passed across Benita's face. A flash of confusion or paranoia. It faded immediately, but Ethan knew he'd seen it.

Buddy said, "What in the world could my Silver Circle belt buckle have to do with the senator's death?" Buddy asked. "I thought he was shot."

"Nothing," Benita said firmly, patting Buddy's hand. "Absolutely nothing." Her earlier confusion was gone. "Detective Delancey has no idea what he's talking about. There are only around twenty-five in existence. They're worth around five thousand dollars each. And fourteen of them are in our safe at the house."

"Fourteen out of twenty-five. Well, that makes them pretty rare, doesn't it?" Ethan asked with a smile. "When was the last time you checked on those you have in your safe? Are you sure you know how many are in there?"

"Oh, good grief," Benita exclaimed, disgusted.

Buddy answered. "I doubt the safe's been opened since the latest Silver Circle Award was bestowed upon a deserving member of our congregation." He frowned at Ethan. "Son, you never answered my question either. Why are you asking about the belt buckles? Does this have something to do with Darby?"

Ethan took a deep breath and prepared to make the Davises suspicious of his motives. "I really can't say," he said. He waved toward the door of the interview room. "Come with me. I'll walk you out."

As he stepped over and opened the door, holding it for Buddy and Benita, he could feel Benita's searing gaze burning the nape of his neck. Good. Now they'd be worried.

He glanced at his watch. Ten-thirty. Laney should be out front, waiting for him. Probably had been for the past half hour. He'd told the desk sergeant to seat her directly on the aisle from the front door to the interview room. He wanted Laney and the Davises to meet face-to-face, and he wanted to be there to observe all three of them. "Well, I want to emphasize how much I appreciate you coming down here to talk with me," he said as the three of them stepped into the hall.

"You don't fool me, *Detective,*" Benita assured him. "You're trying to get a rise out of us by talking about the belt buckles. Well, it won't work. You'll be hearing from Leon about your disrespectful behavior. And you'll hear from our lawyer, as soon as I talk with him about what charges we're going to bring against you."

"Mrs. Davis, I hope your meeting with the superintendent will be more satisfying that this one has been for you."

"Don't you worry," Benita growled. She narrowed her gaze at him for a few seconds, started to say something else, then caught herself. "It will," she said.

Ethan nodded solemnly. "Please don't forget. You need to stay in town, in case we do have more questions for you." He led them through the halls to the front desk. "Thank you again. If you'll excuse me, the desk sergeant has something for me."

He started toward the desk then stopped. "Oh, and by the way, can you call and let me know for sure how many of those belt buckles are in your safe? It will save us both some time and trouble if I don't have to get a warrant."

Benita turned red but Buddy took her hand and she clamped her mouth shut.

Ethan smiled as he walked over to the front desk. On the way, he nodded at Laney, gesturing to her that he'd be with her in one minute. Then he leaned on the high counter and started a conversation with the sergeant.

Buddy and Benita walked between the desks toward the front doors. Ethan turned to watch as the two of them came face-to-face with Laney. When she looked up and saw Buddy, her brow furrowed and she sent a quick, accusatory glance toward Ethan. Buddy saw her and smiled admiringly, as he did with every pretty young woman he saw, but as far as Ethan could tell, there was nothing else. Buddy either didn't recognize her or he was one of the best, slickest criminals Ethan had ever seen. And judging by the contrast between his sermons and his behavior today, he just might be that slick.

Then Laney turned her gaze toward Benita and her eyes widened.

From Ethan's vantage point, he could see Benita clearly. The woman aimed a scathing glance at Laney, then turned to her husband. "Come on, Buddy," she said, sliding her arm into his. "Let's get out of here.

Next time we see you, Detective, or *any* of your officers, we will have our attorneys present."

Ethan tipped an imaginary hat at her. "I wouldn't
have it any other way, ma'am."

Chapter Five

"That was Buddy Davis, wasn't it?" Laney asked Ethan as he guided her into the interview room where she'd waited for so many hours the day before.

"Yes, it was," he said.

"And was that woman his wife? Benita Davis? I've heard she's the real power behind Silver Circle of Faith Ministries."

"She's a piece of work. I can tell you that. What did you think when you saw them?" he asked her.

"Nothing really. I mean, Buddy's build—I suppose he could have been the man in black, but her—what's her name?"

"Benita."

"Right. Benita. She looked as though she knew me and hated my guts."

"Hmm," he said.

"What do you mean, hmm?"

"She could have been jealous because I mentioned your name to them and Buddy remembered meeting you."

"Oh, great. So she does hate me," Laney said. "Thanks."

"You want some coffee? A cold drink?" Ethan asked, choosing to ignore her sarcasm.

She sent him a wry smile. "So now you're playing good cop. Will the other detective, the tall handsome one, be playing bad cop today?"

"Handsome?" Ethan echoed.

He looked slightly taken aback. She smiled to herself. Was he not used to his partner getting the attention from females? Granted, the taller, dark-haired detective had on a wedding band; and did a couple of inches really matter between two guys who were both six feet tall? She'd wanted to goad Ethan Delancey a bit, and she'd succeeded.

"I apologize. Did I hurt your feelings?"

Ethan smiled reluctantly. "No. It's just that I have never once thought of that ugly mug as handsome in any sense of the word."

"Well, you're not a girl."

"No, I'm not. I'm glad you realize that."

"Are you?" Laney didn't know what the difference was today, but Ethan, sitting across the table from her in his white shirt and dress pants, seemed to have gotten over whatever his problem had been with her the day before. In fact, if she weren't mistaken, she could believe that he was actually flirting with her. Not seriously, of course. He was still the cop and she was still the victim, the witness and possibly one of the suspects.

She gave her shoulders a mental shrug. She was probably totally wrong. He probably wasn't flirting at all. He could have had a headache yesterday, or a hangover. Maybe he got some sleep last night, too, and just felt generally friendlier today.

She glanced up and caught his gaze. He looked thoughtful and faintly puzzled. "What?" she asked.

"Wondering what you meant just now. Am I what? A girl or glad?" he asked. "Girl, no. Glad…yes." His smile widened.

She almost gulped. He *was* flirting. The question now was, was he doing it consciously or unconsciously? She decided her best bet was to ignore it. "So is my statement ready to be signed?" she asked.

"Your statement." He blinked, then stood. "I'll be right back." He left, shutting the door behind him.

Laney frowned. That was odd. He'd told her to be at the station at ten to sign the statement, then he'd kept her waiting for over half an hour while he talked to Buddy Davis and his wife. Now he'd demanded she come down here, he'd put her in the interview room, but forgotten about the statement. Strange.

She glanced at the two-way mirror. Was there something else at play here? Was he standing back there on the other side of that mirror and watching her? Waiting for her to do—what? There was nothing in the room except a short number two pencil lying on the table. She sent the mirror a mischievous look and picked up the pencil. What if she defaced the already-defaced table by carving her initials into it? Was that considered destroying city property? Maybe she could write some nasty graffiti on the walls, although the paint was such a musty gray already that her excellent penciled poetry might not even be visible. What if she stabbed herself with the pencil point? Would they put her under suicide watch and make her talk with a psychiatrist? Would they think she was a stronger candidate for killing the senator?

With a small laugh she tossed the pencil down. Maybe Detective Delancey was just absentminded this morning and really had forgotten to get the statement.

The door opened and he came in, hanging up his phone and pocketing it as he did so. "Sorry. We're going to have to do this later. I've been called to the superintendent's office. I have to go immediately."

Laney frowned, seeing his empty hands. "If you have it, I could read it over and sign it while I'm here. You don't have to be here, do you?"

He shook his head. "For some reason the transcriptionist couldn't lay her hands on it. I'll give you a call. Sorry for your trouble." He stood there beside the open door, waiting for her to get up and leave.

"No problem," she said, standing and walking out past him.

Ethan fell into step beside her. "I'll see you out. I'm headed out to my car anyhow."

"Where's yours?" he asked as they walked down the steps to the sidewalk.

She pointed to a fifteen-minute parking place down the street from the police station.

"Okay. Mine's over here in the police lot. We'll get that statement signed maybe tomorrow."

"Not tomorrow. I have to drive up to Baton Rouge for a meeting about Senator Sills's funeral and who's going to finish out his term."

"Okay. Well, we'll get together. When's his funeral—and where?" Ethan asked as he turned toward the police parking lot.

"We're finalizing that today, with his daughters. I'm guessing it will be Sunday morning in Baton Rouge. From what I've heard, his younger daughter will be taking him to Shreveport to be buried. That's where his parents are."

"Any idea who they'll choose to finish out his term?"

Laney shook her head. "Not a clue," she said. "He's divorced, so it won't be his wife. I'm sure I'll know more after this meeting tomorrow."

"Yeah," Ethan muttered noncommittally. "Okay. I'll see you—"

His words were cut off by a town car speeding past, too close to the curb. Laney backed up instinctively and Ethan grabbed her, pulling her back against him as she turned to look at the license plate.

"'*Silver Circle 1,*'" he said as she focused on the vanity tag.

"Oh, my God," she whispered breathlessly.

"Are you all right?" he asked, still holding her close. His strong yet gentle fingers were wrapped around her upper arms and her back was pressed tightly against him. She felt his fast, steady breaths and the lean hard planes of his chest and abs.

"I'm okay." Her voice was shaky and she knew the tremor was only partly because of the close call. Some of it was her sudden, unwanted awareness of Detective Ethan Delancey's fine, hard body. *No, it's not fine,* she corrected herself, consciously pulling away from him.

He let her go, after a brief hesitation.

"Was that really—?" she started.

"Buddy and Benita," Ethan grated. "Benita's probably still pissed at me for hauling them in for questioning. I ought to have them picked up for reckless driving."

"But who was driving? It wasn't either of them, was it?"

"Can you describe the driver?"

She closed her eyes, thinking. "He was larger—muscle I think, rather than fat. He had black hair, kind of curly or wavy. That's all I can remember."

"Good job. I didn't notice the hair being wavy or curly." He was staring in the direction that the car disappeared.

"Do you think they were really trying to hit us?"

"No, he just got as close to the curb as he could, and he sped up as he came closer. They may not have been seriously trying to hit us," Ethan said grimly, "but it was definitely a threat."

EVEN THOUGH IT was only around noon when Laney got back to her house, she felt as if she'd been up another twenty-four hours. The sleep she'd gotten the day before suddenly seemed too far in the past to remember. She had nothing to do tonight except screen and return phone calls, so she'd stopped at the grocery store and bought mascarpone cheese, Parmesan cheese, angel hair pasta and a box of frozen spinach. After setting her purse on the foyer table, she put the grocery bags on the kitchen counter and dug in it for the spinach.

She tossed the unopened package into the microwave and set it for defrost.

Ten-minute spinach Alfredo was her go-to dinner, and today, because she thought she deserved it, she'd bought a bottle of wine. All that was required for the sauce was butter, mascarpone cheese, garlic, spinach and plenty of Parmesan cheese. Within about seven or eight minutes, just the right time to cook angel hair pasta, the meal was ready. Paired with a good dry white wine it was manna from heaven. And if she had enough left over to last the rest of the week, so much the better.

While she waited for the spinach to defrost, she checked her phone. Twelve messages. She ran through them quickly. More acquaintances wanting to know what she knew, a call from a TV station asking for an interview and Senator Sills's secretary reminding her of the meetings tomorrow. By the time she'd reviewed and deleted them all, her eyelids were drooping. She had a long, quiet afternoon stretching ahead of her, perfect for a nap before dinner.

She put the cheese and the defrosted spinach into the refrigerator, then headed down the hall to her bedroom. She'd sleep for a couple of hours, then get up and make the pasta. She was looking forward to curling up on her couch and eating while she watched the news. Then back to bed, and maybe, by the next morning, she'd feel as if she'd finally caught up on her sleep.

THE NEXT THING Laney knew, someone was knocking on her door. Before she came fully awake, she dreamed it was Ethan, coming to check on her again. So when she opened her eyes and realized it was dark outside, she was surprised and, at first, a little disoriented.

It took her a few seconds to remember that it wasn't morning. She'd lain down for a nap after getting home from the police station. But how long had she slept? The knock sounded again, startling her. *Oh, right.* Someone was at the door.

She swung her legs over the side of the bed and slipped on her shoes. She hadn't undressed to nap, so she still had on the shirt and slacks she'd worn this morning. She went into the foyer and called out, "Who is it?"

A soft female voice said, "Hello? Hi in there. My name is Carolyn. I live a few houses down. I think my cat may be under your car."

Laney sighed in frustration. Carolyn sounded young and perky and newly married, and Laney did not want to deal with her. *Sorry. Can't help you if you don't have sense enough to keep your cat inside,* she wanted to say. Instead she settled for a dismissive "Your what?" hoping that *Carolyn* would go away. She didn't want to be pulled into the woman's cat drama.

"Uh—my cat. Please? She's a kitten. Can you help me?"

With an explosive sigh, Laney opened the door a crack and peered through it. A young woman in rather tight blue pants and a striped sweater stood there, smiling warily and holding a cheap flashlight. "Oh, hi. I'm Carolyn." She held out a hand but Laney wasn't in the mood. She hung on to the door.

Undeterred, Carolyn continued. "Okay, then. Hi. We

just moved in and my cat got out when I came home a little while ago. I've been looking for her and I think she's under your car. Do you think you could help me?"

"Have you tried calling it?" Laney asked, not yet convinced that her help was needed to get the silly feline out from under her car.

"Well, yes, I have," Carolyn said archly.

Whoa. Maybe that was unnecessarily rude. "Okay," she said reluctantly. "I'm not sure what I can do—"

"Do you have a flashlight?" Carolyn asked, pointing hers at Laney and turning it on. A feeble glow was all that the bulb could manage. "Mine's dying."

"Just a minute," Laney said and turned on her heel, as Carolyn stepped into the foyer. She had a very good flashlight somewhere. She looked in three kitchen drawers before she found it. When she got back to the door, Carolyn was tapping the head of her flashlight against her palm and then looking straight at it. "Now it's completely dead," she said woefully. She looked at Laney. "Oh, that's a nice flashlight."

"Mmm-hmm," Laney responded as she gestured to Carolyn to lead the way to the lurking cat. Carolyn walked around the side of the house to Laney's car and crossed to the far side. "I think she's closer to this side. Can you bring the flashlight over here?"

Laney rolled her eyes. Yes, she was acting bitchy, but she'd had a difficult couple of days. Much more difficult than losing a cat. *Lost your cat? Well, I was shot by the man who'd just murdered my boss.* Taking a deep breath, she told herself that she should just get into the spirit of finding the cat, because the sooner the cat and

Carolyn were back safe at home, the sooner Laney could get to her pasta and wine.

"Okay," she said, a little more energetically as she walked around the car and crouched down. "What color is the kitty?"

"She's white with a little black spot right here." Carolyn pointed to the middle of her forehead. "So cute and only about three months old." Carolyn knelt gingerly, as if she were afraid her pants would split.

Laney sank to hands and knees, doing her best not to scuff her shoes, and peered under the car. "I don't see anything."

"I'm afraid she could be up under the hood," Carolyn wailed.

"Maybe I should start the engine," Laney said drily, knowing that if the cat were in the engine compartment, cranking the car could be the end of kitty.

"Do you think that would work?" Carolyn asked, wide-eyed.

"No."

"Oh."

Laney thought she saw a hint of anger cross Carolyn's plump face. The expression twisted her bland, wide-eyed countenance into a face that seemed oddly familiar. But it was dark out, and Laney was still in that drowsy waking-up-from-a-deep-sleep haze, so she wasn't completely sure.

Then Carolyn brightened. "I know," she said excitedly. "I'll go on the other side and you stay on this side and shine the flashlight under the car. I'll call her.

Maybe the light plus the sound of my voice will make her come to me."

"Maybe," Laney muttered. "Are you sure the cat didn't run while you were at my door?"

"I don't think so," Carolyn said as she walked back around the car. "Bend down again and shine the light," she said.

Laney did as she was told, doing her best not to wish evil plagues on Carolyn and her cat.

"Oh, look!" Carolyn cried.

Laney stood. "What?"

"It's Binkie!" She pointed behind Laney. "She's running back toward our house." Carolyn squealed and clapped her hands delightedly.

Laney looked at her askance, then turned, but saw nothing resembling a white cat. "You saw her?"

Carolyn nodded eagerly. "I'll bet she'll be waiting at the door when I get there," she said, scurrying up the street.

"Do you want to borrow my flashlight?" Laney called after her.

"No. We're fine."

Laney shrugged and headed inside, closing and locking the door. She opened the refrigerator to take out the makings for spinach pasta. But just as she'd stacked the container of cheese on top of the spinach and was reaching for the butter, the doorbell rang again.

"Oh, no you don't," she whispered. "I am not going after that cat again." She walked to the foyer and called out, "Who is it?"

"Uh—hi. It's Carolyn again. I forgot something."

"What?" Laney snapped.

"Your phone."

"My—" Laney wasn't sure she'd heard right. "My phone? What are you talking about?"

"I found it on the ground," Carolyn said. "I meant to hand it to you but I forgot."

Laney glanced down at her purse. "I wasn't carrying my phone. It must be somebody else's."

"It was right beside your car—on the driver's side."

"That's imposs—" She stopped herself. Maybe when she climbed out of the car? "Hang on a minute." She felt around inside her purse, but she didn't feel the familiar cool rectangular shape of her smartphone. She emptied her purse onto the foyer table. No. Her phone wasn't there. Baffled, she felt the pockets of her slacks. Not there either.

Shaking her head, she stood and unlocked the door. "What color is it?"

Carolyn stood there, holding a phone in a white case. "Here you go," she said with a smile. "This is yours, isn't it?"

Laney took the phone. "It's mine," she said, puzzled. She felt as if she'd just been pranked.

"Thanks again for helping me," Carolyn said, waggling her fingers. "Bye." She whirled and sashayed down the steps.

After closing the door and locking it with a determined twist, Laney stood there in the foyer, looking at her phone. It had a few specks of dirt on it. *Lying beside the car on the driver's side.* It must have dropped out of her purse, although she wasn't sure how it could have.

Oh, well. It was lucky that Carolyn found it. Otherwise it would have lain outside all night, and there was a prediction of heavy showers.

ETHAN WAS ON his way to Laney's house when his phone rang. He'd decided to take her statement to her and get it signed tonight, telling himself that if she were gone all day tomorrow, it would be another day before her official signed statement got into the file, and that was just sloppy paperwork. Plus, it wouldn't hurt to check on her, make sure she was doing okay.

What he wasn't doing was making up an excuse to see her. Okay, maybe he was, but it was for her benefit. He just wanted to be sure she was safe at home, after that incident with Buddy Davis's car on the sidewalk that afternoon.

The phone rang again.

"Delancey. Where y'at?" Dixon said when Ethan answered. It was a common casual greeting in New Orleans, but usually when Dixon said it, he meant it literally.

"In my car, headed—home." He didn't want his partner to know he was checking on Laney. He wasn't sure why.

"Good. Got any brandy?"

"Sure. That bottle of Courvoisier you brought over around Christmas is still there. Why? You have a fight with my cousin?"

"No. Rose's mom is at the house with her. They're shopping online for baby clothes."

Ethan smiled and rubbed a place in the middle of his

chest where he felt a twinge. "How's she doing?" His partner had married his cousin Rosemary, whom he'd tracked down after she'd been missing and presumed dead for over a decade. Dixon had been ridiculously happy ever since, but now that they were expecting their first child, he was over the moon.

Ethan had felt an odd twinge under his breastbone ever since Dixon had told him about the baby. He rubbed the place in the center of his chest again.

"She's fine. Feeling great," Dixon said, sounding impatient.

So Dixon was not inviting himself over to talk about babies or the joys of marriage this evening. That was fine with Ethan. He'd had enough of Dixon's parental joy to last him a long time.

He figured that Dixon must want to talk about something related to the search warrant he'd executed at Senator Sills's home in Baton Rouge. It had taken Dixon and three forensics specialists two days to confiscate all of the personal papers in Sills's house, box and transport them back to New Orleans, and organize them in an empty conference room at the courthouse. "So what's up then?" he asked. "Did you unearth something at Sills's house?"

"How far are you from your apartment?"

"About three minutes," Ethan replied, taking the next left and heading back toward Prytania Street.

"Okay. See you in ten. Pour me a double brandy."

"You got it."

Ethan had changed into jeans and had the brandy poured by the time Dixon arrived. "Come on in and take a load off," he said when Dixon knocked on the screen door after clomping up the wooden staircase to Ethan's second-story walk-up.

"Thanks," Dixon said, picking up the snifter of brandy that sat on the table Ethan used as a bar. He sat in the recliner next to the couch where Ethan was stretched out.

"Have you eaten? Want to order pizza or something?" Ethan asked.

"Nah. Rose has something for me when I get home."

"Chips?" Ethan nodded toward a crumpled bag of potato chips on the coffee table.

"I'm good." Dixon took a sip of brandy. He sighed and settled more deeply into the recliner.

"So what's up?" Ethan set his soft drink down and dug into the chips.

"We executed the warrant on Sills's residence yesterday."

"Yeah, I heard. A lot of paperwork. I guess he was planning on writing his memoirs or something."

"Or something." Dixon took another long swallow of brandy.

"You're not attractive when you're coy, Detective Lloyd."

"I'm getting to it. All in all we brought seventy-three boxes of papers down from Sills's house. It took most of yesterday to load the truck, transport them and then haul them into a conference room at the courthouse."

"Seventy-three boxes. Big ones?"

"Mostly they were those 1.5-cubic-foot boxes that movers use for books."

"Big enough. So what did you find?"

"You know I stayed there all night, right? Got about two hours' sleep on one of the cots at the precinct early this morning."

"Hang on. I'll get my violin."

"Yeah. Bite me. Ninety-nine percent of it was boring stuff. Boxes and boxes of receipts. He must have saved the receipt for every single thing he ever bought. Of the one percent that wasn't boring, the forensics people only gave me what they thought would be relevant to our case, which might have been one percent of one percent."

Ethan sat up and tossed the empty chip bag into the waste can and wiped his hand on his jeans before picking up his cola. "I'm getting the picture. So did the one one-thousandth percent pique your interest?"

Dixon wiped his hand down his face. "A little bit," he muttered. "First. Darby Sills was definitely blackmailing somebody."

Ethan practically did a spit take. "Son of a— Seriously? Who?"

"Damned if I can tell. I wouldn't be surprised if he didn't know himself. His creative accounting is that good."

"Who figured it out? You? One of the forensic guys? Y'all don't have the bank records and safe-deposit box yet, do you?"

"Slow down, Delancey. One of the forensic techs brought me his bank statements this afternoon. She'd started early yesterday and had been studying the deposits all day and night and most of the day today. She's worked out a pattern, but even after she walked me through it twice I still can't find it on my own."

"How much? How long has it been going on? And damn it! Who was he blackmailing?"

"Those are the $64,000 questions. There's a forensic accountant working with our techs right now. I'm hoping he'll have an answer for us soon."

"Could the tech tell how long it had been going on?"

Dixon nodded and Ethan saw a gleam in his eyes. "For the past ten years, according to the accountant."

"Ten years ago. And he put the deposits into his regular account? Man, he had some nerve. They talk about these politicians who think they're untouchable. But Darby Sills took it to a new level. And nobody can figure out who he was blackmailing? Or what the hell somebody did that they'd pay to keep quiet?"

"That's right. I've asked Farrantino to pull any case files from that year and the two years on either side that may have to do with Sills or Buddy Davis. I'm counting on the forensic accountant to find some trace of who Sills's money was coming from."

Ethan thought for a couple of moments. "Maybe you should include Whitley and Stamps. Oh, and get one of those accountants to compare their financials with Sills's. See if anything in their records matches up."

"Good idea. What about Davis's financials?" Dixon asked.

Ethan laughed. "Sure. Why not. It could be good for a laugh. I can see it now, Buddy and Benita standing there with their lawyer, thumbing their noses at us. I'm not sure there's a snowball's chance in hell that we'll ever see a single piece of paper from them."

"We could get a court order."

"I don't know. First hint that we're coming for their records, Benita is liable to start a bonfire that could be seen from space." Ethan paused. "Man, I wish I could deal with Buddy and leave her out of it."

"Why's that?" Dixon asked as he got up to pour himself another few millimeters of brandy.

"He's the polar opposite of Benita. He's easygoing, quiet. Sometimes it seems like he's not even all there. Like he's—"

"Like he's what?"

Ethan frowned. "I don't know. He'll be talking and just sort of drift off."

"Like he's crazy?"

"I don't know. Either there's something wrong with him or he's putting on a hell of an act."

"Why don't you separate the two of them? It's your prerogative as the investigating officer."

"I'm probably going to have to do that. I doubt we'll get the answers we need by investigating them together. But separating them could stir up a whole 'nother hornet's nest. They're big friends with the Superintendent and they'll be in there pulling every string they've got as soon as I even try to put them in separate rooms."

"True," Dixon said on a sigh. He set his snifter down and picked up a manila folder he must have put there when he first came in.

When he sat back down, Ethan said, "What's that?"

"It's the other thing I found," Dixon said. His expression was grim. "I'll let you read it." He slid the folder across the smooth surface of the coffee table.

Ethan caught it before it came to a stop. There was only one sheet of paper in the folder. He read the entire sheet. At one point, he glanced up briefly to find his partner watching him over tented fingers, then he read the entire sheet again.

The contents were shocking to him, although they probably shouldn't be. Con Delancey had never claimed to be a saint. Although from everything Ethan had heard throughout his life about his grandfather, he would have figured the man to be more discreet and respectful of his wife.

"Where did you get this?" he asked.

"Sills's house. I take it you didn't know. Do you think any of your family does?"

"Know that my grandfather had an affair with Kit Powers, the famous Bourbon Street stripper? Yes. Know that he fathered a son with her? No." Ethan laughed harshly. "I think I can say with a fair measure of certainty that none of the Delanceys know that. If they had, I think I'd have heard."

He looked back at the certified copy of the birth certificate of Joseph Edward Powers, then thumped it with his knuckles. "Did you notice the date? Joseph Powers was born the same year I was. Hell, he's only a month younger than me." Ethan didn't even try to hide the bitterness in his voice.

"From what I've heard—" Dixon started, then stopped.

Ethan sent him a sidelong look. "Go ahead. What were you going to say?"

Dixon shook his head. "Nothing. Forget it." Dixon took a sip of his brandy and swirled the glass, watching the golden liquid.

"Come on, Dix. It's not like you're going to say anything I haven't heard before. You think I don't know what kind of man my grandfather was? I mean, in a lot of ways he was admirable. His record of public service is long and filled with innovative programs to help the people of Louisiana. He was generous—he'd give a man the money in his pocket and did, many, many days. But he was a scoundrel." Ethan gestured toward the birth certificate. "No denying it."

"People say your grandmother locked her bedroom door after their youngest child was born."

"I know. I've heard that." He shrugged. "And maybe it's an excuse for what he did. But—"

Dixon didn't speak.

"He was my granddad. It's hard to think about another Delancey out there. A—what? Half cousin? Plus, if there's one, who's to say there aren't more?" He chuckled wryly. "Dozens even."

After a pause, Dixon spoke. "So what do you want to do about it?"

Ethan sighed and closed the folder and set it on the coffee table. "Hell if I know," he muttered, still unable to take his eyes off the plain folder. "Who all saw this?"

Dixon thought. "Maybe nobody other than the tech who brought me the folder. The only label on it said Delancey. The tech said, 'I thought you might want to go through this yourself.' I suppose I could ask him if he looked at anything."

"No. Leave it alone. I want this under lock and key. Nobody is to know about it."

"Are you sure?"

Ethan nodded. "Until all this mess with Sills's death is over—absolutely. Personally, I'd rather not have this information released—ever. But even thinking as a detective investigating a high-profile murder, I know that this piece of paper will only muddy the waters and cause a flurry of gossip and renewed interest in Con Delancey. We can't afford all that distraction if we're going to find Sills's murderer."

"I agree. The question is, do we give it to the commander or do we keep it secret?"

"My vote? Keep it secret. I'll put it in my safe-deposit box."

Dixon looked at him questioningly. "You don't think that's withholding evidence?"

"Evidence of what?" Ethan said on a laugh. "Con Delancey's wandering...eye?"

Dixon stood. "Okay. It's your family. It's your call. Do you want the rest of the folder?"

"Yeah. I'll stick it all in the box. What's in the rest of it?"

Dixon held up his thumb and forefinger, about an inch apart. "Documentation of meetings Sills had with your grandfather. Later on, cassette tapes. Looks to me like he was hoping to be able to blackmail Con. I haven't listened to the tapes, but as far as written records, that birth certificate was the only thing in the whole file that he could have used. I wonder why he never did."

Ethan stood, too, and held up his hands as if framing a screenshot. "I can see it now. Sills tells Granddad what he's got and Granddad just shrugs and says, 'Slap it on the front page for all I care.' I'll bet that's exactly why it's buried in a dusty file. I'll bet Con Delancey told him where he could put it."

"Well, I'd better get home. I just wanted to tell you about Sills's information on your granddad."

Ethan followed Dixon out onto the porch. "Yeah. I appreciate it. Let me know as soon as you get the safe-deposit box. I'm betting that if there's any information anywhere about the people Sills was blackmailing, it'll be in that box. Once we've got those names, then we'll have a real suspect list."

Chapter Six

It was after four by the time Laney finally got on the road back to New Orleans from Baton Rouge. The meetings had gone longer than she'd anticipated. The first one, to discuss who would be appointed to finish out Senator Sills's term, had deteriorated into a three-hour debate between the governor's executive assistant and the president of the senate. The only thing they agreed on was that Laney should work with the new appointee's staff to ease the transition. They couldn't even agree on who would pay her.

That information, she thought bitterly as she exited off I-10 onto Veterans Memorial Boulevard, could have been passed on to her in a phone call.

The second meeting, to discuss the funeral arrangements, was delayed because the senator's older daughter's baby had an earache. By the time it was over, Laney had been excused from any part in the planning or execution of the funeral by both daughters, who also spent quite a bit of time debating. When four o'clock rolled around and nobody seemed inclined to wrap up the *discussion,* Laney excused herself, saying that she had to get back to New Orleans before dark.

Now she drove to the storage building she'd rented when her dad had gone into an assisted-living facility. At the time, it had seemed like a good idea to rent storage space near his home in Kenner so she could move furniture, boxes and books as she had time. Now she wished she'd gotten one nearer her rented house in the lower Garden District.

She keyed in the password at the gate to the storage facility and drove to her building. By the time she unlocked the padlock on the garage door it was five o'clock, and she needed a flashlight to find the two boxes labeled Dad's Papers and wrestled them into the backseat of her car, probably ruining her dark blue slacks and gray blouse.

As she headed back through the gate and onto the access road for Veterans Memorial Highway, a car appeared out of nowhere and sped straight toward her. She tried to gun the engine to get out of the way, but the other car veered at the last second and sideswiped her on the driver's side.

The screech of metal on metal hurt her ears as the impact sent her car spinning into the other lane, where a panel truck barely missed her. Her car slid sideways off the shoulder of the road and finally came to a stop.

Laney sat unmoving, stunned. From the first instant when she'd seen the small car barreling toward her, everything had moved in slow motion. She'd experienced every second as if she were watching one of those super-slow vignettes in a movie. The kind of split-screen action where the driver relived years of memories in the few seconds it took to crash a car or down a plane.

Vaguely, she became aware of a rapping noise. She opened her eyes and saw a man looking at her through the windshield. He was saying something she couldn't understand. After watching him blankly for a moment, she realized he was motioning for her to roll down her window. She pressed the button on the console, but although she could hear an electrical whirr, nothing happened. Once the man saw that the window wasn't working, he gestured toward the passenger side. With a passing thought that this wasn't the man who had sideswiped her, because he had on a white cap and that man had worn a black hat, she lowered the window on the passenger side.

"—the door." The man was talking to her.

She frowned. Had he said unlock the door? "I don't—" she said in a barely audible croak.

He peered at her searchingly. "Are you injured? Bleeding? I need to see if you're all right. I've called the police."

Call Ethan, she wanted to say, but she couldn't make a sound. There was a lump in her throat that felt as big and hard as a stone. She shook her head no, because she didn't think she was injured. Then she swallowed hard and tried to talk past the stone. "Who—who are you?" she croaked, peering at him sideways. For some reason she thought it might be better if she didn't move too much. She felt slightly nauseated and every time she turned or nodded her head, it seemed as though something hurt somewhere.

"I was in the truck. That car pushed you right into my lane. I barely missed you. Was he chasing you?"

"No," she whispered raggedly. "I'd just come—" at that second, for the life of her she couldn't remember where she'd been. All she remembered was the crash. "Where's my purse?" she asked.

"It's right here." The man pointed at the floor of the passenger seat.

"My phone. Call Ethan. Delancey." She tried to shift in her seat and found out, first, that she couldn't move, and second, that the vague pain she'd noticed had suddenly become very specific and very sharp. "My shoulder hurts," she said.

The man grabbed her purse, then glanced up. "Okay," he said. "Just stay right there. The EMTs are on their way."

It took over twenty minutes for the EMTs to get her out of the car. The damage to the frame wasn't that bad, but the door was bent in enough that it kept the lock on the seat belt from releasing. The EMTs had to pry off the driver's-side door, then cut the seat belt.

They checked her vital signs and carefully examined her for broken bones or internal injuries. Once they were satisfied that her only injury seemed to be a bruised left shoulder from the impact, they got her to her feet and helped her walk to the back of the ambulance and sit.

"Okay," the male EMT said. "How're you doing?"

"I'm feeling kind of sick," she whispered. "Sorry."

"Hey, don't apologize to me," the young EMT said with a little chuckle. He pointed to his female partner.

"Just turn your head toward her if you think you're going to throw up, okay?"

WHEN ETHAN GOT to the scene of the accident, he noticed that Detective Stephen Benoit of the Kenner Police Department, whom he'd met a couple of times before, seemed to be in charge. He quickly introduced himself, in case the other man didn't remember him, and explained that the accident could be connected with a case of his and that Laney Montgomery was his witness and a victim in the crime. Benoit gave him a quick rundown of what had happened and told him to stick with him. A crime scene tech came up to the detective, so Ethan took a few steps closer to the back of the ambulance, so that he could see where Laney was sitting.

She seemed unhurt, he saw with relief, except for her left shoulder, which one of the EMTs was carefully manipulating.

From what he could hear of their conversation, the EMT was explaining about the bruised biceps and triceps and what she could expect. Each time he appeared to be finished, Laney would ask another question. Once the EMT tried to brush off her questions, saying the answer was just a bunch of technical stuff that she didn't need to know.

"I do," she said earnestly. "Please. I need to understand."

The EMT patiently explained about bruises and how ice was the best thing for a fresh bruise. As he talked to her, the other EMT taped a reusable ice pack to her shoulder on top of her blouse.

Ethan knew that a couple of hours spent with her did not make him an expert on Laney Montgomery, but right now, watching her as she concentrated on what the EMT was telling her, he was certainly getting a more complete picture of her. She'd been precise and careful in her answers to his questions about the shooting, but now it occurred to him that she was just as precise and step-by-step about everything.

He allowed himself a small smile. He understood, maybe better than a lot of people ever could, where all that need for precision came from. It was her effort to hold on to as much control as she could, even in situations where no control was possible, like right now. He could identify with that. Living in the same house as his father and his oldest brother Lucas, who were always at loggerheads, he'd learned before age ten that logic and careful attention to facts got him a lot further than an explosive temper and a short fuse. He wondered what in her life had taught Laney that lesson. He could see that she was more of a control freak than he was.

It didn't take much imagination to see that she would be hell to live with. But the question was, would she be worth it? *Oh, yeah.*

Detective Benoit stepped up beside Ethan. "How is she?" he asked.

"Looks like just a bruised arm," Ethan said. "Mostly she's just shaken up. You talked with the guy driving the truck?"

Benoit nodded. "He saw the vehicle speed toward Ms. Montgomery's car. Said he heard the engine rev.

The car was definitely gaining speed. It was no accident."

"Did he see anything?"

Benoit nodded. "Definitely. The vehicle was a sports car. Red, naturally. He didn't know the make. Said it was one of those low, fast things. Maybe Italian. He caught a glimpse of the license plate."

"He did?" Ethan was excited. Maybe he could get a lead on Sills's murderer from this.

"Only got two letters and he's not sure of the position of the letters or color or state. But he swears the two letters are correct. He also saw the driver. Said the man had on a black cowboy hat with some kind of shiny decoration on it."

Black cowboy hat with shiny things. Ethan grabbed his pad and made a note. "What were the two letters the driver saw?"

Benoit consulted his own notes. "C and F."

Ethan wrote that down as his brain fed him the obvious interpretation of that partial plate—something to do with Circle of Faith. "I need to run Buddy Davis's plates. I know he drives a sports car."

"Why Davis?" Benoit asked.

"Something the witness told us about the man who shot the senator and her. The C and the F on the license could be 'Circle of Faith.'"

Benoit gave him a skeptical look.

"Look, man," Ethan said. "I hate that I can't be more specific, but my commander wants us to keep certain things under wraps."

"No problem," Benoit said.

Out of the corner of his eye, Ethan saw the EMT hand Laney a little plastic bag with two tablets in it.

She nodded. "Thank you," she said, her voice breaking.

He glanced at Benoit, who nodded. So he stepped closer to her. "Hey," he said with a smile as the EMT closed his emergency box and moved out of the way. "It's all over now. You're fine."

"You came," she said, her voice quivering slightly.

"Of course I did," he responded. Obviously she was a lot more shaken than she appeared to be. Although she'd been at the point of tears several times, she hadn't actually cried during the entire ordeal the other night. That probably explained her tears now. She'd been through a lot and now she'd reached her breaking point.

He didn't want to take a chance on making it worse, so he took a deep breath and put on his "just the facts ma'am" demeanor, figuring that would be better than being too nice or too solicitous. As much as she valued her control, she might not be able to keep from crying. "You're my witness. That means you're my responsibility."

She sniffed, bit her lip, then nodded.

Benoit stepped up and began questioning her, writing down everything she told him. Once he was done, he said, "We'll need to get you back over here to read and sign your statement, Ms. Montgomery."

Ethan spoke up. "If you'll send it over to the Eighth, I'll make sure it's signed and sent back."

Benoit agreed. He thanked Laney and him and told her that one of his officers could take her home.

"That's okay. I'll take her," Ethan said. "Let me ask you a favor. She told you she'd stopped at the mini-storage to pick up some boxes. They're right there in the backseat of her car. She picked them up because they're part of my investigation into the murder of Senator Darby Sills."

He heard a murmur of protest from Laney, but ignored it as he saw the detective's eyes widen. "That's the case you're working on? I thought I recognized the name Montgomery."

Ethan nodded. "I need to take them with me."

"Technically, those boxes are part of this incident."

Ethan grimaced internally. "Technically," he said with a nod, "you're right. I'd owe you one."

The detective regarded him thoughtfully for a moment. "Send me an official request first thing tomorrow," he said.

Ethan nodded. "First thing." He held his breath. He wanted the boxes tonight. If he was right, they were Elliott Montgomery's personal financial records. They might include proof that Darby Sills was blackmailing him.

"Okay," the detective said, nodding. "Go ahead and take them. Need any help?"

Ethan shook his head. "Thanks." He shook the detective's hand again, then got the keys to the car from the tow truck driver and quickly transferred two medium-size boxes from Laney's backseat to his trunk.

While he was doing that, Laney stood and waved off a police officer's help. She walked over to his car. Her eyes still sparkled with unshed tears as she faced him, her back straight, her face flushed with anger. The effect was diminished by the pale blue sling the EMTs had given her for her arm. "You can't possibly believe that my father was being blackmailed."

"So you eavesdropped on my conversation with the detective."

"Of course I did. It concerned me. How could you possibly think Senator Sills was blackmailing *my* father. Go after the dozens and dozens of people Sills *could* have something on."

"Seems to me that Elliott Montgomery could be one of them. And you know I'm checking out everybody who had a relationship with Sills. Tell me something, Laney. Why did you want those boxes, anyhow, if it wasn't to see if his bank statements showed excessive withdrawals?"

Laney stared at him, fury blazing in her blue eyes. "I don't have to answer that," she said. "They are my property, and I don't think you can just *confiscate* them."

"On the side of the boxes it says 'Dad's Papers.' I was going to ask you for them anyway," he said, opening the passenger door for her.

"That does not answer my question," she said icily.

He looked at her. "Let me refer again to the discussion I just had with the other detective."

She scowled. "What about it?"

"There's the answer to your question. I can take those boxes, and I did."

"But the way you told that detective, you let him think I was getting the boxes for you. What if I tell him

I wasn't? Don't you need a search warrant or a court order or something?"

He shook his head. "They were in plain sight. Sorry."

She sent him a scathing look, then carefully got into his car and reached for the seat belt, pausing when she realized she couldn't fasten it with her arm in a sling. "I don't see why I have to wear this ridiculous thing. My shoulder isn't bothering me that much."

Ethan noticed her struggle. He said, "Hang on. I'll get it for you." He closed the passenger door and went around to get in on the driver's side. As he reached across her for the belt, he caught a whiff of something sweet and citrusy. Unable to help himself, he turned his head slightly to breathe in the scent. A soft, choked sound came from her.

Embarrassed, he pulled back immediately, pulling the seat belt with him and quickly attaching it. "Sorry," he said, starting the car as he glanced sidelong at her.

Her right arm came across her middle to cradle the wrapped left arm. She cleared her throat. "Detective?"

"It's Ethan," he said gruffly.

"I don't want you looking in those boxes until I've had a chance to go through everything."

He glanced over at her. "We can look at them together."

"No."

"Then I'll take them to the station and you won't get to see them at all until this case is over."

She sniffed in exasperation and leaned her head back against the headrest. He could feel frustration and anger emanating from her in waves.

"Sorry," he said for about the third time since he'd gotten to the accident scene. "I'm not just being mean. And you don't have the authority to *allow* me to see the contents of those boxes. This is a murder investigation. Your dad's papers are evidence. If I can find out who Darby Sills was blackmailing, I'll be that much closer to the killer."

After a moment of dead silence, Laney said, "Well, I can tell you for a fact that my father didn't kill Senator Sills."

"That *is* a fact," he said carefully. "Indisputable, since your father is dead."

"Oh, my God, do you think I killed the senator?"

"No—"

"You do. Pretty clever, huh? Shooting myself. Wait a minute. The crime scene techs checked my hands for gunshot residue, didn't they? Have you figured out how I managed to graze my temple without getting powder burns on my face or gunshot residue on my hands? Well, let me just tell you right now. I am that good."

He heard the pain and fear behind her angry words. "You know," he said. "You're allowed to be upset. You're even allowed to be scared. A lot has happened to you in a short time."

"Don't patronize me, *Detective*. I am perfectly capable of handling things. But the very idea that you could think I had anything to do with the senator's murder—" Her voice caught. She cleared her throat, trying to cover it, but he wasn't fooled. If he looked at her right now, he knew that he'd see tears in her eyes again.

"So you can *handle things* when someone is murdered practically in front of you, you're shot and two days later you're rammed by a car?"

"Yes," she said. She tried for a determined, confident answer, but her voice was meek.

"Well, you're doing a great job," he said as he pulled up to the curb in front of her house. He jumped out of the car and went around to open the passenger door. He held out his hand but Laney ignored it, climbed out awkwardly.

"Don't bother walking me to my door," she said. "I'll be just fine."

"Will you?" he asked as he closed the car door. "Okay, tell me this. Are you going to take those tablets the EMT gave you?"

"I haven't decided yet."

"Have you got someone coming to stay with you tonight?"

"Why in the world would I need anyone to stay with me?" she asked.

When she fished her keys out of her purse, he took them from her and unlocked the door. He stepped inside and flipped on the lights, then examined her face. "You're pale. You look like you're about to pass out. Is your arm hurting?"

"A few bruises never bother gorgeous cops on TV."

Ethan glanced at her in amusement. "The important word there is *TV.* Again—fiction."

"Fine," she said. She'd never realized how difficult it was to deal with a purely logical mind. She'd always been the most practical person she knew. But Ethan Delancey had her beat by a mile. Several miles.

"I have ibuprofen in that cabinet with the coffee cups." She gestured. "There's cranberry juice in the refrigerator. I'd like half juice and half water. No ice. But if you want something to drink, you can probably figure out where the ice is. I'm going to sit down in the living room. I'm feeling a little woozy."

She sat down on the couch that had been her dad's and did her best not to cry. She was upset. She was scared. Her shoulder hurt. And in a couple of hours, Detective Ethan Delancey would know as much about her father and his dealings as she did. And it was entirely possible that she herself would know more than she ever wanted to know about the man who'd raised her alone after his wife, her mother, died of alcohol poisoning.

"I'm going to get the boxes and bring them inside," Ethan said.

Laney clenched her fists as the front door banged against the wall of her foyer. She aimed a scathing look toward the door, but truthfully, she was more angry at herself. "I should have put the them in my trunk," she muttered. If she'd taken the extra trouble then, Ethan wouldn't have seen them and she wouldn't be torn between two choices—looking at her father's papers in front of a detective or relinquishing them to the police. In either case, she probably wouldn't get them back for years.

But at least if she looked at them here with Ethan, she'd know what was in them.

Chapter Seven

Laney yawned and tried to focus on the bank statement she was holding. She was having trouble keeping her eyes open. "What's wrong?" Ethan asked. He was sitting on the floor with his back against the couch, sorting through papers.

She looked up bleary-eyed. "What?"

"You groaned."

"No I didn't," she said, although she knew he was right.

"You're about to fall asleep, aren't you? You should go to bed."

"I'm not going anywhere and leaving you to go through my dad's stuff alone."

"Don't trust me?"

"Not as far as I could throw you if you were holding both boxes," she said, trying to suppress a yawn.

"Are you hungry? What have you eaten today?"

Laney opened her mouth to answer, but stopped. She couldn't remember. She'd drunk a cup of awful coffee at the precinct early in the morning and had a couple of glasses of water during the day, but food?

"You haven't eaten, have you? I knew it. I'm hungry, too."

She thought about the pasta she'd never made the night before and her mouth watered. "I can make spinach pasta," she said, then looked down at the sling on her left arm. "Or I could if I had two arms."

Ethan rose to his feet. "I have two arms. I can make it if it's not too hard."

She stood, too, and stretched. "It's not hard at all. Butter, garlic, frozen spinach, mascarpone cheese and Parmesan. Come on. We need to get the water boiling for the spaghetti." She led the way into the kitchen. When she turned, Ethan was way too close to her.

Her little kitchen, which she'd always thought of as cozy and comfortable, suddenly seemed as small as a broom closet, with him standing there, towering over her by at least five inches.

He smiled. "What's the catch?"

"The catch?"

"With the pasta sauce? It can't be as easy as it sounds."

She slid past him to open the refrigerator, doing her best to ignore his faint clean scent. "There's a package of angel hair pasta in that cabinet next to the sink, and there's a big pot in the cabinet below the counter." Her voice sounded stiff to her ears, and higher pitched than usual. She cleared her throat as she pulled the thawed spinach, cheeses and butter out of the refrigerator one at a time.

"There's no catch. Trust me, the sauce is just as easy as it sounds," she said, answering his question. "My mother used to make it back before—" She stopped, then went on quickly, trying to cover what she'd almost said. *Back before she died from drinking.* "She always said it was a perfect date dinner. Said my father proposed over a big plate of her spinach pasta."

While she'd been talking, Ethan had retrieved the pot and filled it with water. He set it on the stove and turned on the gas. Then he looked at her. "Perfect date dinner? Good to know."

Before she could interpret the look he'd sent her way, he turned and grabbed a package of angel hair pasta from the cabinet. "This won't take long to cook," he said.

Laney set a skillet on the stove and awkwardly unwrapped a stick of butter, one-handed. With a knife, she cut half off and put it in the skillet. "Sounds like you know a little bit about cooking."

"My dorm mates and I ate a lot of spaghetti and Tony Chachere's in college."

"Tony's? That's all you put on it?"

"Don't knock it. It's pretty good if you're trying to eat cheap."

Laney grabbed a jar of minced garlic from the refrigerator. She set it on the counter and tried to slide the sling back so she could hold it with her left hand. "Okay, that does it," she muttered. "This thing's coming off." She reached behind her head, looking for the fastener.

"Hey, what are you doing?" Ethan said. "Give me that jar." He opened the jar for her and she put a heaping teaspoonful in the melted butter.

"That's a lot of garlic," he said.

"If you don't like it I might have some Tony's," she retorted.

He laughed. Unlike his smiles and smirks, his laugh was hearty and genuine. When she glanced up, his mouth was stretched wide and, she noticed with surprise, he did have laugh lines. They, along with his dark, serious eyes, were just about the only thing that kept him from looking like a teenager instead of a police detective who had to be in his early thirties. She felt laughter bubbling up from inside her. It had been days since she'd even felt like smiling, much less laughing.

She picked up the container of mascarpone cheese and tried to pry the top off, but with one hand, it was impossible. She growled.

Ethan reached over and put his hand on top of hers. "Hey," he said. "I've got all this. Don't get so frustrated." He opened the container. "How much?"

"All of it."

He emptied it into the skillet as she stirred. "Man, that smells amazing."

"It is amazing," she said. The bowl of drained spinach was covered with plastic wrap, which she managed to pull off with one hand. She dumped it into the skillet and began stirring everything with the tongs.

"Should I put the pasta in the water?" he asked. "It's about to boil."

"Sure. The sauce will be ready in about seven minutes or so. That should be just about perfect timing."

By the time Ethan drained the angel hair, the spinach mixture was creamy and hot. She added a generous pinch of salt and handed Ethan the pepper grinder.

"About three turns ought to be good," she said.

He turned the pepper grinder, then leaned over the skillet to take a deep whiff. "Wow. Is it ready?"

She nodded, grinning at him. "Except for the Parmesan." He twisted off the cap for her and she added a generous portion to the mixture. "Now, pour the spinach sauce over the pasta and mix it, please?"

"Yes, ma'am." He picked up the skillet and poured the sauce into the pot of drained angel hair pasta. Then using the tongs, he tossed the two together quickly. He turned to her with raised brows. "*Now* is it ready?"

She laughed at his boyish question as she reached into a cabinet and came out with two bowls. "Dish us up some and I'll grab the jar of Parmesan in case we need more, although I don't think we will."

Within a minute they were sitting at her small dining room table and eating. "I have some wine," she said. "But—"

"Yeah. Better not. You realize we're only about halfway through the boxes."

"I do," Laney said, "but the good news is I found Dad's bank statements."

"Good, because what I've been sifting through are tax records and receipts from back in the nineties. When we finish eating, I'll take some of those bank statements, because that's where any indication of blackmail is going to be." He gestured with his fork. "This is spectacular," he said. "I can see why your dad proposed."

"It's magical food," she said, smiling, too, as she shoved another forkful into her mouth. Tonight Ethan reminded her of how he'd been when he'd come to see her in the E.R. Gentle, kind and solicitous. But after his officious attitude in the interview room at the precinct, she'd decided the pain medication had made her dream that he'd been nice. Still, she could definitely understand why people talked about the Delancey charm, not to mention the Delancey good looks.

Ethan had on a white shirt, dress pants and leather loafers that would probably decimate her salary. It was the same uniform he wore at work, minus the sports jacket, but somehow tonight he seemed like just a guy, instead of a logic-driven, uptight police detective, concerned with *just the facts, ma'am.*

In fact, he seemed like the kind of guy she'd always wanted to meet. Intelligent, considerate, funny. *Whoa.* Was she actually thinking about Ethan Delancey as a man she could date? She felt her face grow warm. She didn't want him to ask her why she was blushing, so she stood to carry her bowl to the kitchen.

"Don't even think about trying to do the dishes. I'll take care of them." He stood and picked up his bowl.

"I'll let you. Isn't it time to take the ice pack off my arm?"

"Probably. How does it feel?"

"Hard to say. It's numb." She flexed it gingerly. "It's not as sore, though. Can you take it off?" She turned her back and held her hair out of the way.

When he touched her neck as he worked the ice pack out from under the sling, she shivered. His fingers were hot against her chilled skin, and she wondered if they would feel just as hot and make her just as tingly if he touched her in other, more intimate places.

"Got it," he said and stepped around her to put it in the freezer.

She had to swallow before she could speak. "Thanks. I'm going to go back to the papers and leave you alone with the kitchen cleanup."

"Are you sure you're up for more sifting through piles?" he asked. "It's after eight. You might want to take one of those tablets and head to bed. The EMT said to rest."

Laney stared at him. "Go to bed? At eight o'clock? I don't think so."

"See. You're already going against doctor's orders. You sleep and I'll finish going through the papers, then sack out on the couch."

"Sack out—? Why?"

"Because somebody's got to watch over you while you're incapacitated."

"I'm not incapacitated. It's just a bruise and I am not going to sleep in a sling. And I'm sure not going to bed in the middle of the evening."

"See. I can't leave. I've got to make sure you follow doctor's orders."

"What you'll do is go through the papers and then go home," she said, angling a disgusted look at him as she headed back to the living room. Sitting down on the couch, she picked up the small pile of papers she'd been going through earlier. From the kitchen came the sound of water running and dishes rattling. She shook her head at the image of Police Detective Ethan Delancey washing her dishes.

Being nice and charming was one thing, but why

was he talking about spending the night on her couch? She'd seen in his face that he knew the excuse of watching over her was ridiculous. But what was his real reason? She didn't know, but she wasn't comfortable with it, whatever it was. She knew she wouldn't be able to sleep if he were out here on the couch. She'd lie awake knowing there was no way in hell he and she would ever get together, but wishing he was in her bed anyway.

Doing her best to shake off the picture of him lying on her couch in his shorts—or briefs, she picked up the first folded and rubber-banded pack of bank statements. She opened it and perused the first sheet. It was for the month of January, a year before her dad had died. It looked like she'd expected it to. Deposits, the monthly fee for the assisted-living facility, automatic payments for utilities and insurance, and cash withdrawals. Nothing unusual. She smiled wistfully as she looked at the withdrawals. He liked to play the slot machines, and went to Harrah's casino near the Riverwalk once or twice a week. She'd often met him there or at a nearby restaurant for dinner.

She paged through the rest of the statements in the stack, which could almost be photocopies of the January one. With a sigh, she wrapped the rubber band around them and set them aside. Then she pulled eleven identical packets out of the box. There they were. Twelve years' worth of Elliott Montgomery's day-to-day life.

Ethan came back into the room as she was dumping the packets onto the floor and delving back into the box.

"What's all that?" he asked.

"A dozen years of my dad's life," she answered, her

voice breaking. "I never thought that checking account statements would be personal, but I can see his everyday life by looking at those sheets." She felt her eyes fill with tears and blinked them away before Ethan could see how sentimental she was.

"You're saying there's nothing unusual. Nothing you wouldn't expect. Withdrawals? Checks?"

"That's right. All those statements, and there's probably only a few dollars' difference between one and the next."

"So that's checking and savings?"

She stopped. "Savings," she said, looking up at him. "Savings. Oh, my God." She started pulling papers out of the box. "I can't believe I didn't remember. After he died, I was surprised at how little money he had in savings."

Ethan's gaze sharpened. "Why?"

"He used to talk about the bonuses he would get from various companies at the end of the year—for doing a good job lobbying for them." She shook her head. "When he went into the assisted-living community, we thought it would take everything he had to buy into it. Luckily, we were able to sell his house and that almost paid for the buy-in. His monthly rent came out of his checking account, just like his mortgage did in earlier years. But all that money that should have been left in his savings account—wasn't there."

"How much are you talking about?"

Laney hesitated. She'd learned a long time ago that most people were suspicious of lobbyists anyway.

When—if she told Ethan how much money her father had saved, what would he say?

He met her gaze and she knew he'd picked up on her hesitation and the reason for it. "Laney, my grandfather was Con Delancey. I'm not going to pass judgment on your dad for what he did for a living or how much money he amassed doing it. All I want to know is how much money went missing from his savings account and when it happened."

"He went into the assisted-living community six years ago. I have no idea how much money he'd put into savings during his life, but at the time we were calculating how much it would cost for him to live there, his balance was around three hundred thousand— No."

She shook her head, not even able to allow the next thought into her head. "I don't believe my dad was being blackmailed. He would never have done anything he was that desperate to hide."

"How much was in the account when he died?"

"I—" she said, then had to swallow the acrid saliva that rose in her throat. The answer to that question made her nauseous.

"Laney? How much?"

"Around twenty thousand." She could barely speak the words. "I wondered what had happened to the money, but I never even thought about—" She definitely couldn't say that word in connection with her dad.

"Wow," Ethan said. "In six years. That's fifty thousand a year over and above his daily expenses. Was he that big a gambler?"

Laney laughed uneasily. "No. I've never known him

to take more than a couple hundred into the casino, and if he lost that, he was done for the day."

"Where are the savings records?" Ethan asked.

"I don't know, but I can't believe that—" A thought occurred to her. "Maybe he left it to some charity—anonymously. I wouldn't know about that, right?"

Ethan shook his head. "I'm pretty sure you would. We need to find those records."

Laney sat there.

"Hey," Ethan said, putting a hand on her arm. "Are you all right?"

She shook her head. "I don't want to find the savings records," she said in a small voice. "I don't want to know what happened to that money. Please, can we stop looking?" She looked up at him and saw an odd expression in his eyes. It looked almost pitying.

"No, we can't. I can't. I'll take them to the precinct and finish there, but I can't stop looking. We know Sills was blackmailing someone. This is murder, Laney. Murder."

"Well, my dad didn't do it!" she cried. There were too many awful emotions churning inside her. Anger, fear, grief, denial.

Ethan took her hand. "Your dad's records might help us find the killer. I understand how much it hurts to find out something shocking about your family. Something you never knew, and that you can't believe they would do."

"Do you?" she said, pulling her hand away, but Ethan wouldn't let it go.

He took her other hand, too. "Yes. I found out, and

I managed to live with it. You'll live with it, too. And if you know your dad, and I'm sure that you do, you'll find out why he did it, and you'll be able to live with that, too."

"I'm afraid of knowing," she muttered.

"I know you are." He sat there, holding her hands and looking into her eyes.

She saw them turn smoky and dark and she felt as if she were sinking into their inky depths.

He let go of her hand and touched her cheek. For an instant, she thought he was going to kiss her and she realized she wanted him to. Desperately. She looked down at his mouth.

"Okay?" he whispered.

To kiss me? "Okay," she responded.

"Good." He let go and turned back to the boxes, leaving Laney stunned and embarrassed.

She'd been expecting a sweet, gentle kiss to go with Ethan's sweet, gentle words and touch. But all he'd wanted to do was get back to searching for proof that her father had been being blackmailed.

"Let's keep going," he said. "We don't really have a lot left to go through."

She should have known. Sure, he was charming and good looking. And those qualities obviously worked to his advantage when he wanted something—like now. What a chump she was, to think he'd wanted anything else.

She cleared her throat. "Okay," she said wryly. "Let's."

They dug through the rest of the papers, looking at

everything. Laney quickly emptied her box, finding nothing. No bank book. No statements. No records of any kind. "That's impossible, isn't it?" she asked Ethan, doing her best to be a trouper. "There has to be some kind of record of withdrawals from savings."

He nodded, not looking up. "Definitely some kind. I suppose he could have thrown them away, or it could have been totally digital. Did your dad have a laptop computer?"

"No. Dad never advanced into the digital age. He never even had a cell phone."

Ethan picked up a large stack of medical bills and statements.

Laney peeked at a couple. "Those are from ten years ago. When he had his first heart attack and had a triple bypass," she said.

"Wait a second," Ethan said, setting aside the sheets. "There's something else here—" He pulled out a small stack of letters, bound with a rubber band. "What's all this? Letters to your dad from you. Where were you writing from? Summer camp?"

"Let me see those," Laney said. "The only time I went to camp was the year I was thirteen. And I for sure didn't write all those letters." She took the rubber band off and looked at the envelopes. "The top two are the only ones I wrote. These others are—wait. They're in Dad's handwriting. What was he doing, writing on envelopes as if they were from me? Why would he do that?"

She pulled the folded stacks of paper from one of the envelopes. "Oh, my God, Ethan! It's the savings account records. He hid them in here." She quickly read through the top one and her throat closed. She covered her mouth with her hand.

"What's wrong?" Ethan asked.

She shook her head, unable to talk. She held out the folded sheets for him to take.

Ethan saw how upset Laney was. And he was sure he knew why. He took the statement from her and perused it. "Hand me the others," he said, and scanned them, as well. Then he looked up at her, and saw her read the truth in his eyes.

"It's true, isn't it?" she said hoarsely.

He could tell by the look in her eyes that she already knew the answer. She was already thinking it herself. Only she was trying to pretend she wasn't. He knew her brain was spinning, had been ever since she'd remembered the ending balance in the savings account, trying to come up with another plausible explanation for those large withdrawals.

He clenched his jaw. He had to say it, because otherwise she would just sit there for who knew how long, doing her best to deny it. "It's true," he said flatly, figuring that if he tried to comfort her right now, she'd lose it. "Given the size of the withdrawals and the frequency, I don't think there's any doubt."

She swallowed and her gaze wavered, but she didn't say anything.

"Laney, of course your dad was being blackmailed. It's the only explanation."

For a few seconds, she didn't move. Then she folded her hands in her lap as her head moved slowly back and forth, back and forth. "What could he have done? He was a good man. A decent man. He raised me by himself after my mother died."

"People can be blackmailed about all sorts of things, Laney. I just found out that Darby Sills tried to blackmail my grandfather about having a child with another woman. That was hard for me to take. That my grandfather disrespected my grandmother. That there's a Delancey out there that my family has never known about."

"That's *your* family. Everybody knows Con Delancey was a rounder and a crooked politician—" Her hand flew to her mouth again. "Oh, Ethan. I'm sorry. I didn't mean to—"

He waved away her apology. "Don't worry about it. If you knew half the things I know about my family—"

She looked at her hands. "I really believed we wouldn't find anything."

Ethan didn't respond to that directly. "There are some huge withdrawals here."

She nodded, seeming to rally a little. "And he obviously went to a lot of trouble to hide the savings account statements."

"Maybe he was embarrassed, or didn't want you asking questions about where the money went?"

"No. I don't think that's it. Look how he printed his name and address and put my name as the return address. That might fool somebody else, but not me," Laney said, her voice unsteady. "He probably meant for me to find these right after he died. I guess I wasn't paying attention when I packed these, or else I was distracted and didn't stop to think that this bundle was way too big to hold the four or five letters I'd written to him."

Ethan sat down beside Laney and took the statements from her hand, sorted through them quickly, then handed her back about two-thirds of them, starting with the most recent dates. "How many years' worth are here?" he asked.

"Twelve years," she answered. "I'm surprised it isn't forty. He saved just about everything."

"Do you feel like taking these and flagging the inordinately large withdrawals on each statement?" he asked, watching her carefully. Although she was extremely intelligent and highly intuitive, he knew that the little girl inside her that still missed her daddy had just received a huge, agonizingly painful dose of reality about the man who'd reared her.

"Sure," she said, straightening her back. "Do you think, if the withdrawals are blackmail, that he was paying them to Senator Sills?"

"I don't know, but once we have the information about the withdrawals, the forensic accountants can compare them with deposits Sills made. So while you flag those, I'm going to find when the withdrawals started."

It took them over an hour to skim through the monthly statements. As Ethan finished with each year he had, he handed the bundle to Laney. Once he got through ten years of statements and started on the eleventh, he discovered exactly when the withdrawals started. So he bundled the oldest two years up and tossed them back in the box. Laney was still reviewing and flagging. She'd slipped her hand out of the sling so that the job was a little easier.

While she worked, Ethan got up and retrieved the ice pack from the freezer. It was almost frozen.

"Is it time for that again?" Laney asked when she saw him with it.

"You're wincing whenever you move that arm. Here, let me put it under the sling." He stepped up behind her and brushed her hair away from her neck so he could slip the ice pack under the sling without getting it tangled in the strands. When he did, she inclined her head slightly and that sweet, citrusy smell he'd noticed in the car wafted across his nostrils.

To his embarrassment, he felt a pleasant stirring deep inside him that heralded the beginnings of arousal. He tightened his jaw as he made sure the ice pack was secure.

He would not give in to his body's cravings. Not with her. She was a victim, a witness, and tonight, she was a grieving daughter and, last but not least, his responsibility. He turned and went into the kitchen and drew a glass of water from her refrigerator dispenser. It was cold and refreshing as he swallowed it. It would be good if he had another ice pack, one he could apply directly to the area that was fast becoming hot and hard, but the thought was nearly as good as the deed. By the time he'd finished drinking the water, the problem was almost gone.

"Ethan?" Laney called.

With a grimace and a stern, if short, lecture about

keeping business and personal stuff separate, he went back into the living room.

"I'm done," she said, gesturing toward the stack of statements on her lap. There were tiny, colored sticky flags adorning every single sheet.

"Are you okay?" he asked. She looked better than she had earlier. The color that had drained from her cheeks was back.

"I am. I'm not sure why. Maybe I'll collapse in grief tomorrow, but right now, I'm kind of creepily fascinated with the amounts of money he withdrew." She shook her head. "Is that awful?"

He smiled. "No. I think your brain is coping by becoming involved with the mundane stuff, the numbers and amounts of withdrawals. Just go with it."

"Okay. So you won't believe how many withdrawals I found. I looked for those over five hundred dollars, because I don't think Dad ever withdrew that much for his personal use. Maybe once or twice, if ever."

"How many?"

"You handed me ten years of statements, so that's essentially 520 weeks, right? Well, he sometimes made withdrawals more than once a week. I counted 848 withdrawals of $500 or more during that ten years."

"Five hundred dollars or more. How much more?"

"Some were as much as a thousand. A few were even larger. Plus, he transferred money from savings to checking a few times a year, usually around $5,000." She rubbed her temple. "I'm still just stunned. I'm sitting here looking at these withdrawals and I still can hardly believe that *my dad* did this."

"I'm going to use the calculator on my phone. Go through the statements and call out the amounts. You can go as fast as you want."

Laney sighed. "That's a lot of numbers. I'm cross-eyed already."

"It won't take too long."

She went through the statements, reading off numbers as rapidly as she could find the flagged entries. "Eight hundred. Sixteen fifty. And seven forty," she said finally. "That's it."

Ethan held up the total. "I can't guarantee I got every single one, but take a look at this. Over $550,000 in ten years."

She pressed her lips together and sent her gaze skyward. He knew the information was devastating to her. After a second, she nodded. "That's probably right," she said. "Your forensic accountants can get the real numbers, can't they?"

Ethan nodded, feeling an unexpected pride in her for rallying, despite the shocking truth that her father was paying blackmail. "Yep. I just wish we had some way of knowing who he was paying. All my instincts say Darby Sills." He paused before asking the question that was on his lips.

"Are you sure you can't imagine what your dad's secret might have been? Nothing sticks out in your mind about your dad and money? Or the relationship between him and Sills?" As he spoke, he stacked the statements and tapped them against the surface of the coffee table to straighten them. Then he picked up the envelopes and a large rubber band.

"No. Dad never talked about money with me. Not after my mother died. The two of them had huge fights about money before she got sick enough that she didn't care to fight about anything." She sighed. "It's no wonder he avoided the subject at all costs."

"You've mentioned your mother a couple of times. Did she die when you were young?"

Laney nodded. She bit her lip for a second, then sighed. "You should probably know everything, if my father's information can help with finding out who murdered Senator Sills. My mother was an alcoholic. A very good one," she said with a sad smile. "Apparently she could drink a lot without actually appearing drunk, until she passed out."

"I'm sorry, Laney."

"And that's what killed her. She died when I was eleven. I know most of this because he told me. She was hiding vodka and drinking about a quart a day. I know—" she said, holding up a hand. "That's hard to believe. Most days by the time Dad got home, she was passed out."

"But what about you?" Ethan interjected.

"I was pretty good at taking care of myself. But one day when she left the stove on and I burned myself trying to turn it off, Dad decided she had to get help. He made her go to rehab. She stayed for about two weeks and was not drinking. But she checked herself out, went to a hotel, drank a quart of vodka and died of alcohol poisoning. It was probably a wonder that she hadn't overdosed before then."

Ethan looked down at the bank statements. Now he

knew. Now he understood. Laney had been forced into the role of adult. Her father had worked and she'd been at home with her mother, after school and in the summer. And so, she'd become an adult, probably a long time before the age of eleven. No wonder she never answered a question on the fly. No wonder she assessed everyone. Children of alcoholics have a warped sense of trust, if they can trust at all. He understood that because of his father, who had been a mean and violent drunk before his stroke.

"I'm so sorry," he said, not only because of how her mother had died, but also because of how her mother had forced her to live.

"I'm good," she said. "I've done a pretty good job of getting over all that. But thanks."

He nodded. She had done a good job. An excellent job.

She pushed her hair back and stretched and yawned. "So you mentioned earlier about my dad's relationship with Senator Sills."

"Right," he said. "I did."

"All I ever knew about Senator Sills was that he and Dad had known each other forever, and about once a month or so, Sills would come over to the house and he and Dad would sit in the living room with the door closed." She stopped for a moment. "I *do* remember them yelling at each other. But I was a teenager and all I wanted to do was listen to music, so I pretty much stayed in my room with my stereo turned up."

"Their meetings could be a clue. Maybe your dad made the withdrawals and then Sills came by once a month to get the money." As he spoke, he stretched the rubber band around the statements and envelopes. When he did, a scrap of paper fell out.

Laney bent down to pick it up. "Something fell out," she said, looking at the small piece of paper. "It looks like one of Dad's notes. He was always writing me notes on torn scraps—" She gasped. "Oh, Dad."

Ethan saw her face crumple. "What is it? What's on the piece of paper?"

She handed it to him without looking up. She pressed her right hand against her mouth, trying not to sob.

Ethan looked at the scribbled note. The first line read, "I hope you find this, daughter. First thing, get away from Darby Sills. He's dangerous."

Chapter Eight

Ethan read the first line again, then the rest of the note.

> I hope you find this, daughter. First thing, get
> away from Darby Sills. He's dangerous. Quit that
> job and don't go back. Take this note and the sav-
> ings account statements to the police. Make sure
> they know how dangerous Darby is. And make
> sure you get all the money back. It was always
> meant for you.

"Meant for me," she said through her tears. "Oh—"
She sniffed, then bent her head and covered her eyes
with her good hand.

"Hey," Ethan said softly. "It's okay."

She shook her head. "He meant the money for me,"
she wailed. "He was trying to take care of me and Darby
Sills stole everything—" Her voice gave out and she
began to cry.

Ethan had no idea what to do. Laney's heart was
broken, not only because of what Sills had done to her
dad, but also because she'd just discovered that her fa-

ther wasn't the superhero and saint that she'd believed him to be.

For Ethan, as soon as he heard what was in the note, his first instinct had been to grab it and the bank records and rush down to the courthouse where the forensic accountants were working. By morning they could have the withdrawal amounts matched up with Sills's deposits. Because as well-meaning as Laney's father had been, he hadn't actually written anything in the note that Ethan could use to prove that Sills was blackmailing him.

But looking at Laney, he knew he couldn't just grab her dad's records away from her and leave. She needed comfort and reassurance right now, and as much as he dreaded having to offer her comfort, knowing what it was going to do to him to be that close to her, he was all she had. So, gently and carefully, he put his arm around her and pulled her toward him. He did his best to keep it platonic and casual.

When he touched her, she stiffened at first, but he forced himself to keep his embrace featherlight. Within a moment the rigidity went out of her and she pressed her face into the hollow of his shoulder, her tears soaking into his shirt.

He said things. Later, he could never remember what, but whatever he'd whispered to her as her sobs faded, they must have helped because she stayed there, in the circle of his arms, for a long time. After a while he stopped talking and just sat and held her, torturing himself by mentally cataloging every wonderful, sexy thing about her. Her soft fragrant hair, her slender shoulder with the sweet curve that his fingers caressed, the warmth of her breath against his skin.

Finally, her breaths stopped hitching and became relatively quiet. A few moments later he felt her sigh, then she lifted her head and pulled away from him. He didn't try to hold on to her, but he did leave his arm draped around her shoulder. She let it stay there, too.

He looked at her with a little smile. "Better?"

She made a face. "I don't like to cry. It just messes up my face and gives me a headache."

He laughed softly and she did, too.

Then she nodded. "Yes. Better." She met his gaze and he marveled at how blue her eyes were. He'd thought from the beginning that they were lovely.

"I think you have the most beautiful eyes I've ever seen."

She blinked and her tongue slipped out to moisten her lips as her gaze slid downward from his eyes to his lips.

He had a sudden need to swallow—hard. Here they went again. Just like before, he sat perfectly still and hoped like hell that she didn't kiss him, because he was already very much on the edge. If she so much as leaned toward him, the tension and anticipation that now zinged through him would erupt into full-on lust, and he'd have to stop himself from jumping on her like a horny teenage boy.

She's your responsibility. Your responsibility.

"Look, Laney—" he said stupidly, because he had no idea what to say. He was just desperate to stop her from looking at his mouth. It worked. Her gaze snapped back to his face.

"Ethan?" she whispered. Her eyes were dewy bright and her cheeks were pink. He brushed his thumb across her flushed skin and her head inclined toward his touch.

Laney saw the question in Ethan's eyes. She had no idea how to respond, wasn't even sure she was reading his expression correctly.

He leaned forward, his gaze moving from her eyes to her lips. Then, as she let her eyes drift shut, he brushed her mouth with his, nothing more than a featherlike touch, but the impact of it was stunning. For that brief second, she'd felt as though someone had lit her lips on fire.

His gaze flitted upward, toward her eyes, then back down and he inclined his head and kissed her again. This time, the touch of his mouth on her wasn't featherlike at all. His mouth was firm, his kiss demanding. Laney took a short gasping breath before he covered her mouth with his and kissed her more deeply.

She let her lips part. Her tongue met his. She tasted him as he tasted her. She couldn't believe the rush of feelings his kiss was evoking in her. She felt it like a river of lava, flowing through her, igniting fires everywhere it went. And she wanted more. She moaned with the yearning.

Ethan went still. "Am I hurting your arm?" he whispered.

"No," she gasped. At this point, if it were burning like the fires of hell she wouldn't admit it. That's how badly she wanted to stay in his arms. That's how badly she wanted him to make love to her.

"Are you sure—?" he started.

She'd had enough of his caution. She leaned forward and kissed him openmouthed, teasing him with her tongue, daring him to kiss her back as intimately as she was kissing him.

He hesitated for an instant, but then with a throaty groan, he met her boldness with his own. He opened his mouth, kissing her fully, deeply, exploring with his tongue in a rhythmic dance with hers. His hand cupped her cheek and his thumb played that magic again across the apex of her lower lip, pulling her deeper into his spell.

Her arms slid up to wrap around his neck. The bruises on her arm ached, but the pain was nothing compared to the exquisite pleasure of his kiss.

After a long time, Ethan pulled away again. This time though, he left his hand on the bony curve of her shoulder. His gaze met hers, searching. She let her eyes drift shut and wet her lips with her tongue. He skimmed his fingertips across her sensitized skin, tracing a sensuous path across the sloping line of her collarbone and on to the small indentation below the column of her throat.

She swallowed and opened her eyes to meet the question in his. In answer, she caught his hand and guided it downward, downward, until his fingers nestled in the hollow between her breasts. He pulled her close and kissed her deeply, leaving her breathless. Then he planted light, erotic kisses along the line of her jaw.

She gasped as he moved upward to nibble on her earlobe, then back down to savor the soft, sensitive skin beneath her jaw. At the same time, he cupped her breast and played with her nipple until it was hard and throbbing.

"Ethan?" she panted.

He pushed her back against the couch cushions, fumbling at her waist. Desperate to feel him inside her, she brushed his hands away and undid her slacks so he could slide them down. Then he rose to his knees above her to undo his own clothes.

Once his arousal sprang free he sank between her knees and pressed it, smooth and hot and hard, against her. She whimpered in yearning. His hand slid between them and he touched her, tested her, caressed her. She felt the flowing warmth that signaled her readiness. He did, too—she knew because he made a sensual growling sound, deep in his throat, then lifted himself and pushed into her with a shuddering gasp.

Laney inhaled sharply as he sank into her, filling her with exquisite pleasure. Without hesitation she lifted herself to meet him and then both of them were frenzied, too turned on to be gentle or careful. They moved as one, not because they knew each other's bodies and preferences, but because they seemed fused together, feeding off each other's passion.

Within what seemed to be seconds, Laney's body tightened in almost unbearable anticipation. As Ethan thrust harder and deeper than he had so far, she felt herself explode into a thousand tiny shards.

Ethan came almost immediately after, with a soft, shuddering cry. The two of them collapsed against the couch cushions, panting. Soon their harsh breaths slowed and softened, and they lay together, languid and spent. Laney trailed her fingers across his shoulders, raising goose bumps where she touched. Ethan's hand rested against Laney's cheek, where his thumb played lightly back and forth, mimicking the flutter of butterfly wings.

When the doorbell rang, Ethan started and Laney stiffened beside him. They'd fallen asleep, still in each other's arms.

"Oh, no," Laney whispered, sitting up and squirming to pull her pants up and fasten them. "That better not be—" She pushed away from him and struggled to her feet, still fumbling with the button at her waist. She smoothed her hands down the front of the pants, then pushed her fingers through her hair to tame it a little. She put her hands to her cheeks, then fanned them with her hands.

"Be who?" he asked as he stood and fastened his pants.

"Oh, nothing. A stupid girl with a silly cat!" she groused as she headed for the front door.

He followed her, grabbing the edges of his shirt and settling it on his shoulders. He wiped a hand across his face, trying to banish the haze of sleep. He had no idea who the stupid girl was or if she or her silly cat might be dangerous, but he wasn't taking any chances. His gun was in his car, damn it. So he stood behind Laney and to her left, prepared to jump the person if needed.

With her hand on the doorknob, Laney called out, "Who is it?" Her voice was after-sex husky and it sent a spear of lust through him. He shook his head and forced himself to concentrate on who might be on the other side of the door.

"My name's Emma. I'm selling candy for our marching band," a small, childish voice said.

Laney's breath whooshed out in a long sigh. She grabbed her purse and pulled out a five-dollar bill.

Ethan stopped her with a hand on her arm as she prepared to open the door. "Hang on. It's almost ten o'clock. Late for a child to be going door-to-door. Step back as you open it. If it's not just a child selling candy, I'll have a straight shot to jump them."

She frowned at him, but did as she was told.

Ethan stiffened as the door swung open, but it actually was a little girl standing on the stoop with a woman who was obviously her mother. The girl smiled shyly.

"What in the world are you doing out this late?" Laney asked, eyeing the mother, who smiled sheepishly.

"She forgot to tell me about it," she said.

"And it's not late," the little girl said, sounding much older than her years. "I go to bed when Mommy and Daddy do. Do you want some candy?" She held up a cardboard carrier.

"Sure," Laney said. "How much will this buy?" she asked, proffering the bill.

The little girl grinned. "Two boxes. And you get a dollar back."

"Good," Laney replied, smiling. "Give me two boxes, and you keep the dollar for your marching band."

"Mommy! She said keep the dollar!"

"I know, Emma. I heard her." The mother mouthed *Thank you* as she led the little girl back down the sidewalk.

Laney closed the door.

"What stupid girl and silly cat?" Ethan asked her as she put her purse back on the foyer table and walked back into the living room.

"Oh, it really was nothing," she answered, making a dismissive gesture. "Last night some annoying little housewife from down the street thought her cat had gotten under my car. She wanted me to come out and help her find it." Laney flexed her shoulder and winced.

"You didn't go out there, did you?" Ethan asked, a faint warning buzz taking hold at the edge of his brain.

"Yes. I thought it might save me from being talked to death." She shook her head. "I'm not even convinced there was a cat. I never saw it. We looked all around and underneath my car. Then finally she said she saw it running back toward her house. So she just headed off down the street with barely a thank you."

"And that's all that happened?"

"Yes," she said. "You know, if she'd waited instead of bothering me, within ten minutes that cat would have been back at her door wanting food. Then, not five minutes later, little Miss Carolyn knocked on my door again. She had my phone! She said she'd picked it up off the ground near the driver's-side door and—get this—forgotten to tell me."

The buzz in his brain grew louder. "How long did it take you to look for the cat?" he asked.

"Maybe five or six minutes."

"And what time was it?"

"When I went outside? I don't know. Around seven or so? When she handed me my phone it was seven-ten."

"So it was dark." He didn't like the direction his brain was taking. Had the young woman gotten Laney outside and distracted her while an accomplice had snatched her phone from her purse? But why would anyone go to all that trouble to take her phone, then give it back to her? "And she wanted you on the far side of your car from the house?"

"Okay Detective Delancey," she said. "What's with the third degree?"

"Where's your phone now?"

"In my purse." She got it and handed it to him.

He examined it. There was only one explanation he could think of for lifting her phone and then bringing it back. "What's your password?"

"Hey," she said. "What are you doing?"

"Give me your password."

She did.

"Damn, Laney. That's the last four digits of your phone number. That's the default password for every phone out there. You're supposed to change it as soon as you get the phone."

Laney gave a small shrug of her right shoulder. "I know," she said. "Lazy."

"Yeah," he said in disgust. Then a moment later, "Not just lazy. Dangerous."

"Dangerous? Why?"

"Your phone's been bugged."

"My phone? Bugged?" Laney repeated Ethan's words. "As in, they can hear what we're saying? I thought a bugging device was—big. Too big to go inside a cell phone."

"This is a totally new technology. It's software-based bugging. They can track your whereabouts with GPS any time the phone is on. They can hack into your conferencing software with their number so their phone rings when you make or receive a call, and they can listen to all your telephone conversations. I've seen it before. Whenever your phone rings or you dial out, the software alerts them and they can record or listen in on your conversation."

She shivered. "I should have known. There was something about that girl. She looked vaguely familiar, but she also seemed a little too eager. Not so much worried about her cat as worried about getting me to help her. So someone walked right into my house, got my phone out of my purse, and I didn't even see them. Ethan, that really scares me."

"It should. Any other time it might have been just a rather annoying incident with a neighbor. But you're involved in a murder. Remember me telling you to be careful? To call me if *anything* unusual happened? The woman wanting you to come help her find her cat qualifies as unusual. You should have called me when it happened."

"I know. I know," Laney said, looking chagrined. "But why would anyone do that? What do they think I'm going to say on my phone that will help them?"

Ethan shook his head. "If it's the murderer, he may want to find out for sure how much you know, or if you recognized him. You said the girl looked familiar. Have you seen her around the neighborhood before? Walking? Driving? Calling her cat?"

Laney shook her head. "No. I'm gone all day and I don't know most of my neighbors. But when I say she looked vaguely familiar, it's not that I've seen her around. I'm not sure I can explain it. It was more like she reminded me of someone. Like you'll see someone who reminds you of an actor, but you can't place which actor it is. You know?"

Ethan nodded without looking up. He was staring at her phone. She'd handled it all day and he'd handled it just now. If there were any usable prints of the person who bugged it, it would be a miracle. But he was going to try it anyway. "Can you get me a paper bag? If you don't have one a plastic baggie will do."

"For what?" she asked. "Wait. Are you thinking you can get prints? I'm sorry, but I wiped the case with a wet cloth when she gave it to me. I cleaned the screen, too. I doubt there's anything left on it."

"I'd still like to try," he said.

While he waited for her to bring him the bag, he turned off her phone. When she held out a small paper bag, he slipped the phone into it, then stuck it into his pants pocket. "I'll take it to the crime lab first thing in the morning. See if they can lift a print off the surface or the keys. It's a long shot, since you cleaned it, but it's worth a try."

"And you'll have the bug taken out?" she asked hopefully.

He shook his head. "I don't think so. No. If we remove the bug, then they'll know we're on to them. But if I leave it bugged, you *have* to watch what you say. Remember, the man who murdered Senator Sills could be listening in." He pulled out his phone. "And when you're driving, I want you to turn the phone off. I don't want them tracking you by GPS. Now, I'm going to call a couple of officers to canvass the neighborhood to find your friend Carolyn. I have a feeling they won't have any luck."

"If she was just distracting me while her partner bugged my phone, do you think he bugged the house, too? Can they hear what we're saying now?"

"I doubt he had time to set a bug in here, but I'll have your house swept. We don't want to take any chances." He quickly made the call.

When he hung up, Laney said, "You're going to have all that done tonight? We won't get any sleep."

And as she predicted, it was after three o'clock in the morning before the last of the lab techs left. Laney felt as though she were sleepwalking. She'd made coffee for the techs but she hadn't drunk any herself, fearful that she wouldn't be able to sleep after they left if she filled up on caffeine.

When Ethan came back into the living room, Laney looked up at him with sleepy eyes. "So what did they find?"

"You want the full rundown? I told you once they finished with your room you could go to bed."

"No I couldn't. Not with my house being swept and scoped and whatever else, like a crime scene."

"Nothing was scoped," he said, smiling.

"Fine. Make fun of me. But wait until after I go to bed. Right now I want to know what they found."

"Okay. Your phone was clean of prints and the techs agreed with me that if they removed the bug or tampered with it in any way, it would alert whoever is on the other end. The computer guy did look at it for a few minutes, to see what he could find. He couldn't find anything he could trace. He said whoever bugged it was good. As far as your house, it's clean. No bugs."

"That's a relief," Laney said. "So what about Carolyn?"

"She doesn't live around here anywhere. My officers knocked on doors all over this subdivision, and the phone tech back at the precinct checked every address and phone number within a mile radius. No Carolyn."

"Wow," Laney said. "I should have had more sense than to play into her little charade. I should have called you. We'll probably never find out who she is."

"Well, I hope we do, because she and the person who walked into your house and bugged your phone are both working for the murderer."

Laney shivered and stood, ready to go to bed. But she thought of a question she should have asked hours ago. "Ethan? These people obviously know where I live. If they—if the murderer wanted to find me and—you know, kill me, he wouldn't have any trouble. So why the GPS and the bug?"

"Think about it. What happened this afternoon? That guy in the sports car knew where you were. He waited for you to come out of the storage lot and then he rammed you. He probably wanted whatever you were picking up from your storage building. Did you tell anybody on the phone that you were going by there?"

"No, I don't—oh, wait," she said. "When I talked to Senator Sills's secretary about the meetings this— well, yesterday morning, I told her I had to leave by four o'clock because I wanted to go by my storage building in Kenner before it got dark. Oh, I don't like this."

"So he figured you'd be getting something from your storage building that pertained to the case. But now they probably know that I've got it, since you had that truck driver call me to tell me about your accident."

"But if I turn the phone off when I'm driving, they can't track me, and if I don't say anything on the phone, they won't know where I'm going."

"That's the plan."

ETHAN TURNED OVER for about the thirtieth time and tried his best to stay asleep. But this time there was more going on than just being disgustingly uncomfortable. His phone was ringing. He sat up, trying to remember exactly where he was and why he'd slept on a lumpy couch. Squinting, he peered around him. This wasn't his place. It was Laney's house. He was sleeping, or trying to, on her lumpy couch. The night before and Laney came back to him in a flash. Odd that it hadn't felt lumpy when they were both on it. Although, as intense and sexy as their coupling had been, he doubted he'd have noticed a tsunami.

When he stood and looked at himself, he remembered that he'd taken off his pants, knowing that he was going to have to wear them again today. They were draped over the opposite side of the couch. He leaned forward to grab them.

"Is that your phone or mine? You have both of them." It was Laney, standing in the foyer doorway with a sheet wrapped around her. She held the two edges together with a hand at her chest.

Ethan grabbed his pants and held them in front of him as he turned around. It occurred to him that for all their intimacy of the night before, they hadn't yet seen each other naked. And now they were standing in front of each other as if they'd never seen each other before at all. "Yeah. Sorry if it woke you."

It rang again at that instant and he groped in his pockets until he found it. It was Dixon. "Hey, Dix. What's up? You're calling awfully early."

"Not that early," Dixon answered. "It's after eight. What are you doing? I ran by your house last night and you weren't there."

"That's right. I'm at Laney's."

"I got your message about Laney's accident, the phone bug and everything, but you didn't mention you were planning to stay there all night. What the hell are you up to?"

Ethan clenched his jaw. "What did you call about, Dixon?" he grated. He saw Laney turn and head back down the hall.

"I got corralled about Laney's accident as soon as I walked in the door this morning. Seems a Detective Benoit of the Kenner Police Department thought you'd have sent him the official request you promised first thing this morning. He said it's for some evidence that was found in Ms. Montgomery's car."

"Well, I considered first thing to be more like nine o'clock than eight. They get 'em up early over in Kenner, don't they?" Ethan said. He heard the water come on in the bathroom. "I'll get that request sent as soon as I get in. We should be there at the station no later than nine. Depends on how long it takes Laney to get dressed."

"Delancey?" Dixon snapped. "I hope you've got better sense than to do what I'm really afraid you've already done."

Ethan was not going to answer that. "That accident was no accident, Dixon. She stopped at the storage facility to pick up her dad's financial records, which, by the way, you'll be seeing today, because her dad withdrew large sums of money every week for the past ten years."

"Ten years?" Dixon's voice grew excited.

"Yeah. How long do you think it'll take to get those withdrawals matched with Sills's deposits?"

"If they match."

"Yeah, right. If they match. But they're going to match, I'll guarantee it."

"Yeah, okay. But even if they do match, what have we got? Obviously Montgomery didn't kill Sills." Dixon sighed. "I'll let you know what I find out. The reason I called was to tell you that we have Sills's safe-deposit box. So if you can tear yourself away from Ms. Montgomery, why don't you come on over to the courthouse and I'll show you some interesting stuff."

"I won't have any problem *tearing myself away* from Laney, Dixon. So get that superior smirk off your face right now. I can't see it but I know it's there." Ethan heard a noise and turned to see Laney standing in the living room doorway, dressed. The hurt look on her face told him she'd heard what he'd said about tearing himself away from her. He held up a finger to signal to her that he'd be just another minute.

She turned and went into the kitchen without acknowledging that she'd noticed him at all, much less seen his signal.

"We'll be there within half an hour, okay?" he said, the irritation obvious in his voice. "I'll see you then." He hung up. "Laney?" he called. "How're you feeling this morning?"

She stepped out of the kitchen into the foyer. "I'm fine," she said coolly. "So don't worry for a second about having to tear yourself away from me. I can take care of myself."

Ethan scowled at her. "Look, Dixon was kidding me, giving me a hard time for staying over here last night. I was repeating what he'd said, that's all. Don't take offense to something I say to my partner. Most of our conversations are a mixture of ribbing and a sort of shorthand that we use to communicate when we're at a crime scene or tracking a perp."

She shrugged. "Thanks for the explanation. Are you taking my phone in this morning? When can I get it back?"

"You can get it back now. One of the lab techs examined it and took prints last night. I cleaned it and left it on the table near the front door."

She retrieved the phone from the table and started back toward the kitchen. "What time are you leaving?"

"I'm not leaving—*we're* leaving," he answered sharply. "Haven't you been listening to me?"

"No, I'd rather not go to the station with you. I'd rather stay here, in my own house, where I'm perfectly safe. You can call me and let me know which dealership has my car. I'll get in touch with them and have them bring me a loaner. Then I can be out of your hair completely."

"Okay, that does it. You're coming with me. There's no way I'm leaving you here alone. I've already explained to you several times that you could be in danger. After yesterday, I'm certain you *are* in danger. Now, Dixon has Sills's safe-deposit box. I want to find out what's in it. Don't you?"

"You mean I can see it?"

"No, you can't see it. But you can wait at the station and when I find out what's inside it I'll let you know."

"I can wait here," she said stubbornly.

"I suppose you could, but you won't," he replied, just as stonily, "because I'm not letting you out of my sight."

THE NEXT DAY Dixon knocked on the door of the small shotgun house on Perrier Street while Ethan stood aside. When the door opened, Dixon smiled. "Hey, Boone," he said.

Detective Boone Carter had been near retirement when Dixon had caught his first homicide—the purported murder of Ethan's cousin, Rosemary Delancey, who was now Dixon's wife. Ethan had never met Detective Carter, but he'd heard a lot about him. The detective had been a legend on the streets of the French Quarter back in the day.

"Hey, Lloyd. Man, you still look wet behind the ears to me. How long has it been?" Boone held the screen door open for them.

"Boone, this is my partner, Ethan Delancey," Dixon said, once they were inside.

Ethan held out his hand and Boone took it. "Yep. You definitely look familiar. Your granddaddy was Con Delancey, wasn't he?"

"Yes, sir."

"Con Delancey," Carter said again, shaking his head. "I'll be a monkey's uncle! You look a lot like him, son. He was a son of a bitch, but he was a grand man."

"Yes, sir. Thank you, sir," Ethan said.

Boone gestured toward the back of the house. Ethan followed Dixon through the small house that had gotten its name because a person could stand on the front porch and shoot a shotgun through the front door and hit nothing but air, if all the doors were open.

"Go on, go on. Out the back door," Boone said. "You'll see what I been spending my time on since I've been retired."

They stepped out the back door onto a concrete patio with a stone fountain square in the middle of it. The fountain was about the size of the kitchen they'd just walked through, and the bowl of the fountain held several koi. Surrounding the fountain and the patio were assorted ferns and other tropical plants.

"This is beautiful," Dixon said.

Ethan whistled. It was beautiful. It looked like a tropical hideaway on a luxurious island. The plants hid the small patio from view of the neighbors, and by the same token they hid the wire fences and peeling paint of the neighboring houses from anyone sitting on the patio.

"Sit down, sit down. Maggie made some iced tea. Help yourself."

Ethan poured himself a glass from the pitcher full of ice and tea and Dixon did the same. Boone already had a glass sitting beside his chair.

He took a swig, then looked at the two of them. "So what's up at the Eighth? 'Cause I know you didn't come here to admire the view."

"It is spectacular," Dixon said, propping an ankle on the other knee and taking a long swallow of tea.

Ethan knew that it was his job to question Boone about the incident they'd uncovered in Darby Sills's safe-deposit box. They'd found a copy of the domestic disturbance report Boone Carter had written that had apparently never been filed, because despite Farrantino's meticulous search of the case files for the past ten years, there was no mention of an incident involving Darby Sills.

Ethan sat forward. "Detective Carter?"

"Boone, son. Call me Boone."

"Boone," Ethan said reluctantly. He didn't feel right calling the gray-haired man by his first name. He'd heard stories about Carter's years as a detective. To him the man sounded like a superhero; and now that he'd met him, he looked like one, too. Still in great shape, Carter had a loose, predatory confidence that Ethan was sure had intimidated even the most hardened of criminals.

"So tell me what you got to tell me son, and I'll see if I can help you guys out at all."

"You know that Darby Sills was murdered four days ago," Ethan started, but was interrupted by Carter's booming laugh.

"Yep," the detective said, grinning. "I knew it. I know exactly why you two are here." He sat forward and rested his elbows on his knees. "Hit me with it."

"Well, sir. Among the contents of Senator Sills's safe-deposit box was a police domestic disturbance report made out by you of an incident with Sills and a prostitute."

Carter was staring down at the patio floor. He nodded. "That's right," he said.

Ethan waited, but Carter didn't say anything else. He looked at Dixon, who just raised his eyebrows and took another swallow of iced tea. So Ethan waited, too, sipping at the too-sweet tea.

"When I heard somebody had shot Darby, I wondered if it had all finally come to a head." Carter shook his head without looking up. "What an idiot."

Ethan frowned. "Who?" he asked.

Carter sat up and picked up his glass. "Darby, of course. He had a lot of problems—couldn't keep it in his pants, couldn't pass up a free meal, no matter who was buying or what kind of strings were attached, and worst of all, couldn't stand to throw anything away." Carter chuckled. "I'll bet y'all found every receipt for everything he ever bought, including gum."

At that, Dixon let out a laugh. "You're right about that. And I've had the pleasure of going through all that."

"So," Carter drawled. "See anything in that safe-deposit box about Buddy Davis?"

"Buddy Davis? Why?"

Carter sent him a wry look. "Just making conversation."

"Detective—sorry, Boone," Ethan said, "is there something you know about Davis that might help us with the investigation of Sills's murder?"

Carter stood and walked over to the fountain. From the wide ledge surrounding the pool, he picked up a small container and sprinkled some food into the water. "Let's see, I guess it's been ten years ago now. What was that girl's name? Oh, I remember. Cristal Waters. She pronounced it with the emphasis on the *AL*. Made sure I spelled it right on the police report. *Like the champagne,* she told me."

Ethan watched him sprinkle a few more grains of fish food, then stand and watch them crowd one another as they fought for the morsels. "I was called to a real skanky house, way over across Rampart. Man, I couldn't believe my eyes. First thing I saw was Darby Sills, hopping on one foot and crashing into walls, trying to get his pants on. Cristal was holding a wet washcloth against her lip, which was split so bad the cloth was red with blood. Her eye was swollen, too, and starting to turn purple. When she saw me, she started yelling. I swear I think it took me a full minute to figure out what she was saying. She was yelling Buddy Davis's and Elliott Montgomery's names at the top of her lungs."

"Montgomery?" Ethan said, a queasy dread suddenly pressing on his chest. "Are you sure she said Elliott Montgomery?"

Carter stopped laughing and scowled at Ethan. "Yeah," he drawled. "I am."

"What was she saying about them?"

"Well what do you think, sonny boy? She swore they were there with Darby."

Ethan winced. This was bad. Laney had been devastated by the thought that her dad was being blackmailed. She would be crushed when she found out that it was because of a prostitute. "Did you find any evidence that either of them had been there? Because there's nothing in the report."

"Do you think it mattered one damn bit whether there was evidence or not? Why do you think that report was never filed?"

Ethan shook his head.

"Because about five minutes after I called in to dispatch that I was answering a domestic dispute call and gave the address, and about two minutes after I walked into that room and saw what I saw and heard what I heard, I got a phone call from the commander, telling me to get Sills out of there and make sure nothing was ever heard about the incident again."

"Who was your commander?" Ethan asked, but Carter was still talking.

"And don't think for a minute that it was the Eighth

Precinct commander's decision. That order came straight from the superintendent."

"Because it was Senator Sills," Ethan said.

"That's right."

"But what about the girl? What happened to her?"

"She never changed her story that those two were there with Sills," Carter said. "Even though she swore that Sills was the only one who'd touched her. But somebody paid her to keep quiet. I don't know if it was Sills or Davis or Montgomery or—even the department."

Could some or all of the money that Laney's dad withdrew have gone to Cristal Waters? It was possible, but Ethan didn't think so. As much as it galled him to think that someone in the highest ranks of the NOPD would pay off a witness to protect a prominent politician, that seemed like the most believable explanation. Second most believable—Sills. Maybe Sills extorted money from Davis and Montgomery to pay Cristal.

Carter laughed. "It would have been a great story, wouldn't it? Those three, the prominent statesman, the famous televangelist and the important lobbyist, all caught with their pants down—literally and figuratively." He turned to the fountain, picked up his box of fish food and closed it, then sat back down and picked up his nearly empty glass of tea. "So you guys think Buddy Davis killed Darby Sills?"

Chapter Nine

By the time Ethan and Dixon returned to the police station, Laney felt as if she were going out of her mind. She knew they'd gone to talk to retired Detective Boone Carter about a police report they'd found in Senator Sills's safe-deposit box. The report had never been officially filed.

It was less than three hours after Ethan had told her he was not going to let her out of his sight and here she was, back in an empty interview room waiting by herself.

She picked up the coffee cup she'd been given by an officer an hour ago. It was stone-cold, of course, and just as muddy tasting as it had been when it was hot. With a grimace of distaste, she set it back down and stood up. The room was small and most of it was taken up by the table and chairs. She walked over to the barred window and looked out at Royal Street.

Last night had been a stunning night, in many senses of the word. The idea that her father really had been paying blackmail to Darby Sills had ripped away the last vestige of illusion she'd had about him. Like most little girls, she had worshiped her father, maybe more than most, since her mother had died when she was eleven and so for most of her life it had just been her and him.

She supposed most children eventually found out that their parents were not superheroes, that they were just people who made mistakes and did things they regretted. She wondered if she was later than most learning that painful lesson.

She knew Ethan thought she was naive. She'd seen it in his eyes. He'd had a hard time believing she'd never wondered about the money her father had in his savings account, or the type of work he did or why he received such generous bonuses. She wished she could explain to Ethan that she'd never known another child whose parent had done the same kind of work her dad had. She'd never had anyone to compare him with.

Thinking of Ethan brought back the memory of the night before and their frenzied lovemaking. It had started innocently enough. She'd been upset, not so much that her father was being blackmailed, but that he'd done something to make himself vulnerable to blackmail. She didn't like to cry, and she'd have given almost anything not to have broken down in front of Ethan, but he'd surprised her. He'd been as tender and solicitous as he'd been that first night in the E.R. So when he'd reached out to comfort her, she'd eased right into his arms. It had felt right somehow, to let him hold her and whisper to her.

Then, when the tender comfort had changed to desire, she'd been as frenzied as he. They'd torn at each other's clothes, coming together with a passion she'd never felt before. Ethan was harsh and demanding and yet at the same time careful. She herself had quickly abandoned all care. For her, nothing had mattered except being as close, as intimate with him as was humanly possible. Their climaxes had been explosive and nearly simultaneous.

For those moments he was not a police detective and she was not a crime victim. There was no murder, no blackmail. The world had dissolved and the two of them may as well have been transformed into pure desire.

But this morning, their fiery lovemaking and their tender aftermath might have been just a dream. In the harsh light of day it seemed insane to think for even one second that they could be anything other than two strangers brought together by the insanity of a violent crime. His job was to solve the murder of Senator Darby Sills and her job—her job was to answer his questions and do her best to identify the faceless black-clad person who had killed the senator.

Once the case was solved, she doubted she'd ever see Detective Ethan Delancey again. As she tried to suppress that depressing thought, her phone rang. When she checked the display, the number was unknown. She grimaced. She was not in the mood for more questions about what she'd seen or requests for interviews. But here she was, stuck at the police station, with nothing to do, not even a magazine to read, so, knowing she was probably going to regret it, she answered the phone.

To her delight, it was the dealership where her car had been towed. With a grateful sigh she gave them her personal and billing information and asked them how long it would take before her car would be ready.

"It's going to be a few days, ma'am," the woman told her. "Would you like for us to arrange a loaner car? You do have that option with your insurance."

She opened her mouth to say yes, but Ethan's concern about her being in danger echoed in her head. "I'm not sure yet," she said. "Can I call back when I decide?"

The woman assured her she could, and told her she'd call her when her car was fixed and ready for pickup.

Laney hung up and called voice mail to listen to her messages. Most of them were the same, but there was a message from Senator Sills's secretary, letting her know that the funeral would be on Sunday, two days away. She saved the message as a reminder and put her phone away.

She'd just about decided to march out into the squad room and ask somebody where she could get a cold drink, and by the way just how long did it take to drive to somebody's house, interview them and drive back to the police station, when the door opened and Ethan came in, his phone caught precariously between his shoulder and chin as he scribbled on a small pad.

"What did you find out?" she whispered, but he ignored her.

"Right," he said. "It's not Waters? Mackey, okay. Phone number?" He glanced at Laney but his expression didn't change.

Laney could hear the female voice on the other end of the phone. She didn't know what they were talking about, but she listened.

"Is there an address?" He set the pad down on the table and took the phone in his left hand, holding it a little closer to his ear. Then he sat. "Can you spell that, please?"

She could still hear the woman but her voice was much more muffled. What she heard sounded like "Burgin." She looked down at the pad where Ethan was writing. He printed, in almost block letters. Looking upside down at the pad, Laney read what Ethan had written: "8830 Bourgin—Meraux." She had an address and either a first name or a last name. *Mackey.*

Suddenly Ethan glanced up at her. She lowered her gaze to her fingernails and picked at a speck on one. Apparently it wasn't enough to fool him because he picked up his pad and stood. "No," he said, in answer to a question Laney hadn't heard. "Hold on." He stepped over to the door and opened it and went through. As the door was closing, Laney heard him say. "Okay. No, the name I have is Cristal, with an I. A prostitute that Sills—"

The door closed, muffling the rest of what he said.

Laney immediately grabbed her purse, digging in it for her phone. She didn't want to miss anything that Ethan said, but she didn't want to forget what she'd already heard either. She turned her phone on and waited impatiently as it booted up. Then she accessed her address book and pressed a button to enter a new contact. Quickly she keyed in Cristal Mackey, 8830 Bourgin Street, Meraux, Louisiana, and clicked Save. While she was writing her brain was racing. "A prostitute that Sills" was what Ethan had said.

A prostitute that Sills had what? Shared with her father maybe? She shuddered, stopping that thought right there. She couldn't even entertain the idea of her father being involved with a prostitute. But what else could have forced her father to pay Sills blackmail? Nothing that she could even imagine. And now, because of all this, she was imagining all sorts of illegal or immoral activities. How much more damage could she endure to the memory of the man who'd born her and reared her for most of her life?

She held her breath and listened for Ethan's voice. It sounded as though he was still talking to the woman. She accessed the web feature and started to type in the woman's name, but at that instant, Ethan's muffled voice changed timbre. Was he saying goodbye?

She stuck the phone under her chair just as he stepped back inside the room, pocketing his phone.

"Well?" she said, leaning forward. "What did you find out from the detective?"

"A lot of stuff," Ethan answered evasively. "And right now we can't even follow up on it, because there's a big press conference in an hour and a half. Commander Wharton says Superintendent Fortenberry feels he needs to update the media about the progress we're making on the Sills case. He wants Dixon and me to help with the prep ahead of time and to be visible on the podium while he addresses the media."

"And you're going to leave me stuck here all that time?" She shook her head. "No. I want to go home. I want to get into my pajamas and get into my bed and sleep for about twenty-four hours. Please."

"Nope. There's no way you're going back to your

house by yourself. Are you not convinced yet that whoever killed Sills knows who you are and where you live?
We talked about this. These people are watching you,
tracking you, listening to you. When are you going to
figure out just how much danger you're in?"

"Okay," she said, trying to keep her voice steady,
"I won't go home. I'll get a hotel room. It won't be as
good as my own bed, but at least I'll be able to sleep."

Ethan was already shaking his head. "We already
know what can happen in a hotel room."

"Oh, come on," she said tiredly. "How good do you
think this person is? Are you telling me the only way I
can be safe is if you force me to sit here in the middle
of dozens of police officers? Well, I'm pretty sure I still
have rights. Do I have to go through this again? Detective Delancey, am I under arrest?"

He glared at her. "Don't start with me, Laney—"

"Am I?" She gave him glare for glare. "Because unless you have something to charge me with, I don't think
you can keep me here against my will."

"How about resisting arrest?"

Laney was so angry her ears burned. "How about I
tell them—" She stopped. There was no way she could
betray him by telling anyone about their night together.
She knew he regretted it. She knew enough to know
he'd be on very thin ice if anyone found out that he'd
slept with a victim and a witness in his case, even if
he protested that she was a more-than-willing partner.
Even if *she* swore she'd been willing.

She knew she could not do that to him, and she was
horrified at herself for even hinting that she might.

"Ethan—" she started, wanting more than anything she'd ever wanted in her life to take back those few words.

But Ethan was staring at her, his expression carefully neutral. She hadn't stopped herself soon enough. He knew what she'd been about to say. "Okay," he said without inflection. "You can go home. I'll call my cousin Dawson and see if he has someone who can watch your house."

"Ethan, I didn't—I would never—"

He sliced his hand through the air in a dismissive gesture, refusing to let her apologize. "The name of the agency is D&D Security. An agent will park near your house and watch it. If anyone approaches, he'll get pictures, description and vehicle license plates. If the person acts in any way suspicious, he'll bring him in. He'll be there to protect you if anything happens."

"Ethan, I swear to you I would never ever betray you. Please don't do this. Don't assign me to a *babysitter*. That's just plain insulting." She had a plan forming in her head and a *babysitter* by any name had no part in it. "Not to mention ridiculous. There's no way that's happening. Besides, it'll cost a fortune. I can't afford it."

Ethan shrugged. "I can."

"I'm going home. If you want to hire somebody, fine. But they will not—" she pointed her finger at Ethan in emphasis "—will *not* tell me what I can and can't do and where I can and can't go. If you stick somebody out there to watch me, they'd better be good, because they just might have to keep up with me."

The muscle in Ethan's jaw ticked as he tried to maintain control. He was angrier than she'd ever seen him. While she wasn't actually afraid of him, he was pretty darn intimidating.

"Don't push me, Laney," he said.

She lifted her chin. Fine. She was angry, too. "Don't push *me*."

"I don't have time to worry about you. You've got two choices. I *will* put you in lockup for your own protection or I'll hire an agent to watch your house *while you* stay in it."

She didn't speak.

"It's your choice," he said.

"My house," she finally answered grudgingly.

"Good answer. When I get off work, I'll pick you up *at your house,* dismiss the agent and take you to my apartment."

"To your apartment? For what?" she demanded.

He stepped closer and looked down at her, his eyes blazing with anger. But that wasn't all she saw in their depths. She saw the same fire she'd seen last night as they came together. It was a fire so hot and yet so compelling that she was at once fearful of being burned and compelled to move toward it. For a moment, standing there in the interview room of the police station where anyone could be watching them through the two-way mirror, she felt an echo of the thrill of his hot flesh against hers and the overwhelming need to pull him to her and feel it all again.

He gave a small shake of his head and an irritating smirk curled his lip. "For your protection," he said with silky control. "What else?"

Laney blew out a harsh breath laced with frustration and embarrassment. He'd drawn her in, then deliberately rejected her. It was like a slap to the face. She stepped backward. "You are a—"

"Watch out, Ms. Montgomery," he drawled. "Anything you say can and will be used against you in a court of law."

She clamped her mouth shut and folded her arms, refusing to look at him. "May I get a ride to my house?" she asked icily.

"Yes, ma'am," he said. "I'll have one of the officers take you, and trust me, I intend to have your *babysitter* waiting for you by the time you get there."

As he opened the door and stepped back to let her exit before him, she remembered her phone on the floor underneath her chair. It occurred to her that it might be a good thing that she didn't have it with her, especially if she was going to carry out the plan that was blossoming in her brain. Without it, nobody could trace where she went using GPS. She tried to ignore the small voice that reminded her that without her phone, she couldn't call anyone if she got in trouble.

As soon as the officer who dropped her off at her house drove away, Laney examined her street and saw no cars parked at the curb. The ones that were in the driveways were either ones she recognized or didn't appear to have anyone inside them. Breathing a sigh of relief, she quickly walked across the street to her neighbors' and used their phone to call the car dealership.

"I would like a loaner car," she told the woman she'd

talked to before. "I can take a cab if you don't have anyone to bring the car to me."

"As it happens, the van is picking up a customer who
lives out your way, so I can send a driver with your car
and the van can pick him up and bring him back."

Laney thanked her neighbor, then ran back to her
house and changed into jeans and a hoodie, figuring
it was more appropriate attire to go visiting on ques-
tionable streets in Meraux than her business pantsuit.
She hoped she'd understood the snatches of Ethan's
telephone conversation correctly, and that 8830 Bourgin Street in Meraux was where Cristal, the prostitute,
lived. She had no idea what the woman had to do with
Senator Sills's murder, but she was pretty sure what
she'd done with Sills himself. For the entire time she'd
worked for Senator Sills, she'd heard rumors that he
liked to pay for sex. According to gossip, his penchant
for prostitutes was what had finally broken up his marriage.

She glanced at the couch and the pillows, which had
matching indentations. The memories of the night before and she and Ethan making love came back to her
in a rush. Closing her eyes, she shook her head, but that
did nothing to stop the thrill inside her as her brain fed
her explicit images of why she'd had trouble sleeping
the night before. If things were different, she'd lie down
on the couch and lose herself in a daydream of the exquisite sensations he'd coaxed from her with his mouth
and his body. Thinking of him, her body trembled in a
tiny aftershock of her climax. She opened her eyes and

saw the sheet and pillow piled on the coffee table, and the beautiful daydream dissolved.

Once she'd closed the front door on the girl and her mother selling candy, she'd turned to Ethan, thinking that he'd take her into his arms again. But that didn't happen. He'd bombarded her with questions about Carolyn and the cat, then he'd called in crime scene people and lab techs and had them go over her house with a fine-tooth comb.

When the forensic team finally left, he'd asked for a pillow so he could sleep on the couch. So much for beautiful, sexy daydreams. There was no time for them anyhow. If she was going to get out of here before her babysitter showed up and make it to Bourgin Street to talk to Cristal before the police got there, she needed to get a move on.

Just as she finished tying her running shoes, her doorbell rang. An arrow of fear struck the center of her chest. Who was it? Stepping over to the window, she peered through the blinds. It was a sedan with dealership tags. Thank goodness.

She opened the door to a man in a light blue shirt with his name on the pocket. He had a piece of paper in his hands. "Ma'am," he said. "Are you Elaine Montgomery? I'll need to see your driver's license please."

She showed him her license.

"Here's your key, and here's the insurance approval for you to get a loaner car. Keep that in the car, if you would. That serves as our insurance information in case of an accident."

She thanked him and grabbed her purse. As she

headed toward the car, the driver walked down to the corner to wait for the courtesy van. She started the car and pulled to the intersection, feeling as though a monster were breathing down her neck—Ethan's babysitter. At the corner, she spotted a large, dark-colored car several blocks down. Was that him? In the other direction, the courtesy van was braking as it pulled up to the corner.

Hurry, she silently told the van. She didn't want the driver around to tell the babysitter which way she'd gone.

It took her about twenty minutes to get to Meraux and follow the GPS in the loaner car to Bourgin Street. She drove down the street, but the loaner car's GPS didn't find 8830. So she parked on a side street and started walking. Getting away from her house without getting caught by the D&D agent was pretty much the extent of her plan, but she figured she could ask about Cristal Mackey at any little shops nearby or give her name to neighbors who might be sitting outside. Somebody was bound to know her, if she had understood the woman's real name correctly.

There weren't many people on the street, and those who were out looked rough. There were young men, boys really, who probably should have been in school but who were dressed to impress in ultrabaggy or ultra-skinny jeans, appropriately sized T-shirts to match the jeans and either hoodies or colors. They loitered at corners or lounged on steps, smoking cigarettes and drinking beer out of bottles wrapped in brown paper bags.

An older woman was sweeping the stoop of her

house, muttering to herself in what Laney thought was Spanish but couldn't be sure. When Laney walked past, the woman looked up and glared at her, bitter hatred in her black eyes.

She tried not to hurry, tried to look cool and nonchalant as she headed on down the street. Most of the buildings were old and peeling. Residences were mixed with shops and abandoned buildings. She passed a sign that advertised apartments to rent. She started to go inside, but on the door was a handwritten sheet of paper that read "Closed."

Sighing, she kept on down the street. Then she saw a narrow house that was painted green and had a few pansies in the front yard. She didn't see a sign with a street number, but it was on the 8800 block and for some reason it just felt like the right house.

She walked up the sidewalk to the three steps that led up to the door of the house. She rang an old, ornate brass doorbell and heard its deep ring inside the house. For a long time she heard nothing except the echo of the bell. There was no other sound, not even any change in the air that might hint that there was someone on the other side of the door.

After at least a minute a pleasant female voice called, "Who's there?"

"Ms. Mackey? My name is Elaine Montgomery," Laney said. "I'd like to talk to you about my father."

"What? Sorry. I don't know him."

"Please. He was Elliott Montgomery. I just have some questions about him."

"Nope. Don't know him."

Laney stepped closer to the door. "Ms. Mackey," she said as softly as she could and still have any expectation of being heard. "I'm alone. I don't want anything from you except to know more about my dad. Please."

There was a long pause, then, "You're alone?"

"Yes," Laney answered. "I promise you."

Another pause, this time so long that Laney almost gave up. But finally, she heard locks being undone. Then the door opened with the chain still on. The face that peered through the crack in the door was very attractive. Her eyes were a startling chartreuse color. She looked at Laney, then glanced around the hall behind her.

When she closed the door, for a split second Laney was afraid once again that she'd decided not to answer, but then the chain clanked and the door opened.

The woman was probably in her early to mid-forties, dressed in a pink pajama set with a flowered robe thrown on over it. Her blond hair was twisted up on the back of her head and fastened loosely with a barrette. She studied Laney for a few seconds, then nodded.

"Come in. I'm Cristy." She stepped back to let Laney in and for the first time, Laney saw the handgun she held.

"Oh, I—" Laney said, stopping and holding up her hands.

"Sorry," Cristy said, pointing the weapon at the floor and clicking on the safety. "Protection," she said wryly as she walked around the island that separated the living area from the kitchen and put the gun in a drawer.

The inside of the house was bright and airy. Tall

casement windows sparkled behind billowy white sheer curtains. Next to the door was a table that held a telephone and a tall hammered copper vase with a narrow neck. As Laney looked around, she realized, as small as the house was, that everything she saw could have been in a special *tiny house* issue of *Architectural Digest.* "Your house is beautiful," she said.

"Thanks," Cristy said, her face brightening into a smile. "I can certainly see that you're El's daughter. "He talked about you all the time."

TWENTY-FIVE MINUTES later, Laney knew a lot more about her dad than she'd ever known before, maybe more than she'd ever wanted to know. But where she'd only pieced together a blurry snapshot of the man who had done something that he'd thought was worth over half a million dollars to hide, Cristy painted her a life-size portrait. Laney heard about a man who had suffered along with the wife he'd loved as she sank deeper and deeper into alcohol addiction and depression, until she'd finally destroyed her looks, her body and finally her life. A man who had taken on the task of raising a daughter alone, and who had fallen in love with a prostitute.

Christine Mackey, who had taken back her given name after twenty-plus years as Cristal Waters, looked at her watch and said that she had to get ready for work.

"I apologize," Laney said quickly. "I didn't intend to stay this long. But I can't tell you how much I appreciate you talking to me."

"I actually enjoyed it. Ever since I saw that Darby Sills was murdered I've been sitting on pins and needles, wondering when the police were going to show up at my doorstep. I knew that eventually getting that domestic disturbance call covered up would come back to bite him. I figured it would get me in trouble, too. But truthfully, I never saw them after that night."

"Them? You mean Senator Sills and my dad?"

"No. I mean Darby or Buddy Davis."

"Buddy Davis?" Laney was surprised, although she shouldn't have been. From the very beginning, there had been plenty of indication that Davis was right in the middle of all this.

"You know—" Cristy said, snapping her fingers. "I've got a picture."

Laney's heart skipped a beat. "A picture?"

Cristy smiled like the cat with canary feathers spilling from her mouth as she reached under her bed and pulled out a box full of photos. "I have no idea why Darby decided to bring Davis and Elliot with him that night. That was the first time I'd ever met your dad or Davis. But they were celebrating something and Darby had two bottles of Dewar's scotch. So after about an hour we were all getting drunk, except your dad. When Darby tried to make him drink more, El joked that he was the designated driver. So I pulled out my camera, which I always did when I had a new client. It was my own personal form of insurance."

"You got a picture of all three of them?" Laney heard the apprehension in her voice. Was there a picture of her father and the other two men *with* Cristal? She wasn't sure she could bear that.

"Honey, no. I didn't mean to worry you. It's not that

kind of picture. I took one of the three of them laughing at some joke while Darby poured more scotch. Then El took one of myself and Darby and Buddy Davis. When it got to be ten o'clock, El said he had to get home because you were going to call.

"That made Darby angry. So he drank some more, and Buddy kept up with him. Buddy started asking me to do things for him and that just added fuel to Darby's fire. Then apparently, it dawned on him that I'd taken the pictures. He demanded the camera and when I wouldn't give it to him, he hit me. He got really violent. As soon as Darby started swinging, Buddy ran like a yellow dog with its tail between its legs and I called the police. By the time they got there, Darby had broken my jaw and was claiming I'd stolen money from him. I was terrified that they'd arrest me, so I threw out all the names I could think of, including your father's." She shook her head slightly. "That, by the way, is when I got the gun. And soon after that, thanks to your father, I quit the business and started working on getting a college degree."

While she'd talked, Cristy had been sorting through the pictures. "You won't believe some of the people whose photos are in this box. Here are the ones I was looking for," she said, holding up two small snapshots, then handing them to Laney.

Laney studied the first photo. It was odd to see her dad laughing and holding a glass up in a salute to a younger Sills and Davis. She looked at the second picture. In it, a truly beautiful Cristy, dressed in a glamorous negligee, stood between Sills and Davis. They were looking at her and she was smiling at the camera. The look on her face made Laney uneasy. She held the picture to the light and studied Cristy's face more closely. "You liked my dad," she said. It was a statement, not a question.

Cristy smiled wistfully. "Your dad was a special man. I know that Darby was blackmailing him."

"You do?"

"El told me. I begged him to go to the police and expose Darby for what he really was, but he wouldn't. He wasn't paying blackmail to Darby for his own sake."

Laney knew what Cristy was about to say. Tears stung her eyes.

"He did it to protect me. He paid Darby and he sent money to me. I never wanted to take it but your father was pretty persuasive when he wanted to be."

"Thank you," Laney said, her heart aching with love and grief. "Thank you so much for telling me that. I couldn't understand why he would let anyone blackmail him. I couldn't believe he'd done something so awful he'd pay blackmail rather than admit it. But he was paying the senator to protect you. Oh, Cristy, you've given my dad back to me." She paused. "Did my dad love you, too?"

Cristy played with the sash of her robe. "He did. But I was Cristal Waters and your dad was Elliott Montgomery," she said with flat finality. "Now I really have to get dressed. I don't want to be late for work. I do counseling at a women's shelter on the evening shift."

Laney started to leave, then turned back at the door. "I don't have my phone with me. Do you have a smartphone? I'd like to photograph those two pictures and send them to my phone, just in case."

"I have a smartphone, but I have no idea how to send pictures. All I use it for is making calls," Cristy said, handing over her phone to Laney. "Send them to yourself. But Laney, I've worked very hard to leave Cristal Waters behind. Please keep my name out of it."

"It might be too late for that. The police know your real name and your address. I got them when I eavesdropped on a detective," Laney said as she snapped a couple of shots of the two photos, then she deleted the photos and the sent files from Cristy's phone.

"Great," Cristy said. "So I was right to be on pins and needles. They'll probably be here any minute now."

"Cristy, call Detective Ethan Delancey at the Eighth Precinct. He's handling the investigation into Sills's murder. He'll take care of you." She paused for a second, then dug a card and a pen out of her purse. "Here's one of my cards." She bent over the hall table and wrote rapidly. "This is Ethan's—Detective Delancey's name and number on the back."

Cristy shook her head. "I can't imagine a situation where I'd want to call a policeman, but thanks for the number." She looked at the card, then stuck it in the pocket of her robe. "I'll keep the card because it's got *your* number on it."

Chapter Ten

The police superintendent had finished his press conference and was taking questions when Ethan's phone vibrated. He'd told dispatch not to call him until the press conference was over. If this was the dispatcher, she was cutting it very close.

"Delancey," he said, stepping backward behind the curtains, away from the crowd of reporters and onlookers. The number on his screen wasn't familiar.

"Detective Delancey," the man said. "I'm Grayson Reed. D&D Securities. I was assigned to stake out this address for you." He read off Laney's address.

"That's right. What's the matter?"

"I've just handcuffed a woman who was breaking into the house. White female, mid-thirties, blonde—"

"What about Laney—Ms. Montgomery?"

"She isn't here. I've—"

"Not there? That's impossible. I had an officer—"

"Detective," Reed said with studied patience. "I've been here just over an hour, but until this person showed up there was no activity inside. The name on her driver's license is Carolyn Gertz. It's a Mississippi license, expired. Probably stolen or faked. I'm having her license plates run."

"Carolyn?" Ethan said. "We've been trying to locate her on a related matter. Where are you now?"

"I'm inside the house. I've called Dispatch to send a police cruiser for my detainee."

"What do you see there?" Ethan asked, terrified that something had happened to Laney before the security agent had gotten there. "Any sign of a struggle?"

"No. Also no purse or car keys. I did find a card on the foyer table that had the name of a local car dealership and the hours of its courtesy van. I believe—"

"Son of a—" Ethan started before he cut himself off. "She got a damn loaner car. Hell, she was gone before you got there."

"That's my conclusion, too," Reed said. "Here's the cruiser now. I'll follow it to the Eighth in my own vehicle and give my written report. Will you be there?"

"I can't say for sure. I may be pursuing a suspect of my own who's driving a dealer car," Ethan said. "I'll have someone waiting to take her into custody. Thanks." He hung up and rushed back to the station. He had to call the dealership and get the make and model and plates of the loaner car so he could track down his runaway victim.

But where had she gone? She had told him she'd wanted to go home and sleep, so why hadn't she done that? He sighed in frustration as he headed for his desk. Dixon was sitting there, absorbed in a report.

"You'll never believe what Laney did," he said, tossing his car keys onto the desk and flopping into the chair.

Dixon looked up. "Um, got a car from somewhere and went down to Meraux to see Cristal Mackey?"

Ethan stared at him. "It's Christine Mackey. Who told you about her?"

Dixon held up a smartphone in a white case.

"That looks like—"

"Laney's phone," Dixon said. He slid it across the expanse of desk between them. "Take a look at the phone log."

Ethan pressed keys. "I already knew she got a loaner car. But how do you figure she knew about Cristal's real name and where she lived?"

"No idea, but the name and address are in her phone."

"Where was her phone anyhow?"

"It was under one of the chairs in the interview room where you were talking to her earlier."

Ethan slammed the phone down on the desktop. "That's what happened. She heard me talking to the officer who ran down Cristal Waters for me. Damn it. I should have been more careful." He stood and reached for his keys. "I've got to go," he said, just as his phone rang.

"Delancey," he growled.

"Detective, it's Holt, head of the lab. One of my techs told me you were asking about a phone that had been bugged."

"Right, I was, but I'm in a hurry right now."

"Give me half a minute. He mentioned that you were leaving the bug in the phone so as not to tip off the hacker. Well, everything he told you that the bug can do is true, but there's more."

"More?" A tingle of apprehension started up Ethan's spine. "More what?"

"Some of these new bugs can activate the microphone on the bugged phone and display GPS locations even if the phone is off. Also, the hacker can see everything in the bugged phone's address book. If the hacker is online when the bugged person enters a new contact into the address book, the hacker can see it in real time."

Dread settled on Ethan's chest, heavy as lead. "Thanks. I've got an emergency." He hung up. "Laney's in big trouble. Whoever bugged her phone knows where she is."

"Where is she?"

"In Meraux, going to see Christine Mackey. I've got to get out there. Call the sheriff of Meraux for backup, will you? Tell them to come in silent and give the deputy in charge my cell number so we can coordinate."

Dixon sat up, grabbing a pen and writing down what Ethan told him. "Sure thing. I'm on it."

"Wish me luck, Dixon. If I'm right, Sills's murderer is on Laney's tail.

LANEY GAVE CRISTY the card with Ethan's number on the back, hugged her and started for the door. But before she took three steps, the door crashed open with a loud, splintering sound.

Laney, gun-shy since Sills's murder, threw herself sideways, shouting, "Get down." She landed behind a table that sat just to the right of the front door. She pushed the table over to provide a bit of cover.

The first figure that burst in through the splintered door nearly stopped her heart. It was him. The man in black who had killed the senator and injured her. He was the same height, with the same long, lean form. He was standing in the same awkward position and brandishing what appeared to be a similar weapon. The only thing different was the mask. This time he wore a black and silver Mardi Gras mask that covered only the upper half of the face.

He hadn't noticed her yet, so she had a split second to examine the mask and the face. What she saw gave her a jolt.

Could she believe her eyes? She wasn't sure. She quickly assessed the black-encased body. The silhouette wasn't just lean, it was skinny. The tight black sweater and pants hinted at spare bones and sinewy muscles, the recognizable body type of a dedicated runner. Her gaze focused on the front of the sweater. Were those small, barely discernible breasts? And what was it about those shoes? She squinted. They were platform boots. High ones. No wonder the figure looked awkward.

The man in black was not a man at all. It was a woman.

In those few seconds while Laney's brain was working that out, the woman in the Mardi Gras mask moved into the room and backed against the wall, motioning for another black-clad figure to enter. This one was taller, larger, unmasked and—Laney did a double take— familiar. She'd seen the man before. But she couldn't remember where, and she didn't have time to rack her brain. She had to concentrate on staying alive, because now, Mardi Gras had spotted her.

But to Laney's surprise, she paid no attention to her. She gestured to the man. He walked over, grabbed Laney by the scruff of her neck and hauled her to her feet. He pushed her against the wall with more than a little force and pressed his forearm against her throat. "Don't give me any trouble, sister," he said.

Despite her terror, and despite the fact that the pressure on her throat was making it a little hard to breathe, Laney almost laughed at his fake *gangster* accent. She held up her hands. "No trouble here," she responded.

Mardi Gras's attention was on Cristy, who was standing in the center of the room. She pointed her weapon. "Okay, whore," she said in a smoky, booze and cigarettes voice. "I know you've got pictures of Sills. I want every shot of him—by himself and with other people." She paused for barely a second, in which Cristy didn't move.

"Did you hear me? I want those pictures—now!"

Laney's hand twitched to reach for the pocket of her jeans where she'd stuck the photos. Hopefully the corners weren't sticking out. And hopefully the man, who was over six feet tall and bulky, wouldn't search her.

"Stay still!" he growled, pressing his thick forearm harder into her neck.

"Oh—" she croaked, grabbing his arm with her fingers and digging her nails into his flesh. "Can't breathe."

He jerked backward, then pressed against her again. "Scratch me again and I'll cut your fingernails down to the knuckle."

Cristy had her hands up, palms out, and was telling Mardi Gras that she didn't know what photos she was talking about. "All the pictures I have are in that box," she said, gesturing with her head toward the box on the coffee table. "In fact, I was just looking at them this—"

"Don't even try to lie to me, you heathen," Mardi Gras said. She brandished the gun, but didn't move any closer to either Cristy or the box. "Put that ratty box in a bag."

"A bag?" Cristy repeated. "What kind of—"

"Shut up and do it! Trash bag, grocery bag. I don't care."

Cristy's face was colorless. She was as terrified as Laney herself was. As Cristy backed toward the kitchen area with her hands still up, Laney struggled against the big man's grip. She sucked in air audibly, exaggerating her difficulty breathing. "Please—" she choked out in a guttural whisper, then coughed.

"For goodness' sake, George, don't kill her yet!"

Laney coughed again and noticed that Cristy was moving steadily backward. She passed the island that separated the kitchen from the living room, and paused. After a second, Laney realized what she was doing. She was reaching inside a drawer.

Laney gasped. It was the drawer where she'd put her

gun. Laney tried to shake her head, but Cristy had her eyes on Mardi Gras. All Laney got for her trouble was another thrust of the muscled forearm into her throat. She cried out wordlessly—almost soundlessly, and dug her nails into his flesh again.

With a growl, he flung her violently away from him. Her back slammed into the wall and she went down, the breath knocked out of her.

At that same instant Cristy took a sudden step to her left, which placed her behind the island. She ducked.

"Hey!" Mardi Gras shouted, taking a step forward.

Cristy raised her head, aimed her weapon and shot. The shot went wildly into the ceiling.

Mardi Gras shot back, splintering the corner of the island, then retreated and ducked behind the open front door. She leaned out and shot twice more.

Cristy rose up to fire back. The bullet went through the wooden door and Mardi Gras shrieked and cursed.

"Got you!" Cristy cried.

Get down, Laney tried to say but no sound came from her mouth. She clawed at the wall and scrabbled to regain her footing. The man pulled a gun and fired at Cristy.

Cristy cried out and went down.

"No!" Laney croaked, her voice barely audible. She got to her feet as the man waited, listening, and the woman kept cursing and calling Cristy names.

Sneaking between him and the table by the door, Laney grabbed the narrow neck of the long copper vase and swung it with all her might, grunting with the effort. She had no idea if she had the strength to swing the heavy vase hard enough to bring him down.

He obviously heard her grunt, because he twisted toward her just as she followed through with her swing and hit him square in the temple. He went down like a rock.

Cristy cried, "Laney!" in a hoarse whisper.

Mardi Gras shouted, "George, finish her off, damn it. I'm bleeding like a stuck pig." She paused. "George!"

While the woman screamed, Laney was crawling over the downed man's bulk and reaching for his weapon. It was huge and heavy in her hands, but she lifted it and backed away from him, pointing it at the door behind which the woman cowered. "Cristy, are you all right?"

"Hit in the shoulder," Cristy gasped. "Can't use gun."

A harsh laugh erupted from behind the door. "Well, whore, it's what you deserve. George. Shoot her and let's get out of here."

Laney aimed the gun, holding it with both hands and sure she was going to drop it any minute. "George isn't available right now," she called out. "If you don't drop your gun and come out I'm going to shoot the door with his gun, and as big as it is, I'm thinking it just might blow a hole in the wood the size of—I don't know— *you*. On the count of three."

A shot echoed out and Laney heard wood splinter as a bullet zinged by her ear. The woman had blown a hole in the door she was hiding behind. Out of the corner of her eye, Laney saw the man stirring. Her arms were already becoming tired from holding the heavy gun straight out in front of her. She glanced at him, then at the splintered door as her mind raced.

Cristy was wounded, probably much worse than Mardi Gras, judging by their voices. George had been stunned for a while but now he was waking up. Laney had no idea what she was going to do now.

The big man lifted his upper body with his arms and shook his head, like a big cat or dog shaking off a nap.

"Don't move," Laney cried.

The man turned his head to look at her. She knew he saw her hands shaking with exhaustion from holding the gun up and out. He smiled, then laughed.

"Stop it!" she said. "Lie down flat."

Mardi Gras peeked out from behind the door. "Don't move, Elaine Montgomery," she said, "or I'll kill you."

Laney knew she was beat. She was no match for the two of them. Her arm muscles were beginning to twitch with fatigue. And she was so worried about Cristy she could barely think. *Phone.*

"Cristy," she said. "Call the police."

"Oh, no you don't," George said, groaning as he worked to push himself to his feet.

"Don't move!" Laney shouted at him. "Do. Not. Move!"

"You don't move," Mardi Gras shouted.

And from somewhere, a third voice—a wonderfully familiar voice—said, "How about none of you move."

It was Ethan. Before Laney could even wonder how he'd found her, he and a roomful of officers rushed in. After that, everything deteriorated into chaos. At one point, Laney heard an officer reading the man his rights as he marched him out the door. Two men with bulletproof vests and rifles disarmed the woman in the Mardi Gras mask not two feet from where Laney was standing. When one of them yanked the mask off, the woman cursed at him.

Laney stared at the unmasked woman in shock and horror, scarcely able to believe what she was seeing. "It was you!" she said. "All the time, it was you." She was staring at Benita Davis, dressed all in black with platform boots and a mask. "You shot Senator Sills and me."

"Oh, shut up, you stupid—" the vulgar word Benita was about to say was cut off when one of the officers yanked on her arm to turn her toward the EMTs. "Ow!" she shrieked. "Police brutality! Help me! Call my lawyer. I demand my lawyer."

Laney opened her mouth, but a hard, firm hand grabbed her arm. She turned. It was Ethan.

"What did you just say?" he asked, frowning at her.

"I didn't say it," she responded. "I was going to but then I—"

"No. What did you say when you realized it was Benita behind that Mardi Gras mask?"

"Oh, Ethan. It's her. I mean it *was* her. She's the man in black. The one who killed Senator Sills and shot me. Look at her in that black sweater and pants. How skinny she is. How bony. It's her."

"But from the beginning you've said it was a man."

"I know. I thought it was. Being so skinny and—I

mean, look. You can hardly see her breasts, and it was dark in that hotel room. But look at her," she gestured toward Benita. "She's skin and bone. And in those sky-high platform heels, she's almost as tall as I am."

Ethan shook his head. "That's not going to be easy to prove," he said. "All the reports, your witness statement, everything assumed the killer was a man. In fact, I was about convinced it was Buddy."

The EMTs had placed a protesting Benita on a stretcher and were carrying her out to the ambulance. Cristy had already been taken out. As soon as they loaded Benita in, the ambulance would take them both to St. Bernard Parish Hospital for evaluation and treatment.

Around Laney and Ethan, people in crime scene jackets swarmed all over the apartment, taking fingerprints, marking small areas with numbered plaques and taking dozens and dozens of photographs. After a few minutes, Laney sat down on a small chair in the corner of the living room. Ethan stood beside her, as stoic as a palace guard. Dixon walked past them, calling out that he was following the ambulance to the hospital to try to talk to both Benita and Cristy.

A few minutes later, Officer Farrantino came up to Ethan to ask him if he wanted her to take Laney to the station. He declined, saying he'd handle her. Slowly the house cleared out.

Laney waited, staring down at the hardwood floor. She knew that Ethan was standing over her, looking down at her. She didn't even raise her head.

Finally he spoke. "You want to tell me what the hell you thought you were doing?"

She didn't move. He was going to have to get it all out. All the anger, all the frustration, all the resentment he held for her. Once he did, she doubted there would be anything else inside him. Certainly nothing positive— nothing caring. She'd probably never see him acting as anything other than bad cop from now on.

"Laney, I'm talking to you."

She sighed, stared at a nail in a plank in the floor for a few more seconds, then looked up at him. "I know you are. I know you're angry and you have a right to be. There is no telling how many laws I've broken, and I'm prepared to face the consequences for that. I don't have an excuse. I wanted to see Cristal Mackey. I wanted to meet her for myself so I could find out what she knew about my father. Turns out she knew a lot—a whole lot that I didn't know. My father did pay blackmail to Senator Sills, but he didn't do it to protect himself. He paid it as protection for Cristal. For her to be able to take back her given name and to make a new life for herself. I knew my father was not bad."

"You knew—" Ethan stopped himself. He was so angry he felt sick. He knew he was on the verge of the kind of life-sucking, debilitating anger that his father had exhibited throughout his life. Anger that had always terrified him and his younger brother and sister growing up. Anger that had given his dad a stroke and confined him to a wheelchair.

Ethan had never wanted to experience that much

rage. He'd spent his life convincing himself that he'd missed that gene. That he didn't have that anger inside him. But tonight, he found out that he did have that much rage inside him. And he found out what it took to bring it to the surface. Laney Montgomery. He took a deep breath. "You almost got Cristal and yourself killed. What the hell did you think you were going to do with that gun?"

Laney pushed herself to her feet, stifling a groan at the soreness in her back and hips from being slammed against the wall. "I took the gun after I knocked George out. Should I have left it there for him to pick up when he woke up?"

Ethan scowled at her. "You knocked him out?" he finally asked.

"With the copper vase. That one over there." She pointed. "I've already told you I'll take the consequences. I'll go to prison if I have to. But I can't be sorry I came here. I found Cristal and she gave me the information I needed. She gave me something else, too." She dug in the pocket of her jeans and pulled out two slightly wrinkled snapshots.

Ethan stared at them, first one, then the other, then the first one again and so on. He swallowed. He tried to speak but nothing would come out of his mouth.

"Where—" he croaked. "How—"

Laney just shrugged.

As the last two crime scene techs picked up their gear and walked out of the house, Ethan stared at Laney in undisguised shock.

"Do you know what this is?" he asked, holding the photos up.

She nodded. "Proof," she said tiredly.

Ethan shook his head slowly back and forth. "I'll be a son of a bitch," he muttered.

WHEN ETHAN STEPPED into the interview room at just after midnight, he found Laney sitting at the table with her head on her crossed arms on the table, asleep. He'd spent the past four, no, five, hours interrogating suspects. He'd started with George Firth, the Davises' chauffeur, who had shot Christine Mackey. George was only too happy to spill everything he knew in exchange for a plea deal. As it turned out, George and Benita had been lovers for years, and Benita had talked him into helping her frame Buddy, who was in the early stages of Alzheimer's, for the death of Darby Sills. Benita wanted the senator dead because she was sick of paying ever-increasing blackmail to him to keep him from exposing Buddy as, as she put it, a "whore-chasing son of a bitch." Benita had been sure that the silver belt buckle would prove that it was Buddy, and that the reason he'd worn it when he'd killed Sills was because he'd forgotten he'd had it on.

When Ethan got through with George, he had a pretty clear picture of Benita's means, motive and opportunity. She'd given Buddy a sleeping pill that night to ensure that he wouldn't wake up, then while she'd taken care of the senator at the hotel, she'd had George waiting outside to drive her back to the Circle of Faith compound and sneak in as if they'd never been gone.

Ethan tried to talk with Benita, but she demanded her lawyer and would not say another word. So he moved on to Carolyn, the woman Grayson Reed had brought in. She'd been carrying her own driver's license, so it was simple to identify her as Carolyn Gertz, Benita Davis's daughter from her first marriage. Benita had talked her into distracting Laney so George could sneak in and bug her phone.

Ethan sat down opposite Laney and rubbed his face tiredly. Laney stirred, but didn't awaken. He knew she was exhausted. He was, too. But he had a job to do before either one of them could get any sleep.

Laney's mouth was slightly open and Ethan could hear her soft, even breaths. He watched her sleep. Every minute or so, she'd jerk slightly and make a distressed-sounding noise. He wondered if she were dreaming about the shoot-out in Cristal's apartment. Thinking about that made his scalp tighten with fear for her. It was a miracle that she hadn't been hit by a stray bullet. He pushed a strand of hair back from her temple where it was threatening to fall over her face, brushing the backs of his fingers across her soft skin.

She opened her eyes.

He jerked his hand away.

"Oh," she said drowsily, lifting her head but leaving her eyes closed. "Sorry. I didn't mean to fall asleep. I just—"

He stood, backing away and leaning against the wall,

hoping he looked a hell of a lot more relaxed than he felt. His unease was not only from interviewing reluctant— and in Benita's case, hostile—suspects. It wasn't only from being so angry at Laney for putting herself in such terrible danger. It was also that when he'd seen her asleep with her head in her arms, he'd been hit with a poignant ache in the middle of his chest. It was painful and sweet at the same time, and he didn't like it.

He didn't want to feel pulled in two different directions when he looked at her. He didn't want to care that she was exhausted, or worry that she might be ill or injured. He didn't want to realize that the only way he could be happy and content was if she was happy and content. He huffed in frustration.

She forced herself to open her eyes, squinting at the bright light in the room. "Look, Ethan, I'm sorry—" she started.

"You're *sorry?*" he mimicked. "Really? Well, that's just great. That wipes away everything you did." Wincing, he tried to ask himself what the hell he thought he was doing, being mean to her after all she'd been through. He realized he had no answer. He didn't know why. All he knew was that he was furious with her for putting herself in harm's way.

"I know it doesn't. I just—"

He sliced his hand through the air like a saber, cutting her off. "Damn straight it doesn't. You ignored me, you ran away from a protected house where I'd placed a bodyguard to keep you safe. You took information from an ongoing investigation—" he stopped and stared at her. "You eavesdropped on an official police conversation."

Laney ducked her head. "I could hear both sides of the conversation," she said meekly.

That was his fault. "I should have been more careful, but," he said, shaking his head. "I've got to tell you, I'd have thought you had more sense than that."

"I didn't mean to cause problems. I just wanted to know if she knew my dad and what she could tell me about him." She paused for a second before continuing. "Do you have any idea what it's like to find out that the father you trusted, that you worshiped, went to prostitutes, did things that made him vulnerable to blackmail, lied to you? Do you know what it's like to learn, within the space of a couple of days, that you never really knew your father at all?"

"You're not alone in how you feel, Laney. I think every adult eventually realizes their parents are just people, not saints and not superheroes. The difference is how you deal with it."

He drew in a frustrated breath. "And the way you dealt with it was to go running off like a—a kid with no sense of responsibility, and get a woman shot."

"How do you figure that I got her shot?" she demanded. "Benita had no idea I was there."

"Oh, yeah? Well, would it surprise you to know that when you typed Cristal's address into your phone, the information transferred immediately to Benita's chauffeur, the guy who bugged your phone?"

"Oh, my God. The phone can do that?" Laney

paused. "That means it's my fault they knew where she was." Her face crumpled.

"That's right. Cristal had taken back her real name, so Benita had never been able to find her. Buddy had told her that Cristal had pictures. She didn't know you were there. She went to Cristal's house to get the photos. Not to protect Buddy. Benita wanted to plant them so they implicated Buddy and helped prove that he wanted Sills dead."

"She wanted to implicate Buddy? I thought they were inseparable. Why?"

"Apparently Buddy is in the beginning stages of Alzheimer's. He's forgetting things, getting confused. According to her chauffeur, who's turning state's witness, she had this big plan to kill Sills to stop the blackmail and frame Buddy for it. Then she'd take over the Circle of Faith ministries and she and George, the chauffeur/lover/computer hacker, could live happily ever after. It almost worked, too. If she'd managed to kill Cristal and get out of there with the incriminating photographs, she might have succeeded."

Laney was staring at her hands. "It was my fault Cristy was shot." She looked up at him. "I've messed up everything, haven't I?"

Ethan shrugged. "No," he said with a little smile. "You didn't screw up everything. You did get the photos. And believe me. It was only a matter of time before Benita and George found her. So actually, by leading them there while you were there to help her, you saved her life."

Laney nodded, pushing her fingers through her hair. "How is she doing? Cristy, I mean."

"Last I heard she was doing fine. The bullet went through her shoulder without hitting the bone, so she's got a nice entrance and exit wound, but no serious damage."

"That's good." Laney took a long breath. "So do you need me for anything else?"

Ethan wondered how he was supposed to answer that question. He looked at her for a long time.

"Ethan?"

"No," he said. "You're free to go."

She stood with a sigh and slid past him to the door and turned the knob. "Ethan?"

He turned. "Yeah?"

"I'm glad I got to know you," she said.

His heart felt as though it had dropped to his toes. "Me, too," he said. "But we'll be seeing each other again."

"We will?"

His head snapped up. Had she sounded hopeful? He studied her face, but all he saw was pale exhaustion. It was all he could do to keep his expression neutral. "Yeah. I'll need to get you to sign your statement and you'll probably have to testify about the photos and about your father's finances, whenever this comes to trial."

"How—how long do you think that will be?"

"Could be as long as several years. It depends on how

good Benita's lawyers are, and whether George sticks to his plea agreement."

She nodded. "So I guess I'll hear from you?"

Ethan looked at her long and hard, then stepped up closer to her. "I could have someone else get in touch with you."

She blinked. "Okay, if—if that's what you want."

"I don't," he said. "Laney?"

She swallowed. "Yes?"

"I don't want you—" His mouth went dry.

Her brows furrowed.

"I don't want you to—" He swallowed and tried again. "I don't want you to leave."

"You don't?"

"You're the most annoying, most stubborn and most fascinating person I've ever met in my life."

"Thank you…" she said cautiously.

He smiled. "I'm sure you probably feel the same about me."

"You are stubborn," she said. "And pigheaded and officious and arrogant and—"

He bent his head and kissed her, hard and long. When he finally lifted his head they were both out of breath.

"And—" she took a breath "—confusing and irritating and—"

"I'll do it again," he warned.

"Oh, no," she said, smiling. "How long will I have to endure this?"

"Well," he said, touching the corner of her lip with his thumb. When he did, she closed her eyes and sighed.

"We do have to put up with each other until this trial is over. It could be years and years—and years."

"Promise?" she asked, lifting her head and kissing him on the lips.

"I promise," he answered, pulling her close. "And here's another promise. Once this trial is over, I'll make you a big pot of spinach pasta and we can see what comes up in the conversation."

Laney laughed and put her arms around Ethan's neck. "I'll hold you to that promise."

* * * * *

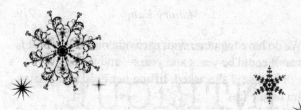

Merry Christmas

& A Happy New Year!

Thank you for a wonderful
2013...

A sneaky peek at next month…

INTRIGUE…

BREATHTAKING ROMANTIC SUSPENSE

My wish list for next month's titles…

In stores from 20th December 2013:

☐ Cold Case at Carlton's Canyon – Rita Herron

& Dead by Wednesday – Beverly Long

☐ Wanted – Delores Fossen

& The Marine's Last Defence – Angi Morgan

☐ Unrepentant Cowboy – Joanna Wayne

& Gone – Mallory Kane

Romantic Suspense

☐ The Return of Connor Mansfield – Beth Cornelison

Available at WHSmith, Tesco, Asda, Eason, Amazon and Apple

Just can't wait?

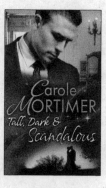

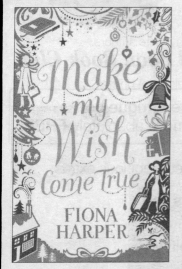

Come in from the cold this Christmas
our favourite authors. Whether you're
Vermont with Sarah Morgan or settli
Christmas dinner with Fiona Harper
won't stop this festive seaso

Visit:
www.millsandboon.co.

vi
or

the Mills & Boon Book Club

Want to read more **Intrigue** books?
re offering you **2 more** absolutely **FREE!**

also treat you to these fabulous extras:

- **Exclusive offers and much more!**

- **FREE** home delivery

- **FREE** books and gifts with our special rewards scheme

Get your free books now!

isit www.millsandboon.co.uk/bookclub
:all Customer Relations on 020 8288 2888

WORLD'S
STUPIDEST
Instructions

Thanks to all the fans of
The World's Stupidest Signs and
More of the World's Stupidest Signs
who sent in their sightings of daft
instructions, and to all our other
contributors. If you're a fan of stupid
instructions or signs, and have the
dubious pleasure of spotting some,
please e-mail them to
jokes@michaelomarabooks.com,
for possible inclusion in future
collections.

THE
WORLD'S
STUPIDEST
Instructions

Michael O'Mara Humour

First published in Great Britain in 2004 by
Michael O'Mara Books Limited
9 Lion Yard, Tremadoc Road
London SW4 7NQ

A CIP catalogue record for this book is available from
the British Library

ISBN 1-84317-078-7

1 3 5 7 9 10 8 6 4 2

Compiled by Bryony Evens

Designed and typeset by
SX Composing DTP, Rayleigh, Essex

Printed and bound in Great Britain
by Cox & Wyman Ltd, Reading, Berkshire

www.mombooks.com

Contents

Introduction

It's an epidemic, and it's showing no sign
of stopping – stupid instructions are
taking over the world!

As ubiquitous as they are ridiculous, the
origins of these daft directions are legion, but
you'll find that holidays are a particularly
great source of entertainment for the
collector of stupid instructions. As the
determined non-English-speaking world
struggles to inform customers of its hotel
regulations, or of local customs, observe the
original language emerging, post translation,
as though tangled in the mechanism of a
ski lift, or mangled beneath the wheels of a
high-speed bullet train!

More often than not, however, inept translation isn't to blame; a vast majority of instructions referring to products and services seem simply not to have been thought through for clarity, or even common sense! As an illustration, take this case of the automated marketing phone dialler used by a sales company in the USA, with its directions to those 'answering' the phone: *'If X is home to take this call, please press one. If no one is home to take this call, please press two . . .'*

Finally, some instructions are just plain unnecessary, pointless, redundant, superfluous and generally meaningless. And they are all here!

To continue reading, please turn the page . . .

Cautionary Tales

In these litigious times, many manufacturers now feel they have no choice but to print instructions for exact use (but on *soap*?), and warn of all the conceivable injuries their product might inflict. Could this be because they are at the mercy of individuals lacking, for want of a better word, a brain? Take, for example, the woman who used a spermicide as a baking ingredient, and then sued the spermicide's manufacturer upon discovering she was pregnant. Unbelievable.

Safe to use around pets and children,
although it is not recommended that
either be permitted to drink from toilet.

On a toilet-bowl freshener

To avoid suffocation,
keep away from children.

On a number of plastic carrier bags

Beware: sled may develop high speed
under certain snow conditions.

On a toboggan

This product not intended for use as a dental drill.

On an electric router made for carpenters

Do not eat toner.

On a laser-printer cartridge

Do not drive with sun shield in place.

On a windscreen cover designed to protect a car's interior from direct sunlight

Take two tablets until passing away.

Label on a medicine bottle in Japan

Caution: knives are sharp.

On a knife sharpener

For proper food safety and quality, use the following directions: do not eat pizza without cooking.

On a supermarket pizza

Twist top off with hands. Throw top away.
Do not put top in mouth.

On a bottled-water label

Choking hazard: this toy is a small ball.

On a child's rubber ball

Not for human consumption.

On a packet of dice

Warning:
misuse may cause injury or death.

Stamped on the barrel of a .22-calibre rifle

Remove plastic before eating.

On a snack wrapper

Shin guards cannot protect any part of the body they do not cover.

On shin pads for cyclists

Dip chips in cheese and salsa.

*Directions for eating tortilla chips
packaged with dips*

Caution, hot beverages are hot.

On a takeaway coffee cup

Do not use for drying pets.

On a microwave oven

Eating rocks may lead to broken teeth.

On a novelty rock-garden set called 'Popcorn Rock'

**Caution:
remove infant before storing chair.**

On a pushchair

Don't drive standing up through the sunroof while you're closing it.

From a car-owner's manual

Warning: do not insert fingers.

On a blender

**CAUTION! – do NOT swallow nails!
May cause irritation!**

On a box of household nails

**Simply pour the biscuits into a bowl
and allow the cat to eat when it wants.**

On a bag of cat biscuits

FRONT

On a motorcycle crash helmet

Warning: sharp blades.

On a packet of craft knives

Do not store explosives in oven.

On a cooker

It is generally inadvisable to eject
directly over the area you just bombed.

From a US Air Force manual

Aim towards the enemy.

*Instruction printed on a US Army
rocket launcher*

**Seat must be facing forward
for take-off and landing.**

*On the back of the pilot's seat
in a NATO aircraft*

Do not open here.

On the bottom of a cola bottle

Turn off motor before using this product.

*On the packaging for a chainsaw file,
used to sharpen the cutting teeth on the chain*

**For serious injuries,
seek medical attention.**

On a box of sticking plasters

Mix with water before serving.

On a can of powdered baby milk

This broom does not actually fly.

On a Harry Potter wizard's broom

Beware of being eaten by small children due to small parts.

On the packaging of Japanese model figurines

Do not take if allergic to aspirin.

On a box of aspirin

Remove clothing before distributing in washing machine.

On a bottle of laundry detergent

Caution: ice cream is cold.

On a tub of ice cream

Caution:
this is not a safety protective device.

On a plastic toy helmet
used as a container for popcorn

Caution! Contents hot!

On a pizza delivery box

Take one capsule by mouth
three times daily until gone.

On a box of pills

Remove wrapper, open mouth,
insert muffin, eat.

On a muffin packet

The appliance is switched on by setting
the on/off switch to the 'on' position.

On an espresso kettle

Do not use on roof.

On a snowblower

Warning:
pastry filling may be hot when heated.

On a box of pop tarts

PARENT: please exercise caution.
Mask and chest plate are not protective;
cape does not enable wearer to fly.

On a child's Batman costume

Instructions: put on food.

On a ketchup bottle

Safe to use in households with pets.
Warning: this product is NOT intended
to be sprayed directly on pets.

On a fabric deodorizing spray

Warning: while cooking
be sure to place crust side down.

On a pizza

Open bottle before drinking.

On a bottle of rum

Out and About

These days, it seems that getting around
by train, bus, car or on foot is becoming
increasingly tiresome. To help make their
journeys smoother and more trouble-free,
commuters need clear, logical instructions,
especially when they are in a foreign
country. With this is mind, here are some
helpful guidelines . . .

At the rise of the hand policeman,
stop rapidly. Do not pass him
or otherwise disrespect him.

If pedestrian obstacle your path,
tootle horn melodiously. If he continue
to obstacle, tootle horn vigorously and
utter vocal warnings such as 'Hi, Hi'.

If wandering horse by roadside obstacle
your path, beware that he do not take
fright as you pass him. Do not explode
the exhaust box at him. Go soothingly by,
or stop by roadside till he pass away.

Press the braking of the foot
as you roll round the corner,
to save collapse and tie up.

Avoid tanglement of dog
with your wheel spokes.

If road mope obstacle your path, refrain from pass on hill or round curve. Follow patiently till road arrive at straight level stretch. Then tootle horn melodiously and step on, passing at left and waving hand courteously to honourable road mope in passing.

Beware of greasy corner where lurk skid demon. Cease step on, approach slowly, round cautiously, resume step on gradually.

Give big space to the festive dog that shall sport in the highway.

*Official Japanese guidelines
for English-speaking drivers*

Avoid overspeeding.
Always avoid accidents

Highway sign in India

Stop: Drive Sideways

Detour sign in Japan

Don't take a chance on ruining your vacation – come to us and be sure

Travel office in Nova Scotia, Canada

In case of flood, proceed uphill.
In case of flash flood,
proceed uphill quickly

One of the emergency safety procedures
at a summer camp in the USA

Children!
No Reversing
Into Playground

Sign outside a school in London

Vertical parking only

Sign in Japan permitting double
or parallel parking

Notice of Take Staircase

Fasten armrest by order,
plese don't ambulate in staircase

Children and old folks take staircase
ought to accompany by keeper

Please don't resort and diaport
at passageway

Strictly prohibit bestride the armrest

Bicycle don't take the staircase

Don't protrude the tartness and
keenness out the staircase

*Notice explaining the correct use of a stairway
in China*

Ask the station employee about a trouble

Instruction at a railway station in Japan

Entrance Only Do Not Enter

On a sign into a car park

Try Bigger and Bigger but keep More and More Slowly

Traffic sign in Tokyo, Japan

Parking Charges

First 20 minutes free

Out Patients

First 4 hours ¥200

Every additional hour ¥200

Please get a punch at window no. 2 no. 3

At a hospital car park in Japan

Warning!
Please don't parking here,
without my guest

At a private car park in Japan

Beware Strawberries

Outside a pick-your-own fruit farm

Exit for soft-cushioned seat passengers

At a railway station in China

The chairs in the cabin are for the ladies. Gentlemen are not to make use of them till the ladies are seated.

Sign on a river-cruise boat in Ireland

Dogs must be carried

Common sign on the London Underground

Beware of People

Sign in a street in Hong Kong

To our customers –

Please keep the followings as the rules in parking areas:

We bear no responsibilities to such accidents as vehicles, men's and parts of vehicles and remains in car to be stolen.

At a restaurant in Japan

28

Beware!
To touch these wires is instant death.
Anyone found doing so
will be prosecuted.

At a railway station in the USA

When two trains approach each other
at a crossing, they shall both come to
a full stop and neither shall start up
until the other has gone.

A law in Kansas, USA

When a lower photograph is click, you can have a good time in a magnification photograph.

From a previous incarnation of the website for Narita Airport in Tokyo, instructing viewers to click on a thumbnail to view a full-sized image

Thou shalt not park here.

Sign at a church in Florida, USA

Cars will not have Intercourse on this Bridge

Traffic sign in Tokyo, Japan

Please shut the fence door.

Sign on a gate in Switzerland

Do not expect on floor.
Resident is forbidden to ride on steppes.
Do not make speech with man
make tram go.
Person without ticket will be persecuted.

Rules in a tram in Prague, Czech Republic

Take care: new non-slip surface

Sign on a newly renovated ramp
at a building entrance in the USA

To Cross Street, Push Button at Night

On a pedestrian crossing in Japan

You Are Here

On a blank wall at Narita Airport, Japan

Don't shit down here

Warning in a Japanese street

Wait for green man to cross

At a pelican crossing in England

Pointless
Product Warnings

Evidently written in a hurry, these surreal and absurd instructions either state the obvious or forbid using the product for its specified purpose; on the whole, they contradict the definition of an instruction! You have been warned.

For use by trained personnel only.

On a can of air freshener

Keep away from children.

On a bottle of baby lotion

Caution: do not use this hammer to strike any solid object.

On the handle of a hammer

Do not wash.

On a pair of socks bought in Egypt

Some assembly required.

On a 500-piece jigsaw-puzzle box

Protect from seawater.

On an ocean buoy

**Visit our site for further instructions:
http://www.pc ...**

*Computer instructions telling user
how to set up their computer*

**Instructional video on
hooking up VCR included.**

On VCR box

1. Remove the plastic wrapper.

*Inside popcorn packaging. In order to read the
instructions, the plastic wrapper must have
already been removed*

Warning: has been found to cause cancer in laboratory mice.

On a box of rat poison

This product is not to be used in bathrooms.

On a bathroom heater

May irritate eyes.

On a can of pepper spray used for self-defence in the USA

**Excessive dust may be irritating
to shin and eyes.**

On a tube of industrial powder

**Bottle exclusively designed for the use of
[X-brand] Natural Mineral Water.
Do not refill.**

On a bottle of mineral water

Warning: may contain small parts.
On a frisbee

Don't use while sleeping or unconscious.

On a handheld massager

In order to get out of car, open door, get out, lock doors, and then close doors.

In a car handbook

This product contains small granules under 3mm. Not suitable for children under the age of 14 years in Europe or 8 years in the USA.

On a packet of juggling balls

Do not peel label off.

On the back of a drinks bottle

Save a child. Push down and turn.
To open: Close Tightly.

On a medicine bottle

Warning:
This product may contain residue of nuts.

On a packet of cashew nut pieces

Tasting! Open it with your hand.
Take off the paper and eat it.

On a Spanish sweetmeat

Pierce with a pin and push off.

On the lid of a jam jar

Warning:
starts healing skin on contact.

On a bottle of hand lotion

Do not turn upside down.

On the bottom of a pizza box,
where the cooking instructions were printed.
Also found on the bottom of a box of glass
ornaments, and on a yoghurt carton

Caution: flammable!
If vapours bother you,
please leave the room.

On a bottle of bleach

Please store in the cold section
of the refrigerator.

On a bag of fresh grapes in Australia

**Do not recharge, put in backwards,
or use.**

On a battery

Battery may explore or leak.

On a battery

**Replacing battery:
replace the old battery with a new one.**

Directions for mosquito repellent

43

**Not suitable for children
aged 36 months or less.**

On a birthday card for a one-year-old

**Remove tissues from pockets
before washing garments.**

*Printed on the piece of cardboard that is discarded
when a box of tissues is opened*

**Do not use the Silence Feature
in emergency situations.
It will not extinguish a fire.**

On a smoke detector

Do not look into laser with remaining eye.

On a laser pointer

If swallowed contact poison control.

On a tube of toothpaste

Warning:
do not climb inside this bag and zip it up. Doing so will cause injury and death.

On a tiny 15 cm³ protective package

Warning: flame may cause fire.

Found on a butane lighter

Do not use near open flame.
On the label of a cigarette lighter

Do not use near fire, flame or sparks.

On a fireplace lighter

Theft of this container is a crime.

On a milk crate

Warning: do not blow dry in sleep.

On a hairdryer

Fragile. Do not drop.

On a Boeing 757 aircraft

Optional modem required.

On a computer software package

Safe for use around pets.

On a box of cat litter

If you do not understand, or cannot read, all directions, cautions and warnings, do not use this product.

On a bottle of drain cleaner

First, carry to fire ...

Instructions on a fire extinguisher

For best results, start with clean bathtub before use.

On a bottle of bathtub cleaner

Cannot be made non-poisonous.

On the back of a can of windscreen de-icing fluid

Hopeless Hotels

Hotels across the globe are a glorious source of badly translated English. One of the largest industries striving for customer satisfaction, the hotel trade is all about comfort, luxury and a home from home. The hotel staff who wrote these signs were obviously trying extremely hard to make their guests welcome, but ended up making their visits memorable for entirely different reasons.

In order to prevent shoes from mislaying,
please don't corridor them.
The management cannot be held.

Hotel on the Ionian Sea, Greece

Be pleased to come lie down
with our masseuse.
She will make you forget all your tired.

Hotel in Italy

Keep shutters close or
monkey make you crazy.

Hotel in Brunei

Bathtimes:

17.30–22.30
6.30–8.30

**If you take outside the indicated time limit,
contact your parents (warden) in advance.**

Youth hostel in Hiroshima, Japan

**Please deposit your valuables
in the management.**

Hotel in Guangdong, China

**Please do not turn on TV
except in use.**

Hotel bedroom

If you wish disinfection enacted
in your presence,
cry out for the chambermaid.

Hotel in Madrid, Spain

Depositing the room key into another
person is prohibited.

Hotel in Japan

Please leave your values
at the front desk.

Hotel in Paris, France

Do Not Use Elevator,
While Causing a Fire.

Hotel in Japan

Caution: when you take a bath,
please close the door and
switch on the fun without fail.

Hotel in Japan

Please keep calm when there is a fire.
The hotel will ensure your safety in shit
with advanced fire facilities.

Hotel in China

In case of fire in your room,
if you can not overpower it:

Leave the room after having
shutted the door.

In case of alarm is given:

If exits are free (corridors and stairs
without fire or smoke):

Leave the room after having shutted
the door, and follow the signalisation
towards exit.

Important:

A wet closed door, watertight with wet
material provides a good protection
against fire for a good lapse of time.

*Extracts from a fire notice in a hotel
in Pas de la Casa, Andorra*

Forbidden to hang out of hotel window. Person which do so will be charge for clean up mess on footpath.

Hotel in Budapest, Hungary

Push this button
in case anything happens.

Lift in a Japanese hotel

All fire extinguishers must be examined at least ten days before any fire.

Safety instructions from a British hotel

If no room in lift, do not perform yourself.
Coolie make lift jump.
Do not burn joss stick in bedroom.
Mouses much like. If mouses annoy,
ask at desk for hotel cat.

Hotel in China

No dancing in the bathrooms!

Hotel on the Gaspé Peninsula, Canada

If telly vice in your room not perform,
do not investigate with screw pusher,
you may get shocking electrics.
Instead attack hotel electric man.

Hotel in Japan

This lift was first all eviator built by Otis
for use in Japan. Very old and curious.
Does not always perform sometimes
will stop in wrong place. If so do,
shout in loud voice for hotel porter.

Hotel in Japan

In case of fire, do your best
to alarm the hotel porter.

Hotel in Vienna, Austria

To call room service, please open
the door and call room service.

Hotel in Istanbul, Turkey

Keep your hands away from
unnecessary buttons for you.

Hotel in Tokyo, Japan

Because of the impropriety of
entertaining guests of the opposite sex
in the bedroom, it is suggested that
the lobby be used for this purpose.

Hotel in Zurich, Switzerland

Please not more than six bodies in lift.
If more than six, lift may shreek or moan
and give up ascent. If such, contact hotel
manager as soon as can.

Hotel in Japan

To speak to a guest in another room, please follow these instructions:

1st floor – add 250
to the room number and dial.

On the 2nd, 3rd and 4th floors –
dial the number required.

5th floor – subtract 250
from the room number and dial

eg to contact room 510 dial 260

(except for room 542
whose number is 294)

Telephone instructions in a hotel in Zimbabwe

When enter lift, push nob for wishing
floor. If lift do not stop at wishing floor,
do not push nob more. Wait till lift stop,
then go back to low floor and attempt
second time.

Hotel in Japan

Do not enter lift backwards
and only when lit up.

Hotel in Germany

Not to perambulate the corridors
in the hours of repose
in the boots of ascension.

Ski hotel in Austria

To move the cabin, push button for
wishing floor. If the cabin should enter
more persons, each one should press a
number of wishing floor. Driving then
going alphabetically by national order.

Hotel lift in Yugoslavia

**Please do not use this lift
when it is not working.**

In a hotel lift

**Cooles and heates: if you want just
condition of warm in your room,
please control yourself.**

*Instructions for an air conditioner
in a hotel in Japan*

Please to bathe inside the tub.

Hotel in Japan

Is forbidden to steal hotel towels please.
If you are not person to do such thing
is please not to read notis.

Hotel in Tokyo, Japan

If you wish breakfast, lift the telephone
and our waitress will arrive. This will be
enough to bring up your food.

Hotel in Tel Aviv, Israel

In case of fire,
try to use the fire ex-ting wisher.

Hotel in Japan

Please hang your order before retiring on your doorknob.

Hotel in Ankara, Turkey

Light pranks add zest to your services, but don't pull the customers' ears.

Rules for hotel chambermaids issued by the Japanese Tourist Industry Board

Visitors are expected to complain at the office between the hours of 9 and 11 am daily.

Hotel in Athens

About the window in the guest room:

It isn't possible that it is possible
to open a window at the guest room
(on the safety)

About the laundering:

The wash becomes a finish the
evening tomorrow at the front desk
until 7 o'clock at night of the day.
(It becomes the evening tomorrow
in the morning even if it has.)

Hotel in Japan

Please dial 7 to retrieve your auto
from the garbage.

Hotel in Rome, Italy

Guests should announce the abandonment of theirs rooms before 12 o'clock, emptying the room at the latest until 14 o'clock, for the use of the room before 5 at the arrival or after the 16 o'clock at the departure, will be billed as one night more.

Hotel in Sarajevo, Yugoslavia

Gives you strong mouth and refreshing wind.

On the packaging of a toothbrush in a hotel in Japan

It is kindly requested from our guests
that they avoid dirting and
doing rumours in the rooms.

Hotel in Italy

To make international phone, dial 00
and wait to receive a bong.

Hotel in Osaka, Japan

You are invited to take advantage
of the chambermaid.

Hotel in Japan

You Did *What* With It?

Why would anyone use their products for the practices some manufacturers feel it necessary to warn against? And, in some cases, HOW? The following examples are better summed up with these serious words, found on many Japanese products: *'Not to be used for the other use.'*

Do not use orally.

On a toilet-cleaning brush

Do not eat.

Warning with polystyrene packaging

Do not spray in eyes.

On an underarm deodorant

For use on animals only.

On an electric cattle prod

Not to be used as hedge trimmer.
On a push-along lawnmower

Not dishwasher safe.

On a TV remote control

Do not insert curling iron
into any bodily orifice.

Warning: This product can burn eyes.

For external use only.

On various brands of curling tongs

Not to be used for drying hair.

On a blowtorch

DO NOT use soft wax as ear plugs or for any other function that involves insertion into a body cavity.

On a box of birthday cake candles

Do not use orally after using rectally.

Instructions for an electric thermometer

Warning: children can drown in bucket, do not place kids in juice.

On a large bucket of pickles used in fast-food restaurants

Do not feed contents to fish.

On a bottle of dog shampoo

Appliance should not be used to pick up lit cigarettes.

From the manual of a vacuum cleaner

Do not spray in your face.

On a can of spray paint

Do not use as a ladder.

On a compact-disc storage rack

Do not spray into electrical outlet.

On a hose nozzle

No small children.

On a washing machine in a launderette

Caution: avoid dropping air conditioners
out of windows.

On an air conditioner

Do not use as an ice cream topping.

On a bottle of hair dye

These earplugs are non-toxic,
but may interfere with breathing
if caught in windpipe.

On a packet of earplugs

If swallowed, promptly see doctor.

On a 4-pack of batteries

**For external use only,
not to be swallowed.**

On suntan lotion

Do not attempt to swallow.

On a mattress

Do not use near power lines.

On a toilet plunger

Do not use on food.

On a bottle of washing-up liquid

Do not use in shower.

On a hairdryer

Do not use under water.

On a toaster

Do not use this as a projectile in a catapult.

On a CD player

Do not place this product into any electronic equipment.

On the case of a chocolate CD

Warning: do not use on eyes.

In the manual for a heated seat cushion

Do not use house paint on face.

*In a credit-card commercial which depicts
a couple buying paint*

Do not use intimately.

On a tube of deodorant

Do not put in mouth.

On a box of fireworks

Do not put lit candles on phone.

On the instructions for a cordless phone

**Do not dangle the mouse by its cable
or throw the mouse at co-workers.**

From a computer manual

**Warning! This is not underwear!
Do not attempt to put in pants.**

On the packaging for a wristwatch

**Do not allow children to play
in the dishwasher.**

On a dishwasher

Not for highway use.

On a 13-inch wheel on a wheelbarrow

Cheap and Cheerful!

The worldwide demand for useless gadgets and toys has grown so great that 'bargain retail outlets' (or 'pound shops', to their customers) flourish in every high street. In order to supply the kind of items that every household needs at a price that's right, manufacturers often cut corners. Despite instructions being vital for installation, assembly and even safety on many of these products, the first expense to be spared often seems to be the translator's wages . . .

Multi-Chopper for Herbs & Vegetables

Mode of Job for Multi-Chopper:

In order that the article has minced could be perfectly cut, Knocked Vigorously on the bud Superior hand Opened.

The most or less great number of knocks determines the fineness of cup. The rotation of knives is made automatically and regularly.

For the cleaning, to pull the inferior bell and to release the recipient Superior. Well to rinse the machine, if possible to the running water.

Reassembly in Senses inverts. All parts metallic are executed in a materials has the test of the rust.

Simple Cleaning

Effective and quickly

Cutting well View Control

*Near-incomprehensible instructions
accompanying a vegetable slicer
made in China*

Care must be exorcised when handring
Opiticar System as it is apts to be sticked
by dusts and hand-fat.

*Instruction from the manual for keeping
the drum of a fax machine clean*

Super Laser Yo-Yo

Attention:

Don't put into mouth
to prevent from choking.

Don't tie the string around neck
to play in a rough way.

Don't leave the string alone
with children under 3.

Don't throw the yo-yo at people.

Be aware of people coming close
when you play yo-yo.

Be careful of the mental parts
when dissemble the yo-yo.

*Safety instructions from the packaging on
a yo-yo*

PUZZLE BALL

Let's decompose and enjoy assembling!

HOW TO DECOMPOSE

Easily though it into the floor have fun.

HOW TO ASSEMBLE

2. Hold A1 hand. Put A2 and A3 on both side of A1.

2. Slide B1 and B2 on both side of A2 & A3.

3. Slide C1 for the side of B1 though the side of B2.

From a Christmas-cracker toy

Don't let a child close on
during exercising.

If you feel vomitive, dizzy or any
uncomfortable condition during exercise,
stop exercising immediately.

Away from the dangerous things (glass
wall, angle of table, sharp things ... etc)
during the exercise.

The knees should be closed together the
pad. Can't relax at any time when you
exercising.

Safety instructions with an exercise gadget

ATTENTION TO ITEM:

Abecedarian at the complanate arid flat ground coast please. handlers at gliding, it would be best draw on helmet and kneecap, shin guard and protect artifice, for fear accident injuries from falls.

Avoid by all means at sanded or lapidarian place and busy a section of a hightway coast, for fear happen accident.

At use be indispensable to check up screw whether become flexible, altitude changeless move about buckle and foldaway speedy lock whether locknut.

Warn: the manufacture not be propitious to under 6 year of children and elder use.

Cryptic safety instructions accompanying a micro-scooter

Operate it on the loosen condition of levers without confirmation can cause the handle pole bent and cause incident.

Do not resolve and refit the product optionally due to safe reason.

Be attention to the environment around and abide by the traditions.

Do not operate when you are in poor health or bad spirit.

Instructions from another micro-scooter

Do not attempt to open cassette case as it is exquisitely fixed.

From the manual of a cassette recorder

SAIYAN WIELD WAYS AND MEANS

setting pre ceiling of way and means

WARNING

With appertain rotor of screw setting
pre ceiling on the under standing that
screw no wield. May wield two-faced,
pressboard securing. wield pre to begin
with wiping ceiling of bilge dasto.

Thread of length need half as many again
as tad.

Open toy of batteries shuck. Verification
batteries, +, – whereafter stow down.
to a certainty need locknat lest take
place accident.

Hook through toys apside of hole.

Needs swithes shoving NO.for pre arrows specifying of orention shoving.Pack it up time,withbold toy pate,need switches shoving OFF.

Prythee no sport with stingy or play asperity game.Winding finger have got bloodstream not walk.Throagh of peril.

Tad disport of time grown man tatelage.

Till the cowcomes home.Wield toys damage,burn-in prythee wind to a close wield.

Give attention to open/close toys,therefore take place peril.for instance slipup batteries wield result in the emission of heat rupture liquid.vent itself prythee pay attention.

Play at sith to a certainty bolt up power supply fetch out batteries. Batteries no electification dissolution,plunge ioto aquaor fire.

Not trust for tad batteries lest in advertent eat off. In the event of accident without loss of time plythee pillroller tuke order with.

May pre house the seamy side volitation!!!

Instructions on the packaging of a Japanese toy

MENUAL

QX-1004 Ver 3.2.A

Thank for order 4CH PCI Sound Card(QX-1004),It's easy install to your PC system as follow step:

Turn off your PC system power.(disconnect the power cable)

Open the PC case(please becareful the screw,we need to use it assembly again), and find out the PCI slot.

Remove the PCI slot pannel cover(nomatter it with screw or not,if with screw please keep the screw if not with screw plaese check the system parts box and find out the screw),and plug the QX-1004 on PCI slot with right position,please check the QX-1004 bus(gold finger) is all plug into the PCI slot,put the screw to fix the card on the case.

Close the case with the screw you just disassemly the case,and plug the power cable .

Plug the speaker(up to 4pcs),microphone,aux in,MIDI/game connect.

Turn on the PC system power and booting just same as before ,find the CD driver (come with QX-1004) put into computer CD ROM DRIVER,and install again,the software will install itself.

If anything not correct plaease install again with very carefully.

Thank again to puchase our QX-1004,please fell free to give us advise how to inprove our product.

Instructions with a computer sound card

Assembly Procedure:

1. Be tights part E with part I together by fitting M. Also can be installation handle part J in this side.

2. Be tights part D with part H together by fitting M. Like a step No. 1. And may be installation handle in this side too.
   – Use corner fitting to be holds the Bottle rack.

3. To connects the both side legs with Back frame part G. Then ware Wire tray along the position itself and tighten each corner.

4. Assemble wood top with drawer divider. And bring part from Step No. 3 turn around to back of wood top

(from picture) then tights wood top with housing and ware all casters to position.
Be CAREFUL top wood face!
When this step finished turn around it again.

5. Input the Drawers.

6. Test stranger & use on.

On a handy kitchen trolley

Please use quality batties.
Don't use bad batties, or any problem is not any contact with our CO.

Japanese packaging

Can't invert with laugh to laugh begin
you are useful automatize as poke as
shaky as shaky as laugh during the use
open the lif of tep and take two cells
(no. 5) in the box. If you want to stop
laugh or don't use for a long time
you must take out the cells
(this seller have no cells)

On box of a Vietnamese laughing tip-toy

Give me coins and I will enjoy you.

From an automated toy children's money box

Preposterous Proclamations

Some instructions simply defy explanation.

Here is a selection of the best – or possibly the worst – of these.

Strain yourself or push at the time of
contraction and two hours later
a baby will come out.

A swell will be checked if there is,
by pushing shin.

If your weight gains rapidly, it is a sign
of swell or fatness.

If you pick up around your nipple
come out I cm high, and it'll be alright.

You'd better begin your sexual
intercourse after the delivery after the
one mouth check-up with a doctor.

If you want to do a vowel movement
don't stop.

After you vomit, you rinse your mouse
and if you can eat, eat.

You can do Üfoo, foo naturally when you open your mouth slightly.

Brasure can be for maternity one or nursing bra, so that your breast can't be oppressed.

There are many differences of ideas in family but she felt family bondage after delivery as a wife.

Advice for pregnant women at a Japanese clinic

Insert coin

Select product

Pull knob out fully

Sign on a condom-vending machine in England

Please do not close face to monkeys.

Sign on the primate enclosure at a zoo in Japan

Report the clerk when you find out fire.

Shopping centre in Japan

It is forbidden to enter a woman even a foreigner if dressed as a man.

Temple in Bangkok, Thailand

Push button. Foam coming plenty.
Big Noise. Finish.

Launderette in Japan

Refuse to be put in dustbin.

From a government office in the UK

When you have finished your meal,
return used food.

At a language school in the USA

Please Keep chair on position and keep table cleaned after dying. Thank you for your corporation.

Sign in a café in Taiwan

Why not rent out a movie for a dull evening?

Sign in a video shop

STOP! This is the last rung.

Printed in English, French and German on an aluminium ladder

For your convenience, we recommend courteous, efficient self-service.

Sign in a supermarket in Hong Kong

Dangerous drugs must be locked up with the matron.

Sign in a hospital in the USA

Please leave a pet outside.

Outside an ice-cream parlour in Japan

Visitors with reading difficulties should proceed to front desk for information.

Sign in a community centre in England

Please call us!
We will provide you with any emergency.

Advertisement for a babysitting service in Japan

Anyone throwing stones at this sign will be prosecuted.

Sign at a country estate in England

Don't press the glass to get hurt.

On a shop window in Taiwan

**No exit for boys
except for disposal or rubbish.**

School notice

To stop the drip, turn cock to the right.

On a tap in a restaurant in Finland

Remember to flash the toilet.

Instruction on a Tamagotchi
(an electronic pet toy)

No smoothen the lion.

Sign on the lion cage at a zoo
in the Czech Republic

Watch batteries while you wait.

In a jewellers in Japan

Swimming is forbidden
in the absence of a saviour.

Sign at a swimming pool on the French Riviera

Caution! Don't lean on the gate.
The gate would fall down when lean on it.
It occurs you Trouble.

Notice on a gate in Japan

Drop your trousers here for best results.

Sign in a dry-cleaners in Bangkok, Thailand

Do not use the diving board
when the swimming pool is empty.

Sign at a swimming pool in Sri Lanka

Entrance on Back Side please.

On the window of a shop in London, England

NO HOT ASHES!!

*On a wheelie-bin inside a cemetery
on the Isle of Man*

Danger
If you fall in the pond, you will be boiled.

At a hot spring in Japan

Full payment and all menu choices
should be received 2 weeks
before the reservation.

*From a Christmas-party leaflet
in a pub in London, England*

For restrooms, go back
towards your behind.

Sign at an airport in Japan

We close this door for a wind blow hard.
(Keep warm inside)
Please come into the other door.

Notice in a shop in Japan

DO NOT USE

*Printed on a handle die-cut into cardboard
packaging for heavy computer equipment*

Please do not put wet aardvarks on the counter.

On the counter at a social security office

**If your child has run out,
please take another.**

*Sign over a supply of envelopes for collection
at a Sunday school in England*

**Ladies, leave your clothes here and
spend the afternoon having a good time.**

Sign in a laundry in Rome, Italy

**Please do not allow children
to lock themselves into these cubicles
on their own.**

*Sign on the inside of a toilet door, only visible
to parents after the door closes, England*

Please leave these toilets as you
would wish to find them.

Wipe the seat.

Use toilet brush to clean the bowl
thoroughly.

Ensure flush is properly used.

Please do not leave the cleaners
with an unpleasant job.

*Sign put up by an over-officious cleaner
in an office block in England*

Mice! Do not leave crumbs.

In a church hall in England

| Restrooms | Please wait for hostess to seat you. |

Adjacent signs at a restaurant in the USA

If you cannot find what you are looking for on our menu, please ask our waitress what you would like.

Menu at a hotel in England

For your safety this game is not allowed
for those who suffer from hearts,
diabetics, nerves, high pressure
and pregnants.

Sign on an amusement-park ride in Saudi Arabia

Eat your fingers off.

The KFC slogan, 'Finger lickin' good',
when first translated into Chinese

Bite the wax tadpole.

The Coca-Cola brand name,
when first translated into Chinese

Ladies! Have a fit upstairs.

Sign in a tailor's shop in Hong Kong

Besmear a backing pan, previously buttered with a good tomato sauce, and, after, dispose the cannelloni, lightly distanced between them in a only couch.

Instructions on a packet of convenience food from Italy

Please don't handle the fruit. Ask for Debbie.

Sign in a greengrocer's in England

Please attach 2 recent bust photos (taken within last three months).

On a Taiwanese visa-application form

Children must be kept in your car.

Sign at a recycling centre in England

Ladies are requested not to have children at the bar.

Sign in a cocktail lounge in Norway

Epilogue

Despite there being plenty of genuinely stupid instructions in the world, never forget that, no matter how sensible instructions may be, there are always people who will turn them into stupid ones, as this final true story illustrates.

A woman was at a bus stop in London on a bright sunny morning and noticed an older lady shading her face and shrinking back from the sunshine as best she could.

'Are you OK?' she asked the old lady, with concern. 'Have you got a problem with your eyes?'

'No,' the old lady replied. 'It's this medication I'm taking. I'm having real trouble following the instructions today. I read the label and it says "Keep out of direct sunlight."'

All Michael O'Mara titles are available by post from:

Bookpost, PO Box 29,
Douglas, Isle of Man, IM99 1BQ

Credit cards accepted.
Telephone: 01624 677237
Fax: 01624 670923
Email: bookshop@enterprise.net
Internet: www.bookpost.co.uk

Free postage and packing in the UK.

Other Michael O'Mara Humour titles:

All Men Are Bastards	ISBN 1-85479-387-X	pb £3.99
The Book of Urban Legends	ISBN 1-85479-932-0	pb £3.99
The Complete Book of Farting	ISBN 1-85479-440-X	pb £4.99
Complete Crap	ISBN 1-85479-313-6	pb £3.99
The Ultimate Book of Farting	ISBN 1-85479-596-1	hb £5.99
The Ultimate Insult	ISBN 1-85479-288-1	pb £5.99
Wicked Cockney Rhyming Slang	ISBN 1-85479-386-1	pb £3.99
Wicked Geordie English	ISBN 1-85479-342-X	pb £3.99
Wicked Scouse English	ISBN 1-84317-006-X	pb £3.99
The Wicked Wit of Jane Austen	ISBN 1-85479-652-6	hb £9.99
The Wicked Wit of Winston Churchill	ISBN 1-85479-529-5	hb £9.99
The Wicked Wit of Oscar Wilde	ISBN 1-85479-542-2	hb £9.99
The World's Stupidest Criminals	ISBN 1-85479-879-0	pb £3.99
The World's Stupidest Graffiti	ISBN 1-85479-876-6	pb £3.99
The World's Stupidest Laws	ISBN 1-85479-549-X	pb £3.99
The World's Stupidest Men	ISBN 1-85479-508-2	pb £3.99
The World's Stupidest Signs	ISBN 1-85479-555-4	pb £3.99
More of the World's Stupidest Signs	ISBN 1-84317-032-9	pb £4.99
The World's Stupidest Last Words	ISBN 1-84317-021-3	pb £4.99
The World's Stupidest Inventions	ISBN 1-84317-036-1	pb £5.99
The World's Stupidest Sporting Screw-Ups	ISBN 1-84317-039-6	pb £4.99
Shite's Unoriginal Miscellany	ISBN 1-84317-064-7	hb £9.99
Cricket: It's A Funny Old Game	ISBN 1-84317-090-6	pb £4.99
Football: It's A Funny Old Game	ISBN 1-84317-091-4	pb £4.99
Laughable Latin	ISBN 1-84317-097-3	pb £4.99